Statue New London Harbor, Eugene O'Neill, age 7

THE ORIGINAL LIE

Mind-Dream Ship's Bell on "The E. O'Neill"

By

RICHARD HEIM

The Original Lie
© 2007 Richard Heim. All rights reserved.

Cover Copyright 2007 Richard Heim. Photograph © 2007 Richard Heim

This is a work of fiction. Names, characters, places and incidents, other than those of Eugene O'Neill and persons in his family or those contemporaries with some connection to him and his work, real places in and around New London, Connecticut and incidents actually taking place and connected to him in some way, are the product of the author's imagination or used fictitiously. Any resemblance to actual persons living or dead, events or locales, except as listed above, are entirely coincidental.

References by the narrator to his family members, past, present, his acquaintances, events and circumstances in his life are based on such family, acquaintances, events and circumstances in the author's life.

Published by Polygon Publishing
P.O. Box 1545, Palm Desert, California 92260

ISBN 978-0-9764768-3-2

DEDICATION

To my father, Joseph, blamed falsely at age three for his own mother's cancer death because he often sat on her lap and rocked his head against her breast.

From this shameful condemnation, he never recovered.

Jamie and Eugene, you are not alone.

TABLE OF CONTENTS

PROLOGUE

She dropped him into a deep pit. Then came the afterbirth. He laid there with a large awareness and from then on, he perceived the world and all that was in it with deep-pit eyes. He cerebralized it endlessly.

The public and the powers soon enough cheered and saluted and fell in behind him in a long parade and if you look outside your window, you will see that it is still going by.

FORWARD

This is a work of fiction containing the experiences and perceptions of an older man, a retired professional, with the phenomenon that is and was Eugene O'Neill. Much of the presentation is a glimpse inside the sole character's mind as he drives from New Jersey to New London, Connecticut, the boyhood nightmare home of the playwright. Similar family defects make him uniquely able to see what others do not; have not, about this "Institutionalized" saint. It is based on persons and events in my own life.

The book amounts to a view thru once-black eyes of the pathos life of Mr. O'Neill who struggled to the end, and of the non-technical, non-production aspects of his work and the public reaction to it. The continuing missteps of mankind, so amply laid out in the plays and in their creator's life, are everywhere today. In a certain sense, he represented the epitome of such missteps in kind and in cause although many people stay unaware of the latter. O'Neill's tragic experience mirrors the archetype of the same in humanity. These uninformed masses might agree on the descriptions of the conduct and circumstances involved, but few understand how and why it all comes about and fewer still accept the remedy revealed.

The narrator goes back to New London in 2006, one hundred years after O'Neill entered Princeton University, and he searches for the spirit and the essence of this man now long gone, as part of an effort to find and develop a detailed reckoning of the erroneous views, theses, conclusions and ideas about him and mankind. He knows that all of these were tainted by the playwright's desperate background. Then there is the still widely accepted perspective held by the public and critics, also tainted and also supported by similar personal experiences that are trance-forming.

No part of this deals with the staging genius, innovations, technical aspects, theatrical expressionism or revolutionizing of American theater. O'Neill's ability to shock and entertain are not challenged. But a host of untruths abound and nowhere is one to discover how people's lives, the underlying reasons, get so tangled and despairing or just how they can untangle it all. This book challenges and dissolves all the old perceptions and claims made by the world, the critics, the public and the prize-givers and one must conclude that this last group was also unaware of such considerations and were simply bowled over by the novelty and intense dramatization of human misery. A good example of O'Neill's offered claims for that misery is what he thought of as "cultural alienation" and the perils of "Theater life". He failed to see that whole persons are not changed by such influences. The former, they try to change themselves by steady, amiable examples and the latter is withstood easily and not succumbed to because whole people are rock solid and not swayed from that by any loose ways of ordinary theater folk. That, too, they try to change for the better. Many things that he saw as primary problems were only symptoms and these include items like alcohol overuse, miserliness, dictator-like ways, loose morals, theatricality and the "homelessness" of theater life, all indicators of child mistreatment and the original lie.

It is true that he did claim to discover the *remedy* for family misery (ie. The final parts of *Long Day's Journey Into Night*) but those are naïve and do not fly. O'Neill's death in 1953 occurred while he was more or less in the same pitiful state that he had always endured and his admitted struggle to understand mankind as well as himself all of his life is a concession that he indeed failed to uncover the root of the agony that pulled him down for sixty-five years. It continues to pull mankind down today and there is no hope in most peoples' viewfinder although the answer is simple and reachable. O'Neill knew of but failed to grasp Zarathustra's words by Nietzsche that "You must have chaos in you to give birth to a dancing star". Nietzsche was speaking of that answer, that remedy. It is free-fall grieving and pain which removes the life-ruiner installed by closet kin.

O'Neill's entire existence was pain-avoidance except in 1939 to 1941 when he delved into his inner torment to write about it. The product was *Long Day's Journey Into Night*, an attempt to resolve his anger and resentment against his family and to forgive them. The effort did *not* help him to shed his ghosts of pain because the endeavor was so blocked by distractions. He seems never to have discovered the real cause for his plight and his adult carryings-on, both as a man and as an artist (and father and husband) can be summed up by the label "cerebralizer". The title, *"The Original Lie: Mind-Dream Ship's Bell On "The E. O'Neill"*, expresses the beginning of that real cause and shows how O'Neill's methods of dealing with people were *typical* for all who struggle as he did. But this work is *more* about how society and the experts *err* than about the playwright himself who is now a distant character and viewed by many as overrated and irrelevant. It is a lesson for mankind to grapple with and advance on. The absolutely rampart state of the world with its lying, cheating, blaming, pettiness, irresponsibility, substance-abuse, juvenility, hatred, religious strife, wars, obesity, famine, self-dealing, and more, along with the awful status quo of religion, rife with delusions, falsity and sectarianism, all cries out for clearheaded heroism, but who will ride to the rescue?

An absolute pity of a mismatch to O'Neill's real genius was the languishing in his final days in Boston, in that hotel, without any healing. Had he grasped the true answer, one has to wonder what marvelous thing on a stage he could have wrought! That is gold that will be forevermore left in the darkest mine.

Richard Heim
August, 2007

CHAPTER ONE:
CITY FIN

It seems a most curious thing. No matter what I ponder or recall or what I see and hear, what is nostalgic to me, it all stays upon a museum shelf on both sides of my center, my consciousness. It can be the warm air flowing over my bare body. It is May and fragrant-pregnant on the deserted Rhode Island beach. Yet looming, not in my thoughts but in quick experiences, I am then at my apartment window and the river and a snowy ice and the braced hawks. Easter is far away. That sort of polarity snatches away a 'sanity' and installs in its place a slammed realization. It must be like birth. Beforehand, it is, again, May, but during is an unwitting and unwelcomed passage, while the aftermath soon becomes the delight of a new sensation.

It all plods on without true memory. At first is vaulting and spearing ahead with the slowdown much later in life, yet the overall phenomenon stays equal. Every day is fresh insofar as it is unlived but the years of heaps can squash it down. Nevertheless, when falling asleep at the end, the novelty lingers as one had not until that very moment endured such a thing.

The times that I dug my scrawny fingers into the sand there, in Rhode Island, cold and alone, and thought about him down the road, his house, so revered, so celebrated, but what do they know or care? It's neatness in the Eugene O'Neill puzzle is all. I rode past in 1994 and was myself taken in by the local fever, the statue at the docks, the misery projected by reputation. Then, there was the Eugene O'Neill Theatre, tucked on a corner of a wilderness kind of road. It sounds so grand, but the man, the soul, the guts, the destroyed child, like every little child of such monsters, was he lost forever to the public sweep? New London knew the boozer, the drunk, the dandy-like intellectual with all those books, the brother to Jamie O'Neill and his partner on Bradley Street in the debauchery, the self-centered creature son of the famous actor, difficult and often sour, the great talker although usually quite shy, gaunt, shifty, dressed up. New York knew the rebel, the budding writer, the semi-eccentric Village resident, full of new ideas and spreading old ones as well while keeping company with some of the avant-garde. Such was the New York of Eugene O'Neill after 1915 and not the derelict of the 1912 suicide try on Fulton Street. But the child, the lonely, ruined, little face, made crooked just to survive, where was the fascination and concern then? The grown up alcoholic, destitute inside, hagged to belong to something, anything, and to fight away the memories even as they were being made each day, faltering under the mounds of horrors of all the days, who could save him or know him or even approach him? He had been cemented.

I glanced at my watch as I drove north and it occurred to me that my head was overflowing with O'Neill. It was a new preoccupation. I had my senses awakened by a PBS-TV piece on him only a month before. It was quite dramatic and detailed.

That father-actor, so well known and chased after, such a national "treasure" for people's needs to escape their inner blight, was but a cog on an endless rotator. His road routine was pressed into Eugene and the realm of theater life, theater thinking, were an element for him to help fill in his void. Later musings on this and tries at theater involvement might have been Eugene taking on part of his father's identity but more likely, were engaged in merely to please or to get him to accept Eugene finally for the child that he was born to be, not that the kid ever really knew what that was. A mistreated youngster *never* gives up hope that abusive and neglectful or abandoning mothers and dads will someday, somehow, turn it around and get it right and love them finally and cherish them unconditionally. That is why attempts to get miscreants to place the blame where it should go, on the offender parents, is usually unsuccessful. To do that would be to admit that that hope is ill-conceived. The devastated human being prefers to put the souls of such mothers and fathers in an insulated place and to keep them there until that miracle comes around. It *never* does, or seldom does. James O'Neill never really came around and was never really confronted by his son except in a superficial way such as the decision by Eugene at age fifteen not to go to church anymore. There was a physical tussle but little else. It was true that mistreated kids will blame parents incidentally or refuse to speak to them, but the placing of *real* blame so as to identity the true root of the child's life messes and to affect some positive disposition leading towards wholeness is not made of that.

Eugene's father would almost certainly not have any real regard for his son, the unwanted child, had the budding playwright not garnered such good reviews from his first Broadway production in 1920 of *Beyond The Horizon*. One must wonder as well if the play would have even seen the light of day had O'Neill not been the kid of a renowned actor and star of the Count of Monte Cristo production for decades already. It is so that Eugene befriended the well known writer, H. L. Mencken, while living in Greenwich Village, and that he was instrumental in getting the play sold to the powers that be on Broadway, but still, it is a valid query whether the writer, too, was impressed with the nexus to James O'Neill and that without that, no such career movement would have happened for Eugene. After getting off the highway for gasoline, I got back on and continued my thoughts.

It was there on that beach that I suddenly remembered my college sweetheart, who lived in Dover, New Jersey, and whose mother bragged that her family was related to Eugene O'Neill. That was in 1961 0r 1962 and I can still see her sitting there in the family room/library on the main floor, cigarette burning, whiskey in her hand and something 'important' on her lap, Will Durant, maybe, going on and on while I just looked on and thought about how similar it all was to my own alcoholic, addict mother. There seemed to be almost an exhalted filial posture in this and, because at the time, I had no idea who Eugene O'Neill was, it just rolled off my back. It seems to me now forty-five years later, that she might have said "cousin" or "distant cousin".

Children who grow up with such eternal hope have to put the aggression somewhere. It rushes out or leaps upon others. It can gush at the slightest comment. There has to be a register inside them that glows when the rage is acted on even if the target is wrong. Then, the occasional holiday gathering where the real targets might be lurking, that scene might reveal a bullseye but it is prompted usually by drink and a ruined festivity is the usual result, a kicked mother or some punch in the eye.

In 1928, Eugene gave up alcohol on the warning by an analyst and one has to wonder if his already writing-oriented life was to then become obsessed with the pastime and to include exclusion of other people in large part. Was there a parallel between this and his mother's withdrawal into her morphine habit? It is widely known that Ella was unavailable, physically *and* emotionally, to her son and the rest of the family really. I know that my surrendering of a tobacco addiction, heavy at that in 1975, was replaced simply by another. That was alcohol, and by the time I got to 1991, it was an integral part of my routine. So the substitution concept seems alive and well.

But Eugene O'Neill was *driven* to be obsessive about his work by a lot more than the wagon that he had climbed on. Although his drinking did quell the harpies, the sobriety was a stage for more than their return engagement. The utter and ultimate need to matter is what drives a man to produce what he produced. Then, there was the fact that it occupied his otherwise turmoiled mind, it gave a sense of belonging to something (and someone; his readers and playgoers) when his was a gnawing existence of belonging to nothing and nobody, it helped with the abject loneliness that plagues all children of alcoholics and addicts even in a crowd, it was somewhat of an ego boost and it was a prime example of a human doing in place of a human being. The Nobel and four Pulitzer Prizes show the degree and depth of *something*, but the question is what outside of technical, production, expressionist and other nonsubject content aspects. The revolutionary changes in American theater cannot be denied but the alleged breakthrough portrayals of emotional matters I question strongly, although the artistic drama *was* strong.

Eugene's parents made sure that he did not matter. His father was an overbearing alcoholic ego maniac who found 'salvation' on the stage. It was his whore. Ella, the mother, was withdrawn, desperate, in love with the narcotic life. Eugene was a constructively abandoned child. He was unwanted from birth and made to feel worthless, a bother, not fitting in anywhere and not entitled to affection or stability. James and Ella were themselves mistreated kids who also did not matter and they were accomplished self-dealers. In a way, Eugene was set up to be an addict. The cigarettes and the alcohol allowed him to 'feel' what his parents treatment of him denied him to feel: well-being, comfort, self-esteem, power, worth. So powerful was this substitute, that the untoward health effects were meaningless to him. Only the relief mattered. The shoved aside child does not care about health or longevity or normality. Removing the ache is all that counts and when he was still too young to find solace in chemicals and other devices, he looked to the power, the freedom, the excitement, the dynamism, the escape offered by the sea. Its most immediate presence was the Thames River and New London Harbor right across Pequot Avenue from the summer cottage occupied when the father and mother were not on tour.

Suddenly, I remembered the time my sister who lived in Old Mystic explained the pronunciation to me of "Thames". I rode onward.

Just across the Thames from where his boy spirit was crushed lie the bodies of my mother and sister. That Groton cemetery never pulls me but as I sit and mull it all over, a kind of sweep comes and my senses flash back and forth across that bridge like lightening. My mother was the callous drinker, the shamer with ease, but timid simultaneously and inept in all but the household. To this day, I have no real feelings for her much as Eugene was missing the same from his own inept "Moma". Her daughter, my alleged sister, didn't inherit the bottle but did fall prey to the addiction monster and that finally did her in.

The strong and able Canada geese can fly right up to an office window and look in but they are unable to partake of what they see. And so it is with the put upon child or the grown up drunk, parading it all before the world, netting prizes, some to die for, but what of it? The misery stain seems indelible and nobody, not one son-of-a-bitch can get them steered to where it can all be banished forever. Yes, more successful plays, more throngs to attend and cheer, more rave reviews, more controversy over content, every new Broadway spectacle, the geld rolled in but the pain, the old, steadfast companion, never rolled out! His lost "faith" was just a poke in the night, a dribble on the bib of a childhood indoctrination by the church. His mother, Ella, was always going on about her lost "faith" and so this seems like a familiar family theme. However, Eugene must have very soon realized after age fifteen that whistling in the dark does little good when the wolf has you by the lips. And then there was the blaming of Eugene by his mother for her morphine addiction. Such a confounding influence upon a child more devastating than that, especially when it was untruthful, it is hard to imagine. This kind of maltreatment by a parent will turn a child into a subhuman every time and for Eugene, this status pops out in many ways, not the least of which was his self-characterization as one of the "fog people" who are always stammering and never belong and are unwanted.

He tried desperately to get his pen around such a fate. He truly wanted only to love and be loved, as do all children, but that kind of life was plainly to be withheld and with what was left, Eugene valiantly attempted to eke out *something* to show his imagined worth. Thus the journey beginning in 1913 to be an artist or nothing. There might have been some residual element in this from his Catholic upbringing insofar as dedication to an ideal, in his case, creation of art in the form of plays for in that early period, there seems to have been little of the motives that drove him later on. Near the end, he came up with such world-renowned pieces as "Long Day's Journey Into Night" which was a desperate attempt, after his abandonment of the strenuous project of the cycle of plays, eleven in all, to delve into the agony that resided in him forever and to try to resolve all of the turmoil and confusion growing out of his family debacle life starting at his birth. He and the public claimed that he succeeded but that is false. Likewise for "The Iceman Cometh" which was heralded as an exposition of man's inherent weaknesses and the devices required to live with them, but that production was scraped off the bottom of a life that could not help but see things in such a crooked way. It is full of human *untruths*! One of these is that illusions are the very substance of human life and another is the 'impossibility' of man's pipe dream of finding the secret life! There certainly was no real healing in either work for him. The state of Eugene's life from about 1943 until his passing ten years later is the proof. All talk of a "reconciliation" between O'Neill and his father occasioned by that first Broadway success in 1920 is wishful thinking. Yes, the old man was impressed and did wish Eugene well, but the long history of abuse and neglect such as theirs cannot be reversed without a lengthy period of emotional transactions during a recovery process. It had to feel somewhat good and even refreshing to the two of them to be on "good" terms over that play, but true healing is the product of something that neither of them ever dreamed of. In fact, neither Eugene or his father (or the rest of the family) ever really knew who they were, what they wanted or what they felt, not in the sense that whole people know such things. Relief was the order of the day for them all and that was *every* day. More than one Eugene O'Neill "expert" has publicly displayed a woeful ignorance of all such considerations and branded the relationship as "happily reconciled". Naïveté resides everywhere! That relief slant to living is what was behind the famous O'Neill line about "Being always a little in love with death". In the end, near August 1920, the atmosphere between James and Eugene had been cleared of domineering, tyrant anger, belittling, rejection mode and replaced with the sort of resignation that overtakes most who face imminent death. It was salve on a burn and there were words of advice to the young man about being true to the best inside of him, but really, Eugene O'Neill had absolutely no idea what that thing really consisted of. And, two weeks after the father's passing, it is easy to imagine the son slipped back into his former trance and numbed out self. A low level of consciousness seems to be fate of such warped and ruined children. It acts sort of like a protector. A life of false thinking and fake behaviors awaited our hero and this style of existence was anchored mightily as a substitute for grappling with the original lie and its aftermath. It was kept deep and 'hidden'.

I noticed that I had a couple of hours drive left to hit New London.

There are lines by O'Neill to the effect that he would have been so much more successful if he had been born a fish or a seagull and that brings the question up about whether it is better to be born and abused than never to be born at all? Or, what of the terminally ill child? Can one with heightened consciousness look at such a kid and feel the delight of its purity instead of the crushing tragedy? For sure, there is a robbery of the treasures that we all seek, or the things that we want but which are false due to a defective parent-child relationship, but who can say that 'fulfillment' and long life are essential? The ill child is one side but the ruined child is quite another because he *can* be cured. However, no one will listen because the road back is fraught with ruts that seem intolerable. Who goes down a road of pain, of relived nightmares? Nobody does! Eugene's trip down such an avenue was too disciplined and controlled and distracted to count for much in the way of unwinding the mummy. There was a lieracy harnessing about and that was first and primary. Grieving what was done to him was not a concept in his ken, nor in the world's really. Alcohol, marijuana, lying, denial, and the like all come to the rescue and the pain and agony remain on the throne. There is no true feeling of pain but only being ruled by it in the nonvulnerability sense. That is what drove Eugene to his nesting place to begin with the aerie of chaos, depression, nonhuman aspects, cerebralization, alcohol, tobacco, running away, becoming the artist, "mattering". Meanwhile, his real self stays in hiding, shaking like a leaf. More shaming, abuse, crushed hopes and emotional abandonment are kept walled out. Most people do not grasp this and Eugene was at a loss to understand himself and would take that yoke to his grave. All his energy was spent in coping including the writing, which was a substitute for real living, real mattering. Never was there true glee or fulfillment. That Nobel in 1936 meant no more than a cigar. In fact, it put undue pressure on him to shine when he felt like quasi-death, thrust his future into a spotlight that was wholly unwelcomed mainly because he would have to measure up, behave like a champion. He had other pressing emotional circuses going twenty-four hours a day in his brain and being a Nobel hero did not let him alone. He could not be the subhuman creature when the world expected a super one. It might have even reminded him of his father's demands. A handy excuse kept him from having to go to Sweden to accept the prize from the King: he was too weary!

A cruel affair must have been what Eugene felt when he was attacked by that Parkinson's-like disease that made his hands shake. This was not only a slap in the face by a reminder of his mortality, it also threatened to take away his teat, his 'love', his continuous distraction. Now he would have to struggle even more, never mind the upheavals of childhood turmoil and torment and defeating loneliness, now the job was as if he had had weights tied to his pens or pencils by Satan as a joke!

This life development might have actually propelled O'Neill towards real grieving as nothing brings a body around faster than a crack in the puss or a broken leg. The false structure, not really even noticed anymore, crumbles and the authentic person, cowering inside in dread, rolls out into the open if only for the occasion. Wrinkles, diminished or lost potency, aches and pains, all haunt a man but the shakes such as he had, that must have been quasi-devastating!

My own recovery from child mistreatment came to mind.

Most people did not and do not really understand Eugene O'Neill, nor did he understand himself or grasp his early world of horrors or the aftermath. He is, too, an epitome because of the typicality of his situation. He was like millions of other children who were and are the victims of like predecessors, emotionally abused and neglected, winding up *completely false* while the public sees only a "nice" family there! And the complete falsity *exactly matches* the *original lie;* it does not overshoot it or undermatch it. Seldom is there actual physical abuse although some might exist some of the time, the vast majority of the damaged little ones are done in by hands-off stuff. That public, however, always thinks of physical maltreatment when it comes across the idea of child abuse.

The drive to matter is what drove O'Neill to produce what he did. This is so for most artists outstanding in their fields except for some propelled by insanity of an organic nature. Unlike the excellent ditch digger, propelled to the matter by faster, deeper product, the creator thrusts his hopes with the likes of innovation, expressionistic stuff, novelty, absurdity, and outrageousness. These last two line up with that original lie as well and the striving artist exists with the same pusher that makes a young boy or girl yearn for approval from a disapproving mother or father. Then, there is the fact that James O'Neill was forty-two years old when Eugene was born in 1888, so he hardly qualified as being at a fatherly age but was more close to a grandfatherly one and this too robs the son of something. Maybe some of Eugene's isolation feeling sprung from this. No doubt, however, the old man's haughty role as The Count of Monte Cristo carried over to the two sons, Jamie and Eugene, and they were apt to resent it all. Never was there any "pal" feelings between father and sons in this family. By such things are children wound up and let go on the sidewalk that is the world.

If O'Neill was a tobacco addict in the end there in Boston, and we have his third wife, Carlotta, saying that he could no longer hold a cigarette without burning himself, then he was not cured at all and no or almost no ghosts were banished by any of his great efforts in spite of what the public believes. Grief work removes addictions. It also removes neuroses (nonorganic) and phony roles and made-up behavior. Eugene was a master of that. I had been as well!

Being completely false does not stop an artist from portraying in a truthful way the state of humanity's misery but it *does* block any revelation of *how* it got that way or how it can get *free*. That is a virulent sign of Eugene's throttling and continuing emotional demise right up to the final passing. When cured, the real self emerges and is oceanic, euphoric, mostly from relief. I was. It lasted for months when a plain old resumption of ordinary life took over and that could have graced our hero, but he was denied any blessing of recovery. The head is abandoned as an outpost and full emotional vulnerability is restored. Of course, everything hurts when unpleasant but the positive elements register as never before and glee is actually experienced once in a while! I cannot help but wonder if his instructions to Random House about keeping *Long Day's Journey Into Night* sealed up for twenty-five years after his death was not only to spare persons but mostly to avoid while he was still around, the future ordeal of a public scrutiny of this most hurtful aspect of his history forcing him to relive it. Such a motive would also indicate a lack of curation for the most part. He was still essentially just a kid with his foot nailed to the floor by his parents and really only living an existence of variation circles. The internal distractions coupled with the dishonest conduct of those around him and the myriad devices and things in his world that offered, falsely, to relieve it all, all elements unknown or unyielded to by the whole among us, kept Eugene in a never-ending nightmare. As for the dysfunctional child grown up and gone thru recovery, there is still that ACOA magnet pull and I feel this for him in many ways. For those unfamiliar, "ACOA" is standard jargon for "Adult Child of Alcoholic" (or "Addict" or "Abandoner" or "Abuser"). He was a prisoner in a kind of *a jungle* that James and Ella put him in and his entire efforts and life were spent wandering around looking for a way out. His talk was jungle talk. His concerns and doubts were jungle thinking. His actions were of the bush and most of Eugene's totality was deep jungle thicket and he was way off the path! An instinct clash is behind this. World acclaim and clamor to the contrary, even works like *Long Day's Journey Into Night* or *The Iceman Cometh*, fierce drama to be sure, riveting and intense, nonetheless were full of *false, jungle stuff* and the product of that kid going around in circles desperate for the right answers.

The talk of "jungle" reminded me of *The Emperor Jones*, his 1920 offering on Broadway that brought international recognition, and I have to say that the story and the details behind it impressed me tremendously! Then there is the fact that it was composed on only three sheets of paper! All of the theatrical devices, the masks, the dreams, the constant tom-tom beat, ever increasing the tempo, the primitivity, the regression of memory to the past coupled with progression of psychological understanding, the romantic idealism, all of it just a marvelous artistic indulgence. On the minus side, however, the play seems to tag as defects in man, such as self-superiority, what is really only a symptom of victimization of the original lie unless mental illness is involved. A very pointed example is the view by O'Neill in the late plays, like *Iceman*, where romantic dreams are exposed as delusions and not characterized as either evil or beautiful but called, unbelievably, 'The very substance of human life'! Nowhere are they seen as *symptoms* of induced emotional illness. The prizes only underlined the proof that the planet was comprised of inhabitants who also hid in that wild wasteland.

Suddenly, I asked myself "What kind of a civilization uses a human being by calling him a 'National Savior' and the match of Ibsen and Chekov when in fact, he was a national tragedy, a boiling pot of 'insanity' on a child who is famous for wanting to be born that seagull or fish, who was always a stranger, unwanted, one of the fog people?" That poor kid, theater waif, plagued by a false mother who put false blame all over the place and a machine father without feelings, "soared" to make stage offerings that were pointed to by astounded critics and audiences and celebrated as revolutionary. Revolutionary though they might have been. O'Neill's works clearly revealed a very troubled and crooked person at the helm. They used him. They shunted aside his obvious need for help and instead gobbled up the entertainment, the shock, the horror of their own lives plainly portrayed or the pity for others that they were reminded of. O'Neill's private life was spread around soon enough so that a continuing meter was there for all to read. His missteps of a personal nature kept the public aware of his sickness, yet his utility was heralded and his need was not attended to or even sympathized with. All the opinionated and strong statements by him about man's weaknesses and victimization at the hands of fate were believed by many or most and so forth and they were dead wrong. Moreover, nowhere did O'Neill show, nor could he with his then current awareness or the public's, really, just how it was that these human tragedies came about or what remedy existed. One has to wonder what he figured was behind the tragic flaw present in every Greek hero in the ancient Greek plays that spelled the downfall in the end. Surely, he did not see the plain truth in that. Unless organic, those flaws were merely *symptoms* of beginnings similar to O'Neill's and were entirely *preventable*.

The kind of society that does such things are those infected with the same sickness, although the various symptoms occur in combinations that are not predictable. Using others for entertainment or shock to feel something or novelty to relieve boredom or for plain old amusement has always been the way. Never mind that the sports or theatrical or political or comedy or musical hero leads a questionable moral life, is a child abuser, an alcoholic, a drug addict, a womanizer, an adulterer, is in favor of violence or intolerance. Just look at the roster of famous persons over the last fifty or sixty years and one will see that this seems to be the rule. A U. S. President comes to mind, as does a famous painter or a baseball hero or a 1940's singer that was the rave or another U. S. President or a New York Mayor or a be bop inventor or many, many modern music figures. It seemed clear to me that in this way that society is a macrocosm of the kind of family that occupies *Long Day's Journey Into Night* or the other works by O'Neill. Everyone is either superhuman or subhuman and nobody is just human. All of the struggles revealed in O'Neill on stage are symptoms of the original lie and its offspring. These are rage, despair, meanness, trickery, self-dealing, false roles, guilt, addictions and neuroses, all uses of devices to survive and so forth. Juvenility is rampant. The masses that made O'Neill's plays count were and still are in need of being led by the hand. It is scandalous. His mother, Ella, could lead the pack with her lament "If only I could find my faith again". This is pitifully immature and simple-minded and it is as if she had been looking for a lost puppy. The same brand of behavior moves the tobacco addict who swears that he cannot give it up and then finds himself depressed over that. It is a sham. He smokes because he cannot get that feeling in any other way and it fills in some awful void and need that plague his life. The relief is the only thing that counts and a shorter life, a stinking body, an illness-ridden health history do not matter. Who wants a longer life when this one stinks itself? Such addictions as this one are not physical to any real degree in spite of what they say. I know first hand. I was heavily addicted and I beat it without any real symptoms. Of course, another one took over: alcohol.

Any audience identification with the O'Neill portrayals, especially *Long Day's Journey Into Night* were mostly a harp struck inside of hearts of gloom. Never do they really grasp what ticks in him or in the characters themselves, let alone see that a remedy exists and is glaringly omitted. While the presentation of the family members is no doubt accurate insofar as they were stand ins for O'Neill's real family, the "how" they really got that way and the "why" of it is missing. Conclusions at the end about what is really going on and the human factors responsible are wholly bogus and merely desperation by the author for an anchor and an end to the emotional ordeal of having belonged to that clan and of carrying its pain. He carried it to *his* end. I marveled at how much I had picked up about this man, his works, and just how his living and concepts dovetailed with mine, my past.

The "illusions" theme of *The Iceman Cometh* is really the same sort of thing. People labor under or resort to all kinds of pipe dreams, life lies, illusions, fake behavior, to survive, all the while miserable anyway underneath the surface. The play claims to state that mankind *cannot* survive, be happy, content, without this owing to certain *innate* characteristics. More bogus stuff! No awareness is there as well of the magic of a way out. I do not refer to Hickey's way out because *that* is based on a voluntary surrender of the masks of falsity, which is positive, but it will not turn the trick. Only an emotions-based transaction can do that and O'Neill never truly came close to one of those except for his "ordeal" in creating *Long Day's Journey Into Night*, and I have thoughts as to why *that* failed. In Iceman, the characters attach each other, shame each other, trick each other, hurt one another but they never go in for the real target, the parents, who created their misery, having inherited it themselves in like fashion. Nobody there seems to see this and the idea of *required* pipe dreams to deal with life is ludicrous. If the play were simply a commentary on how life is for many, many folks, that would be accurate, but it goes way beyond that in its bold and incorrect diagnosis of mankind. I am reminded of the presentation of the death penalty in this country today. It is as if everyone were blind. Television broadcasts news of it as though it were weather and no one grasps the utter damage that this spectacle does to children. Among the several outrageous effects from such a thing is the instilling of a fear of death in children. Death is a natural part of life and a blessing in the end. To fear death is to die as many times as O'Neill died over his tormented lifetime. It also shows kids that the value of human life is not *absolute*, which is absolutely horrible to teach. Then there is the prospect of retribution and state-sponsored violence. These are blessed by the exposure of this hideous penalty to children. The residence in the head in place of the vulnerabilities allows persons to "consider" the many arguments against such a travesty and then still vote for it on a hidden, private agenda. It was what brought Jesus down, yet they all go to church and praise him as the Prince of Peace. Later that day, they assent to the death penalty in a family discussion because some church leader says that it is alright in certain circumstances! Talk about an *illusion!* It was so plain to me now that the pain carriers, the fractured, toil in the field of constant unhappiness and really cannot get a grip on what is really behind it. These serfs stay down no matter what is up and such fate is the opposite of that carried by whole people, "up" no matter what goes wrong that day.

This struggle has a pointed example in O'Neill's 1906 first year at Princeton during which he ignored his studies, cut classes and met his brother, Jamie, in New York City on weekends for whoring and drinking binges. These two activities, class and schoolwork requirements versus partying in the way that he did are the opposite state of mind, yet engaged in by him simultaneously. Unless O'Neill was forced to go to college by his father when he really did not want to go at all, he had to have felt that a Princeton education would give him an ego and self-esteem increase and, maybe, pave the way for some kind of career success. Yet he acted like it did not matter and in this, I am reminded of myself getting the boot from another New Jersey university after one year for the same reason. I just did not care. I did not know, but O'Neill *must* have known, the degree of study required at Princeton or any college, really, yet he persisted in his ways. Talk about illusions and false behaviors. I figured that a similar thing was O'Neill's actions with respect to marriage and children. The illusions seem rampart there. His first, to Kathleen Jenkins in Hoboken, New Jersey in 1909 was an "impulse". He abandoned her one week later and set sail for Central America at his father's insistence. The second was to Agnes Boulton. That produced two children, Shane and Oona, to be added to the first one by Kathleen, Eugene, Jr. . This second holy union was thrown over the side when he decided that Carlotta Monterray was for him and he wed her in Paris in 1929. The effects would be devastating on these poor kids.

Everyone knows that the scene for Iceman was the Fulton Street bar where O'Neill lived as a derelict after returning from Argentina. There he nearly drank himself into oblivion followed by a near-successful sleeping pill attack on himself. This was 1912. So, his life even at the age of twenty-four was dramatic, reckless, loose and full of illusions-based conduct. A lot was pain avoidance by chemicals. In 1913, he resumed living in New London and declared his intention to be an artist or nothing and by 1916, his routine was writing obsession in place of any other real life. Again, more illusions behavior.

In 1915, Eugene moved to Greenwich Village and fell in with all sorts of interesting and intellectual people. Of course, 1920 brought that Broadway fun for him and then his father's passing in August of that same year. His brother, Jamie, died in 1923 at age forty-five, ten years his senior, in a facility in Paterson, New Jersey, from the effect of decades if inebriation which included near blindness! A year before, his mother, Ella, passed away, having beaten her morphine addiction, and so, Eugene lost everyone in the immediate family within two years. He was now alone in that respect but their ghosts were well entrenched inside his head and it would be almost twenty years before he would even begin to try to face it all for relief purposes. Misery lived between his ears and no prize could touch that. He did have some power and it is noted that he managed to make the Broadway big shots accept his work on *his* terms so it must have been quite important to them. Perhaps it was the experimental nature and revolutionary aspects of it all that made them fall in line for Eugene. He could write, though, and lots was poetic.

A person who is stuck in the kind of emotional prison that O'Neill was in, in spite of a family, a home, two children there, one far away, and Broadway pointing to his literary prowess, still comes up with stuff such as "homesick for homelessness and irresponsibility". The ruination that racked him was not about to allow a lining up of shattered pieces or any snap to attention on mere Pulitzers.

The medical advice that Eugene surrender the bottle at age forty resulted in his even deeper burrowing into writing to the point of retreat. He was quite burdened by his loss of the Catholic comfort but even more so by fears that he was only a pseudogenius and not capable of any masterpiece. The arrival of the third Pulitzer in 1928 for *Strange Interlude* did little to quell this demon. And the very next year, he was off to Paris with Carlotta with Agnes, Shane and Oona left in his wake. This new love was somewhat of a seductress, a false front, formerly played the role of Mildred in *The Hairy Ape* many years earlier, and had herself been deserted by her own mother when she was a child. That made *her* an ACOA and a perfect fit for Eugene. She persuaded him that he was entitled to great comfort and a different kind of life and he ate it up like the child that he was inside. Eugene visited Carlotta on multiple occasions on the Eastside of New York City where she had a lavish apartment. He was still with Agnes and the kids when his flirtation, back and forth, with the new one was making everyone unhappy. Eventually, their marriage in Paris was to last a stormy twenty-four years and he was a difficult husband. O'Neill appears to have abandoned during this period his efforts to "find his faith" and in its place, he began to focus on what was rotting inside him. While they were residents of Sea Island, Georgia, he came up with a candy-coated version of his childhood in New London and elsewhere and called it *Ah, Wilderness*. That was in 1932 and the next creation finished in 1933 and staged early January, 1934 at the Guild Theatre in New

York City, *Days Without End,* got such bad reviews that it made him withdraw completely out of anger and resentment and to, perhaps, punish everybody. I winced at this. When the Fall of 1936 rolled around, he had created a tentative cycle of nine plays already, and he and Carlotta moved to Puget Sound. Soon, that Nobel was announced but his condition allowed him to not travel to Sweden and by December, he was hospitalized where the prize was brought to his bedside. Talk about proceeding on one's own terms. That was December 17, 1937. At this juncture, they lived in California, and they returned there after his hospital discharge which was not always a sure thing. Because O'Neill felt bogged down by that cycle, he having now outlined ten of the eleven plays that he wanted, and he realized that he could never finish it, so he instead began work on things that involved his rotten insides. This was Spring, 1939. It was around this time that he got a diagnosis that he suffered from Parkinson's-like disorder.

Long Day's Journey Into Night became the immediate product of that focus thru gut wrenching recall and examination of his awful childhood on Pequot Avenue and it was finished in 1941. Yes, he did suffer a lot, there was much turmoil and tears, he became exhausted but nowhere is there a clear indication that anything curative came out of it. The pain that he was carrying, his parents' pain, cannot and could not have been removed with ease or in a rush. Only grief work can do it. He might have had snitches of it, some revelations, but the emotional transaction that is the real remedy cannot be a cerebral exercise. My guess is that some large amount of his tears was out of morbid depression and not grieving although an overlap was possible. But the discipline required to complete that "masterpiece" was enough of a distraction that it blocked full grieving and absent full grieving, one kids oneself. An even greater *masterpiece,* the rebirth of O'Neill's authentic self, long ago crushed and replaced by an imposter, awaited but that shining trophy was not to be had.

Statements to the effect that O'Neill had ridden himself of his pride (false pride) and his self-pity in the decade or so leading up to the time he wrote *Long Day's Journey Into Night* are incorrect because those personality defects, if you will, are symptoms of maltreatment as a child and nothing removes them short of the emotional transaction of grief work. The same has to be said about the prospect of his gaining of "compassionate understanding" towards his family members (represented by the Tyrones) although understanding is cerebral and recovery is not. The achievement of the latter allows the former to occur and without recovery thru grief work, no insights amounting to "compassionate understanding" of misbehaving persons is likely. Some identification with them might be, but no amount of true compassion can be because that is a genuine feeling and these poor people were forced out of their feelings beginning with babyhood and they reside in their heads only.

As to whether the playwright managed to *transcend* his former drive to place himself autobiographically in his works so as to rid the later ones of this personal involvement, I believe that what he did do was evolve into being less judgmental and more observing. That is about it. *Transcendence* is rising above so that in the case of good and evil, for example, the struggle between them is merely observed and neither is identified with. It could be the product of mere bewilderment.

It has been noted by experts that the morphine addiction of Ella O'Neill and the character that represents her in *Long Day's Journey Into Night* was intensified by the fact that there is *no real reason* for the addiction. It makes me blush to hear about such nonsense. *"Real reason"* for addiction is that the mood-altering effect of the substance, here morphine, is overwhelming insofar as it creates and holds feelings (temporarily) that whole people feel as a matter of daily fare. The relief of such an experience in the addict is all-important and no amount of body-damage or warning or punishment really registers. Ella O'Neill was an abused child and grew up to marry a child-abusing husband. She lived in an otherworldly haze and was quite juvenile. The morphine to her was like a Godsend because it allowed her to feel peace, well-being, comfort, stature, all things that euphoria brings. "No real reason" indeed!

It began to rain and my wipers were seriously old and streaking, so I had to strain to see the road but it lasted only about ten minutes and then the sun came back. This sort of snapped me out of my thinking-fog and made me realize that I was driving as a robot and not focusing on the road per se. Yet, the fog went on.

It suddenly dawned on me that O'Neill probably obtained *relief from bitterness* when he wrote of the Tyrones and the confessions and revelations about his father's miserliness and personal theatricality, his brother's meanness and hardness and his mother's withdrawal and dream world trance. Hearing the *reasons* for behavior that hurts us can remove the sting of it but any damage done to a child by reason of such behavior, especially over a long period, cannot be removed without grief work. Understanding the why of the maltreatment is a start, however, towards that special state of giving up control over tears and blocking out all distractions to allow free-fall. If O'Neill says he got *more* than relief like that, he was faking it. It was wishful thinking just as in *Ah, Wilderness.*

Proof of this prospect, I was certain, lies for the world to see. O'Neill's life was never purged of addiction or emotional turmoil or marriage failures or the emotional shakiness that prevented driving a car or continuing estrangement from his three children, two of which did themselves in. They got this from their dad!

The end of this play is bogus in that it pretends to reflect *illumination, peace, the joy of belonging* (though there might have been some of this if even to a horribly defective clan) and support *euphoric freedom.* None of this is ever possible in the abused child grown up unless recovery is had at the end of about three months hard crying and grieving to produce the biochemical changes needed.

The public and the powers that be might have been shocked or lulled or both into a conclusion that Eugene O'Neill had shown the way, the road for tormented souls to find peace and wholeness. He did not. No place is there any indication that he understood how a beaten child grows up to become a child beater or why a battered wife stays on year after year or how it is that a family composed of hatred and hateful acts nonetheless refuses to split up. All we get are celebralizations and explanations that fall far short. *Forgiveness* is fine but it is not any answer. That all are *innocent* is fine, too, but no key. How is the ruination of a child even possible (absent organic disorders) and what is the cure? *Novelty* of O'Neill's works no doubt had a hand in all this because nobody had until he came along ever seen such graphic human misery on a stage and with such skill, power and imagination. A large majority had such stuff hidden in their inner vaults and these plays allowed them to feel some relief in that they saw that others understood what festered in them. But that is not remedial. It was a misery loves company thing.

That was my life, too, and I felt so lucky as I drove towards New London that I no longer suffered under that yoke. I pondered the details of the *original lie* and how it gives birth to the *ultimate life-lie* which is the *ultimate illusion,* namely, that everyone who is not a whole person, a large majority, is welded to the notion that they can think their way out of any emotional dilemma or misery. They cerebralize about dysfunction and believe that the right track is only a matter of thinking the right kinds of thoughts. So, when they learn that all of that is crap, that only an emotion transaction can deliver them from the clutches of addiction, neurosis and false lives, and that an unfettered free-fail is required without distractions or crutches, they usually project denial.

O'Neill's efforts in *Long Day's Journey Into Night* were not to embrace pain but to escape it. However, he might have had an intuition that it had to be cried out, *not thought out*, but that suffering was so intense that he thought that he would break. This is common. I felt, too, I thought to myself, but I did not break. I was restored to wholeness after two months of nonstop tears. Eugene, therefore, was engaging in another artifice when he resisted outright grieving except to the extent that a play can not be written while the author is out of control. Anyway, his mission was a "thought mission", a cerebral examination to try to figure it all out and to find relief *that way*. He was desperate to *understand* those who were supposed to love him as a son, a brother and to *forgive* them for the awful life that they inflicted on him and each other. That enslaver is subject to little change by discovery and major overthrow comes by giving up to the pain and resisting it no more. That kind of discovery is really not critical anyway because it is all duly registered in the hidden, cowering child inside. He will direct the recovery show. It is extremely interesting that Eugene O'Neill himself is quoted as saying that "Truth goes deep, so it reaches you through your emotions. They are instinctive". This seems to be an indication that he realized that instinct rules emotions and that they are primal and not really subject to alternation by falsity and, further, that *truth* reaches a person through these emotions. But what he did not grasp, and I do not fault this, is the idea that latching onto one's emotions and letting them run amok, not in hysteria which is neurosis, but in healthy grieving, was the answer to his prayers for relief. The *truth* of the monkey on his back was available for him to learn and cure with had he known that free fall emotions would do the trick if given enough time. But Eugene O'Neill was full of neurosis and it is no wonder that he could not discern that difference. It is noteworthy that any professional assistance that he sought with regard to his emotional turmoil and drinking completely missed this. Such is the state of psychotherapy even today I am sad to say.

Because James and Ella O'Neill were addicts, he, alcohol, she, morphine, they set up their sons to follow suit. It is almost always the cause. The emotional damage inflicted by the parents causes a great need in the child and the addiction fills the bill as artificial feelings of power, relief, self-esteem and joy. In a way, Eugene *became* his parents. The void in an abused and neglected kid means no true identity and the identity of the mother and father are used to fill that in. Also, they are the tormentors and a phenomenon occurs, similar in prisoners of war, where the victim joins the wrongdoer's ranks by adopting his identity. It is a way to imagined safety. I shrink from the memory of this, my alcoholic family and their cronies, my grandfather, so decadent and pitifully cynical, mean, and his daughter, my mother, and her son, my half-brother, now forty-seven and mellowed quite a lot.

I was just now coming to New Haven on Interstate 95 and every time I did that, a change would come over me as I remembered Yale University, my six weeks there for the Connecticut Bar Examination review course in the summer many years before and then the day of reckoning that awful July when the actual ordeal was at hand! I could not have known, but I passed easily when 34% did not.

That presence at Yale and the one in 1994 when I lived in Hamden, home to Thorton Wilder, and bummed around New Haven nearly every day never imagining that my feet went right where O'Neill's son's went now amazed me. He was a strong Greek-Classics scholar there and made Phi Beta Kappa. Then, the playwright himself got an honorary doctorate around his fortieth birthday when he was the guest of the president at the Yale-Dartmouth football game. So many famous and prominent persons have roots at Yale!

I recalled suddenly that my time in Hamden was nearly always consumed by painting and I was cranking out nearly four a week! Then, there was Joseph Campbell, one of my heroes, whom I discovered on PBS-TV. He filled me up, and many were the days and nights of actual loneliness where I would ponder Campbell and the wonderful way that he *raised* me up.

Then there was the historic part of New Haven, the Revolutionary times and events occurring right there on the Green. Nearby, was the sight where I was sworn into the Connecticut bar.

Soon, the road was slanting to the right towards the east and all that New Haven was seeped away and I noticed that I had about an hour left to drive. I gave a silent salute to Interstate 91, which went due north towards Hartford County, the place where I withstood and contributed to mightily in the judicial system for twenty-three years.

By the time Eugene was seventeen years old, he was a ruined man, an animal, desperate, lonely, miserable, bitter, lost, pitiful, a con artist. He probably seemed different that that in public: learned, freewheeling, conversational, happy-go-lucky, colorful in his language and tastes, but it is usually that way for children caught in his kind of web. They say that he was shy, even to the point sometimes of being rude, but the tantrum was always there under the surface, and a whole host of tantrum reasoning by a drunk is behind his many conclusions about mankind and human nature which were almost laughable except for the tragedy of it all. From that age until his death at age 65, he was more or less the same: disowning any true role of father, flitting from romance or ideas of same to new adventures there, reckless, substance-dependent, seeking, searching to grasp what was wrong inside, ever mobile and ready to establish new quarters, difficult, sour, depressed, anxious, shaky, driven, worried.

As I stopped the car to get out to stretch, I saw clearly that in spite of his monumental ability to come up with ideas for stage productions, the vast variety of themes, his prolific prowess, the novelty, the innovation and experimentation, O'Neill never presented the *germ* that was within the reach of *all* who suffer as he did and from what he did. Although it lurked inside him and them, its flowering is and was always suppressed. No matter that his creations garnered a Nobel and three Pulitzers while he lived, shocked audiences and moved them deeply, and greatly reshaped American theater, he never was hit by the revelation of the remedy to it all. He had, it would have been a tiara-topping diamond. That he himself never benefited from the cure, I marshaled the evidence rolling across my mind: first, his tobacco addiction right up to the end of his life proves that he was still suffering and still a fractured person; addictions fall away upon recovery; then, near his death November 27, 1953, O'Neill made a statement to his wife, Carlotta, "Born in a hotel room and. God damn it, died in a hotel room". His birth was in New York City in 1888, Barrett House at Broadway and Forty-third Street and his death in the Shelton Hotel in Boston. The *key* here is the use of *profanity*. It shows a lack of peace, an agitated and fearful state of mind, and it expresses a *rage* that he still carried and rightfully so. Such anger is *not* carried by whole people or abused children who grow up and go thru recovery thru grief work. It was simmering. It is made of childhood bounty violations, being made to feel worthless, being hurt by the ones he loved by instinct, having to stay with the abusers out of necessity and a fear of being alone. People who curse used to be innocent. It is bitterness with a voice. Third, near the end, O'Neill had ample opportunity to have *something* with his two children, Shane and Oona, Eugene, Jr. already having committed suicide, but he really did not. This is a sign of continuing turmoil. Carlotta got his estate in its entirety although he did leave Spithead in Bermuda to the kids quite a while before his death, so that they did have that. He did disown Oona because of her marriage to Charlie Chaplin and Carlotta did interfere with any meaningful contact with Shane due to his radical thinking.

Fourth, it was a generally accepted idea that his plays were all Eugene O'Neill ever really cared about and that while he was deep in the period of creating them, it was obsessive and excluded much of all else. This would be typical for any child who went thru what he did if there were a special talent a hand. Being an artist ruled his existence. It was what he perceived was a way to boost the inadequacy that lived as a tenant for free in his head and heart. He carried a notion that he, indeed, was a genius, and that there was some masterpiece in him, but the fears of falling short, of being the pseudogenius, drove him relentlessly. And, this very same *obsession* amounted to one of the *blocks* to free-fall that might have helped him during the times that he got up the nerve to dig and delve and search the awful, hideous, hidden muck that contaminated his existence every day on earth. He might well have presented the "answers" to it all at the end of *Long Day's Journey Into Night*, but again, they were bogus and desperation-born; next, around 1943, after O'Neill had completed *The Iceman Cometh* and *Long Day's Journey Into Night*, he is said to have remarked that if he took sedatives, he'd feel like a "dull dope" and that if he did not take them, he'd have maggots crawling inside his skin and that the "inner shakes" were harder to bear than the "outer shakes". This shows that he was anything but cured of the affliction that James and Ella forced upon Eugene. Such statements are by a man who was not cured or whole; Moreover, O'Neill admitted that he *never* resolved his inner conflicts, one being that of 'true nature' vs. 'acquired qualities'. Then, even though he could no longer write after about 1943 due to his tremors, O'Neill still continued to try to find out, understand, what made people tick and what made his family history so terrible. This shows that he did not know and had he been restored to wholeness, he would have.

Seventh, his instructions to Random House about the sealed copy of *Long Day's Journey Into Night* never being published until twenty-five years post his passing, aside from considerations of the effect on persons involved and still living, shows that he probably *feared* having to endure a public reaction to it and *dreaded* any reliving of that family history by way of inquiries and follow up criticisms. It was a guard. The creation itself was aimed at relief but because of *distractions*, there was, again, no free fall; had he been cured, his joy would have been trumpeted.

Eighth, the *distractions*: One cannot effectively grieve the loss of one's authentic self and take the weeks or months required if there are distractions and crutches. His addiction to at least tobacco was just such a crutch. If there were sedative use also during his brave examination of his life during the creation of *Long Day's Journey Into Night*, that would be another. But the distractions were myriad and they had to have shunted the waiting benefit from all his tears at delving into the awful, painful years at the hands of self-dealing, emotionally unavailable parents with the hatreds, false blaming, shaming, belittling, boundy violations, loneliness and pettiness. So, while a haggard, weeping, exhausted man did appear at the end of many of those days, the following kinds of elements prevented much good from coming of it:

a.   His efforts were ego-driven and not recovery driven and thus he was always aware of the effect of his efforts rather than at the mercy of free fall grieving; there *was* a desire to gain total relief but it was pain endurance as a *price* to come up with the play and not pain embracing to recover his lost, real self;

b.   His efforts were also masterpiece driven, engaged in fear that he might not be a genius but only that pseudogenius;

c.   A desperate need to matter, present all his life, drove the creation and this as well was a distraction from grieving; Escape from being nobody, nowhere, belonging to no one and no place pressed him always;

d.   A need to feel and sense the power that all ACOA's lack was another motive for that play and this, too, was a distraction;

e.   The discipline required to produce a work of art cannot prevail when in free fall, and that was another impediment; details of scenery, costumes, stage directions, lighting, other technical matters, not to mention effective dialogue, all need the playwright's attention and intense focus;

f.   Eugene was understandably distracted by Carlotta; she lived there with him, she was his shield from loneliness; she supported him and there would always be a natural tendency for him to give "account" to her day to day, night to night; she also put up with him and he must have felt remorse at times over that; also, Carlotta's main motives in this marriage of codependents, enabling each other, were to be married to a famous man and a genius. There had to be some pressure in that on Eugene, however subtle;

g.   The war in Europe, begun in 1939, was a major concern to O'Neill and he followed news accounts of it and was distressed by it; this distracted him;

h.   The tremors in his hands greatly upset O'Neill and this, too, distracted him.

Next, The Iceman Cometh was written in 1939, the same year that O'Neill began work on Long Day's Journey Into Night, and the idea of the Hickey character attempting to get the bar patrons to surrender their illusions and to live without guilt proves that the author was still in the clutches of child mistreatment. If there is guilt in a person and it comes from a false life or a false face, it cannot be removed simply by giving up the falsity. First of all, surrendering that, although a good first step in real recovery, will not last if unaccompanied by the grieving process. The false life creeps back because it "works" and because the person really knows no other way from shortly after birth. Also, guilt cannot be removed by thinking it away. If it is born of a misdeed in a whole person, say by way of injury to another by negligence, that guilt can be relieved by forgiveness or by certain restorative efforts aimed at the victim. But "guilt" in a fractured person is not a real thing anyway but merely part of the false emotional existence. Perhaps, that "Guilt" can be alleviated by certain imagined eradicators like dedication to a "victim" but that seems like codependence and nothing more or just face saving. The fractured person is living outside of his or her vulnerabilities and feelings and true guilt cannot be felt by them. The illusions part, removable only by recovery thru grief work, is a stain on every mistreated child, abused, neglected or abandoned, Hickey might as well have asked them to fly out a window by waving their arms. O'Neill's conclusions that those illusions, pipe dreams, are *required* for man to survive owing to his weaknesses as a species shows his being in the dark about his own defective engines. It is pure cerebralization. Hickey's dark secret, that killed his wife because he really hated her and not to, as he said, to help her, to save her from suffering, is more of the same. It might be great theater and a poignant portrayal of the layers of falsity possible, but it is no kind of ultimate revelation. That life is in paralysis without life-lies is nonsense conjured up by a desperate alcoholic, dry or not. It could *seem* like paralysis, but the real defect is in the fractured soul. Illusions are just devices. Further, the themes presented about God and redemption and salvation show more mere cerebralization by an uncured mind as well as a low level of consciousness attendant to the intellect of all such defective thinkers as O'Neill here. A lack of spirituality is universal in the fractured person although it might seem otherwise for some who are obsessive about religion. It is an imagined savior and not more. Only attainment of wholeness can bring back the *natural* spirituality that *is* innate. And the theme of an "abyss" is ridiculous. It is mere desperation, though understandable. Finally, the idea that in the end, everybody is trapped with everybody else, trapped by the past, by the "guilt", by innocence, by pitying, by forgiving but not forgetting, again proves that O'Neill had not recovered from his childhood ordeal emotionally. Yes, they are locked in by their pasts but it is not intractable. It is wholly subject to correction.

Tenth, the Roman Catholic upbringing of O'Neill has its place in this. The dogma is like a mantra. Had he been some other denomination or religion, it is less likely that his efforts over the many years searching for the lost device would have added up so. Spirituality was removed from him by early abuse and the indoctrination put in its place was an insult, actually because it was projected by parents without spirituality and just going thru the motions, onto a child with none and following suit just to survive. No wonder that he was *haunted*. Whole people do not suffer so in their musings on God. But the fractured, if they engage in anything religious, have to know every little detail. The stories are unbelievable and ludicrous. Unabused and unneglected people grow up to have a natural sense of what God is and what salvation and redemption are made of and they do not pine over the mystery of it all and the universe and the seeming inconsistencies in life and the naturally occurring tragedies like the deaths of innocent children. Also, they do not require advance knowledge about any afterlife. O'Neill's struggle in this area is just another sign of his continuing defective state.

Then, *Long Day's Journey Into Night* shows *many* hints that its author was not recovered, at lease by 1941 when this work was completed. The language about being more successful as a fish or seagull than a man means that he was not a whole man. The talk of being one of the "fog people" is another. Then there is the "stammering" comment and the always being a stranger comment and the never belonging comment. His beautiful and touching and haunting descriptions of becoming the sea, dissolving in it, becoming moonlight, belonging, no past or future, a wild joy, serenity greater than life, being drunk with the beauty of it, becoming the sun, the hot sand, the secret itself are all signs of hope for Eugene even though he was speaking thru the character, Edmund. It showed an ability to be spiritual, a peek thru the window of that antithesis of the O'Neill lifelong torment and struggle, but it is not a sign of having been cured. The fact that he let this play out of his control to Random House meant that he agreed with its content and that content was anything but indicative of a recovered victim. He spoke of it being "terrible to face and forgive" with respect to the Tyrone family, a substitute for his own there on Pequot Avenue. But real forgiveness is not terrible but comes with ease when wholeness is reached. Yes, it *is* terrible to face it in the beginning when a life has been spent numbing out or running away inside, but the characterization of his comments indicates that there was no real healing in the writing of the thing or the delving into his past. He might have fancied that he forgave everybody that he portrayed them *without judgment*, but he was *driven* to find relief. He might have accurately shown each family member fact-wise, but so what? Mary, the mother figure, has to be listened to by the other family members because of her *beauty!* This is an excellent symbol of how the world operates. Surface counts and gets you through and truth does not. But this is not the true world but only this rotten one that O'Neill thought was everybody! He cast Mary as *needed* by the other family members but she returns to her morphine habit and defeat and degradation. This was his way of showing that nobody owns anybody else in this life or the next. It seems to be an O'Neill device to relieve distress and agony inside him. Ella, the real life Mary, was a fractured girl and woman, was bent early in life on becoming a nun. She, like her son, was always searching for her lost faith. Nowhere in the end of this play is the message of true emotional recovery or its workings and that is another hint.

The theme of self-hatred runs throughout this work but, again, where is the root of it, the true source, and what does it really mean? O'Neill does not hit on this nor the path out in any genuine manner. Twelfth, add the fact that O'Neill had been all along and continued to be well after the 1939-41 span was too emotionally frantic and frail to drive a car. This shows that he was not a whole or even nearly whole person.

Finally, another critical piece of evidence was his and Carlotta's nearly simultaneous "nervous breakdown" and physical breakdown in 1946, which had them ending up, coincidently, in the same hospital. This was caused by tensions and failures to control things that each felt threatened by such as Carlotta's reaction to her husband's flirting with young actresses. Carlotta's who had been married three times before O'Neill, which shows emotional instability and damage from an abusive childhood, even deserted Eugene from jealousy. Their day-to-day marriage was often stormy because both were fractured people and not yet or ever cured. The very fact of staying with Carlotta after 1941 proves that O'Neill was not recovered or cured because whole people do not, cannot, stand to be with fractured, codependent ones whose neediness is like a flashing neon light. The flirting shows codependence and pursuit of sexual novelty, hardly appropriate for a married man.

I next realized that many have observed that O'Neill's plays are full of truths and revelations and that none of it is made up. Nowhere is such notation more frequently applied than in *The Iceman Cometh* and *Long Day's Journey Into Night*, and I am certain, all of it is based on his actual experiences in New London as a child and the aftermath. But the level of consciousness held by the public and the critics and the award-givers was quite low in 1920 and beyond and it is not much higher today. Maybe it did not rival that of the gorilla in the cage in The *Hairy Ape* in the way it regarded the roles and characters in the late plays. The ape's drives and perceptions were primitive and base; pain avoidance and pleasure seeking and not much more. Moreover, it is kept in that prison without regard for his feelings merely to make money and satisfy the lust for novelty, excitement, danger and so forth. In this way, the gorilla is not that much apart from O'Neill. No one gave a hoot for his suffering or defective dignity. He was just a curiosity, a device to take the public mind off of their own ball and chain, to entertain, to induce feeling where there was none. O'Neill scared them or titillated them and so, *they used him*. To be sure his artistic skills are amply evident in the portrayal of human interactions in the world in the Ape and later plays, but they all are missing that crowning jewel. No place does a body see any hint that the miserable author knew, past what I have already set forth, a whit about recovery or that the vast majority of miscreants and n'er do wells in the world were *made* and not born. I wonder if O'Neill actually saw himself as that ape, emotionally imprisoned, used by society, immersed in a climate of ubiquitous rage, misdirected hate, anesthesia, anxiety, depression, false roles, crookedness for gain, struggle against authority held by the law or the employer and always the outsider, never belonging. He yearned for the oceanic paradise. That struggle was a phony substitute for one against the parents. Marvelous is the use of music in the Ape to balance the roughness. A concertina is stolen by a ship hand who does not play but who indulges a futile grasp at gaiety, refinement, power and freedom, as though such things could be garnered by dishonesty! All the characters seem to be corrupted by the same thing but each displays it in a different way such as the sly-eyed seductress, Mildred, who casts men off with glee after using them. The men tending the coal furnace on board labor under pretty unpleasant conditions. The character called Yank boasts "I'm the one who makes her go" in his ape-like manner. The blow to Yank is palpable when Mildred rejects his masculinity and calls him an ape. Following shortly is a stern lecture to her while she bathes by another, older woman but the dose of moral reality rolls off her like the soap bubbles. Eventually the Apeman is caught by the law trying to get at sly-eyes to "smash her before she smashes me". They put him in a cage and break him down with a high pressure water hose. He is reduced to a child like trance, defeating him the way that chronic abuse defeats every child. He himself had been lectured on moral reality by the ship's captain, but it, too, rolled off. The "toys" manufactured by mistreating parents just keep going and going until the wheels finally fall off. Sometimes, those wheels magically pop back on and the charade goes on indefinitely. Yank is the ultimate coal shoveler and that is how he matters and controls. His satellites are hopelessly locked in around him as are those of Mildred. They are all hangers-on to the power that they see in that center. The maniacal shoveling is a symbol for the human doing instead of the human being. His illusions are readily cracked when called "a hairy ape" and his worthlessness grabs him by the throat just like when his parents first instilled it. For the instant, his shield of denial falls and the enraged little child violently rises up. But when the troublemaker faints at Yank's advances and dominance, a neutralization occurs and he is reduced to stroking her hair and face. Soon, he backs off and returns to the same old life, making the ship go, but now *he* possesses the whistle that the superior shipmate used to blow to control the coal shoveling like an imagined slavedriver and Yank's mates are mirthfully fooled as he twinkles his eyes. That furnace is life and it requires attention without letup. Sly-eyes is life, too, in all of its fickle ways and the beauty in her face, her lines, her ways, allows great power while her guile gets her what beauty does not. But, really, she herself is used as well and in the way, is the *female ape*. As an aside, Eugene's father might have been in the Monte Cristo cage and his mother, Ella, in the beauty cage, both used by others, as was Carlotta by Eugene.

Relief is what Eugene O'Neill sought every day of his life and that is what is painted on the face of Yank when the girl faints in his grip. She is entirely controlled by him and perceived no longer as a threat. Of course for O'Neill, "relief" came in the bottle, a cigarette, sedatives, false life. The valiant attempts to find it in the writing of *Long Day's Journey Into Night* were condemned from the start because he was examining pain and not really seeking it. It was his cerebralization remedy and it fell far short. O'Neill had to understand deep inside that he was way off the path, that what they had done to him and his heart had to be *cried out*, but the same digging in of the heels that anchors denial also blocks out of control emotions like that and chaos was what he was running *from*. It is quite understandable that he would never run *towards* it! Besides, that long-term solution, taking months ideally, was not his usual prescription for pain. O'Neill was used to quick relief such as whiskey or pills, relief in the moment. Immediate gratification was also a factor.

The mission in writing that great play was not a therapeutic one so much as it was a literary one, to get that masterpiece finally for his ego, his desperate striving to matter, by using the most dramatic stuff he had in himself! The considerations about forgiveness, probably genuine, were tag-along really. O'Neill was steering a *great ship*. The hull was reinforced in Sweden and the three masts made in New York City at Columbia.

Certainly, there could have been the "laxative" sensation while he was deep in the delving. Although one cannot expect a picnic of pain, there can be a certain "pleasant" sensation accompanying the reliving of the childhood misery. It would be similar to the moment on the toilet when the constipation gives way. Yes, it does stink and it sounds horrible, but a wonderful sense of clearation and relief comes and maybe even a mild feeling of well-being. We can never be sure but it is very clear that he did not drown in the unhappiness so as to trigger the authentic grieving required. He kept his head above water while he steered that ship. In that way, he drowned one thousand times instead of just one. His efforts were a partial mountain climb but when he died in 1953, he was clinging to a crag, still on the way up, stuck and cynical. The wounded little boy was still in hiding and he died there. I feel deeply for him and cannot help but sense some connection to him. *Long Day's Journey Into Night* was born the same year as I was, 1941, but I, unlike that author, got lucky and made the same delving. Mine was, however, unwittingly and the result of pain being *forced* onto me. It sent me where I had to go, where Eugene sort of trod but recoiled from. Mine was the same family of drugs and alcohol and emotional violence and shaming and grim playfulness. I was unbelonging as was he. I was in a trance like his "fog". I fit in nowhere and struggled every day of my existence like him. I *see* Eugene like few others are able to. I am now descended from that same mountain and the same age that he was in 1953 at the final point. Now, as I drive back to New London, I ponder those horse and buggy days of long ago. Something quakes in me. Now, when I am at that same sea, it becomes all the points that Edmund as character recited but without the desperate slant. Now, the mystery is so much grander and humbling than O'Neill ever could have tapped into and raptured over. It is so much more profound, the danger so much more keen, the refreshment exhilarating, the power unavoidable, the fishlike feelable, the surreal floating and soaring unimaginable in its delighting, the roots of humanity so much more discernable. It is like the first dose of a mother's eyes that turn away and strike the first blow, only it is the *intensity* and not the *tragedy* of it.

I drove along and suddenly came upon in my mind that little, bronze statue of him on a rock in New London harbor. Then I hear a visitor there in the summertime and she gawks at Eugene and remarks how nice it is. "No, lady, it's not so nice, you are caught in a web of lies".

CHAPTER TWO:
UNRIPENED

Lord knows, just lying around doing nothing day after day, one barely has an original thought. But driving, especially a long distance, the only occupier is the road and the danger that hangs over the head, nutcase, blowout, whatever, is soon dulled and only the trip's end is sought. It is in this frame of mind that a topic of recent interest might bloom into all sorts of things, insights, comparisons, that could otherwise be lost forever. Such a theme, that nearly all people, adults, are hopelessly suspended and stuck in a juvenile state, struck me not long ago. Now it was nearing 11:00 a. m., I yawned and thought that because this is true for nearly all persons, to one degree or another, there is a general unawareness of the thing due to lack of contrast with emotionally whole adults. They are rare.

It seemed so clear to me but not to all that such a state is evident everywhere. The relationship with the government, any level, is one of parent-child. Laws instruct what citizens must do nor not do and the consequences for disobeying. Swimming in too rough an ocean can get an adult arrested. The parent-government knows better and apparently, method of suicide for compos mentis adults is *not* off limits! One wonders what O'Neill would make of that! Ditto for freedom of employment. The parent takes away an adult's right to work for whatever compensation he can command and it insists on price fixing labor by minimum wage laws. This steals freedom and is a substitution by the State for adult judgment. Then there are the judges who scold defendants and lecture them as if a speech will overcome the defect that is in place that fosters stealing, cheating on taxes, drunken driving and so forth. Never does one see a judicial focus on the roots of crime. Only the symptoms are attacked and it is always parent to child. An unique brand of this is the death penalty. The State inflicts this sort of violence onto a receiver or Defendant but the penalty itself is collective, juvenile-state rage and is a substitution for the real target, the parents who forced children out of their vulnerabilities and into their heads. It reminds one of the totalitarian government which is always a parent-child system. Most of the world recoils from infliction of death as a penalty but it remains an American stain.

I saw now that relationships in religion are the same thing but they take two forms: clergy-parishioner is one, and the claims made by religious "authority" is the second. "Father" to denote a priests or reverend and "Mother Superior" in the Catholic faith are prime examples. The masses are referred to like children, be it Christian, Jewish, Hindu, Islam, Buddhist or other faiths. It strives to comfort them in a juvenile manner and it instructs what is proper and what is not. It assures about "horrors" such as death, what comes after death if misbehavior was at hand in life, and generally attending the flocks to ward off the boogie man in the dark. It is always handing down or looking down. Then come the claims. They reflect the juvenility of the clergy, the religious status quo, as well as the receivers and believers of the claims. It is a *world by magic* phenomenon, normal in the under age nine child, but not in adults. However, it is prevalent in adults who are under age nine emotionally, stuck there by parental mistreatment which blocks maturation. For kids who are very young, daddy disappears or mommy disappears in the morning and there is no concept of what is going on. Then at the end of the day, the working parent *magically* reappears. Again, the kid does not grasp work or need to earn money and so forth. This also explains the myriad of juvenile activities abounding on earth like tarot cards, superstitions, "fate", fortune tellers, astrology, hexes, palmists. It is a world by magic there. In religion, the magic stays. Satan is believed as a real entity and not just a metaphor for mental illness, which is what evil, is. Concepts of "Devine intervention" are similar. It is entirely acceptable for the clergy to deal with the masses from a parent-child position only if God is really the "parent" and they are giving voice to that. But ideas like changing events by prayer instead of limiting prayer to its real function, focus, acts of community, and consciousness raising, is world by magic nonsense and followed only by juvenile-state people although they will deny it and, maybe, blacken your eye if challenged. The religious authorities spread this butter over their congregations, which wallow in it until their church burns down. Then there is a crisis of faith. "My goodness, did we not pray enough?" This state of mind does not grasp that God is a destroyer as well as a creator. The mystery is too great to be of use to the neediness, so it is tampered with. Man's origin, fate, destiny is well detailed by persons who have no channel to the great mystery, but the juvenile *need* demands answers.

There might be another source of adult juvenility loose on earth to graft itself upon the abused masses, namely, the nature of nature. Mankind cowers to the likes of lightening, floods, earthquakes, volcanoes, tidal waves, fierce storms, and there might be a tendency to assume the emotional posture of a helpless child to such "parents", especially ones of whim and cruelty, and this could maintain a sense of juvenility instead of taking such elements for what they really are and in stride the way that whole people take death.

The unripeness is all around us. A man is caught speeding and he puts on his best downcast face for the officer much as a real child snagged with his hand inside the cookie jar. An alternative cover is babbling and the apprehended individual might resort to all kinds of stories about traffic, his life, and his problems. Danger brings it out, confrontation does the same, and unexpected developments do it, too. Then there is the rage. The enraged juvenile has temper tantrums right in the middle of his adult life. Violence erupts the same way. It comes from being made to feel worthless and violated and is bottled up because it is unacceptable to let it show all the time. "This is the usual way", I said out loud.

Now I was firmly headed east and a sweep came as if a freedom pulled me away from those New Haven and Hartford County memories and thrust me into the likes of Harkness State Park. My move to Hamden was preceded by a time in New London where I tried to paint but felt blocked. Substituted were the outdoors, the ocean and Harkness! A wonderful place it was. Why there must have been 1000 feet of coastline on the saltwater, Long Island Sound, with sand and trees and a wide-open expanse of lawn that reached back hundreds of yards to the access road.

Centered and near the water was the boarded up mansion with gardens of the owner eons ago, Edward Harkness, a tycoon in the early twentieth century who, is is said, was hated by Eugene O'Neill for his involvement with other more well-known magnates of industry, and perhaps for other reasons. They *were* neighbors of sorts with the Harkness complex lying just west of new London.

My mind suddenly turned to a time when it used to be July and me, barely clad, and running when the sun held the air in a 90-degree spell. This twice a week ritual consumed an imaginary oval on the lawn in front near the road and I was the marathoning 'warrior' until two miles had been done. Other moments were more serene and lulled away by the waves, the constantly changing shell variety or the girls! It was sort of a desert of thirst with relief all around but never could I connect for a drink! Loneliness! When approaching Harkness from New London, one had to drive past the Eugene O'Neill theatre and when I did, there was never a thought or concern. I knew the name but not a lot else save the old girlfriend's connection to him.

Other common aspects of the unripened adult are the use of fantasy and imagination to deal with reality. This might include the pipe dream life put forth by O'Neill in *The Iceman Cometh*. In that reality, the lion changes the art of the zebra by adding red. The gentle, graceful gazelle is made ugly and ruined by the appetite of the king. Because the juvenile mind cannot bless it and resorts to denial, walls of hardness, it fails especially insofar as such protections are applied in life every day.

Immaturity in the employer-employee relationship is rampant although it does not have to be. Except for laws governing same, employers dictate and employees ignore at the risk of losing the job, dress code, hours, shifts, behavior, and expression and often, these are perceived by the employees as parental orders and chafted at or begrudgingly followed. Stealing at work is a juvenile device to "get back" at the "oppressor".

Unripened people clamor for immediate gratification. When they are age ten, that is expected but when twenty, it is a symptom. The same is true for irresponsibility, codependence, shamelessness, egoism and rebellion.

Unripened parents cannot bring forth whole children. Fractured children grow up to repeat the cycle unless a *trance-breaker* comes in like death without offspring or recovery through grief work with reclaims of authentic self. Intelligence is not a factor and the principle applies to the brilliant and the retarded. Many geniuses were emotionally retarded and very juvenile.

"Who sees this?" , I wondered. Illusion-use, fantasy, common and normal in the child, is used by adults who are the product if ill treatment by parents on a chronic level, or absence by parents, be it neglect, abandonment in fact via death of the parent or deliberate abandonment, or constructive abandonment by walling the kids out and being emotionally unavailable which delivers the message that the children are worthless. Mistreatment is the product of mental illness in the parent or a history in the parent of having been the victim of abuse as a child. *Pipe dreams* to survive are *false conduct* in adults who are still juveniles but who hold adult powers. Illusions are not required for man to get along in life and are not based on anything *innate*.

I was certain that Eugene can be thought of as an epitome of what juvenile-state parents can do to a child. One has to wonder what O'Neill's life and work would have consisted of had he been reared by whole parents instead of fractured ones. Certainly, the motivations that drove him to produce what he did would have been absent. He had a sort of a *life and death struggle* going on in his emotions and the agony of being James's and Ella's son was a constant distraction. *Escape* for Eugene was daily fare. So was pain relief, trying to matter, trying to belong, fighting the awful notions of worthlessness and apparent meaninglessness of his life and, later, of mankind's. Of course his father's artistic bent and theatrical experience and fame all had a part in spurring O'Neill on to do what he did and had he had a whole father and mother, such paternal influence could have gotten Eugene in the arts anyway but the drama, the desperation, the product that shocked and moved the public, these things garnered the Nobel and the Pulitzers even if the conclusions by O'Neill as to *root* of the misery and the absence in his plays of reference to *remedy* of an authentic kind are glaringly erroneous or gross inadequacies. Eugene remained inside the web that his mother and father wove for him starting in 1888 and was not aware of these things.

I could easily see that James and Ella O'Neill were patently *unripened* human beings and their lives and minds were fraught with juvenility. James, an Irish immigrant, was steeped in poverty and that alone was likely a symptom that his own parents were in an emotional struggle. His own father *abandoned* him and his mother and went back to Ireland. Poverty, unless the result of things like weather affecting crops, is usually chronic in families or nations. James was warped when it came to money and who among us with a poor background would not be? Such a thing set him up for his sentiments about the lifelong harnessing to the Count of Monte Cristo and "If only I didn't have that damned play!" That "Damned play" made James rich to the extent that he was able to buy the rights to it outright, buy expensive clothes for the family, own a Parkard when most people did not have a car, buy a cottage on Pequot Avenue in New London and a lot of other real estate in that city in anticipation of making a killing with the plans to make New London a seaport for transatlantic traffic to rival Boston and New York. James blames the play for keeping him in a cage with the sure buck. He cites his earnest desires to do more Shakespeare and the grand praise that the famous actor, Edwin Booth, had heaped upon him for James' role as Othello. *False* is the posture of this man regarding this situation. *Phony* is his excuse and it is boldly so. True, however, is the note that the public after while would not *let* James O'Neill perform in any other role than The Count.

Then there was the barroom behavior. He was well known around New London's hotels and regular bars, a storyteller, a buyer of rounds of drinks, a loaner of money when he was drunk although he could carry himself well. He loved the public attention on and off the stage and ate it up regularly. This made him feel that he actually mattered. James O'Neill was an alcoholic and a typical one at that. He was self-centered and manipulative and grafted on top of that was the actor with all the dramatics that such talents bring. Inside, he was still a baby. His wife and sons were baggage and he dealt with the baggage as he could. Not very amusing are the published accounts by so-called O'Neill experts and critics that describe James O'Neill's treatment of his wife as loving and sensitive. Alcoholics are manipulative and self-dealing. James' actions in life were largely fueled by his codependence. Love and sensitivity are not possible in such a defective personality and are reserved for the whole among us.

The money gave relief to James O'Neill, as did the bottle as did the adoration by his fans. He was not apt to give any of it up and that entrenched emotional posture was carried along by his domineering ways as a parent, a husband, an egomaniac and a gad about town. James' gambling habit was also juvenile behavior.

Whole people never pair up with fractured ones and James was no exception. His union with Ella, Eugene's mother, was a perfect match. Her remarkable beauty was a jewel in his crown but she was not a human being, just a jewel. It gave *her* the power that only beauty can bestow. It was the great mover, the sly pusher, the wave maker and a perfect mask for outright treachery. Ella was falsity personified. Her Roman Catholic upbringing laced her fully with the indoctrination that has Ella holding on for dear life against never-ending turmoil and confused crutchery. Her "faith" took the place of a real person and her moaning entreaty "If only I could find my faith" is such a striking shamelessness that it protrudes like a charm or a cure-all device quite apart from anything truly religious.

Next is the terrible falsity of false blame. Ella lost her younger son, Edmund, before Eugene was born and so heavy was the guilt on her leaving Edmund with his older brother, Jamie, age seven, in the care of her mother in New York City while she was on the road with James' touring, she ended up blaming the seven year old for giving the baby the measles that killed him at age one and a half. Such an outrageous pit to put a child in is simply beyond imagining. Even if it had been true, the placement of blame can but destroy the child and it did. Jamie drank himself to death at age forty-five when Eugene was only thirty-five.

Ella had attempted to blame her later morphine addiction on Eugene because the doctor prescribed it for postpartum depression. She also blamed her husband for much of her travails. This made me think of my own mother's ways.

As a young girl, Ella tried to fill up the void in her soul by imagining that she would become a nun. It was perfect. Structure, discipline, human contact, a mission and an identity were just what she needed to deal with chaos inside. It never came to pass however and the stern direction of the Catholic Mother Superior for Ella to try out the gay, romantic life first apparently made Ella see the light.

Once addicted to morphine, she was usually upstairs in that cottage in dreamy land. No more pain but downstairs, the pain was festering! Once, when she needed a fix and could not secure the stuff, Ella tried to drown herself in the Thames! Selfishness and juvenility could have no more pointed a demonstration than that.

Ella never had *real guilt* over the death of baby Edmund because fractured people live outside of their vulnerabilities. That kind of "guilt" is the penny that bounces off of the bedspread and hides. It is false guilt and the world is saturated with it. One prime example is the lone survivor of some tragedy who feels "guilty" that she made it when the others perished. Another is the wacky concept of "an embarrassment of riches". It is a false and a fake notion and grows out of the immature emotional state.

It is possible that Ella *did* feel something when Edmund died because that kind of trauma tends to shock a person back into her feelings, but it does not last. The bastion of former protection is so strong and stubborn that it will not be denied and it rushes back after a short time, so desperate is the suffering without it. The pain of living in one's true feelings is unbearable for someone like Ella O'Neill and that is what drove her from that place as a very young child to start. She'd have to stay in the pain to have any hope to reclaim her real life. She did not and could not. Her withdrawal from reality and from the family interaction in any meaningful way made Eugene's daily life "unreal". Morphine is a wonderful drug and my memories of it are splendid but it ruins any chance of carrying on a life and Ella's withdrawal was just that-no life. One has to note that her son as well had a habit of withdrawing in life when he encountered bumps in the road such as the poor reviews that some of his plays got. He did it to "punish them."

With James blaming the damned play and Ella blaming Jamie and Eugene, it sounds like a fight in a sandbox. While they were on the road touring, Ella was relieved of the heavy responsibility of caring for two young children. That is rank juvenility in escape from the burden and deprivation of what those babies needed most, attention of the feelings kind. All the things needed: love, support, discipline, structure, praise, understanding, tolerance, all held away from Jamie and Eugene and in place of that was egotism, selfishness, absence, undermining, mercurial faces, shaming, criticism, conflict, intolerance, coldness, immaturity. What a mother's love confers upon a boy is indescribable and the suffering that is put upon him by its vacancy is as well. The strength, the humor, the warmth, the example that James ought to have granted to Eugene was, too, a void. What chance did he and Jamie have? A lonely, little figure meandering down Pequot Avenue, because what else could he do, was what they all must have shaken their heads at as Eugene neared the cold-stare cottage. Didn't anybody get alarmed or moved? Was it the usual fare: "family seems alright, never noticed anything much out of the ordinary"? So, he grabbed hold of the only friend he had and that was falsity and it was adopted without hesitation. That is how the cycle goes. The one person who *did* seem real to him, Sarah Sandy, hired by the O'Neills to care for Eugene when he was under seven, was snatched away from him when they decided to sentence him to Catholic boarding school in the Bronx in 1895. She used to read to him, take him places that stimulated his intellect and imagination, give him human caring. The terrible loss of Sarah had to cut Eugene deeply and made him bitterer. Nobody cared because they were all self-dealing children themselves. So, there he was, a fully formed and confirmed juvenile, condemned to remain so forever. He was unwanted and Ella was so scared of what God would do to her for having Eugene after Edmund's passing, she completely expected to be *punished* for having s child! This is blatant *world by magic* stuff! The same could be remarked for James' statements on his deathbed in 1920 in New London that this world was rotten, no good and that he was going to a better place. What does that do to his son? How hardened and callous does a soul have to get to reach the limit? Eugene's own moment to match it was coming!

I saw that there were about thirty miles left until New London and I turned on the car radio and thought of other things. The city came into view soon after and I made a slight wave of my hand as I drove on towards Charlestown, Rhode Island, to get a motel room for the night.

CHAPTER THREE:
NEW LONDON:
A REVISITATION

My next-day arrival began with a fever: "Kindred spirit, I am here. Three times a husband, you and I, booze and drugs, silent muttering in the crowded bars, handy with the word, son of the Sea, lost at home, New York in the blood, peripheral Yale connections, escapes to Morocco, near-suicides, nighttime cascades on paper, bearer of the rare smile, 'Motherless', "Fatherless', hanging around State Street, sibling lost to each of us by addiction, blew a bundle on real estate, experts with the false front, Irish, English, Scotch, Welsh."

One can still go and see the light that was shining into his eyes. I did it today. The sun came up at 6:14 a. m. and I tell you, it pulled me halfway out to sea! Immediately the water was different; it came alive. The darkness on it sneaked away and suddenly, it was lively and brightening. The air became fresher and saltier and a funny kind of gladness descended.

The skydiving seagulls over the town cried out the truth, then darted and maneuvered. Some took up the countenance of pigeons in the tall eves and on the roofs but no one was fooled.

My deprived stomach was gnawing at me now that it was two hours past breakfast hour, but I was on the road and only a short time from leaving the Charlestown motel. There was some wait yet before the only diner that I could spot, Monica's, was to open. I felt deprived actually and had planned on The Whaler, which seemed to me to have been in New London forever. But it was gone! It had disappeared with all the rest that had transpired there, went on right there, years and decades and centuries.

When I was in residence in New London for eight months in 1994, a toasted corn muffin with grape jelly could always bring me around at The Whaler when I required a break from my painting on plywood or canvass. The coffee, however, was a different matter and I could still recall the look on the face of who ever was in charge when I complained that it tasted like cigarette ashes. "Insulted" would be understating it and I received an undeserved scowl. Maybe that is why it was gone?

The ever-present seawater is down at the low end of town and is a force on a body any time that one's eyes catch it by accident. Since I had time to kill, I drove down Pequot Avenue along the harbor and parked my station wagon a little way from the cottage and walked towards it going south. His broken, tiny soul trod right where I trod. It was now 6:30 a. m. . His glance was downward and his guts turned. It was abjectly lonely. Not one hundred yards from his house was a sandy shore that bore the sunlight and the cast of untold mornings there. It had to be the same in 1888, in 1895, in 1913 and in 1920. The rocks and stones that are two feet deep, under my feet as I walked along, are unmoved, the same as under his when he was seven or ten.

Eugene was gone. When I looked at his photograph as a grown man, I get a shiver. The dark mustache, the semi-scowl, somewhat of a cross between Boris Karloff and William Powell, there is a sinister element. I see the liar there, the emotional phony, a manipulator, self-centered, hardened, and I recoil. My alcoholic grandfather comes to mind or my cousins or my ex-law associate. It actually produces a feeling of being threatened! The lanky legs, the same look on his face in many of the pictures that the public sees, the beach scenes, all of it I found to be somehow unsavory, shifty, gaunt, pseudo-aristocratic, quasi-preppie, sometimes a beaten down look inviting pity from anyone who'd fall for it. Then there is the sullen, spoiled look and perhaps, eccentric as well. Then, there is the cigarette stink, the desperation cast upon that visage, the crookedness of his center.

All of that I put aside on this morning for I was in a gentle review and seeking only the child. His form set upon that rock, if one looks harder, has in its face the question: "Why bother taking my picture or dressing me up like this: why don't you just cherish me?" As troubling as is the grownup face of O'Neill, the scariness is stt invited my kindness. One picture of the adult Eugene, taken in 1921 at a beach gathering at Peaked Hill Bar, Provincetown, Massachusetts, shows him sitting on the sand and third from the left. There, he looks a lot like me or my cousin, Runcie. At times, I get the creepy undertaker effect from his photographs. Then there is the shakiness, not so much in his presence but more in the hands and the reactions. I speak of his pre-nerve disorder days. Strongly I sense the anxiety and depression in him simultaneously and recalled that in myself. Always there is the feeling that Eugene is looking back at you from inside a tube from another planet or other worldly place where he is in solitary confinement. He seems unstable, child like, afraid, neurotic, nonplussed.

I rode back to the center of town. As I looked up at the mighty First Church of Christ on State Street, founded in 1642, I knew that *his* eyes fixed on it although his was not a Protestant faith. Its immense spire snatches the imagination and defies all to look away. Across the street is the Baptist Church of 1804 and you just know that he had to have brushed against it or nearly countless times as he walked up or down from the top Courthouse part. The New London Library is there, too. Down at the other end was another gaze stealer, the Nathan Hale Schoolhouse, nearer the water. The plaque reads "1774-75" and it is rather small and red. Directly in front of that, standing in a kind of a base set in the middle of the street, is the magnificent military monument erected when O'Neill was but eight years old. The 1896 obelisk is quite high and made possible by the Lawrence family and dedicated to the soldiers and sailors of New London. Prominently displayed is the famous statement by James Lawrence of Boston during a naval engagement in the War of 1812 where he said "Don't Give Up The Ship!" Eugene *had* to have been inspired when his eight-year old eyes caught that!

Wandering back up State Street and away from the harbor, I came upon many sites that are well known connections to Eugene, his father, James and his brother, Jamie, and it seemed eerie to be there on an ordinary day and to remember all that had gone on. The quietude of the moment made it seem surreal or nonexistent, sort of like a trick of time. As I gazed all the way up towards the Courthouse, I wondered aloud what became of the Lyceum Theatre where James O'Neill played his famous role for the locals and where his son had staged some of his own works such as *The Straw*. Eugene did consider it a not so friendly town and many of the residents looked at the family as Irish riffraff, servant class folk. Maybe the Lyceum has been down Bank Street. I saw no remnants of it.

Next, I tried to imagine or see where the Second Story Club was located and met regularly. Eugene used to attend and partake of the books there that he could not find elsewhere as easily. Then there was its social side with the avant-garde forming the core with the townspeople looking down their noses in dismay.

Eugene and his brother, Jamie, were frequent visitors to the whorehouses up on Bradley Street and which, it is said, were winked at, more or less, by the New London Police when it suited them. That did nothing for the brothers' reputations and added to the heavy drinking by the older O'Neill sibling and other conduct by the two. Respectable local girls were well advised to steer clear. I did not discover the exact site of the brothel, but recalled the topic in

Long Day's Journey Into Night as a source of downfall for O'Neill.

It was easy for people to see that the O'Neills had money since the boys were well fitted with tailored clothes and the family had a chauffeur and a coachman. Ella, the mother, often wore hats and outfits that indicated high quality.

Some way up State Street is the Crocker House, on the left, and still operating. It was at one time the hub for the well to do and the local, prominent businessmen, cadets from the nearby Coast Guard Academy and the very rich such as the Morgans, the Astors, the Whitneys and William Randolph Hearst, all visiting from their yachts docked in the harbor or Thames River. That onslaught was usually just in summer. James O'Neill was a regular at the Crocker House, days and nights at the bar, and was well known because of his acting fame and fun loving ways, especially when imbibing. A lot of the local real estate that he bought up was bargained for at this bar from another New London resident who was usually pleased to see James. James did end up taking a loss on most parcels however. The brother, Jamie, a heavy drinker and ten years Eugene's senior, has his own rut at the Crocker House and was well known to entertain companions there often with stories and jokes. As I passed by the front, I got a shiver and suddenly remembered going inside in 1994 when I was searching for living quarters before I ended up with an apartment much closer to the hospital. I could, on my revisit, still recall the staleness of the smell and the people lurking and the furniture. It turned me right off back then and again now. But, my poor stomach was in revolt at this point so I walked back down to Monica's Diner, as it was just 7:00 a. m.

Only a couple of men were waiting to get in. Once I was there for five minutes, though, it was almost full! There had to be thirty people seated. Before too long, I had my badly needed coffee, egg whites, dry rye toast and home fries, the last item usually being not very delicious in public eating places, so I prepared to ignore the potatoes. So glad to be wrong was I! They were quite good and I wolfed it all down. Maybe it, too, was the mood I was in being there in O'Neill territory and on the hunt. And the atmosphere was quite friendly and uplifting, the people, the waitress. I even caught myself humming! Very unusual for one-way past his habit of a 4:00 a. m. breakfast.

Back out on the street, I turned left and sauntered up to the Thames Club, just past the Crocker House and on the same side. As I walked, I noticed the Mohican Hotel on the opposite side of the street. It is a very large building and still in business. Ella stayed at The Mohican during the time of her husband's funeral in August of 1920 and Jamie lived there at one time as well as being a guest on occasion. The Thames Club was founded February 8, 1869, and as I approached its oldness, I got another one of those weird sensations because so much had gone on there, so much envy and tension and prestige and now, it lies quiet, an ordinary building. Although it was begun by New London businessmen as an exclusive club, James O'Neill managed to be admitted. His club mates were rich and well known citizens of New London and it is said that he frequented the place in the summertime up to three times a week and often purchased drinks for any members there at the time. He himself was, of course, well known as an actor, but a subtle current of disapproval prevailed over his vocation and "breeding".

Leaving that site and continuing to the top of State Street, I came to the corner of the library and went inside. I learned that the original section of the building had been open since 1892. It was quite attractive architecturally. I then knew that I was in the very same spot where a young Eugene could often be seen with a load of books under his arm coming or going into that edifice. His choice of reading materials made many of his acquaintances envy Eugene but some of the locals disapproved. It seemed to me that some of the very same volumes that he had handled were still around somewhere inside and that his fingerprints might well still be on some of them. I all of a sudden remembered that none of this was evident to me back in 1994 although I was familiar with the O'Neill name and vaguely aware of some of his ideas as a playwright and the Eugene O'Neill Theatre nearby. But not even the name on the street named after him right smack in the downtown rang a bell.

Next, I walked across the street and back down until I hit Union Street and I turned left and walked up it. Shortly was the grand and old New London Post Office building. "It was right here" I told myself, "That he rushed to with his latest creations to mail them off to Washington D. C. to the Copyright Office back in the days when he was heady with the writing power and was worried that somebody else would come up with the ideas that came out of him. This struck me hard because *I* used to do the same thing only it was musical compositions, mostly rock and roll, when I was twenty-five or twenty-six years of age. *That* would be about Eugene's age when he did that, somewhere around 1914-1915 before he left to go to live in Greenwich Village. I, too, was worried about losing my "masterpieces" and was going to the New Jersey post office near my house in Denville regularly. A very nice metal sign with a brief history of New London, founded in 1646, helps visitors learn a bit about the city if they happen to be near the post office and see it across the street.

From there, I wandered back down to State Street trying to find something, feel something, a spirit, a hint, a sense of how it was for him breathing the air right where I was as if his essence could somehow linger. Crazy stuff, I know! Some kind of idea came to me regarding the tricks that the past can play in making the present resemble it, imitate it, especially with respect to the "No talk rule" that is ensconced in most alcoholic families. That is a tenet that keeps the false structure from tumbling. Nobody speaks of father's drinking or mother's indiscretions.

Soon I was back down by the water, near the statue modeled after a picture of him in 1895 when he was just seven. It would not be long before a young Eugene was to be found right there at the pier and docks and harbor pestering old ship captains about their seagoing experiences and sea lore. He marveled at the sights of the schooners coming into New London in the early 1900's with their square rigger majesty competing for space with the training boats for the cadets, Navy boats and yachts belonging to the millionaires. It would not be long before those old schooners would vanish from the scene forever. I wondered if Eugene ever rowed his rowboat up to this very place and if he ever thought about Mark Twain and if his, Eugene's, boat were painted dark green. Maybe he pretended that it was part of the marine goings on!

It is said that both Jamie and Eugene were rather defiant as teenagers but I thought in my heart that they were only digging in their heels against a very shameful poisoning that was their home life. It seemed to be, right there, the likely spot that the Harvard-Yale boat races were held and the spot where Eugene took part in the very festive atmosphere and activities that occurred each summer. So much of him had been right there where I was spending that ordinary day. It was, or so I hoped, creeping and seeping into me. All of a sudden, a funny feeling came over me. I looked way over, in my mind's eye, towards the present day highway, I-95, and I recalled with pain a December, 1967 morning when I was leaving Norwich and New London, to follow after my future wife and her young son who fled the day before from our "hideout" without telling me. I had come home with a Christmas tree and discovered the apartment that we shared empty. We were in love and on the road in secret with her then husband searching for us and apparently on our trail as it had led from New Jersey to Alabama to New York City and then to Norwich. My heart sunk and I cried and cried. I could still recall driving back to New Jersey that sad morning and passing under the overpass in New London on the highway as the radio played "One Less Bell To Answer" by Fifth Dimension.

I turned back towards the little statue and for some reason; the image of my brother came to me. He never got married as was the case for Eugene's brother, Jamie, and *he* was an alcoholic just as was Jamie. Actually, mine was a half-brother and an *unwanted* child. He still speaks of it to this day and it reminds me of Eugene's unwelcome arrival in 1888 and his mother's reactions. I wondered then which child suffered more at the hands of such an outrage, my brother or Eugene and if either of them were hurt more than Jamie who was blamed for his baby brother's death.

Another memory flooded me at that point. It was 1994 and I had met a very nice girl on the boat from Montauk to New London and I discovered her identity and address and called to tell her that I had done a special painting for her and that I wanted to meet her to give it to her. That kind of approach rarely fails. We did meet some days later near the railroad tracks in town where the boats from Long Island come in and she was gracious about accepting the art, but she declined my implied invitation to have more.

Eugene had been a reporter for a New London newspaper for a short stint and I remember concluding that he had to have walked in some of my exact footsteps on that day. But so what? Why is that so critical? More crazy stuff.

The carrying on on Bradley Street by Jamie and Eugene fascinated me and I wondered if Eugene shunned "normal" girls or if they steered clear of his neon sign of emotional neediness. At any rate, he did not have to invest any of his own emotions or self with whores. It was "safe". One recalls Eugene O'Neill's observations about prostitutes being like the earth.

People look but they do not see. I imagined that many New Londoners saw Eugene, his façade, as the real person when in fact, he was extremely troubled and in a mighty struggle inside. The loneliness I know. It plagued him. It plagued me. The permanent cry lies just beneath the surface. The fake-it life comes to be a "religion".

I had had enough of town for the moment and so I drove my station wagon along the water towards Pequot Avenue and towards the awful place. A sign proclaims that it is a national historic site. Big deal! Where's the sign for the ruination of an innocent baby? Or are gorillas supposed to just shut up and stay in that cage? In the area are many stately houses, such as Montauk Avenue, and these must have belonged to such as ship captains and industrial magnates or bankers. That part, I thought to myself, offsets the skid row aspects of New London. Not far from Monte Cristo Cottage is the lighthouse near the corner of Pequot and Guthrie Place (I dislike saying "Parkway South"). I wondered how much of a pall existed in that city when Eugene was there and if *it* ever pulled him down even more?

Near that lighthouse I suddenly spied a full moon low in the sky in the south. Did *he* ever see this in April like me and did *it* become one for the Misbegotten? It was eerie, unreal, and otherworldly and it made me ponder. *I* was here in this place, on *his* road seeing *his* places and *his* things and what does a man ever really know? I did know that Eugene played on the large rock masses that formed the river shore beach areas. What kid would not? I turned around. "Oh, yes, there it is: mean house".

Suddenly I remembered that only days before I had read *Anna Christie*, his second Pulitzer piece. I did this not to be entertained or to get at its content, but rather, just to connect to Eugene somehow, touch his person as it was laid out on the pages. Maybe, it was that the play was touted as a sea tale and I was standing right there at water's edge that made me think of *Anna Christie*. It was only 67 pages and I recalled wondering what the Committee saw in it to elevate the thing beyond the other drama entries. It then occurred to me that it must have been the novelty that forced the contrast.

For some reason, I saw it and still do as candy-striped, candy cane-like and a neat package of a thing. For days afterward, I could think nothing else but Anna and Chris and Burke and the barge and Jimmy-the-Priest's and Boston and Provincetown outer parts and fog and the "Devil" and violence and struggling and lying and vacillating and more lying (self-deception), and God talk and parental irresponsibility with rationalizations and minute breakthroughs for Anna upon the sea for the very first time, and the phony blaming and hardness from hopelessness, and hypocrisy and imagined tidying up by O'Neill in the ending areas. He has Anna confessing prostitution in St. Paul and knowing her utter worthlessness because of it, yet somehow, she still gets Burke to want her for a wife and she pledges to keep a house for him and her father, both of whom accidentally signed on to the Londonderry bound for Cape Horn. Chris, the father was at "Dat Irish fallar" all play long, denigrating and threatening him and plotting his demise lest he wrest newly found Anna from him after his fifteenth year abandonment of his daughter. Burke, the symbol of human range from violence-life and boastful control of others to deep God talk and Catholic notions about the sea, blames the sea, hates Burke and hates what families go thru because of the sea. He wants better for Anna but her morally precarious position does not let her pick and choose. A scenario of her keeping the house for them both until they return together is a bit much and the play is quite naïve in its implication of a happily-ever-after result. I shook my head at Eugene then. Where are the *causes* of this victim, victimizer, chaotic string of lives that you have paraded before me? And what suddenly makes it all go away so as to allow such harmony and future glint? Anna's stern stand about being treated like a piece of furniture is good and in one's face. The men who saw the play or read it way back then had to notice. Maybe O'Neill did *not* intend to portray happily ever after. They *did* belong!

I wondered if the Pulitzer Committee was even *aware* of the causes that make peoples' lives do what Anna's and Chris' and Burke's did? Did they know even what it takes to get rid of those effects? I was sure that they did not. Still, I did not quarrel with their award here. It could be that a lot of reliance was made on circumstances expanding consciousness, on revelation and realization by the characters, on elimination of real-world cares like poverty allowing Anna not to be a whore any longer but that seems far-reaching. She could have made it in a dime store clerk's job, no? The answer is that her prostitution was made possible by her worthlessness feelings, those rammed home by an abandoning mother (thru early death) and a runaway father! These do not disappear with marriage or money or the father's return. Nor does Burke's way of the fist get dissolved by a wife and a "stable" home. Then there is the false blamer, Chris. Only abject loneliness is abated by a daughter's hand but the root of his conduct remains firmly planted and viable, be it mental illness or the effects of his own parents on him long ago.

Anna Christie did stick with me though, "Py yimminy!", and I do give deference to O'Neill on it. Oh, yes, the feeling of personal connection came. Now, I was looking for the same in the air, the streets, the new London way. Oh, yeah, Eugene, did they really have movies in Boston around 1910?

There is some kind of wildness in New London. It beckons and it did that to me that morning in the new light, the high cries, that globe hanging, the rippling, the silence, the yearning. Connected is the pull of that sea, its smell, like the smell of a girl, necessary and unchallenged. There is limitlessness. It is not like other cities somehow and perhaps it is the unique history, the whaling fervor, the commerce, the military and Naval presence, the pre-Revolutionary war life. The bright air, the shimmering, the sunlight, the stabs in the ether, why I was ready at that moment to put to sea!

Those words carved or inscribed on the monument and the Nathan Hale Schoolhouse must surely have poured down on O'Neill. He was no dummy and his imagination had to have stirred. Nathan Hale is known to all the world and his presence in the downtown of New London is no small matter. He was hanged for us! Did Eugene get the majesty or glory from this stuff and was he pulled in by it or just into a bar?

For a break, I drove up to see my old apartment and on the way, passed Lawrence and Memorial Hospital. It was the last place that I ever saw my mother who departed this life there in 1985 from alcoholism effects-bled to death internally from lack of clotting factor from damaged liver. My estranged sister, that way all her life really, died there too but hers was from addiction. Eugene must have been in there countless times during the spring and summer of 1920 as his father lay dying and wasting away. Now his old man was tucked away with his mother, Ella and brother, Jamie in St. Mary Cemetery. I decided to go over to St. Mary graveyard on Jefferson Avenue, a place that I did not know about in 1994. One comes upon the scene rather quickly from the center of town and sees that it is a sprawling place. The main gate is on the left and is very tasteful and inviting. There is some kind of a grand majesty at St. Mary but I could not put my finder on exactly what is responsible for the feeling. Maybe it is the size and nature of the monuments, the layout, the large openness of the tracts that makes it so pleasant. I parked by the cemetery office and grounds building and was quickly directed by a very nice man to where the O'Neill site was. He told me that a film crew had been out there the year before. I drove the short way and found the stone right away where James O'Neill had spent the last eighty-five Christmases. As I walked towards it, I thought to myself "I've come to tell you about the statue of your son, Eugene, as a child, since nobody else has likely done that. It's at the harbor at the end of State Street and was put there because of his amazing notoriety, all come about since you passed in 1920." I really felt like saying a lot more, how he was fifty per cent of the root of his son's terrible life, but I kept my craw shut and just gazed at the tombstone which is kind of large, maybe four feet wide and three high and set on a larger base stone. It sits among thousands of others in what I estimated to be hundreds of acres of land lying on both sides of that road.

This moment struck me sharply for I was right away confronted with the names on it and which I knew from my study of the family and the totality of the feelings. *Here* was Edmund! Baby Edmund wrenched everybody's' heart in 1885 and provided fertile ground for falsehood and fake blaming. He was right there beneath my feet and only one and one-half years old. Then I saw the name Bridget Quinlan who was Ella's mother and who had the two children in 1885 when the measles came to claim the baby while the parents were on the road. Bridget sent a wire but the death came before the O'Neills could reach the kids in New York City. So, here *she* was, right before me. It amazed me! It was like a package of history all bound up, sealed up neatly for me to savor. Maybe that is the wrong word. Bridget's dates are 1829 to 1887. At that moment, it occurred to me that cemeteries produce in me a feeling similar to what the sea does and no other kind of place matches it. A certain majestic solemnity and quietude comes across even if the two kinds of places bespeak of death and overpowering forces.

At the top left of the gravestone is the name of "James O'Neill, Actor" and the dates were 1846 to 1920, while right under him appears Ella O'Neill, 1857 to 1922. Top right was "James O'Neill 2nd", 1878 to 1923 directly over the name of Edmund, and the two are identified as "Sons of James and Ella O'Neill". It hit me kind of hard that Jamie, the drunk, the severely wounded child who was outright *blamed* for killing Edmund with his measles, who died nearly unable to see in that Hoboken, New Jersey facility, he was *condemned* to be here by his own parents. It seemed so tragic, disfiguring to a little boy. My God! Here he was collapsed in finality, the dirty tricks of nature smote his gentle, baby heart and now a full time resident of St. Mary. My throat was tight because my own brother or half-brother was kind of the same put upon creature. He is still around, though.

I took one last gaze at the stone, the engraved large cross extending vertically almost the height of it and separating the two sides and having flanged ends, and then I left. "This is a very real day" I thought to myself as I approached my car, "And it will be followed by more of the same, but one day, it will all run out and I will fall myself and my own eternal wanderings will have to be confined to a spot like this". Then I remembered the cemetery in Groton, so very different from this both in physical aspects and in my emotional reactions there, which is usually almost nonexistent. Apparently I had similar feelings, or no feelings, for my mother as Eugene had for his own. Both were inept and addicted. The last time that stuck in my mind visiting my mother's grave was March 25, 1994, except for a farewell time in 1997, which was brief, and I had little trouble leaving the scene. I recalled wandering around, seeing other stones, dates, names, families, abbreviated stories, all carved for eyes that are no longer. One had a wreath of "Merry Christmas" and I got tears for the sweetness of it, the oddity, the out of place aspect in March, the loneliness so pointed. I returned to my mater's site but couldn't speak a word, not even a "Goodbye". Could she have been all *that* different from my father, buried in Morristown, New Jersey, whose tomb I went to the year before and from which I had great trouble leaving to my great surprise. Some stones near my mother's were from 1942 and the styles popular then touched me nostalgically. Some from 1910 or 1874 amazed me while others with lichens announced fathers and daughters, and children. The trees were undated.

I drove away from St. Mary Cemetery and back to town where I felt a draw to Pequot Avenue again as if there were something there to be discovered or frightened by, I was not sure. Again, I parked across the street from the cottage and got out to stand nearby. By now the sun was up quite a bit more and the moon had assumed its place as the lesser critter. All of a sudden, a ringing in my head came and I remembered the last words that I ever heard my mother speak in the hospital. She said "I feel so alone" and that made me think of Ella O'Neill saying "Sometimes I feel so lonely". I could not recall if that was a line by a character in *Long Day's Journey Into Night*, the mother figure, Mary, or if it was an actual line spoken by Ella O'Neill and related to us thru her son's pen.

Snapping back, I thought that the boarding school decision made tears for little Eugene right here where I was standing! "Child of the Gay Nineties, man of the Roaring Twenties, see me here, come down if you are a spirit and you can do it. I am special and I know all about your Hell. *We* can show the world what is really wrong!" But I knew and I know that they will not listen. They are too afraid to hear us out and they cannot take heart and find the courage to maybe see a path out that was in a blind before. Eugene *never* saw the answer although the world applauded him without letup and still is to a large degree. He wanted to be certain that he indeed did strike the answer to his agonies but he was in error for the most part. When the King of Sweden announced a gift in 1936, O'Neill must have become even more certain that he was on the mark. Of course, the 1941 "masterpiece" and *The Iceman Cometh* offering had yet to be created, but his work to that point did touch on themes that drove him to claim hitting paydirt. It was mostly iron pyrite. I wondered if O'Neill ever connected the thing that King Gustav had for him with the Cab Calloway song "Minnie the Moocher" who had a dream about the King of Sweden who was giving her things that she was needing. Eugene also had in his belt the three Pulitzers to bolster his claims of insight to mankind's woes. Of course, these four awards could have been largely based on dramatic accomplishment and technical prowess and design and not so much human insights, but I doubt that. It is much more likely that they were aimed at O'Neill's claims about innate human weakness and that kind of rubbish because the world was unaware then much as it remains today. Folks still *kill* in the name of God!

I then thought of *The Great God Brown*. That is the work where O'Neill proclaims that "Man is born broken. He lives by mending. The grace of God is the glue". A shudder ran through me. Can he be serious? Can nobody see? Man is *not* born that way. His parents break him, if he is broken at all and that happens starting with the infant receiving the original lie. Maybe an exception would be if he were born mentally ill, but then, God's grace would not mend it. Such a distorted claim by him is born of desperation alone!

Then I began to think about the third Pulitzer heaped on this man. I believe the year was 1928 and the piece was a singular one, the 9-act production known as *Strange Interlude*. It covered a twenty-five year period in the life of Nina Leeds and the thing took two nights to perform each time. It is easy to see why the Pulitzer folk fell for this piece. It was strikingly innovative in its stream-of-consciousness presentation and actors and actresses speaking directly to the audience in asides. Then there was the impossible-to-look-away aspect made irresistible by its author's terrible, dark life. That allowed him to create characters and events and a story that reflected a greater source of deep misery-ken and the awful places that the mind of man is forced to endure. Few if any other dramatists had such a wellspring. Also was the risk that he took in presenting such a structure hardly ever before stumbled upon in the theater if at all? Those very characters, in *Strange Interlude*, were considered by many, at the time, to be very, very strange themselves and extremely moving. Then there was O'Neill's sincerity that came thru in this play which many considered to be ultra passionate and probing and deeply burning and more intense and unrelenting and bizarre than any dramatist in the country. One can tell that the author of this and many of the others had a desperate *stake* in the play, almost as if his very sanity or survival was riding on the correct and screaming expression of his own terrible ordeal.

Nina Leeds is involved with three men, essentially, and the way O'Neill developed the tale to exhibit what he considered the lot of womanhood on earth he ended up just loving the thing, its depth. The idea for it came from a story he had heard in Provincetown in 1923 and it has been suggested that O'Neill borrowed other ideas for the piece from Freud and from James Joyce. Suffice it to the note that the theme of *instability of human relationships* was an overriding one along with what has been dubbed the erosive workings of time. Frustration and love and hostile leanings form a network here which have Nina playing both a victim and a victimizer. Notions of the G. B. Shaw creation of "Everywoman" are also said to have crept into Eugene's mind in the writing of this Nina character. An abortion of her child is made "necessary" by fears of the appearance of the insanity she discovers in her husband's family. She then tries to have a substitute child with her lover, Dr. Edmund Darrell. A fantasy engulfs Nina that all three of her men are melded into one and that they merge into he. One is a homosexual that O'Neill is said to have modeled after the painter, Charles Demuth, whom he knew from Provincetown. The character was named Charle Marsden, the second part of that handle being from the friend of Demuth, the famous Marsden Hartley!

As for the theme about human relationships and instability, I had to say again that it is one invented by desperation and inability to explain the chaos that one observes in the world between people and nations. O'Neill tries to nail down this loose end by ascribing such instability to innateness. It is anything but innate. It is the immediate product of child maltreatment but I guess that the prize-givers and the public and the critics either languished unaware or simply balked at such notions. Another, similar, concoction by our playwright was that man is born afraid, but *I* am afraid that it is bogus as well and the invention of a man so fragile emotionally that he cannot cope with the idea of driving his own car and he did never do so! Then, there was his bouts of hysteria when parted from his wife, Agnes, for as little as a week!

I stared over at my parked car and then back at the cottage and then I walked up the steps and on the pathway towards the building. When I reached about twenty feet from the front part, I stopped, as if treading on a dream, and inhaled a deep breath. "Here, right here". I said out loud "Is where Eugene got fifty cents a day from his father for trimming the hedges and to teach him the value of a dollar." Then I wondered how much a shot of whiskey cost at the Crocker House Bar the same years as that yard work and pondered the "value" of any such dollar for that!

I was and wanted to focus on the child and not the monster adult, the drunkard, the bitter spiter, the grand cerebralizer, the phony, the dandy. It was the young creature that was covered in *fresh blood* that I was after. Headed for the Bronx with all those nuns, any carefreeness that he cherished was now pinched by the awful deprivation of Sarah. How much more can one do to a boy? Yet, a much colder road lay ahead. They'd both be off on a troupe, not that he'd miss that, but he'd be stuck in New York with chores, lessons, dreariness, false discipline for its own sake, no content. The seagulls here would have to do without his love.

I became affected by the yellows, the pinks, some in the sky, others in the water and a few on the houses and buildings down Pequot Avenue. It was quite pleasant and uplifting in spite of the concerns on my brow. Maybe Eugene captured that same light in his own senses? I hoped that he had.

Soon I went back to the harbor pier area downtown. There, a body can almost see the people from 1642 milling around and whose words we might not readily recognize today. Sailors and seafarers of all sorts had to have thronged down this way, bundled up, gear in tow. Their shining faces spoke of the coming freedom. No more wives to bitch and yell. No more cold stares or favors withheld. No more hiding the liquor or pitching it out and no more backtalk!

"Tis the sea, laddie, and it comes to save my soul!"

Those very wives complained bitterly, but the men, they won't give up the ship!

CHAPTER FOUR: JUDGMENT DAY

The New London County Courthouse has been since 1794 at the top of the hill where State Street begins and I sat on a curb nearby and gazed at the old part which is clapboards and recalled my days of lawyering in Connecticut and times when I had cases pending before the Superior Court there, though they were few. Most of my career was in Hartford and Tolland County areas. I did defend my brother there in the 1970's on charges of burglary for his breaking and entering to steal liquor from people's houses and *not* money and he ended up with a lighter sentence than might have otherwise been imposed, I believe that he did a year in Montville or something like that and I can still remember visiting him once in a while and the heavy mesh between the prisoners and the public. Then, there was another time when he was prosecuted in the same Court for a similar felony and my mother was there playing the lost child role to deal with the expert lawyer that was handling this particular offense for my brother. I clearly remembered her entreaty "I'm so worried about how I'm going to pay you". The gracious lawyer said "Stop worrying, that's my payment". So, it worked!

Soon I was brought back around to Eugene O'Neill and I wondered if *he* ever got in trouble and ended up in that Court. I began to think about some of the themes presented in his plays and of the various claims made by him both in the works and in public statements of one sort or another about humankind and all the difficulty that seems to plague people and relationships and the consternation about religion and God and so forth. I sort of went into a daydream where he was arrested and prosecuted for making phony representations about human weaknesses and innate problems and thereby hurting mankind. The critics and the public seemed to be buying this stuff in the 1920's, 1930's, 1940's, 1950's and beyond and I became *swept* by the enormity of the public lie. With my eyes closed, I imagined myself in a Courtroom in the old part and witnessing the proceedings, which went as follows:

Marshall: Oyez, oyez, oyez, all rise, the Superior Court for the Judicial District of New London at New London is now in session. All persons having business before the court or ordered to appear herein shall give their attendance according to the law. The Honorable Maurice Desruisseaux presiding. Good morning, your Honor.

Judge:　Good Morning, please be seated. (Indicates to the clerk that he wants a file which is handed up to him), this is the matter of State of Connecticut versus Eugene Gladstone O'Neill (recites the docket number) on one count of violation of the Connecticut General Statute (recites the statute citation) prohibiting falsehood hindering humanity. Is the defendant present?

State's Attorney:　He is, your Honor, and may the record show that he is seated at the table to my left.

Judge:　Is the State ready this morning?

S. A. :　State is ready, your Honor. I don't know if O'Neill..... .

Judge:　Mr. O'Neill, I note that you have elected to proceed without an attorney and that that wish was granted by me prior to today. Do you still wish to go forward on your own, sir?

O'Neill: I do, yes...please...I am an intelligent.... (cut off)

Judge:　Are you ready to proceed today; do you have witnesses here and do you have any physical evidence that you want the Court to consider?

EGO:　I am...er...I am ready to go, Judge, sir...please...

Judge:　Mr. O'Neill, I want to repeat for the record that you are charged with a very serious offense and the penalty can be quite severe, we went over this last time, you recall, and we also discussed that you had a right to a jury trial where the State has the burden of proving, in either kind of proceeding, each and every element of the charge beyond a reasonable doubt. Do you still wish to waive the jury and go on with a Court trial?

EGO:　Do not want a jury, please and yes, I know that it is serious although I do not agree with it...(cut off)

Judge:　You'll have plenty of time for that, sir, to argue that. Are your witnesses here, Mr. O'Neill, in the Courtroom?

EGO: I did not bring any, judge…I…. .

Judge: Are there witnesses that you wish to have who are not here?

EGO: No, sir. I want to testify for myself and I can tell the whole story…

Judge: You seem to be a very intelligent person, quite gifted I understand, won some awards?

S. A. : He got a Nobel Prize, if it please the Court and …(cut off)

Judge: And a Pulitzer, as well, I have heard!

EGO: Three…your Honor… three Pulitzers (proudly)

Judge: Three! Goodness, we have a celebrity here (catching himself and looking down at his file). Now this count is similar to crimes that you no doubt have heard about such as war crimes or genocide or crimes against humanity.

EGO: Yes…. . but not (cut off)

Judge: But not as serious as those, correct, those crimes can carry a death sentence while this one has a maximum of life in State's prison,

EGO: (silent but grabbing his throat)

Judge: Now, the matter of ….

EGO: I didn't do anything wrong! …yes, I…I get it…….

Judge: You understand that you have a right not to testify against yourself, yes? incriminate yourself, you understand that, Mr. Defendant O'Neill?

EGO: Yes, sir, but I *want* to testify…that is. . I mean. . that's all I have . .

Judge: Very well, now I am going to appoint an attorney to represent you but his role, at least for the time being, will be just to sit beside you and to offer his confidential advice if you need that or the …. there is a duty to conduct a fair trial and it is just better this way.

EGO: Well, I guess I can't stop you, judge…

Judge: You're being held downstairs in the lockup, is that right?

EGO: No, it's not right. I'm not a criminal…I didn't do. . (cut off)

Judge: I meant are you being held down there…well, I already know that you are, but it is satisfactory…the conditions and all?

EGO: No, it's not satisfactory (sarcastically), it's cold and clammy…

Judge: How many witnesses does the State anticipate calling, Mr. State's Attorney?

S. A. :   That depends, your Honor…it depends on whether or not the Defendant is going to exercise his right not to…

Judge: He's already said he wants to speak under oath…

S. A. :   Yes, but the State would want to call him as its own witness if he does not object…

Judge: You understand this, O'Neill…the State wants to call you as its own…

EGO: Yes, I am ready to testify now…please, let's not wait. . I want to…

Judge: By the way, Mr. O'Neill, there is no statue of limitations on Falsehood Hindering Humanity and that is why you were picked up here in Connecticut while you were, uh, visiting, is that it? …I know you expressed some irritation on this point, sir…

EGO: The first day of summer comes whether you are ready or not, (quietly)

Judge: I beg your pardon…did you say something?

EGO: Yes, why I am under arrest for this now…I…I see why…

Judge: (stands up) How do you spell my name? (he asks the courtroom)

ALL: D-E-S-R-U-I-S-S-E-A-U-X (in unison: the clerk, the marshals and staff)

Judge: (sitting back down) Right!

        (The Defendant looked askance at this and did not deem it very amusing)

Judge: Now, I note, Mr. O'Neill, that you attended Princeton…when was that?

EGO: I went for one year, Judge, after which I pursued other avenues…

Judge: Didn't like it?

EGO: They kicked me out…

Judge: Really! And for what reason, may I inquire?

EGO: A little too rambunctious, I guess…

Judge: I asked because Princeton is my alma mater, you see. Anyway, I guess that is a relief to get out of the prisoner's uniform, eh?

EGO: Quite right…I can tell you, it's not my style…you see…

Judge: I note for the record that everyone in the Courtroom, quite a lot of people, seem to be here to watch this case and that the press is well represented, and I want to issue a caution that no disruptions will be tolerated and wacky screwiness is, likewise, forbidden.

Clerk: Your Honor, I believe that Mr. …Attorney Brindle has come in….

Judge: Thank you. Mr. Brindle, I have appointed you to represent the defense in this case as we discussed some time back, and you understand that your place is beside the Defendant at the defense table as silent assistance because he is representing himself. You may assist him if he asks or you deem it necessary. You okay on this, attorney?

Brindle: Yes, your Honor, I recall the parameters we (cut off)

Judge: Very well, then, have a seat at the table…Now, Mr. O'Neill, you said that you want to forego your right not to testify at this trial, yes?

EGO: I have nothing to hide. I have done nothing wrong and I want to speak to the Court about all this…

Judge: Okay, the State may proceed…uh, I understand that the State has several subpoenas in this matter and that, well, let me ask, are those witnesses here, did they respond to the subpoenas?

S. A. :   They're all here except for one and she called to say (cut off)

Judge: Okay, well…you'd better keep them here…it is my guess that you did not count on the Defendant testifying and now that he appears ready to do just that, you might not need all those witnesses, am I right?

S. A. :   I'm not sure at this point, perhaps you are right…I'll have witnesses stand by.

Judge: Any person under subpoena by the State of Connecticut in the O'Neill matter, you are to remain in the Courthouse or you can sit and watch but do not leave until the Court excuses you.... Proceed please.

S. A. : The State calls the Defendant...uh, as its first witness...

Judge: Please come up here, Mr. O'Neill and raise your right hand...

(The clerk administers the oath to the Defendant and he is told to sit)

Clerk: Please state your full name and spell it and your address.

EGO: Eugene G. O'Neill (spells it out and gives his address)

S. A. : Good morning, Mr. O'Neill. Will you please state your date of birth?

EGO: October 16, 1888, New York City.

S. A. : And for the record, you *are* the defendant in this case?

EGO: I am, yes, but I didn't (cut off)

S. A. : And you plead "not guilty" correct?

EGO: It's true...I am not guilty...yes...

S. A. : Please state your profession.

EGO: Playwright...I write stage productions of a dramatic nature.

S. A. : And you have written many plays over the years, correct?

EGO: Yes, many...

S. A. :   And some have earned you prizes of a grand nature, have they not?

EGO: They have...the first one was... (cut off by judge)

Judge: Do not answer a question that has not been asked, Mr. O'Neill. Just listen to the question and answer only that, okay, sir?

S. A. : And tell us please what the first award was, which play and when?

EGO: It was for a play about two brothers in love with the same gal, 1920 entitled *Beyond the Horizon* and it won a Pulitzer Prize...it was on Broadway, you know....... oops, I'm sorry...I...

S. A. : And the next prize was what work, what year and what theater staged?

Judge: Please, Mr. State's Attorney, just ask him *one* question at a time. Okay?

S. A. : Sorry, your Honor.... what play was the next to win a major award?

EGO: Morosco Theatre, that's it!

S. A. : I beg your pardon. . what did you say?

EGO: I was trying to remember the name where *Beyond the Horizon* was first...

S. A. : Very well, sir, what play won next?

EGO: That would have been *Anna Christie*.

S. A. : That's the title, the name?

EGO: You mean that you're never heard of it? Gee...I...

S. A. : I'm sorry to say that this job does not allow me much time to study literature or plays or Broadway history, no, sir...*Anna Christie*?

EGO: Indeed...debuted at the Vanderbilt Theatre in 1921, New York...

S. A. : And the next one...wait, *Anna Christie* won a prize. . what was it?

EGO: Columbia University...Pulitzer Prize for drama, you know..... and the next one was, let's see now. . uh, oh, yes, Strange Interlude...funny...that's what this seems like...strange...

S. A. : A Pulitzer for that one, too?

EGO: Correct...the year was 1928 and the place was New York again, the John Golden Theatre...quite a thing it was, took over five hours, you know no one had ever seen anything like it... (his voice trailing off).

S. A. : Wasn't there one more big prize for you, Mr. O'Neill?

EGO: There was...I got the Nobel Prize...that was in 1936 and I, I didn't...

S. A. : A Nobel Prize! Imagine that! Seems we *do* have a celebrity here your Honor.

Judge: Please, keep your comments to yourself and just ask relevant questions!

S. A. : Sorry, sir, if it pleases the Court…

Judge: It will please the Court if you just proceed in a regular fashion and forget about the Defendant's fame…

S. A. : Well, your Honor, the Defendant's fame is really part and parcel of this case since he is charged with falsehood hindering humanity and that kind of offense is hardly possible by a person that nobody listens to…

Judge: Yes, I see your point, but just go ahead…ask the next question…

S. A. : And what play was the Nobel for?

EGO: Oh, it wasn't for any particular one. You see, it was, I imagine, for the totality of my work to that time… Actually, I was annoyed by it. .

Judge: Annoyed? That's peculiar…

EGO: Well, I guess I'm peculiar…that's the answer to that…

S. A. : Did you have to go to the old country to receive that?

EGO: I was suppose to, but I declined…I was too weak, you know. Ill health. They brought it here, to the USA.

S. A. : They gave you a Nobel Prize here instead of in Stockholm?

EGO: I was hospitalized and they…they just gave it to me in bed there.

S. A. : Now, Mr. O'Neill, you know or you realize that it is and it has been a natural curiosity of people resident here in this State, especially in New London, but elsewhere as well, to read your works or to read about them in books and the media and to go to New York City to see production of the plays and that they all would be affected by them in one way or another, is that not true, sir?

Judge: That is speculation; the question is stricken.

S. A. : Well, your Honor….. . Mr. O'Neill, do you know that citizens of this State and this city of new London have read and seen your plays, yes or no?

EGO: Yes, I do know it, and they have, of course…

S. A. : And did you not intend readers and audiences to be influenced and affected by what you wrote, the content of the works?

EGO: That's why I wrote them…to explore various themes and issues pertaining to man and mankind and God, the human condition...er... and ideas such as hidden motives, unconscious thought, emotions-driven acts, archetypal stuff. Then there was the distortion was delusion inherent in the romantic imagination of man.

S. A. : Are you familiar with any particular persons who you know of who have seen and or read your plays that resided in this State at the time and *were* affected by that content in any way?

EGO: Yes, but I cannot recall any one name right now.

S. A. : But you are saying here and now, under oath in this Court, that you are aware of persons who have read and seen your plays and who were subjected to their so called themes and messages and that they either did so in Connecticut or resided in this State at the time though they may have seen the productions in New York?

EGO: Sure...my parents, for instance, and friends, and acquaintances, and curious New Londoners, and old pals, and other locals, and a librarian although I cannot recall her name anymore, and people I knew from just having lived here way back, you see? Oh, yes, and some of my works were staged at the Lyceum Theatre here in town. That was very long ago!

S. A. : And did you ever learn what effect any plays had on any of those folks or a particular person?

EGO: I could tell, yes, from comments of various sorts and reactions and that.

S. A. : Please describe any that you remember.

EGO: Well...let's see, many seemed to be depressed, frightened or alarmed. Some appeared worried, you know, not happy, like, maybe they saw themselves in the plays...you understand that?

S. A. : Saw themselves? Did you model any characters after local residents?

EGO: I don't care to say that, I, uh, (paused)

Judge: You must answer, Mr. O'Neill.

EGO: Well, I guess, subconsciously, I mean they have an influence on me when I knew them or came in contact with them a lot.

S. A. : And did you intent for audiences to be…what did you call it…could we have that read back, your Honor, please?

Judge: (To Court reporter) Yes, read it back…

Reporter:"Well, let's see, many seemed depressed, frightened or alarmed, some appeared to be worried, you know, not happy, like maybe they saw themselves in the plays. You understand that?"

S. A. : Did you intend for the people to have those reactions?

EGO: Yes, I did. I described the human state of affairs, the sickness in society today. . it is awful and I wanted to describe it, take it apart and show its workings, you know…intend to shake them up…yes, to alarm them, yes, certainly.

S. A. : And what was the title of the last major play, major in your view, to be seen on Broadway…the title and the year of debut?

EGO: *Iceman Cometh…The Iceman Cometh.* The year was, let's see, uh…it was The Martin Beck Theatre…it was, uh, 1946, not so long ago.

S. A. : "Cometh"? Isn't that a little Biblical?

EGO: I don't know, oh, I suppose so. . it could be…

S. A. : And please tell the Court what other major works you had staged in New York City and the year of debut.

EGO: Well, there was *Desire Under the Elms* and that was in 1924, then, there was *Mourning Becomes Electra*, 1931, *The Hairy Ape*, 1922.

(uproar of laughter in the Courtroom)

Judge: (pounding his gavel) Order! Order! I'll tell you just this one time, I will not tolerate interruptions such as that in my Court…any more of that and I will be finding you all in contempt and you can discover that "cold and clammy" place the prisoner here has reminded me of! Go on, Mr. O'Neill.

EGO: Then there was The Emperor Jones at the Playwright's Theatre in late 1920. It sort of made me very famous, very unusual play, innovative, drums, etc.

S. A. : And I think that you said this but I would like it to be clear, that some of your works were staged right here in town, the Lyceum you said, the same place where your father, the distinguished actor, God rest his soul, performed for many years his Count of Monte Cristo role?

Judge: Mr. State's Attorney, do not insert personal comments or views.

S. A. : Yes, your Honor, I…I am sorry…I…

Judge: Again!

S. A. : Yes, again.

(The Defendant happened to glance out a side window of the old Courtroom, which windows were quite high and large, and he saw someone on a ladder washing the panes and the fellow was wearing a clown's head! Eugene shuddered and rubbed his eyes but it was still there and he wondered if he was in a dream. Then the clown looked like he had sneezed and when he pulled aside the mask to wipe his nose, it could be seen that the man's face looked like Eugene's face. It was terrible to see and his spine tingled and hurt him. This went on for quite some time and as he went from window to window, it greatly distracted Eugene and he had trouble concentrating on the questions to him. It appeared that nobody else saw this clown or if they did, they were afraid to speak up).

S. A. : Mr. O'Neill…Mr. O'Neill, can you hear me?

EGO: Sorry, I was….

S. A. : Did people that you knew go to see your plays at the Lyceum?

EGO: Plenty did.

S. A. : Thank you. Now, I notice that you are quite well dressed. (O'Neill had a light, grayish-tan tweed with orange flecks and a cravatte of deep maroon on a shirt that was darker pea green. His shoes were of copper and gold, sort of a saddle shoe style).

EGO: Thank you, I always…

S. A. : And this shows that you are not in the poorhouse, yes?

Judge: Relevancy?

S. A. : To show that he is well off, that he has made a lot of money from his works and gained a good deal of fame and derived a large economic benefit from making people worried, alarmed, depressed, upset and that you see, Judge…

Judge: Not an element of the crime. It is not required that the defendant derive compensation from the plays, only that the staging of them and the publication of them in books and so forth tended to and did amount to falsity that hindered or tended to hinder humanity.

S. A. : Very well, your Honor, I'll move on…

(At this point the defendant stood straight up from his witness chair and said out loud "X-U-A-E-S-S-I-U-R-S-E-D" and everybody was caught off guard, especially the Judge)

Judge: What was that, Mr. O'Neill?

EGO: Your name, Judge. I spelled it backwards. (proudly)

Judge: I beg your pardon?

S. A. : The State is not amused, your Honor, I…

Judge: You are out of order, Mr. O'Neill…

EGO: (shouting) Oh, Ah, Wilderness! Guild Theatre, 1933…yes!

Judge: I'm finding you in contempt of Court, Mr. O'Neill, for ridiculing the Court!

EGO: (looking contrite) I'm sorry, Judge…sorriest…

Judge: I order you to stand up and to raise your left foot off the floor for one-half hour and do not let it touch the floor, you understand?

Brindle: Objection, your Honor. This is most unusual and I think that…(cut off)

Judge: Sit down, attorney or I'll find *you* in contempt as well!

(after only fifteen minutes, the Defendant could no longer stand on one foot and he complained to the Judge)

Judge: I find you in contempt a second time, Mr. Defendant O'Neill, and I sentence you to occupy the witness chair with both feet off the ground for the remaining fifteen minutes.

EGO: I may be a Nobel Prize winner, sir, but not even I could levitate like that, why, why I....

(the courtroom erupts in laughter)

Judge: I don't expect any levitation, just sit down and hold them off the floor!

EGO: Yessir! (mocking the Judge)

Judge: Proceed.

S. A.: Now, getting back to, uh, did you not become famous as a result of your plays, Mr. O'Neill?

EGO: I did.

S. A.: And would you not agree with me that hundreds...no, thousands of people have gone to see productions of your works over the many years from 1920 until the present time, sir?

EGO: Oh, I would say so, yes, tens of thousands I guess.

S. A.: And that would be mostly in the adjacent State of New York, yes?

EGO: I suppose...yes...

S. A.: Now, would you also concede that a fair percentage of those tens of thousands were residents of Connecticut at the time?

EGO: That sounds correct, yes...I guess...I'm sure.

S. A.: Can you give us an approximation of how many people from this State actually saw one or more of your plays in New York or in Connecticut?

EGO: Well...that's hard to say, but...

Judge: How is that germane?

S. A.: Your Honor, if it please the Court...one of the elements in the charge is that the Defendant must have knowingly issued falsehood tending to hinder humanity and that such occurred in this State or involved residents of Connecticut at the time.

Judge: I'll allow it. Go ahead and answer that, Mr. O'Neill...

EGO: Uh, Uh, I'd guess... (cut off)

Judge: No, do not guess, estimate fairly, if you can...

EGO: I'd estimate about one thousand or three, maybe, close to that.

S. A. : Or it could be higher, couldn't it, sir...I mean...think about this... people on A Saturday night or a Sunday afternoon seeing one of your plays on Broadway, visiting the City from Connecticut. It's close by, maybe a couple of hours drive or a nice train ride, yes?

EGO: I suppose...

S. A. : And the number of persons physically in Connecticut while reading one of the plays. . pretty common occurrence, no?

EGO: No, I wouldn't say so...people don't read plays, they usually are not meant to be read, they're designed to be watched, you know...except for students maybe in high school or college studying literature or people involved in local productions, a theater group, you know what I mean...

S. A. : But that number right there, readers and actors and students, that would add up, too, wouldn't it, sir?

EGO: Not nearly as high as folks actually taking in a Broadway show... those theaters are packed and you can hardly get tickets...(voice trails off)

S. A. : Yes! You can hardly get in, isn't that right, Mr. O'Neill?

EGO: Well, it use to be, not so much anymore...

S. A. : But during the 1920's thru the 1950's, yes?

EGO: Yes, definitely! May I have some water please?

Judge: The Marshall will pour some for you. Drop your feet, Mr. O'Neill.

        (the water was poured into one of the paper cups there in a stack and the Defendant reached for it with a shaking hand and a semi smile)

EGO: Thanks...and thank you Judge for letting me put my feet down...I promise to be good.... the clock is.... my, my! these women are beautiful, just lovely here…lovely (referring to women seated in the front row)

Judge: Please, just refrain from such out of order comments. Okay?

EGO: They serve the men well, don't you think? (asking the judge)

Judge: Please continue, Mr. State Attorney…

EGO: It serves their drives…

Judge: What was that, Mr. O'Neill, drives?

S. A. : Could we have a read back?

Judge: Ask the next question please.

S. A. : (looking cynically amused)So, now, the estimate please!

EGO: What?

S. A. : You were about to estimate the number out of those tens of thousands of people, how many, approximately, read your work in Connecticut or were from here and saw it in New York?

EGO: Oh, I'd guess maybe, out of how many?

S. A. : *You* said tens of thousands total.

EGO: Maybe, half or a third…yes, a third, like a third woman, on the side, yes, a third of them, yes…(smiling broadly)

S. A. So, your answer is about thirty-three hundred people?

EGO: Sure, why not! (picks up his cup which is now empty and playfully turns it upside down as if to show everyone how dry he has become)

Judge: No demonstrations, please!

(the defendant then made a joking slash motion across his throat with his finger but the Judge missed it)

S. A. : Now, Mr. O'Neill, you have admitted that you have gained considerable fame as a result of your plays and those four wonderful prizes that we have heard of, and by the way, they carry besides prestige, a considerable sum of money, too, is that not the case, sir?

EGO: It is, well, the first one was one thousand dollars and...

S. A. : Yes, I am certain and, Mr. O'Neill, would you not say that a part of
        the fuss, if I may, over your long string of works is that reporters and
        critics and all types of personalities have pursued you and required
        explanations or else have given their condemnations, yes?

EGO: They hounded me...I hate them!

S. A. : But you answered them, responded to those inquiries and gave a
        lot of insights and opinions about the plays, what they meant, the
        themes and so forth, stuff about the state of the world and the "ter-
        rible" state of mankind, right?

EGO: It seems to me that I did that, yes...

S. A. : And the times that you made such statements, you knew that there
        was a high likelihood that they'd be published or spoken of on radio?
        TV?

EGO: I guess....

Judge: Don't guess! Say that you do not know if you do not know!

EGO: Well...yes, they were always talking about this scandal or that theme
        or some other thing that was looked down on as outrageous or sub-
        versive or wonderfully exposed or whatever.

S. A. : But you were fully aware of, were you not, that many of the things that
        you said about mankind, the problems that face us all, the causes, the
        very nature of life and the tragedy and the relationships and religion
        and fate and traps and despair and depression and so forth, that the
        public was eating this stuff up? You knew full well that it was paying
        attention to you and your words, yes?

EGO: Yes, I did know about that. . it sells tickets, you know!

S. A. : Now, many of your views, opinions, were directly meant to be ap-
        plied to problems that mankind was suffering with, problems such
        as your own kinds of personal difficulties, yes?

Judge: No, no foundation...please, I have to make sure that this man's rights
        are safeguarded, we have to have a *fair* trial...

EGO: Flattered...

Judge: Don't be…it is my job especially when one is self-represented.

EGO: Like the fool?

          (the Judge ignored him)

S. A. :   You have suffered in your lifetime from many, many problems and emotional ailments, isn't that so?

EGO: I suppose so, yes, that is where I get a lot of this stuff, what I see around me and what I feel…my own experiences inside myself…

S. A. :   And so a lot of the views and opinions and representations given out by you were made of the very same fabric as your own misfortunes?

EGO: I don't know what you mean by "fabric"!

S. A. :   In other words, the statements made by you knowing that they would reach the public, be it in the media or in your plays, they were coming from the warped insides that you carried?

Judge: I'll strike that…do not use that word without foundation.

EGO: No, it's alright, Judge, he's right. I was warped. Who wouldn't be in *that* house?

S. A. :   You are answering a question that has not been asked!

EGO: Sorry about your teenie toes there. (sarcastically) (the courtroom explodes in laughter and the Judge allows it)

S. A. :   Do you admit that yours was a troubled childhood in *that* house?

EGO: Of course.

S. A. :   "Sexually?"

Judge: Sexually?

EGO: Oh, yes, the stuff I've done about sex and the turmoil on the earth over such a simple concept, like in *Desire Under the Elms…* what's the question again?

S. A. :   In your opinions and view, uh, given out to reporters and such, a lot of that based on your own misfortunes? You yourself were suffering from the very same ailments, moral ones, emotional ones, addictions, agonies inside I think you said somewhere, right?

EGO: I've got a million of them!

S. A. :   So how is it then that you could reasonably expect to give out objective and accurate stuff and not false or tainted ideas? Where did you get the gall to conclude that you would be qualified to do that?

EGO: What the hell?

Judge: I'll declare a twenty minute recess.

(court went into recess and everybody in the room began standing up and milling around; some pointed at the defendant as he was led downstairs to the lockup by two marshals where he sat nervously with them and then joked about getting a beer)

(court was reconvened about thirty minutes later)

Judge: (gesturing)You may proceed.

S. A. :   Remember my last question, Mr. O'Neill?

EGO: Yes, I'll be damned if...(covers up his mouth with his left hand) Sorry...I made a boo-boo...I recall, yes.

S. A. :   Where did you get the gall?

EGO: I'll tell you where, sonny, I'm an expert at gall...when you've had it shoved down your throat all your life, you get used to the taste you see, sonny (very sarcastically as his face turned a red as a beet).

S. A. :   That's no answer and I move that it be stricken as unresponsive, your Honor!

Judge: I'll leave it on the record...it's connected.

EGO: (answering without a pending query) All my life I have known these people and I know what it is like in those trenches that I dug in my plays!

S. A. :   And what people are those? (sarcastically and grinning)

EGO: Well...what people are *you* talking about?

S. A. :   Your Honor, this witness is hostile...besides, I ask the questions, not him and. . (cut off by the judge)

Judge: Of course he is hostile, he's the defendant...Mr. State's Attorney!

S. A. :   (giving in)I'll tell you what people…the ones struggling, in a throat vise with addictions and drinking and crookedness. Are they not the people that you wrote about and still are?

EGO: Sure.

S. A. :   Well, then, answer my question!

EGO: What one, sir? (thinks at the State's Attorney's silence)You know, sir, there's life in the high Arctic, plants and animals, and it's there because it *can* be there and not by any design. Up in the white, life is not like in the tropics, no siree, it is suffering and deprivation and then relief. Those outside that cruelty cannot come close. That's where *you* are, Mister!

(the Judge looked at the Defendant incredulously but did not speak)

S. A. :   (seeming abashed)Your Honor, this man is obviously stalling, playing dumb, or maybe he's not playing. (courtroom laughed)I ask the Court to *order* him to answer me!

EGO: Oh, that question…I forgot for a moment…yeah, where do I get the gall… I thought I'd already spoken to that, Mister, I was one of them. Who could know better than one who was there, been there?

S. A. :   Yes, I know, but my question is where do you get the idea that your dysfunctional background has not impaired your ability to see the roots of the sickness in society even though you may accurately describe the symptoms? You are or were a victim of that very sickness. How did that not rob you of your charity?

EGO: It just didn't, that's all!

S. A. :   May I suggest to you, sir, and to the Court, that your expertise with suicide. . . You do concede a suicide attempt in New York in 1912, yes?

EGO: Unfortunately, yes…

S. A. :   Your experience with that, with being an alcoholic…you concede that as well, Do you not?

EGO: Not anymore, I don't…no!

S. A. : You're reformed maybe, but you are still one, no? the alcoholic per-
         sonality?

EGO: No!

S. A. : The alcoholic personality is self-centered and manipulative. Do you
         say so?

EGO: Uh….

S. A. : Wouldn't that describe your father, James O'Neill, the famous Monte
         Cristo actor…was he not ego-driven and running your life?

EGO: That is also unfortunately so…

S. A. : So you did not get the same personality from him?

EGO: No! I didn't manipulate anybody!

S. A. : You're not self-centered, sir? Think.

EGO: Well, when you are famous, people make up things about you, make
         you to look like that, you see?

S. A. : They didn't make up your abandonment of a pregnant wife, Kath-
         leen, in 1909 so you could traipse off to Central America on some
         wild, gold prospecting scheme, did they?

EGO: My father was behind all of that.

S. A. : So *he* manipulated you. (not asking)

Judge: Where is this going?

S. A. : I am trying to show that the defendant knew full well that his themes,
         comments, views, addictions, depravity, self-murderousness, all of it,
         were made by him from a defective mental state or emotional one
         and that he knew or had reason to know that his views, quoted in a
         detailed manner and widely read or seen or heard, would be taint-
         ed, inaccurate, off the mark, colored, self-serving, promotional and
         reckless. He had impaired credentials, your Honor and …. (yielding
         to the Judge)

Judge: Well…

S. A. : This man struggled to the very point we are at today here and now to understand man, and himself, all of the miserable baggage that's got mankind bent to sink to the bottom of the sea.

Judge: We've not heard any evidence of that ...please!

S. A.: Isn't it a cold fact that as we sit here today, you are *still* an addict, hooked on tobacco, still on pills (cut off)

EGO: I have a severe disease, that's what the pills are for...the shakes! (angrily)

S. A.: I am referring to sedatives, sir...and is it not a fact that you cannot even drive a car, have not for decades, because you are too nervous to deal with traffic?

EGO: I'm afraid so...afraid...you see I...

S. A.: And it *is* so that you have been quoted as saying that you *still struggle* to grasp man's behavior and the awful fate that usually does him in; also you are grappling with the alleged instability of human relationships, yes?

EGO: I do continue to look for those roots of sickness. . I do...

S. A.: So then, does that not *prove* that your themes, the analysis, the explanations in such great detail, heaps of theories on human weakness, all were embarrassingly off the mark, inaccurate, tainted by your crap-colored glasses, If you pardon my thoughts (courtroom erupts in giggles)

Judge: The Court will *not* pardon that, sir. No! No more!

EGO: Well, I know what you are driving at but *I did my best*. I also have been quoted as saying that I tell the truth as best I see it or feel it.

S. A.: But in matters of emotional illnesses, mental disorders, addictions, neuroses, alcoholic personality traits, is it not clear to you as you now sit here in New London, that any kind of accuracy or true insights in such analysis depend to a critical degree on objectivity and sobriety? Are you not now and over the years little more than a child advising his playmates that they avoid the hospital because it is scary and they cut you?

EGO: Say! You should have been a writer, sir, why I ...

S. A.: Believe me, Mr. O'Neill, this job entails more writing than anybody would ever guess…

(the defendant stared at him as if in a fog)

S. A. : So, I am a writer, just not like you…now…didn't your first wife have a son and is it not so that you shunned that child for eleven years?

Judge: Really?

EGO: I didn't know she was pregnant…I…

S. A. : But you consummated the marriage, didn't you?

EGO: Of course, we were together only one week, though…a mistake…

S. A. : But you had sex with her before the marriage, no?

EGO: Yes.

S. A. : Now tell us that in such a matter as this, a holy matrimony, that you knew that it was a "mistake" after only *one week*? I'd call that self-centered, wouldn't you, sir?

Judge: Please! Ask one question at a time…

EGO: My father *pushed* me to go to Honduras…I did not know about the baby boy!

S. A. : But you did hear about it all in a New York bar, true?

EGO: I guess…

S. A. : And you avoided that child for eleven years!

EGO: I couldn't…I was…I'm sorry…

S. A. : Now, you did this all again, didn't you. Didn't you get another girl pregnant and marry her…Agnes Boulton, your second stab and you ended up with two more kids, Shane and Oona, to neglect and mistreat and abandon, yes, Mr. O'Neill?

(there was a sort of ruckus at the rear of the Courtroom and it seemed like it was where the reporters had been standing for lack of seats. Then a loud sound shot across the air kind of like with a buck rabbit after he completes a mission)

EGO: (straining to see what had occurred) We were not getting along and

I thought it best for the children. You see, I... (cut off by the next question)

S. A. :   I, I, I...you, you, you...it's always about you, isn't it, Mr. O'Neill? Isn't it a fact that that had nothing to do with the "Best interests" of those kids...that you hated being around children...that Shane was a neglected child often found wandering off by himself or so introverted that he was practically withdrawn? Wasn't he found alone at a very young age down by the water at Spithead in Bermuda while you and Agnes were doing whatever you were up to up in the house? Was that not *typical* for your involvement with the children? Weren't you a Bohemian, sir?

EGO: Hey! Fuck you! ...I won't...

Judge: Mr. O'Neill! That kind of thing will land you in a cell for certain. Now, no more obscenity, please! I understand you're upset, but this is a Court of law!

S. A. :   Didn't you really leave Agnes and the kids to go off on another "adventure" to Paris with a wench named Carlotta?

Judge: Mr. State's Attorney, I just got through lecturing *him* on obscenity and here *you* go with words like that. No more or I'll see you are seated next to him in that cell. Do I make myself clear?

EGO: Carlotta is my wife, sir, and I'll thank you to refer to her in a respectful manner!

S. A. :   So that was your third marriage then?

EGO: Yes and this one will last.

S. A. :   Now, did you not have TB in 1913?

Judge: Relevance?

S. A. :   To show the Court that he was laboring under a great *illusion* about the cause of that ailment, and...

Judge: Go ahead.

S. A. :   Were you not of the belief that that disease was a *punishment* from God for your past wicked ways.

EGO: It's been reported that way, yes…

S. A.:   But didn't you believe it?

EGO: I guess I did…

S. A.:   Then we have it right there…you were *delusional*, and you admit wicked ways as well!

EGO: (remained silent with his head drooping)

S. A.:   Now, sir, I am sorry to have to bring this up but your son by Kathleen, Eugene O'Neill, Jr., he ended his own life at age about forty did he not?

EGO: Unfortunately.

S. A.:   And that was in 1950, was it not…by razor blade in a bathtub?

EGO: Yes. (looking very sullen)

S. A.:   And you refused to attend the funeral, correct?

EGO: I didn't think that I could face it, face everybody…

S. A.:   So you admit that there were awful things for you to struggle over and to face?

EGO: Yeah…feelings that I was a failure as a father and horrible doubts that I might have been behind his death…(defendant let out a choked sob)

S. A.:   Well, for eleven years you failed. And what about after that? Wasn't the unmistakable message to your son that he did not matter?

EGO: Crazy, huh? That's what I carry…that I never did either…

S. A.:   So, here you have that awful anchor around your neck and you consign it to your firstborn to drag him down…what kind of thing is that?

EGO: (obviously hurting) I paid for his funeral, though…(choked again)

S. A.:   Before your 1912 suicide attempt, and I guess that got passed on as well, in New York City, Fulton Street, wasn't it? Anyway…did you not carry on the life of an absolute bum, a binge drinker, a derelict, a gutter animal?

EGO: Sounds like me (fake smile on his face)

S. A.: So that was another example of your life being totally out of control?

EGO: Unfortunately, yes…I have tried my best. I can look myself in the mirror on that! (defendant starts to cry) Your Honor, please, could we…

Judge: What is it, Mr. O'Neill?

S. A.: Just more pity stuff, I'm afraid, cornered so pulling *that* card out!

Judge: Just a moment… go on, Mr. O'Neill…

EGO: I just wanted to ask the Court…it would help everybody here to understand, even you Judge, if we could go down to Pequot Avenue. It's not that far, maybe five minutes by car, and it would be where all this took place…I mean everything that…

Judge: (stands up) How do you spell my name (to the staff)

All: D-E-S-R-U-I-S-S-E-A-U-X (all chanted in unison)

Judge: Just making sure that they are all alert! Now, what's this? You want us to go down to where, what avenue, Mr. O'Neill?

S. A.: It's his boyhood home, your Honor, and if it pleases the Court, I don't think we have time for such nonsense…

Judge: You're right, we don't have time for nonsense and that is what your objection is, Mr. State's Attorney. What's the address?

S. A.: 325 Pequot Avenue, sir, his summer home as a boy.

Judge: Will you approach the bench, State's Attorney?

(the judge has a short conference with him and the defendant who is leaning over towards the two; he does not want anybody hearing about this in case he orders it; a trail of followers would be likely from the onlookers and reporters)

Judge: (whispering to the parties) Why would you want this, Mr. O'Neill?

EGO: (whispering back) Because it would help me, assist me to explain, to show what it was like existing under the terrible dark cloud all the time, year after year, how it hurt me, warped me…my father, the drugs, my mother's weakness, hysteria, my poor brother, Jamie, and me…*me*!

Judge: (in a low voice) This is a very serious charge. I will allow it…how's two o'clock sound, gentlemen? After lunch. (beckons to a Marshall to join them) Mr. Marshall, we'll need you to drive us in a State vehicle and we'll leave from the rear entrance…two o'clock.

EGO: Can't we go at night, when the darkness has come, when the fog rolls in?

Judge: When the fog rolls in…what in the world…?

EGO: That would more closely resemble, follow, match my feelings, the way it was for me…(cut off)

Judge: I'm afraid that won't do, Mr. O'Neill, why we'd have to be working after hours, cannot do that, we recess at five o'clock I'm afraid, sir. Two o'clock is the order and it will be no longer than one-half hour and you, Mr. State's Attorney, you drive your own car and leave from the back. Okay?

S. A. : Very good, your Honor.

Judge: Proceed.

S. A. : Now, Mr. O'Neill, you resided in Greenwich Village in New York City beginning in 1915, is that right?

EGO: Yes.

S. A. : And there you hung around with a bunch of radicals?

EGO: I would not say so, no.

S. A. : Isn't it true that you used to frequent places where anarchists hung about, poets, philosophers with revolutionary bent, ideas fermenting?

EGO: It was a free country!

S. A. : And you *yourself* were advocating the overthrow of the capitalist system?

EGO: You mean oppressive political system! (lecturing tone)

S. A. : No, I mean *economic*… let's not alter the plain meaning of words!

EGO: Well, however you characterize it, I did advocate that, yes, because it was grinding down the little man to powder, don't you see that?

S. A. : And he was *chained* to those factory machines, right, that's your story?

EGO: A man has to feed his family.

S. A. : But you wanted to squash the very machines that were doing just that, feeding his family…do you see the crookedness?

EGO: In what way?

S. A. : What do you think would have taken the place of that factory job to provide wages if you crushed that system, huh?

EGO: Why, the government, of course!

S. A. : Sounds communistic to me…is that what you are, a communist? The government is supposed to work for the people, not the other way around!

EGO: But I pulled away from that view…anyway…I…Uh…

S. A. : Of course, some people have to run the government, that is alright, but as owner of the means, it's crooked, do you see it?

EGO: I don't know…I don't know anything lately.

S. A. : You claimed to know that you were, and I quote you, "Not cut out to be a father".

EGO: Well, I guess I was not…it seems…

S. A. : You admit to putting three children, at least three, on this earth?

EGO: Eugene, Jr., Oona and Shane. Yes.

S. A. : But not "cut out" for it!

EGO: You know what I meant…you…

S. A. :   Let me guess: you meant that after trying it out, you didn't want to buy it, so you just let it drift away!

EGO: I would never put it *that* way! I tried…I…

S. A. : You tried? You *failed*, right?

EGO: Unfortunately…

S. A. : So then, does it not prove that you remained ego-driven, delusional, self- centered, addicted, irresponsible, confused, (cut off)

EGO: Do not take heart in my dirty laundry, Mr.... (mutters to himself)

S. A. :   Mr. O'Neill, you realize that you face a severe penalty upon conviction, right?

EGO: So I'm informed.

S. A. :   And you've pleaded "not guilty", correct? Innocent, right?

EGO: As the German man said as he held up a bar of soap: "I might be a heinie but I don't stink!"

(the Courtroom absolutely erupted in laughter and shouting and a few cameras even went off although they were supposed to have been confiscated by the State Marshalls beforehand)

S. A. :   (before the judge could get a word out) Mr. O'Neill, is it not a fact that all of your themes, or most of them, the views, the analysis of what you termed a "sick society" were just a reckless effort born of inner desperation and seen from a damaged viewpoint *and* were just down and out *false, wrong*?

EGO: Preposterous!

S. A. :   And is it not true, sir, that all those people who you have *admitted* that saw the plays or read the plays and were either from Connecticut or did so in this State, all thousands, were affected by that falsity?

EGO: I do not agree...not affected...there *was* no falsity!

S. A. :   But you just got done a couple of hours ago, or so, telling me and his Honor that it was your *intention* that they be affected, scared, alarmed, depressed, worried and so forth, recall that? (the defendant squirmed around in his chair pretending to find a way to get more comfortable)

S. A. :   Well, sir?

EGO: It's a free country, ain't it? (using slang for defiance)

S. A. :   No, it is not, not if you are going around behaving like that, using false ideas and views and themes to upset people and scare them, no it is *not*...and as a matter of fact, sir, the State will show you and the Court that you have violated the law against falsehood hindering humanity...that is, setting mankind backwards on vital notions such as blame, shaming, family turmoil, use of self-deception, illusions, pipe dreams as you think of this, shall I go on, sir? (sarcastic tone)

EGO: Don't I have a First Amendment *right* to say what I want?

Judge: Yes, you do, Mr. O'Neill, except when the use of speech, including books, plays, presents a clear and public danger to the public welfare, such as advancing the idea that it is *normal, innate,* acceptable to use the phony excuse that one is *required* to use falsehoods to survive emotionally, that it is the nature of man to need this, you see?

EGO: Uh?

Judge: It *prevents* people; in fact, it is the rope to grab to avoid facing reality, from shedding the awful legacy of childhood abuse and neglect such as that which you claim to have suffered.

EGO: (in a weak voice) But I was only reporting what *I* experienced myself.

Judge: It acts as a block to public progress on this ancient problem and it stands in the way of a general acceptance of the notion that citizens who are adversely affected by parental misconduct of a chronic nature can nonetheless find a remedy, a cure, instead of being condemned to a life of drugs, alcohol, divorce, crime, wife beating, job failure, traffic violence, gambling away the rent money and other social ills that sap the vitality of our nation, no, the *world*, and which are not organic disorders...

S. A. :   I could not have said it better myself, your Honor!

Judge: That's why I'm up here and you are not. (kidding voice) But seriously, Mr. O'Neill, that kind of thing, the false dissemination such as you have been charged with, it blocks the spreading of *truth* and that mankind can *indeed* find that relief by going into a recovery process, painful though it can be. It is a kind of crime against humanity!

S. A. :   You've admitted, have you not, that there is a terrible sickness in society and that it gets passed around, passed down actually, father to son, on and on, yes?

EGO: No! I don't admit it. I proclaim it! (in a loud voice that startled the judge)

S. A. :   And it was just this kind of sickness that you yourself passed on to your own three children, one of which is already dead at age forty just as you yourself attempted in 1912. Lucky that what you've done to *them* is not charged against you specifically, sir!

Judge: Enough of that!

EGO: Well...I don't know of any connection...I...

S. A. :   What about Shane? Has he not had a life of drugs and addiction? Have there not been awful missteps for him and is it not true that Oona has married, when she was eighteen, a man fifty-four? Famous comedian? And have you not shunned her since, your own daughter?

EGO: I think that I have that right, a right, have that right! Maybe she'll come to her senses if I refuse to have anything to do with her...teach her...

S. A. :   Like teaching the value of a dollar, sir? (smugly)

(Eugene was silent)

Judge: Excuse me, I was trying to think of another pointed example to tell the defendant about, one of falsehood holding back humanity. I think that a good one is the totalitarian government or dictatorship one which treats its people like children instead of adults. One way might be the discrimination against certain classes of citizens of that system such as women...making them dress a certain way...or a radical group, making it behave in a separate way...that is falsehood if it is rage-based or shame-based or fear-based, you see, Mr. O'Neill?

EGO: Yes, I do, your Honor, and thanks. (slightly sarcastic)

S. A. :   Getting back to.... Mr. O'Neill, didn't your children get their troubles from you?

EGO: I don't know that...

S. A. :   Well, what effect do you suppose it has on a kid when he is ignored by his own father for eleven years, or in the case of Agnes, when they are deprived of a father's love by one who admits that he was "Not cut out to be a father"? You held yourself away from them emotionally!

EGO: I was just reserved.

S. A. : Like your mother was just reserved...upstairs on a morphine trip. Like that?

EGO: (silent and gloomy)

S. A. : You have been withdrawn from anything unpleasant or demanding all your life, yes?

EGO: I guess so. I tried my best... (head hanging down)

Judge: It's time we broke for lunch. I'll see you gentlemen for the matter we discussed at the bench side. Okay? (holds up two fingers meaning two o'clock)

All the spectators filed out of the Courtroom, some were buzzing, others, laughing, but some were down in the mouth. The press, scattered among them, professed that a great story was unfolding here. They seemed to be taken with the unusual aspects of the case, the notoriety of the Defendant, a Nobel Prize recipient and a local personality. Many had lunch at the usual eateries and went on about how fair or unfair the judge was. Some saw that the State was "picking on Eugene". About half thought that he was absolutely not guilty of anything and they were outraged at the idea put forward by such a "crime" as they put it cynically. Some spectators actually knew the defendant from when he lived in New London up to 1915 and talked about Eugene O'Neill Drive.

The Courtroom had been locked up for lunch and was dark. The prisoner was in his cell and refused to eat. He did smoke quite a lot and looked pale. Judge Desruisseaux ate his brown bag meal in chambers fielding telephone interruptions while Court personnel mostly gathered in the lunchroom. At 2:05 p. m., at the rear of the Courthouse, the Judge, two State Marshalls, the Court Clerk (Assistant), a Court reporter and the Defendant wearing handcuffs but no leg irons all piled into a large, white van owned by the State and drove off with the State's Attorney following in his own car. The driver, instead of driving down State Street and then going right to go along the water, took a more secretive route and wound up coming out by the lighthouse. The van turned left onto Pequot Avenue and as it got closer and closer, Eugene's face grew paler and paler. He was visibly shaking and the Judge saw this with concern on his brow. Too soon, the van reached a spot where all could make out the National historic Register sign on the front lawn at 325 Pequot. The prisoner's eyes closed and he appeared to be "asleep". The van was parked and the driver got out, opened the door for the Judge and the Clerk and then the other Marshall got out and guided the Defendant down the step of the vehicle. The reporter followed them in a state of readiness in case the Judge instructed her to begin recording on the record conversation or orders. It was not anticipated, however. as the Marshall who was holding Mr. O'Neill by the arm walked towards the steps from the street up to the front lawn of the cottage, the prisoner said, as he pointed with his joined arms.

EGO: I can see..... . uh.... (and he suddenly raised his arms way up high and to his left as if trying to scratch his left ear but in a sort of a wild, hypnotic kind of a motion and then he broke loose and bolted across the street towards the water's edge which was only thirty feet or so)

Judge: Get him! (shouting)

(The others commented crazily with stuff like he would swim to Long Island. One of the Marshalls thought to himself that O'Neill runs just like a "girl", "wails like a baby". Eugene reached the water in no time and he dove in head first, cuff arms outstretched. He went under and did not come up. One Marshall went in after him and was struggling to move with all his uniform wet and heavy. Soon, though, he came up with a handful of Eugene, covered with gunk, algae, soaking wet, half-conscious, muttering, crying, delirious, his beautiful suit and shoes ruined.)

Judge: That's enough of a viewing for me! Let's take him back and reconvene in thirty minutes!

(on the ride back, some personnel were angry with the drowned rat but others seemed sympathetic)

Court Reporter: What enables one plant to turn soil, air and water into a pineapple and another growing right next to it, to turn the very same things into a potato?

(The others looked at her like she was from Mars. Then somebody said that they had read a long time ago about O'Neill's mother trying the same thing, trying to drown herself, and wondered if it had been the same place. Eugene pretended not to hear any of this and sat quietly with eyes shut tight and head tilted. Back at the Courthouse, the growing unrest at the locked doors and the clock nearing 2:23 p. m. was growing louder. Nobody wanted to miss anything. The doors were opened at 2:45 p. m. and everybody streamed in complaining and indignant. They got no explanations. The Judge took the bench and wondered to himself what the world would think about a Nobel Prize winner being here like this, here in a prisoner's uniform which was necessary because his street clothes were unusable. He pondered whether O'Neill had tried to escape or drown himself. Court was called to order and the State's Attorney was motioned to resume his case on direct.)

S. A. :   Let the record show that the defendant is back in the witness chair, that he now dons his prisoner uniform and that this was made… (cut off)

Judge: Stop it! No reference to any activity that we…you know! (the courtroom buzzed at this but simmered down quickly to hear) You're still under oath, Mr. O'Neill…proceed, please. Are you okay?

EGO: No. I'm not "okay". (angry)

Judge: Out there, I am sorry that that had to occur…

EGO: Why can't you all just leave me alone? I have not hurt anyone…leave me in peace…let me go for Christ's sake!

Judge: Unfortunately, we cannot do that. I do appreciate your willingness to testify, your choice, and to tell us the truth and the Court will decide in the end whether you are guilty or not based on the evidence. A lot of evidence is to come yet and you, yourself can produce whatever evidence and witnesses you wish as part of the defense, you understand?

EGO: Yes, I do. (resignedly)

Judge: Very well. Proceed please.

S. A. : Haven't you made statements in public to the effect that you present the truth as you see it, or better, feel it?

EGO: Didn't we already go over that?

S. A. : Correct! And in that regard, Mr. O'Neill, my question is this: How do you know that what you present or what you feel is actually the truth…I mean…in other words, how do you avoid the cerebralizations of a contaminated child growing up?

EGO: Contaminated? What?

S. A. : Affected by abuse and neglect chronically…you were, no?

EGO: I was. I guess so. (sadly)

S. A. : So, you were and still are under its spell, right?

EGO: I don't know that I would say "spell"…I…I carry around an awful thing inside of me and it never goes away unless I have a drink or take…

S. A. : Yes…and I have read statements by you to the effect that…to that effect, so my question now is, being contaminated by that agony, how do you avoid cerebralizations that all contaminated people use?

EGO: I don't know (thin voice)…I just do, that's all…what do you mean by cerebralization?

S. A. : That means the practice of thinking one's way in and out of everything and explaining it all away…having an answer to everything… that's you, is it not?

EGO: Eh?

S. A. : You run your whole existence by way of acumen or supposed acumen instead of by feelings and vulnerabilities, don't you?

EGO: You call what I do out there on Pequot no feelings? I told you, I present the truth as I feel it! That's not feelings?

S. A. : Don't you really mean "sense" of it? You are not really in your true feelings, are you?

EGO: Certainly I am, why…I…

S. A. : Your dad died in 1920 and our mother two years later and your brother one year after that, 1923, and they're all buried out on Jefferson. Did you ever cry one tear over that?

EGO: Did I cry over them? …I wanted to…I

S. A. : That's what I am talking about…outside your feelings!

EGO: Oh…

S. A. : That agony that you speak if, depression, anxiety, obsession, so forth, those are substitutes for real feelings, vulnerabilities is a better word. You understand me now?

EGO: Sort of, I…

S. A. : So you agree with me now that you do not, cannot avoid the cerebralizations that all abused and neglected children indulge, yes?

EGO: Maybe…I guess, I don't…maybe…

S. A. : To put it another way, sir, when you speak in public or make statements to be read by that public or write your plays, how do you know that the "Truth" as I see it or "Feel It" is not mere self-dealing, born of desperation to have answers to that agony and all that is turmoil inside you from the past?

EGO: I don't know how…I just…I don't know how/

S. A. : Let me put this idea to you: Isn't the Greek tragedy a subject that you are intimate with and well versed in, correct?

EGO: Of course.

S. A. : Aren't they where the hero is brought down by some tragic flaw, really bogus insofar as that flaw is implied to be unavoidable if not innate?

EGO: I don't know. I never considered it like that…bogus…the classics,

S. A. : Is it not possible that as you sit here and now that any such tragic flaw is just as likely to have been induced by bad parents as it was born?

EGO: Possible, give me an example…can you?

S. A. :   Let's say that our Greek hero suffers from fatal and false pride, his undoing. Isn't that likely to be a symptom of child abuse not to mention curable?

EGO: False pride? Like a boastful person or a showoff? Ego-driven?

S. A. :   Yes.

EGO: It *could* be, sure.

S. A. :   And that kind of flaw in a Greek play, a tragic flaw, is not innate but induced, you agree?

EGO: It could be innate, say if a symptom or some organic disorder like... an organic emotional disease...

S. A. :   Perhaps I used a poor example, but what I am driving at is this: all of your public pronouncements, statements, characterizations on the nature of man, the *trapped* condition that he is in, the "*damnation*" that is his due, the *despair* that racks him, the *struggle* that he has with *reality* and the effects of that, according to you, on the realization of mankind's ideals such as faith, creativity and love, all of that, and the turning of such ideals into hatred, destruction and skepticism by way of frustration, could you have been mistaken in all of that?

EGO: How so?

S. A. :   It's simple; your representations about all of that along with such ideas as in the core of *The Iceman Cometh* about man's weaknesses requiring the use of illusions by him to survive or ideas such as man being *born broken*, are you not now able to see that a large part of such notions by you were *false,* that any such "defects" in mankind are not inborn, not fate, not angry gods, not damnation, not being trapped as a predestination, but only conditions induced by parents' misconduct or nonconduct or absence and that your own family history is a pointed example of it *and* of the cerebralizations indulged in by you when coming up with such stuff?

EGO: Well, when I made all of those statements, wrote the stuff, I was in no way saying that man's doom had any connection to anything truly avoidable...I always insinuate that they were his fate, his due.

S. A. : And that extends to *religion* as well, does it not? Aren't your themes about a world with no God or with vengeful God or power, about lost connections to God, is that not the same thing…a result of something that *was* avoidable and *is* avoidable…namely, being on the receiving end of parental misconduct or nonconduct resulting in becoming warped and robbed of natural spirituality?

EGO: I am a Roman Catholic, sir, and I have never thought about my religion in terms of anything except that the world and heaven either is as I was   taught or it is wholly without God, period!

S. A. : Have you not made rash statements about "being mad at God" or "angry with God" and did you not give up church at age fifteen because God did not answer your prayers about your mother's morphine habit?

EGO: True. They were not "rash", however!

S. A. : Not rash? Would you not say that such a position is grossly paranoid in the delusions of grandeur persuasion? I mean, where did you get the you know what to be "mad at God"? That's hard to believe! God is what God is and none of it depends one iota on your receiving his favors or his violence, does it? Wouldn't it be more accurate to be mad at the Church? It is what taught you about the world-by-magic formula in place of the world by logic one, is that not true?

EGO: I don't grasp your idea…world-by-magic?

S. A. : Sure! You think that you can get your mother to stop using drugs by mumbling words? Is that not magic's baliwick?

EGO: I have no more words for you, sir…(insulted)

S. A. : Do you see now, see that that Iceman idea about needing pipe dreams to   survive and that truth is death, I think you said, see that that is just your own desperation to find an answer, any answer, just so there would   be no more void, which void is part of your agonies?

EGO: I…I…well…(hemming)

S. A. : Is it not so that part of the turmoil in you is the state of knowing not what's really wrong and so you took your best shot at explaining it from all the evidence you chose to sift thru, feeling in your own way truthful and objective, and coming up with the likes of Iceman?

EGO: (crestfallen) Gee, I never looked at it like that… but I say it *again*, it *was* the truth as I really saw things, felt them! (assuring)

S. A. :   You might have felt in your soul that it was the truth, but if I suggest to you now that it really was an *untruth*, false, would you be more likely *now* to agree with me, Mr. O'Neill?

EGO: I don't know…I don't want to hurt my case…my defense…

S. A. :   What sense does it make now, here, in the clear light of day, clearer light, that human beings actually have an innate need to self-deceive?

EGO: I see what you're driving at…sort of…I guess

S. A. :   So then, can you not see now and *agree* that those themes and issues as in *Iceman* and other plays and other statements made to the public, they were in hindsight really a patch job, the best that you could come up with *thinking your way out of your agony. . .* in other words, cerebralizing?

EGO: It seems so, yes…

S. A. :   Thank you, Mr. O'Neill, thank you! Now, do you know what codependence is?

EGO: No.

S. A. :   Let me define that. A person is born codependent and it is normal in all children. It means that their sense of self-worth comes from the actions, expressions, words by others and *not* from inside of themselves.

EGO: Okay. (not conceding anything in his voice)

S. A. :   And when such a child is chronically abused, often only subtly, and neglected, they never lose that trait whereas kids growing up in a whole environment largely free of abuse and neglect *do* lose it. That occurs at around age sixteen or so when signals of self-esteem come from the inside.

EGO: Okay, I…

S. A. :   Now, a lot of your plays and themes, as well as your public statements about them, describe that for human beings, relationships are tenuous at best, unstable, and human frailties prevail, that human weaknesses abound. You speak a lot of the fear of death. They seem to be morbid fears. You lament the struggle of man to come to grips with his trapped condition and the "absurdity" of it all, yes? You communicated a lot of this stuff in letters to the media and friends, yes?

EGO: Indeed, sir!

S. A. :   Isn't that just a *drunk* talking?

EGO: (insulted and turning red)

S. A. :   Or the *son* of a drunk? The way that you put it all, the explanations of *how* things are and how they work and the seeming inevitability of the doom and damnation, the despair, the destruction, the dire loneliness, the impossibility of belonging to anyone or any thing, all that, do you *now* see that all that, coupled with the codependence thing, is rooted in the mistreatment of youngsters, neglect, abandonment by the parents whether it be subtle or overt?

EGO: Uh…(thinking)

S. A. :   Can you not agree with me now that all of that is made up bandages, that there is no such thing as "fate" predetermining events or outcomes and that there is no trapped condition really or damnation and no innate despair and doom and that many of the weaknesses that you expose are really just *symptoms* of that abuse and abandonment. The same goes for frailties. And let me bring in your grand idea that human nature is fraught with *perverse complexities.* Aren't these all symptoms of a largely avoidable phenomenon?

EGO: Uh, I suppose that I might have overlooked such a *slant.*

S. A. :   Is it a *slant* or is it the rock truth? Your strong and repeated themes to the contrary are false, phony, born of your own understandable but *illegal* efforts to find a road out of Hell, to grab a little bit of peace? Do you not today see that your efforts to find relief and that would include a manufactured importance so that you could feel that you mattered, belonged to something, anything, that that was and is hurtful to the public and it holds the public back from any kind of progress on the emotional front, a hindrance to humanity, a crimp in the hope?

EGO:　　I couldn't stand to have anything like *that* on me…my conscience!

S. A. :　Well, the State of Connecticut has charged you with just *that*! When you write, people believe it. When you speak, the world pays attention and if you say whistling in the dark really is a valid defense, the poor masses who continue to struggle in that darkness will seize onto what they hear if it comes from the likes of you!

EGO:　　I *have* achieved a degree of notoriety, yes…

S. A. :　But you are *hurting* them. They want nothing more than to blame it on fate instead of their mothers and fathers. Unless they are the victims of an organic disease or some accident of nature, these haggard people are *in fact doomed*, but it is not any kind of legacy on earth. They are being doomed by you by your thrusting out candy of false manufacture! *That* is what you are charged with sir and I ask you, I beg you to see it and to fess up now, for your own good and that of the future.

EGO:　　(rubbing his face and obviously weary) I don't know about confessing to anything like that…why I am a good person and I…

S. A. :　I know that it hurts to say that you are wrong, made a mistake, acted out of self-interest. That kind of relief is intoxicating, I understand. But, *they*, them out there, they need you, they need it…for you to fess up!

EGO:　　(seeming confused, tired, threatened) I want to help you…

Judge:　It is not your job to help *him*, Mr. O'Neill. The State can take care of itself and I will not allow the State to cajole you into a false notion that you are under any duty to assist it in a trial that is aimed at putting *you* in prison for life.

S. A. :　All I am saying and asking, your Honor and Mr. O'Neill is for you to admit or deny that what you threw out on the street in Iceman Cometh was confection for the emotionally starved and whether you saw it then or see it only now, please confirm or deny that, sir!

EGO:　　I don't know…I…I don't know about that…

S. A. :　Your Honor, I ask the Court to order him to be responsive! He has to know, know what he feels and thinks, confirm or deny it, please!

Judge: But the State's position is that he does not know what he feels!

S. A. : "Feels" in the sense of perceives, your Honor, not in the psychological way...

Judge: Yes, proceed, Mr. O'Neill. Answer that last question...confirm or deny it.

EGO: Candy to the what. Emotionally starved? Well, they are starved, so what?

S. A. : That is not the point. The point is that you threw false candy to them and that it enabled them to continue lives fraught with drink, drugs, lying, fibs to the self, life-destruction...a ticket to a long future of despair instead of a message of hope.

EGO: "Hope" was a name in *Iceman*, you know!

S. A. : But your efforts squash any hope of hope working. Yours is a message of no way out of the degradation...admit it!

EGO: I admit *that*...there is no way out! *That's* why I am famous, for saying it!

S. A. : But they, those wretched souls in that bar, they cerebralize just like you are accused of doing. They are you in a sense. As a matter of fact, you got the very idea for The Iceman Cometh from that bar on Fulton Street in lower Manhattan, where you swallowed a bottle of sleeping tablets in 1912 to end it all yourself, right!

EGO: Everybody knows that! (face shows pride)

S. A. : So, aren't you one of *them*? And how in hell...heck...can you come up with any kind of thing describing all of that and analyzing it in an accurate way when you are nothing but one of them and stuck in the same muck?

EGO: I am much smarter than the average bum, that's how!

S. A. : But thinking the way out when you yourself are the prisoner, does *that* reach out and snag the ring of keys?

EGO: There you go again...Mr. author (smiling bitterly)

Judge: Mr. O'Neill, stick to answering the questions and not being argu-
        mentative please…

S. A. : Isn't it the emotional transaction that gets you out, Mr. O'Neill and
        not the thinking transaction?

EGO: I have no idea what you are referring to. (defiant)

S. A. : Trouble is, nobody, not you or anyone else, has the *nerve* to go thru it!

EGO: Still don't know what you are talking about, do you even know?

Judge: That'll do!

S. A. : Haven't you insisted over the years that the emotions are the route to
        truth and that emotions are *instinctive* ?

EGO: Sounds like me, yes.

S. A. : So why balk at that now, why not admit it and stop stalling so that we
        can all get out of here (frustrated)

Judge: Mr. State's Attorney, that is improper! No more talk like that *please*!

S. A. : All those people in that bar, they all carry on fantasies about God or
        no God, power or no power, meaning or no meaning to life, quit-
        ting or not quitting, hating or not hating, drinking or staying on the
        wagon, and you have told them all that they need that to survive!
        This stuff is now public and a part of the public's consciousness and
        it hurts everybody because it is not true! There is and was even a
        widespread belief that this play expresses an *ideal* of compassionate
        understanding by man for his fellow man. Misery loves company is
        not compassion and, these souls, do not understand anything!

EGO: Prove it (defiantly)

S. A. : How can you sit here and with a straight face tell us and the world
        that mankind is born with such a defect that he requires falsehood to
        survive?

EGO: Ever seen a mother bird pretend to be wounded so as to lead a preda-
        tor away from her nest of hatchlings, huh? (A loud applause broke
        out in the Courtroom and the judge scolded them but seemed to like
        the retort)

S. A. : Yes, *that* is falsehood to survive, I see it, Mr. O'Neill, but that is different. That is not human beings who have high intelligence and can survive by being honest and good.

EGO: Ever see a wounded soldier pretend to be dead at the point of a bayonet? (Again, the laughter and clapping arose)

S. A. : Yes, but that is an extraordinary circumstance and not a lifetime of action such as you portray in Iceman!

EGO: (seeming defeated suddenly)

S. A. : Come clean now, please, it'll go better if you tell the truth!

EGO: Who's version?

S. A. : I recall a quote about you, sir, don't remember where I read it, but it was something about you offering the world your "Significant bit of truth". Do you…does that ring any bells?

EGO: Many!

S. A. : Well, then, let's focus on *that* version, shall we? Suppose you tell us about *that* kind of truth.

EGO: I was referring to the insights that my plays have projected to the world and I was, I guess, self-effacing there.

S. A. : How so?

EGO: Well, I was understating it, you know, so as not to sound too bold…

S. A. : But what truth were you projecting?

EGO: Oh, I think that the world knows and that you know as well.

S. A. : But the Judge does not know and we need to get it on the record, you…

EGO: They didn't recognize me for stating falsehoods!

S. A. : Who?

EGO: The King of Sweden, that's who, want to grapple with him?

S. A. : That's impudent, your Honor…please instruct…

Judge: Yes, Mr. O'Neill, no more of that…please…

EGO: And the board at Columbia, they didn't award me three of their jewels because I was a fake!

S. A. :   So, that is your defense?

EGO: Uh…sure (light bulb going off in his head)…yes! That's my defense!

Judge: Time for statements of defense theories later, sir, not now!

S. A. :   So, you are testifying under oath that your themes and plays and statements, such as the outrageous stuff that I just recently asked you on from *Iceman*, that all that is part of your significant bit of truth because of your four awards?

EGO: Why not? They're not dummies, you know! (grinning in victory)

S. A. :   But what if *they* are blind and contaminated just like you and just like those poor patrons in that bar, Mr. O'Neill, what then?

EGO: Don't be ridiculous, *they* are not contaminated by anything!

S. A. :   Aren't your plays really more about describing the plight of mankind rather than telling what the causes are?

EGO: No!

S. A. :   Is it not your philosophy, Mr. O'Neill, that no matter how long a person has sunk, like the bar patrons in Harry Hope's Bar, that there is nonetheless always one dream left?

EGO: I have said as much, yes…

S. A. :   Didn't you portray Hickey's wife as long-suffering and "loving" him so much that she'd forgive his transgressions and infidelities?

EGO: I did.

S. A. .   And is it not a fact that those poor slobs at that bar really saw their pipe dreams as true dreams in light of their characterization of Hickey as "insane"?

EGO: I guess you read the play?

S. A. :   Yes, and isn't there something in there about "To hell with the truth", that it has no bearing on anything, that it is irrelevant, that the like of their pipe dreams is the thing that gives life to the whole bunch of them, be they drunk or not?

EGO: I was expressing the ambiguity of truth, of human motives (voice trails off)

S. A. : Mr. O'Neill! (shouting) "Ambiguity" of truth! ?"

Judge: There had better not be any "ambiguity of truth in my Courtroom, sir…I warn you! (very sternly).

EGO: No, sir, your Honor, I was speaking literarily.

S. A. : Yes, literarily, you see that the truth can be ambiguous?

EGO: Of course (in a lecturing tone), as can much of man's motives and ideas and thoughts and carryings on…

S. A. : How about a priest or a rabbi or a U. S. District Court Judge… uh, no offense, your Honor,…would you say that these persons possess thoughts and ideas and motives that are ambiguous and, perhaps less than truthful?

EGO: In matters of love or hate, emotions, romance, etc., sure…

S. A. : But *that* is not "To hell with the truth", is it? *That* isn't truth having no bearing on anything…that's what you wrote…the word "Anything", Mr. Defendant! (loud voice).

EGO: (Looks down and seems afraid to meet the State's Attorney's eyes).

S. A. : Are we not really mulling over what's really inside of you, what you carry in the disease or disorder sense and not any *objective* notions of what truth is and its role? ?

EGO: I was portraying the problem of showing such a thing as you suggest in a world that has no absolutes, our world, this world…

S. A. : No absolutes, sir? You mean like rearing children in love and discipline and steadiness, like telling the truth all the time, like paying for a newspaper even when the merchant is in the back room and nobody would find out that you stole it? Absolutes like those, Mr. O'Neill? (in a demanding tone).

EGO: (remained silent)

S. A. : Well?

Judge: Answer the question, please!

EGO: My drive, my literary and philosophical idea there was that the pipe dreams held onto by those poor folks were more sane, more "life-giving" shall I say, than the kind of self-righteousness that passes for truth and absolutes in the world today...

S. A. : So, then, when you claimed that "To hell with the truth" was the idea, that it has no relevance, you were saying it figuratively and not literally?

EGO: I was projecting that much is pushing onto the world as "truth" when it is the opposite, clouded, ill-motive-oriented, and, yes, even ambiguous! I was saying to heck with *that* kind of crap but not to the kinds of things that you listed as examples. Who would Be against those?

S. A. : Who? (sarcastically) Who, Mr. O'Neill? (again) Who (sharper)? Why do you think that the world is in such chaos, Mr. Defendant? Suppose you tell me your reason or idea on *that*!

EGO: (taking too long to answer)

S. A. : I'll tell you the answer, sir, *you are*! You are the reason for it and that is why you face this serious charge! (on his high horse) the claims that you have made in these plays, this play, *The Iceman Cometh*, is a pack of untruths! Yes, the descriptions of how people are, live, deceive, carry on, cling desperately are accurate in some sense but the justifications and the root causes are either morally awry or just missing, sir!

EGO: I don't know how to respond to that...

S. A. : You have idealized social intercourse vis a vis these kinds of people under the guise of compassion and understanding and thereby become a plain old enabler...an enabler, sir, just like Hickey's wife!

EGO: Hey! Don't sell those two things short, sir (as a tit for tat)

S. A. : You are selling needles in a balloon store, Mr. O'Neill. Real understanding and true compassion are nearly vanished in Harry Hope's or any other setting that embraces such misery. People who live on pipe dreams, illusions, the smokers, the drunks, the skunks, etc. do not really understand anything except pain relief and pain avoidance. It's misery-loves-company drooling, Sir, not "understanding"! It's fear of being alone and wrong, Mr. O'Neill, not "compassion".

EGO: Well…(befuddled)

S. A. : These poor slobs do not even know who they are, let alone what they *feel* or what they really want.

Judge: I don't hear a question.

S. A. : Do you not now see that Harry's Hope's patrons feel only "pain" and the "thrill" of escape from pain?

EGO: They suffer because there *is* no final secret, no unimaginable dream of beauty over the horizon, Mr. State's Attorney, do *you understand* and have a *compassion* for what that means?

S. A. : But why does it have to be "over a horizon", sir? Why does it have to be a "dream" of beauty? Why not the absolutes I listed?

EGO: Because that is not how this world operates. Can't you see that?

S. A. : Oh, indeed, that is why *you* are on trial…you foster it, encourage it and your enormous status is the engine that must be shut off! People believe you!

EGO: I only know what I feel and it is a rotten life and a rottener World and illusions and pipe dreams are the lubrication (cut off)

S. A. : They are excuses and not more!

EGO: I disagree.

S. A. : All the hand-wringing about man's "fate" and dreaming the ideal but failing and falling under sin and such things as materialism is really just baby stuff. Man is whole to start out and not plagued by such nonsense until parents ruin things with their self-dealing or worse!

EGO: I cannot see that really, my plays describe the roots of (cut off)

S. A. : What else is there in there besides that?

EGO: I railed against materialism, that's in there. (sarcastic and defiant) That's the American way of life and I think it stinks! The very process of possession and gaining *more* possessions is self-destructive and in the end, dispossesses!

S. A. :   Anything else?

EGO: Are you telling me that the Pulitzer Prize Board awarded me three times and were totally unaware of fakery as you allege?

Judge: You are not to question the State, sir! Proceed!

EGO: (rashly) Are you having the nerve to suggest that the Nobel Committee labors under blindness?

Judge: That's enough, Mr. O'Neill, I can place you back in that cell to cool off!

S. A. :   What else is in there?

EGO: Moles…I don't know…rats? (angry)

S. A. :   In the plays…what other significant bits of… (cut off)

EGO: I have made as a theme the quest to break free of illusions and to unite with the "spiritual force" and to discover the genuine identity of a person.

S. A. :   Funny you should mention that, Mr. O'Neill because I was only recently reviewing the anticipated testimony of one of the State's witnesses, here today, on that very same subject.

EGO: Oh? And who would that be…do I know him?

S. A. :   Her, Mr. O'Neill, her…

EGO: A woman? Gads!

S. A. :   Genuine self? Do you know what that is even?

EGO: Of course…and I am not the ogre that you make me out to be… the genuine self is that which flows from purity and not from utter skunkity!

Judge: "Skunkity" sir?

EGO: Sorry…I get carried away…

S. A. :   Isn't that the real theme here, that you got carried away…you began well-intentioned enough, however, the lies that came quickly to you found ample fertilizer and the whole thing bloomed out of control, is that not the truth, Mr. O'Neill?

EGO: Nonsense! I have also preached about human compassion and that it is *better* than truth! Deal with that!

S. A. : But why can't those two coexist?

EGO: I don't know…maybe…but they never do, really they…

S. A. : And what about all your efforts to grapple with death, your awful dread of it, the so called "meaninglessness of life" and the "absurdity" of everything including death. What is that if not a blow to the children who must come to fear death because of you when death is a natural and welcome part of being alive!

EGO: (silent)

S. A. : Well? I'm waiting.

EGO: (sheepishly) yes, I suppose that that is true…it reminded me of feelings that I had to push out, push away a long, long time ago…

S. A. : It set you back, did it? You understand me?

EGO: I do. Yes…sort of…but it hurts to be reminded…

S. A. : Then think of the hurt on others, the setback to the whole human race when you put that stuff out on a stage. They gobble it up, they cling to it for dear life. You make everybody terrified of dying instead of being grateful that there's some end to getting out of bed every day!

EGO: Never could think of it that way…*never* (loud voice)

S. A. : But you see my point? Death cuts *you* off of any chance to inherit the *real* legacy and the chance to get rid of that agony even if just for *one precious day*. Isn't that the *real* fear?

EGO: (sobbing) Yes, Oh, yes, that hits me square in the eyes! My rotten life, they stole her, Sarah, and that was the last straw, kick in the balls… the awful acid loneliness was my due, my reward for being a good kid… and nobody cared! (sobs deeply) (The Judge looked very sympathetic)

S. A. : Your Honor, I believe that Mr. O'Neill is in a very much deeper kind of a prison right now and that he always has been really, and that his being here in New London only emphasizes the bars, strips away the denial that has allowed him to carry on elsewhere. Any jail that the Court might put him in would be superfluous, really...what do...I... uh,

Judge: I grasp your sentiments, but we are sworn to uphold the law.

EGO: Reality defeats man's attempts to arrive at freedom and happiness. Reality is the prison...

S. A. : You see, Mr. O'Neill, you have harmed even yourself, held your own self back, hindered that, too, so in a way, that is great enough punishment except that the law cannot stand idly by and watch a thing like that in its rancid bloom. If it is a continuum of rottenness and falsehood and the innocent to come are victims in the waiting, it must act. It must put a stop to it, prevent it as well as expose ongoing putrification as in your own case. And, if I may say, your Honor, as an aside, please indulge me for a moment, but the defendant here seems to be a microcosm for or of that sick world. He is a potent symbol of it. All of its insidious elements are intact and operating in him.

Judge: I see that, but that is not evidence and we are limited to evidence.

EGO: Evidence? Will I put in my own brand?

Judge: Your turn at defense is coming.

S. A. : You *are* trapped, Mr. O'Neill. There is a cocoon of wretched falsity that has been spun around you by your parents and you exist in there with a plastic smile, do you feel it on your face, sir?

Judge: Strange question!

EGO: Correct! That is what I am...no hope at all, not for me, not for man!

S. A. : Be that as it may, Mr. O'Neill, that very same kind of binding up by cords of falsehood, pinning down hope, strangling freedom, taking the good people, the ordinary folk like those sitting out here in this Courtroom (gestures with both hands) and turning them into transparent jailbirds, that's what parents do. But *you*, you are the ultimate jail keeper because you make sure that the jail keys cannot be found. In fact, plays like the *Iceman Cometh* stand for the idea that those keys no longer exist on earth. What say you to *that* preposterosity?

EGO: I don't know (stalling)

S. A. : All the shocking eloquence that made your writing-days so bearable, who pays the price for them? I'll answer that for you, we do, Mr. O'Neill, and *that* is why this prosecution was brought. It's to stop you and serve as a potent example to others who might dare as you dared!

Judge: Put it away (speaking to the State's Attorney)

S. A. : What's that, your Honor?

Judge: The soapbox...put it away!

EGO: It is patently inhumane to cut off a man's tail!

S. A. : Your Honor, I ask that that kind of obscenity be discouraged, I...

Judge: Obscenity? Nuts, yes, but obscene?

EGO: That's what I get if you keep me in prison for life...

S. A. : And what do *you* cut off of a child when he or she gets the effects of these plays and the message of hopelessness, meaninglessness and all the rest, answer that, Mr. O'Neill!

EGO: I don't know...

S. A. : Your works, your life behind the works, they all represent a type of a jewel of dysfunction that is glinting, gleaming, shining into those kids' eyes. The falsity of it, paste, harms them even more than their parents did because it glitters them right out of any possibility of returning to where they began, at the innocent stage, before the miscreants got their crooked little fingers into the baby pie!

EGO: Uh-huh...(amused)

S. A. : It is lulling them all into accepting that it is alright, Okay, to be the way that they've ended up with addictions, false roles, devices, and lying, lying, lying and denials up the you know what. Can you defend such a thing as that?

EGO: I don't have to ...I...I...

S. A. : *That* is why this crime is so grave, not capital, but...

EGO: Not capital! (shouts) No, not that!

S. A. :   The confounded child is set upon the sidewalk of life, wound up like a clock, and he marches up and down State Street or Main Street, and all eyes wiggle every which way. That is what you're meddling in, Mr. Defendant! Do you admit that it is so?

EGO: I only wrote…I wrote only of life as I saw it, as I knew it…it was the truth as I feel it.

S. A. :   The State is not necessarily claiming otherwise. It *is* claiming that in spite of the bona fides or not of what you *felt*, it was dead wrong and harmful. It was in fact *not the truth*! Do you see that now?

EGO: I'm having trouble seeing, is it getting dark in here?

Judge: (standing up) Spell it! (the response was thin and disjointed and scattered) Maybe we'll have to stay after today and practice this, huh, gang? (a low murmuring was heard…a grumbling sound)

EGO: May I answer the last question?

Judge: Please.

EGO: No real answers to any of life's major questions can ever be found, at least not those touching upon the frustrations, failures, sadness, despair, and none of the answers that I have come across ever come close. Man is too frail to stand up against the stark state that reality is. Take God. What is the nexus between sex and God, passion, love, that cosmic force that runs thru all of life and that drive us to yearn physically? It is a wonder in itself and it *alone* is invaluable in fending off the barbs of loneliness and hurting inside if only momentarily. Is it God? I put that to you? And what of the glaring inconsistencies in life? What about that? One man gets into Harvard and another digs ditches. One is a grand athlete and another crippled by disease. Where is the answer there? We are all of us plain victims, victims of mankind's innate human vulnerabilities and, it seems, unable to hold up against that, that reality. We are too weak and ineffectual and we thereby and therefore merge into dreamland's world to cope. Do you see that?

S. A. :   But that is all just your warped perspective, again, made in desperation and (cut off)

EGO: I'm not wacky screwy or crazy screwy, whatever word was used here…I did it all for a reason, you know!

S. A. :   Yes, I recall, you've stated the reason: to scare people, alarm them, and all the rest.

EGO: I see it as my duty to speak the truth as I perceive that and to get the *targets* of that truth to perk up their sad, battered, little ears and if I have to throw some fright their way to show how life really is, if I am compelled to alarm the hell out of them, so be it! The end supports the means, as they say. I seek to clear up the confusion in the world...show how it really is, how *terrible* life can be and to shock them into really seeing!

S. A. :   Yes, you do show by your plays and by your own life how terrible life can be, but that is not what we are about here today. We are here because of the fakery in your conclusions as to the *reasons* behind that awful state of things, the conclusions are wrong and warped and false and a virulent danger to society. What say you to that? Is there any confusion in you as to the purpose of this prosecution?

EGO: Persecution is more what it is. How do *you* get so lucky as to see the *real* roots and *I* do not ? Answer me that, boy!

S. A. :   I can see what you do not because I did not come from a household like yours.

EGO: A wild turmoil of agony resides neath this prison garb and it drives me just as savagely to try to lasso it, corral it, contain it and brand it so as to find some *relief*. (begins sobbing again)

S. A. :   Why don't you take a moment Mr. . . . (cut off)

EGO: (thru tears) I am not some Polish madman...Wladislaw Craziskiewicz...! (The Courtroom fell apart in laughter at this tension-breaker and the Judge finds that he, too, cannot help himself).

S. A. :   Very drole, sir, but it is not so, what you have stated. In the beginning of your writing endeavors, you suffered from a large hole inside, a vast void that *drove* you almost like a madness. It pushed you to try to gain a sense of belonging to some thing if not someone and to try to *matter* when your senses told you that you did not. Wasn't the new life project, after your Harvard stint for one year, one of immense value to you, even desperate value and did it not at least *distract* you from those "wild agonies"? Later on, did it not become an attempt by you to heal up that void, making yourself better even though you were no trained psychoanalyst? And didn't the notion of some type of *productive* life spurred you on to become nearly *obsessed* with writing to the point where it *excluded* nearly every other pastime and daily routine? Did it not, after some success in the start of things, grant you a tremendous ego boost, a sense of *power* that you never wielded, yearned for hurtingly?

EGO: Well, yes, I suppose that I *did* feel driven by some of those things, but…it was wonderful for me, like finding a gold nugget, or a …

S. A. : And, sir, isn't it also so that such a project as writing plays excluded and ruled out anything meaningful with your children? When the accolades began pouring in, were they not vehemently resentful that the successes of their alleged father were poppycock and made of the same nonsense and treachery that had befallen them at his hands?

Judge: Do *not* provoke the witness, please, but, go ahead and answer anyway, Mr.….

EGO: My children? I was not aware of any connection of their conditions to my own work, no!

S. A. : Didn't they have a loud, untoward reaction to the public airing of most of the stuff that they recognized as their own family rot? Did they ever bring this up?

EGO: Shane was shy like me. Oona never did what you suggested. Eugene, Jr., well…he was a *very* bright child, always ahead of me, why I was even afraid to talk to him for fear of being one upped. Very sad, that…

S. A. : Were they afraid to approach you on this?

EGO: How should *I* know?

S. A. : So then, you admit to being so out of touch with your own three kids that you had no way to tell if they were afraid of coming to you with a comment about this crap!

EGO: (remained silent)

S. A. : Would you say that your literary work was primarily to boost your ego, get emotional relief, help the world or what, sir?

EGO: That is all foggy to me now. But a good deal was to try to get at the persistent monster inside of me.

S. A.: And what about those cigarettes?

Judge: Pardon…what is the relevance there, please?

S. A.: Relevant because they, along with any pills, sedatives, booze or past booze habits, all part and parcel of Defendant's emotional state and mental being and aimed at him getting relief.

Judge: Go ahead. Answer the question.

EGO: I gave up drinking…in 1928. I guess I was about forty…

S. A.: But wasn't that the out of the fear that a doctor put in you?

EGO: He told me that I'd have egg white for a brain…

S. A.: But you kept on with the other stuff?

EGO: Yeah, smoked all my life mostly, and the pills are to keep me from jumping out of my skin…a guy like me needs *something*!

S. A.: Weren't you terrified that if you didn't give up the bottle that you wouldn't be able to write anymore and that idea was inconceivable to you; you were horrified at the prospect. It would have taken away the only thing that you had left, kind of like Sarah Sandy, and you panicked?

EGO: True…yes, scared the shit…oops, sorry…

S. A.: So you quit out of being terrified…

EGO: It was a *discipline*.

S. A.: Oh, a *discipline* was it (sarcastically), and was that the *same* discipline that allowed you to take three wives, beget three kids, cut them off from yourself physically, emotionally, ignoring them, you sailing all over the map, moving from residence to residence all over the place?

EGO: Say, what are you trying to do, assassinate me?

S. A.: No, I *am* trying to prove to the Court that you acted in writing those plays over the decades to serve your own selfish needs and *obsessively* at that although I do not dispute the *agony* that you bore, still do, especially after seeing you over on Pequot like this. (catches himself) (A loud murmur arose in the Courtroom)

S. A. :   (covering his error in tipping off the spectators)It is and was almost like the *drunken driver*. He drinks to take away the pain, his powerlessness, feelings of worthlessness and he is glowing and he feels "happy" and he gets behind the wheel...(cut off)

EGO: But you know that I don't drive, sir...

S. A. :   (ignoring him) and he drives along and he then fails to see that little girl or little boy walking along there on Angel Boulevard and he smashes that little body to smithereens. *That* is what you are charged with here, Mr. O'Neill, smashing to hell all the hopes of humanity to swerve out of the way of the *Iceman Cometh* nightmare by learning about and then undergoing treatment for the very sickness that everyone agrees is rampant (shouting).

EGO: I never ran over anybody.

S. A. :   You serve up a platter of stuff that they devour and they get fat and they *stay* fat on the illusions, those pipe dreams. These poor slobs have had a taste for them going all the way back. They kept the 'sanity' with those morsels of insanity...and it *is* Wladislaw Crazikiewicz!

EGO: But you keep forgetting...the Nobel Committee and the (cut off)

S. A. :   No, *you* keep forgetting! Nobody is immune from the trance. The very *novelty* of your work probably bowled them over, struck everyone so hard that they forgot about the falsity that every crook exudes though he swears that his tracks are covered!

EGO: But don't I get any credit for *their* part in this? The attention that *they* paid to my stuff, to me, made my work so much more in demand, famous and far reaching and so, if I *did* hurt anybody, *they* are partly to blame!

S. A. :   Well...I suppose that they might be looked at as accessories but I do not know if we have jurisdiction (pondering out loud),

Judge: It's incidental...move on please!

EGO: I cried and I raged and I (catching himself)

Judge: There is no question yet, Mr. O'Neill, wait for that.

S. A. : You never once attribute that "trapped condition" of mankind, the hopelessness, the meaninglessness of life, the absurdity of death and all the rest, to the abuse of the baby or infant or toddler, do you, sir? Not one time is there any reference to an instinct clash and the never ending journey that kids are chained to after that, the secret yearning that there will be a miracle, a turnaround. Meanwhile, they live in total denial thus saving a seat at the miracle table for mommy and daddy. And as they wait, everyone else around them becomes the target for the rage, that crying and raging that you just now spit out. The innocent take the punch of that. More parental garbage and damage and pain and isolation and shaming rain down while that wait goes on interminably!

EGO: No, I haven 't.

S. A. : Haven't what?

EGO: Cast it all in those terms...

S. A. : Not in *any* terms, Mr. O'Neill.

EGO: An eighty-nine year old man whose teeth are worn down to the gums looks up and sees that luscious apples are still growing on the "vine". Why is that Mr. State's Attorney? (before he can be interrupted) I'll tell you. It's because *they* are waiting for *him* to fertilize the earth! (The Judge leered at the witness but the State's Attorney ignored this and continued)

S. A. : It would have been maybe not so bad if you had coupled your messages, false though they were, with at least some grain of the real root. At least that way there would have been *some* merit, some small value in educating the suffering hordes instead of being a *pure hindrance!*

EGO: Didn't I help out all the droves of alcoholics and help humanity *that* way? Didn't I help humanity in my brilliant paralleling of their lives, the euphoria that achieve, with the human condition, the constant battle with disappointments, the crushing of their hopes to escape reality at hand and the awful dissipation and self-destruction and death... such as my brother, Jamie. . . boozed into the ground at forty-five!

Don't I get credit for all that…that the life of mankind is the same life as the alcoholic's?

Judge: You are not to question the State, Mr. O'Neill…please wait for a question.

S. A. : I move that the last answer be stricken, your Honor.

Judge: Leave it.

S. A. : Please note my exception…

Judge: Noted.

S. A. : None of that alcoholic stuff is valid anyway, is it, Mr. O'Neill?

Judge: You ask that it be stricken, yet, you now rely on it to form a query?

S. A. : Sorry, Your Honor. Anyway, that parallel is bogus, Mr. O'Neill in answer to the question that you are not supposed to be asking. The absolute falsity is just astounding! How in t he world did you ever come up with such a thing?

EGO: In the gutter. (quasi-proudly)I have been called an enigma, a mystery… that must count for something, no?

S. A. : That you might represent an unknown quantity to the public, I do not dispute, in fact, sir, that might be all the more reason for them to be very wary of you. However, they do not seem wary. They appear to eat up every bit of O'Neill stew that you whip up, well most of it, with nary a worry about *arsenic. But poison there is, sir, and you put it in!*

EGO: But I spoke, speak, through my emotions, my deep feelings, and I projected the theme that I see as truth the thing that you claim I am void of. That truth goes very deep inside of me and it reaches me, anyone, through the emotions and *that* is not false, sir (triumphantly).

S. A. : Maybe some of what you are now saying is so, but it is a very small part of what we are about here today. We are more concerned with the substantive messages that your works and your public statements project. *Those* are the falsities that offend. They are the ones that you dreamed up in a desperate try to "lasso" all the demons! (challenging).

EGO: But you are missing a great breakthrough…that man is a hero of sorts and that he struggles, to no avail, with the monsters of his own inconsistent emotions and *this* plagues him and ruins him.

S. A.:   A man's own emotions ruin him? That is preposterous. That is like saying that if a man walks out into a road and is stricken down by a car, that his legs that carried him out there ruined him! Also, you just said that *truth* reaches you, anyone, through the emotions! But they ruin him?

EGO: Very literary.

S. A.:   Contradictory emotions are not the meat of any *real* struggle but are usually just *symptoms* of the dysfunctional child grown up to inherit adult powers on the world stage. By the way, Mr. O'Neill, have you not made certain claims about man's *control* of his emotions?

EGO: You know more about me and my work than I ever would have imagined.

S. A.:   Is that a yes then?

EGO: Yes, I have made that type of observation and statement, yes…(just then, there was a slight commotion in the back of the Courtroom and a voice called out "Why is he in that uniform?")

Judge: Order, please, I'll have none of that!

S. A.:   (after judge motions him to continue) More falsehood, I'm afraid, Mr. O'Neill. One is not well advised to control one's emotions unless he or she is out of normal, that is, emotionally disturbed. It is as ridiculous a notion as telling somebody what to feel. A mirage! That thing that you pose is a *false device* used by the put upon, the despairing masses and has no place on the grandstand of truth, sir!

EGO: But those perverse complexities of human nature…(cut off)

S. A.:   Once again I must protest, Mr. O'Neill. That is another one of your pitiful devices…an idea that *you* think sounds good but it is baseless. People are complex, I grant that but there is no perversity in it, nor perversion. The only perverse thing that we are concerned with here today is the perverse things that parents do in their self dealing… do to their innocent children!

EGO: (remains silent and looks disturbed and shaken)

S. A. : What it is reported that *your* mother and father did to *you* and your
         poor brother, Jamie, *that* is where, I guess, you get such a notion.
         Perverse innately? I don't think so, Mr. O'Neill. It is the very kind of
         thing that people do and will and can seize on to justify their con-
         tinued rack and ruin upon others and the world collected in great
         masses, it forms, in forms of parental rage and child rage, nations
         that prefer war. It is the formula for the mire that is the Middle East,
         was Nazi Germany, was the Crusades insofar as the killing, and de-
         ferred rage is the great engine of personal and state defeat!

EGO: But a man is a victim of the ironies of life and a victim of himself.

S. A. : That poppycock will not be the basis of any valid defenses here, sir.
         Ironies may abound, I admit that, but whole people see them as just
         how the universe is. There is no more to it than that except to those
         whose pitiful state needs more and then they, *you*, just make it up!
         Man is a victim of himself? What does that mean, you tell me.

EGO: His inherent weaknesses defeat his ideals, his better part.

S. A. : That's nonsense and I would recommend you for a bachelor's degree
         in nonsense if I were a university dean.

Judge: Please, ask questions, do not lecture him…you know the rules.

S. A. : Your stories hurt people, Mr. O'Neill. Your version of the world cock-
         eyed and it is holding the race back. Do you admit this now?

EGO: I report it as I see it, remember? And life manipulates us all and is
         cruel and tragic, a rotten trick on me and *you*, brother, and will *you*
         admit that?

Judge: I could find you in contempt again, Mr. Defendant, do not ask ques-
         tions under any circumstances unless you do not understand a ques-
         tion put to you!

EGO: Oh, yes, I forgot…I forget, this is, you see I…

Judge: Do that again and I will sentence you in contempt of Court to spend
         some time in that cottage at 325 Pequot Lane and I will see to it that
         the front windows are all blocked out so that you will be blind to the
         water!

S. A. :   That's 325 Pequot Avenue, if the Court pleases, your Honor.

Judge: Yes. At this point, we will take a fifteen-minute recess. (At this pros-
          pect, the Defendant began to shake wildly and swoon. He dropped
          down off the witness' chair and slumped halfway onto the floor at
          which two Court attendants held him up and took him downstairs).
          (Court came back twenty minutes later).

Judge: Court will come to order. (turning to the defendant who was reluc-
          tantly back in the witness chair)Mr. O'Neill, you are still under oath
          and I hope have regained your composure. I did not mean to alarm
          you, sir, only to stress the importance of just listening to the ques-
          tions and then answering them truthfully. No wild statements!

EGO: I get it. (speaking in a much thinner voice now).

S. A. :   Now, Mr. O'Neill, I am going to refer again to your last major play,
          The Iceman Cometh, and point to your portrayal of something that,
          at first, seems to be wholesome and constructive and not contami-
          nated by falsehood, to wit: the character, the main one, Hickey, who
          comes for his annual visit to the bar, only this time, instead of mak-
          ing jokes and generally being his entertaining self, gives the idea out
          to the bar rag folk, if I may, that he has at long last found happiness
          and that it consists of having no more masks, being real and throw-
          ing off all pretenses that he used to wield. He has given up his prior
          life of falsehoods. Does that sum it up at all?

EGO: Pretty well, sure...

S. A. :   Okay, but then you have Hickey fall down. You make him, make it a
          farce by revealing that he has killed his wife, that he dons the mask
          of justification by stating that he did this out of *love* and to relieve
          her when in fact, he really *hated* her. Those bar patrons are greatly
          relieved themselves when they see that that can now go back to their
          former pipe dreams and illusions and blame Hickey's ravings on a
          madman, right?

EGO: Right!

S. A. :   But *that* is a false message, isn't it...I mean Hickey's mode of salva-
          tion or happiness is the true one and if you meant only to show the
          world *how* the world is, that's one thing, but the implication, the last-

ing and strong impression that you leave with this Broadway piece is that such a thing is the *norm*. You say that it is satisfactory and inescapable. That *there* is the true falsehood! Come on now, fess up! Do you see that now and can you be a man and admit this?

EGO: (The defendant remains silent during a moment, then turns beet red) God damn you...God damn you to Hell, you bastard, you are making a mockery of all that I am, all that I have striven to produce with years of hard work and struggle, trying to pin down man and *his* struggle! (the voice is still thinner and slightly defeated)*Failing!*

S. A. :   Failing? Did you say that...failing? (urging his voice over the witness)

Judge: I have no choice but to find you in contempt of Court. Mr. O'Neill for...

EGO: Oh, please! I beg you, please do not put me back in that place. It's dark it's indecent, it will kill me again...I could not bear it. No more, moma, no more...please judge, that hellhole is my home...I'm sorry...I'm the Irish one here, always flying off the handle, yes, that's it, too much of the happy juice, I am at your mercy, please! (breaks down crying).

Judge: I warned you about chaos in my Courtroom.

EGO: But that is what man inherits. That is what his life is, Judge...chaos and I am sorry to (sobbing) tell you this but...

Judge: While we take a moment, let me suggest to the State that it might well consider a charge of *attempted escape* in connection with the incident this afternoon. (The reporters in the Courtroom absolutely crumpled their faces and leapt out of their skins at this news)

S. A. :   I am not sure, your Honor. Perhaps it was an escape from life and not from custody...after all, the prisoner *was* handcuffed and how in the world could he swim away from us like that?

Judge: But this man's a swimmer. Don't you read? He could have easily floated on his back and kicked his legs...do you see the physique on him? He's still strong enough to make headway in the water even without arms.

S. A. :   Very well, sir, we'll take a look at it (patronizing the Judge)(The Defendant oozed terror at this suggestion and seemed to just wilt).

S. A: Can you hear me Mr. O'Neill?

EGO: Y-yes...I...

S. A. : I wish to ask you... (cut off)

EGO: Could I have some more water, please...it's time for my pill... (Marshall pours some for him)

S. A. : What pill is that?

EGO: Sedatives...I need them...

S. A. : Do you have a valid prescription?

EGO: From my California doctor, yes. (shows the old bottle) There's no fish in this water? (Courtroom again erupts in giggles).

S. A. : Now sir, if you are again ready, are you familiar with a Life Magazine article that appeared December 2, 1946 which discusses your work and makes a comment on the nature of tragedies. It provides that tragedies, great ones, are contradictory to the spirit of American Democracy *and* that they are incompatible with the American belief in *progress*.

EGO: I seem to recall that sort of talk, yes (wiping his eyes).

S. A. : And my question to you is: do you agree with that assessment? Do you see your own tragedies as being against American progress?

EGO: Hell, no! (catching himself)...heck no! In *Desire Under The Elms*... (cut off)

S. A. : But what I am suggesting to you now is that Life Magazine had it correct and that the very same ideas that they project form the basis of the case here against you. See that?

EGO: Huh?

S. A. : Isn't your message of damnation, despair, destruction, hatred, tenuousness of human relationships, fate, dirty tricks by life, trapped people, reality destroying the ideal, being mad at God, being puzzled over God, alienation, loneliness, lack of belonging, human frailty and weakness, frustrations as a block, skepticism, self-deception, alcohol life as a symbol of man's fate, the animal in mankind and the awful specter of death, all of that born in your own private hell of desperation?

EGO: No...I mean, well...I...

S. A. :   Regards to the public, the playgoers, the play readers, the consumers of your pronouncements in the media or about you, like Life Magazine, and the world in general, isn't all of that a false message propounded by you that such a fate for man is inescapable?

Judge: I think that he's answered that three times already. You're smacking mosquitoes with a sledge...please, move on...please!

EGO: I wrote it as I (cut off)

Judge: No question pending...wait...

S. A. :   But *you* were that drunk behind the wheel. To boot, you never hinted at, let alone revealed, any remedy...the fact that such a thing *does* have a cure in large part. You go along insisting that there is no answer and the world bows down to it! Do you see it now and agree?

EGO: I agree that I tried my very best. Maybe I did not understand all that you state now and I am not now insisting that you are *completely incorrect*. All I can say is that I wrote what I knew and that obeys the first rule the trade, to write about what one is familiar with. It goes along with the first rule of auto mechanics which is do not push on a wrench or the one for carpenters, measure twice, cut once.

Judge: That's enough...

EGO: One learns a lot of miscellaneous stuff when...(cut off)

S. A. :   So you are now saying that the allegations filed against you about most of the things we went over here today might be true and that I might not be "incorrect" entirely?

Judge: He admitted to that and several others of the allegations along the way but strongly denied others.

S. A. :   If I tell you that I believe that your heart was sort of in the right place, would that grease the way for a further admission, at least to the extent that you are and were not competent to make all of the judgments,... bad word, strike that...representations, claims, about man and mankind and being trapped and born broken and all of that? Better add the requirement that the weak human needs those illusions and pipe dreams. Is it easier for you to fess up to all of that now and see that much of your work involved needed but manufactured explanations for the misery that seems to seep thru most of your characters?

EGO: I suppose so…yes, it would…I only want to do the right thing, I …

Judge: To save time here, he's also admitted to the publication of his works insofar as exposed to Connecticut citizens or persons in general inside of the State's borders.

S. A. : Thank you, your Honor. That's all I have for the witness. (Defendant tries to leave the witness chair).

Judge: Wait, Mr. O'Neill. You have the right to cross-examination. Ordinarily, your own counsel would do that to test the testimony for bias, errors, credibility and so forth…motives and that.

EGO: Do I cross myself?

Judge: You may explain any answer that you gave under oath if you believe that it needs clarification or if it left a wrong impression.

EGO: (thinks to himself for a minute) No, I didn't say…I do not believe that any of that is required. I am satisfied with my testimony.

Judge: Very well, Mr. O'Neill. You may step down. You know that you have the right to present your own *defense* evidence?

EGO: Oh? I will?

Judge: Certainly. When the time comes, I will instruct you.

EGO: (voice cracking) *Please!* Please don't put me in that place…please!

Judge: Don't worry about the…that place…Mr. O'Neill… Call your next witness.

S. A. : Well, your Honor, the State has, as the Court knows, witnesses here under subpoena and some voluntarily, but it does not seem that they will be necessary because the Defendant has testified at length and has made certain admissions and, it seems to the State, given a basis for all the elements of this offense to be found proved beyond a reasonable doubt, so…

Judge: So? So the State rests?

S. A. : Except for one matter, your Honor. The State asks that the Court take judicial notice of the fact that out of the thousands of persons that the Defendant *admits* have seen or read his works and all of the public statements by him over the years, all of which were made in Connecticut, or read there or books read there or in the case of plays seen elsewhere, seen by Connecticut residents at the time, that a substantial portion of those persons were adversely affected by the false and misleading messages contained therein, or any omitted.

Judge: Would it not be more accurate to ask the Court to take that notice in a way that, well, notice that these plays and statements do tend to hinder humanity?

S. A. : Very well, sir…I…

Judge: The Court so finds. The issue of whether or not they are in fact false is a fact issue to be decided by the Court after all the evidence is in.

S. A. : Correct.

Judge: Mr. O'Neill, do you understand any of this?

EGO: (looking like a dumbbell) Not really…I…

Judge: A Court can take judicial notice of any notorious fact that is relevant.

EGO: Are you all telling me in a subtle way that *I* am notorious?

Judge: Not at all, only that the fact that any alleged falsehoods in your works or public statements tend to hinder humanity, that's all.

EGO: Oh.

Judge: The state has rested, Mr. O'Neill, so it is now time for any defense that you will want to present.

EGO: I'm a good person, I didn't do it…I…

Judge: (interrupting him) No, not defense *argument.* That will come later. Do you have any defense evidence like testimony, witnesses, documents, and so forth, as was explained to you the last time we were here when you entered the plea of "not guilty"?

EGO: The people *want to believe* (loud voice)

Judge: Take the witness chair again, sir.

EGO: I was just up here (as he retakes the seat), this seems dumb…no offense.

        (There was mild Courtroom laughter)

Judge: You may…you are still under oath…testify as to any facts that you think are a good defense and are relevant or introduce any tangible things like papers and so forth that support the defense.

EGO: I don't know…all of the things that I said already…the Court will not ignore that if it helps me? All that I said *is* my defense evidence.

Judge: You do not wish to add anything?

EGO: I swear under oath that I am a good person…never hurt anybody and all I ever did was present the truth as I saw it. I come from a good Victorian era, straight and proper. I tried to make people *think, feel* when they do not *want* to feel because it *hurts* them to feel.

S. A. :   Objection, your Honor. That is false testimony. The Defendant is charged with… strike that. The objection is that intentions are no defense and what Mr. O'Neill intended cannot save him if the falsehoods are in violation of the statute's prohibition on hindering humanity. Also motivation is not a defense. He thinks that he prompted people to want to feel something that hurts them or what have you. That goal is no defense if the any falsehoods contained in the subject works violate the statute.

Judge: Yes, I agree. The motives may have been laudable in the Defendant's mind and his intentions as well but the bare bones of the law here is number one, was there a falsehood or falsehoods and, number two, did they hinder or tend to hinder humanity. Objection sustained. Go on, Mr. O'Neill.

EGO: In my works, I attacked Puritan mores and all of the falsity of *those* kinds of people and their own crooked lives. That was dissemination of the *truth* and that is the opposite of the crime charged on me, yes?

Judge: Please continue sir.

EGO: And I…(interrupted by Attorney Brindle)

Brindle: Your Honor, I am counsel of record, appointed by you, to sit quietly by the Defendant to assist him so that a fair trial could be ensured. But he is up there and I cannot help him now without interrupting to address the Court on a matter that we passed by a few minutes ago.

Judge: What was that, attorney?

Brindle: Judicial notice. The Court was asked to take notice the way that the State's Attorney's motion was worded but the Court adopted its own brand of wording and the matter taken by judicial notice ended up being, and I quote, "that these plays and statements do tend to hinder humanity". Then your Honor went on to say to the defendant that the Court would decide as a fact issue whether or not there was falsehood after all the evidence is in.

Judge: Yes, that is not right, is it? I see your point.

S. A.: Your Honor. (angry)

Judge: No, he is correct. How can the Court take such notice *now* that the plays do tend to hinder humanity if there is not to be any possible finding until the end of the trial whether there is any falsehood to begin with. So, I will strike my order of judicial notice. Now, Mr. State's Attorney, do you wish to make a new motion in this regard?

S. A.: Yes I do, sir (red in the face)…well, not a new one, but I renew the State's original motion and that wording, if we could have that read back please? (Judge motions to the Court reporter)

Court Reporter: "Shall I read all of it?"

Judge: No, just the part that the notion is suppose to embrace.

Court Reporter: That a substantial portion of those persons were adversely affected by the false and misleading messages contained therein, or any omitted.

Brindle: Same objection…no finding is yet possible as to falsity and…

S. A.: But he's (indicating the witness-defendant) admitted to falsity and…

Judge: Gentlemen, let's wait until the evidence is in and then address this.

Brindle: I reserve one other aspect to be argued at that time, your Honor, and that is the issue of notoriety, which is required to (cut off)

Judge: Very well, you may address that aspect as well. Continue Mr. O'Neill.

EGO: (looking lost in the atmosphere of legal arguments) and...I...railed against middle class complacency and opportunism and materialism, ugh! I saw and portrayed the idea that most Americans were living a degenerate life. That was truth, wasn't it? Doesn't that counterbalance any so-called falsehood?

Judge: Proceed.

EGO: *And* I shook up the American theater; everybody said so and *I* gave it a transfusion and made it fun, scary, stimulating, valuable, a force for social change.

S. A.: Objection! That's a conclusion.

Judge: I'll allow it...Before I forget it, I want to put on the record *again*, as I did at the preliminary hearing, that this charge, on conviction, carries a mandatory life sentence *with* the possibility of parole, and that the Defendant was fully aware of the fact and chose to waive defense counsel's handling of the case and chose to defend himself. (At this, the defendant began shaking again.)Proceed.

EGO: I...I...I...feel awful. Let me...I want to finish so that I can go and lie...lie down (sweating visibly and shaking more).

Judge: We can take a recess.

EGO: No! Please...let's finish up this...I was saying...I forget...I...I...Oh, yes...if *I* am guilty of falsehood holding back people, what about the government?

S. A.: Objection!

Judge: The Government?

EGO: It does the same thing all the time. Nobody prosecutes them. So, *I* get my example from that (brightening up).

Judge: Explain that please.

EGO: Man performs miracles all the time! *And* he knows not how! He makes the baby and it comes out perfect, but they know not how! (proudly insightful)

Judge: Mr. O'Neill! . . . stick to the defense…you…just proceed.

EGO: (seeming close to hysteria suddenly) The government sends us off to war while the police send men into local war and the firehouse sends men into fires and explosions.

S. A. :   Objection!

Judge: Continue, Mr. O'Neill…objection overruled by the way…

EGO: These things that the powers do, it does to the injury of those babies (seeming to connect up the previous two pieces of testimony). They worry the kids to death until dad or mom comes home from that war or that crime scene or that fire! Or worse, when they *never* come back home and their fathers are gone forever and they are left to be four or six or three and no father. Then they are warped and hurt. *That* is a falsehood because the government does not have to take men and women for the military or for police work or firemen if they have minor children who will be scared sick, though they are dreading to admit it, or worse, left as partial orphans. That is a falsehood that hinders humanity every day in this world… just read the paper, Mack! It's child abuse and child neglect as *public policy*. It perpetuates juvenility in adults, too! (The judge looks incredulous and sits rubbing his chin and waits for more)Then there is divorce. That is all the time hurting kids but…

S. A. :   The defendant is *estopped* to assert any defense based on divorce hurting children, though it irreparably does, because *he himself* got a divorce from Kathleen Jenkins, his first wife, who was pregnant with his first child in 1909 and that child was hurt deeply by it and, it is on this record, committed suicide in 1950 with a razor blade…

Judge: No, I want to hear…

EGO: The government allows it. Nobody blocks the *untruth* that divorce is. It's supposed to be a *contract* with the State, *your* State, Mr. State's Attorney and it is for the protection of kids but people are allowed to just *breach* it at will and the law lets them drift apart and the kids always blame themselves. Where's the moral truth in that? *There's* a hindrance to humanity, sir (leering at the Judge).

Judge: Where are you coming up with all this, Mr. O'Neill?

EGO: I don't know…maybe from listening to the State's Attorney, maybe it is rubbing off on me?

S. A. : It doesn't excuse what he did…the government is not on trial here!

EGO: (ignoring him) And what about the government letting people act like children when they're…when they're adults, how's that a truth?

S. A. : I object. He's making the State's case…er…argument…

EGO: (ignoring him) What about children who are beaten, on the receiving end of violence? The Government does not stop that. My words are hardly any threat to humanity compared to that! Hitting children, call it whatever you want…spanking or whatever, hitting them delivers the important message that they do not matter and that violence is a tool that the powers deem acceptable! Hypocrite *I* say! Hypocrite State's Attorney! *False.*

S. A. : I object!

Judge: Continue, Mr. O'Neill.

EGO: *My* works stress individualism and dramatized it. That is a human *good* is it not? And I was against Marxism…even though I was attacked for wanting to oust capitalism, still…and I was against complacency…

S. A. : Object! We went over that already.

EGO: (continuing to ignore the State's Attorney) And I was a great and grand example to our own dear nation when I asserted that the USA was the greatest *failure* in the world because it is engaged in the eternal game of trying to possess its own soul and having something *outside* of that at the same time! Where else is humanity going to get stuff like that, from Mars? (courtroom laughter)

Judge: Go on.

EGO: And I pointed to the sorry human race for its own benefit, that it was unable to see the true secret of happiness. (quoting the Bible) "What shall it profit a man if he gains the whole world and loses his own soul? There's truth for you. It's not falsehood! I was interested only in the relationship between God and man and *not* man and man. *That* is truth. Man's precarious position and his inability to belong are directly connected to this.

Judge: I don't understand that.

EGO: (ignoring the judge's query) I have spent my whole life, long years
          of struggle, looking for a solution to my and man's frustration and
          despair. If *that* is not honorable and the *truth*, what is? I ask all of you
          (gesturing turning out towards the seated spectators). I may be just a
          ghost, a sea ghost, one within another…and I may seem frail to all of
          you, but to the real God, I am the essence of nature and a full bloom
          of it. Or, I am the fog. It rolls in and confounds. Then it rolls back out
          and illuminates by default…that is *I*, gentlemen of the jury.

Judge: No jury here, sir. And you really do confound like the fog. You truly
          do… at times…

EGO: My weariness will be dissolved into the great, green-gray sea and I
          will, finally, be at peace, and I wish you all well, gentlemen!

Judge: Go on…oh, does the defense rest?

EGO: Done!

Judge: Cross?

S. A. :   In the interests of saving time, no cross-examination.

Judge: Any other defense witnesses or evidence, Mr. O'Neill? One last
          chance.

EGO: (in a reedy voice) I guess not.

Judge: Okay, the defense has rested, Rebuttal? (looking over at the State)

S. A. :   Well, I have all my witnesses still here, your Honor, but I am not
          thinking of rebuttal…no, no rebuttal…but the State claims unfair
          prejudice in that the Court's vacating its ruling on the judicial notice
          might mean that the State will have to put on fact evidence re: the
          effect of the alleged falsehoods on humanity, so…could we please
          argue and dispose of that judicial notice issue now before I let my
          witnesses go?

Judge: Sounds sound. (Attorney Brindle stands up and comes over towards
          the action) The State wants the Court to take judicial notice, without
          fact evidence, that what…tell me again…

S. A. :   That the kinds of falsehoods that have been already supported, no, proved, by evidence on this record, disseminated in the manners and over the time span testified to by the Defendant, that those falsehoods can be deemed to hinder humanity without proof of the fact by evidence *because* it is a *notorious* fact and not subject to challenge.

Brindle: That is where I come in, your Honor. The defense says that such a thing is anything but a notorious fact and is, in fact, generally unknown or little known by the public.

Judge: Go on.

Brindle: Actually, *that* might be the reason that this man got so many awards from learned bodies for his works even though they *might* have contained made up themes and theses and explanations and so forth. So, even if *lies*, outright lies are laced into his plays, if they are not known to cause that alleged hindrance notoriously, the Court cannot take judicial notice of that!

Judge: Go on.

Brindle: A better example of a falsehood that would hinder humanity that could be the subject of judicial notice under the right case would be the matter where a scientist invents a cure for cancer and refuses to disclose it, although his colleagues acknowledge the feat. If the government declares that it is to become public property for the good of mankind subject to just compensation, and the scientist nevertheless still so refuses and then puts out sidestepping falsehoods, *he* might be prosecuted for this same crime and the Court could easily take notice of the effect.

S. A.: All very amusing and interesting, but unnecessary, I'm sure...

Judge: No, I find that the subject matter of *this* motion is appropriate and that judicial notice is proper in the context of the motion and the Court takes judicial notice as requested.

Brindle: Reserve an exception, please...

Judge: Noted. (There came a rustling sound and a mild commotion in the Courtroom as many sensed the end of the trial. They seemed worried about the outcome).

Judge: Please, the State's summation. (Whereupon the State's Attorney summed up all the evidence points that he deemed favorable to the State's case and that a "guilty" verdict was supported by the evidence).

Judge: Mr. O'Neill...summations?

EGO: I have nil to say, I am afraid (began shaking again and appearing increasingly worried and pale)

Judge: Very well. I shall retire to my chambers and have a decision shortly, perhaps thirty minutes or so. Thirty minute recess. (Whereupon the Court went into recess. The Defendant seemed to faint dead away on the carpet in front of the bench and Court personnel revived him with smelling salts and propped him up in a chair. He laid his head on the defense table and waited. Someone thought that they heard whimpering) The Judge came out early, about fifteen minutes later and reconvened Court).

Judge: I have reached a decision on guilt or innocence. Will the defendant please rise?

(Mr. O'Neill stood up and started to shake and tremble violently. He put his hands up to his face and then over his ears. The Judge began to recite but the defendant commenced to shriek and wail and cry out. He was terrified of being put in a jail for the rest of his life, his sorry existence. He also had hallucinations about being forced into that cottage. The marshals tried to calm him as did his Court-appointed counsel, Mr. Brindle, but it did no good. He swooned and moaned and yelled out a thing that nobody could comprehend. It was impossible for the defendant to hear the Judge's words and he had to be carried out without ever having heard them.

I snapped out of my daydream, looked up at the 1794 Courthouse plaque and rubbed my paralyzed face. Then I walked towards my car.

CHAPTER FIVE: DARK WHITE

Sometimes a masterpiece can be a half-truth, maybe in contrast to other works by the same hand that are untruths, and a series of same might add up to only that: a half. People are not born "broken" or in pieces, halves, and if left to normal forces, will pursue life, not chase relief. I see this unquestionably.

Those that can see know, however, that there is a predominance on earth of the fractured soul and that this seemingly inevitable pile controls the doling out of what is labeled "normal" or "acceptable". It also blesses that kind of "masterpiece".

A great chasm separates the crying human need from the barely visible remedy. It also separates the blinking eyes from the realization that there is any real need or root of misled lives.

Today one is stuck in the twenty-first century while Eugene O'Neill remains in the Twentieth and Nineteenth and in the case of me, the overlap covers just twelve years, 1941 to 1953. Although our residences in Connecticut and New London never coincided in time, the vision that he painted in *Ah, Wilderness could* have belonged to him at any point where he might have partaken of the product that emerged after my emotional paroxysms which led to a cementing back together of just such a pile of pieces. That was about age fifty, the very same that O'Neill was during his painful revisitations to his past upon crafting *Long Day's Journey Into Night*. We were apples from the same kind of misery tree.

Eugene O'Neill never achieved wholeness, except at his birth, by reason of that ordeal of delving into the Pequot Avenue nightmare because his mission was not pure. His goal *was* partly to escape the clutches that that cottage maintained on his throat, but the primary aim was to produce that "masterpiece" before his failing health could put an end to his engine's prolific performance. That struggle impressed me but was no excuse.

Age fifty or so is optimum for recovery work because the iron protections erected in youth are rusting considerably, yet the hope for the future fulfillment remains strong. I was that age in 1991 and he was around 1939.

My experience was terrible and lasting but effective. Carlotta's descriptions of his remind us that he, too, suffered much agony of revisitation, but, again, his was only a half-way lying down in the road because of the host of distractions whizzing by that made him get up to account every time. Therefore, his "recovery" work, unwittingly, was a balk and the proof is in the life that he lied after Long Day's Journey Into Night was done. He never reclaimed his authentic self. The agony that called O'Neill home lived on until his last conscious day in Boston.

Had we bumped heads at the correct juncture, time aside, a true recovery might have been delivered to him by way of kidnapping, physical or persuaded. All his life he struggled to get to the bottom of things, the despair, the permanent sadness, but in the end, he failed. Oh, the experts might tell you otherwise, that O'Neill managed to get a handle on the forces that plagued him, that he made some kind of peace with the Furies, but those mouths belong with the blinking eyes.

On more than one occasion, I strongly considered a like kidnapping of my drug addicted sister who lived not more than a few miles from Pequot Avenue. But I knew that the law would track me down at the insistence of her husband and children and that my motives, rescue her from the *trance* that our parents put us in and from which *I* had miraculously escaped, would not hold up in Court. If done correctly, however, and there is no fear of consequences, kidnapping of a fractured person to *force* them back into their vulnerabilities works marvelously. Outward Bound uses the right technique although there is no imprisonment of subjects with them. The setting that they employ, usually wilderness, acts as a kind of prison though because the people being administered to cannot flee. The surrounding area is wild and unlimited unless one hikes for tens of miles.

So an abduction of Eugene at any age really would have worked unless aspects of his misery were organic which it does not appear they were. His was a homegrown defect tended daily by James and Ella O'Neill.

Mine would have been a special status because of our commonalities. *I* had a vasectomy because there was no room for children in my "affections" and the selfishness was just too massive to imagine! Whether it was a match for yours, Eugene, we will never know but it *was* similar. A dream that came the other night was most unusual and it made your situation with Jamie come to mind. It was a unique, warm, fuzzy-feelings event. My sister and the attraction made me amazed because *nothing* like it had ever happened in life or in the nighttime clouds. After so many decades of treating her as a non-entity, this was hard to fathom and I could attribute it only to a fifteen-year post-recovery lag. Sibling clash is really one between the parents.

We tried being nice. We tried being rotten. We fit in nowhere and no one ever beckoned. Always, always, always was the inner nagging, the missing part—the glee. Even graduation from college brought nothing. Nobody came. Law school in Boston years later produced the same. It seemed like success was doomed to fail. The nobody role stuck like a stain.

Eugene O'Neill knew about the *authentic self* idea because he said so, that it needed to be nurtured. But he believed that that was nearly impossible. The same can be said for his notions of the *genuine identity*, free of "masks". No stronger "mask" ever leered outward than that donned by my said sister who walled me out from fear of a recovery confrontation that she *knew* intrinsically would hurt like hell. That lasted nine full years until her demise-shortened life. It came crashing down in New London. The other Lawrence and Memorial tragedy, my ma, unfolded *before* I possessed airtight "kidnapping plans". Now I am old and she is mold. Too late! She was always in a panic and weak…the original lost child. Now I say the same to *you*, Eugene, I am old and *you* are mold. Both beyond my reach forevermore except in this offering to the future, as a father grants a gift to his child, maybe a turning point in his life of few years, of a long and rocky experience coupled with understanding gained the hard way.

Such misobservations as reality thwarting unification with the spiritual force or frustration blocking realization of the ideal where man lies choked on hatred, destruction and skepticism would fall far away on Eugene's recovery. He would easily see the truth and the mistruth. The death-headed monster would be metamorphisized into a natural creature welcomed in the end. No more trapped condition, no more damnation or alienation, no more claws of fate raking inconsistencies across his face and no more frailty would stalk Mr. O'Neill.

Had I encountered him in the street and offered up a friendly hand with a permanent smile, he would *not* have agreed to embrace the misery that he was constantly fleeing from, but rather, Eugene would have shackled himself to the locked iron door, such is the way for a trenches-hardened beetle, accomplished liar and possessor of the face, whatever type, needed to escape! His internal distraction would have ruled his outer direction.

The folks…those responsible for this, their kind has not been diminished very much during the period from 1888 to 1912 to 1953 or even now. One has to wonder whether O'Neill's present deafness in the grave is any more profound than that which he sported out on that street? Standing on the spot where "Papa" gave him that fifty cents for yard work to teach him the value of a dollar makes me wonder deeply about the value of a hug! There was no scale to weigh it, however. When one is that age, things seem a lot more solid than they really are. Dinner every night, guaranteed delicious, the kitchen, the table, the four seats, the familiar "jokes", the wonderful lawn and yard and trees, the summer heaviness, the green beyond belief, all pretending to be uplifting and wholesome. I could drive there in a half an hour, stand in the street and gaze into that yard, maybe reach out and place my hand on one of the hickories, but I'd only cry. That would *not* be because it is gone but only due to the "violent" interruptions that took it all beyond the flowing way of all things. The burrs and angles protruded everywhere back then, still when one is fourteen years old, the regularity of it all anchors somehow and the hard parts are taken so much as a great looking girlfriend with a limp. Letting go is not thought of . So, those tears would never be dried by recovery. Their ready presence is and should be a fact because the up- rooting of my family in pieces is and always will be hurtful as a memory. Desertion of me and my father, by my mother and my sister, in 1957, triggered a breakdown and severe physical disease for my father. His eventual paranoid symptoms thrust *me* out of that house in 1963 when I questioned the missing knives in the silverware drawer and was told that he was not about to let me *kill him*! His own private hell and damnation were frothing and scalding. Yes, *I* could have helped you, Eugene. Did *your* father ever ask you to shorten his life with the shotgun in the basement? My guide station could have directed you deeper down than anyone wants to go where the fear lives and seethes, where nightmares lurk and breed, where the child crying out in the darkness gives up his soul *as you did*. Yes, I went to that fifty cent spot and I shed a few for you, but you were chained to it, child *and* adult and could never do the same! Blocked! Yet those masses worshipped you, you, the blocked one, and they all pointed and chanted "Theatrical God"! The prominence that befell you was really made up of other people's misfortunes, their fears and their recognition of themselves as "trapped" as you put it. It was all laid out on a stage for the first time and portrayed with such intensity and drama. The techniques were novel but where do you lay out the false thinking, false being, the bounce around of that aligned with cheating and enabling, all as a *substitute* for facing reality and not a fly in its salve? Where was the instinct clash? Where is the *sane* road out?

You labored over *Long Day's Journey Into Night* for two years but recovery takes only two months. The original lie had you by the balls and the ultimate life lie was a poison in your blood. It was as if you were stuck in an elevator where the overhead fan was out and the silence allowed you to hear the otherwise covered groans and squeaks and banging of the cables and you freaked out, scared to death, cowering on the floor in the corner, *babbling* stories to explain it all! Yea, the vast assurances on *love*, ruination, damnation, weaknesses, God, were all false! "Love mixed with hate, guilt, resentment is a *phony stew* and it does not exist. Where is the *selflessness* that is the germ of holiness? Not convenient, that? Then I thought that the very same perceptions about "stupidity" are abounding. Listen to the comments like "he's an addict because he's dumb" or "she stays with him to get beaten up again because she is a jackass". O'Neill fans look at James, his father and the fact that he was a brilliant actor, so roundly successful and even had a U. S. Supreme Court Justice at his 1920 funeral, yet they cannot understand how a man in that position could be a self-destructive alcoholic. All are *rooted* in the same thing, though those people do not know it, nor did Eugene. A monster was handed to the father, James O'Neill, when his own dad fled the United States and deserted him. He passed it on to his own kids, gift-wrapped abuse and emotional unavailability. Had I got him in that street, there could have been a successful *unwrapping* to reveal the plum of wholeness inside. It stays juicy and sweet no matter what transpires, goes wrong, on the outside life, the quince part. The blind falter and are sucked in at every turn while the seeing so easily do just that. The world spread out before them is taken for just what it is and is not caramel coated by desperation but that is what you did, Eugene! The Hairy Ape "dilemma" about mankind wanting to ride the rails of advancement and growth while preserving the joyous part attached to the animal and unsophisticated stages of long ago is nonsense. It presupposes an abandonment of what it is to be human. Robotization comes to mind but progress and growth are never connected to that. If they are, it is *not* progress. Growth coupled with retainment of joy and the "animal" level *is* possible. Inner peace is possible but "Yank", the Hairy Ape, found peace only in dying. *He* was defective by the way of upbringing and it rode him to the end. It *could* have been different. His rejection of American democracy and other aspects *could* have been unthinkable had he been allowed to grow up whole. Meanwhile, materialism is *not* soul-destroying as portrayed. A ruined soul and possessions-based life are both symptoms of the same thing: a fractured, not a whole, person.

Eugene, you spoke of digging at the roots of sickness in society and *you*

felt it existing and the death of the "old God" and failure of science and materialism to give us a satisfactory *new God* for the surviving primitive religious
instinct so as to find a *meaning for life* and find comfort for the *fears of death*.
That was pure despair speaking. Although the critics raved and the academ-
ics saluted, it was just a bowl of pitiful soup because there is no "meaning"
to life. Life just is. Whole people see it. Fractured ones cannot unless recovered. The truth would be more like a *"fear of no death"* since without it,
an interminable nightmare would be on our backs. The *real* fear is that you,
all fractured souls, will run out of time before the end comes to set things
right re the instinct clash set up by the misbehaving parents. Also, is the fear
that any miracle of them turning it all around will not have time to happen.
Their death cuts that short and so does yours. Maybe you were paraphrasing
something that Joseph Campbell noted: we die to our animal selves and are
born to our spiritual ones, but the hairy version seems to miss that point by
insisting that the "joyous" parts of man is lost when he graduates. This notion
is warped and is in error.

Unknown to you, *Long Day's Journey Into Night* was presented on stage
a few years after your passing in 1953 and the world seemed to salute the
falsity. You were *sure* that it was the resolution of the fictitious life that you
endured as a child and the world's as well but that was a bent view and
wrong. My birth in 1941 was the same year that that play was finished by
you, Eugene, and my existence was greeted and saluted as well and just as
falsely. The family bestowed upon my poor, little, unsuspecting heart a large
dose of crookedness and self-dealing. Maybe we were linked by a speck of
a diamond that jetted out of its kimberlite and got planted where it would
do the most good. Meanwhile, they over there on Pequot Avenue never let
you be human. As with me, they always made you into the thing that did
not count, the robot running on rules and *we* carried it into adulthood.
Our fates were split, however, as *I* reclaimed the authentic self, my genuine
identity, in 1991 and ended up the way that *you could have* and *you* ended
up the way that *I* could have, hopelessly mired in ruination and unhappiness to the death. Maybe at that moment in 1953, a spark leapt out of you,
skidded off my alcoholic grandfather's head onto my alcoholic mother's
and onto my own where it was incubated and nurtured until now? I can just
see you now: glaring and looking down your nose at me, selfish, spoiled,
mean, cranky, controlling, about to either erupt at me or slink off. But when
you wailed, when you sweated, when you cried and cried and buried your
head in your hands, day after day, telling Carlotta of the ordeal, past and

present for you, *you came as close to living in your feelings* as you ever had in your life since the *first sneak attack* in your face made the cheeks of your soul red and pink, Your withdrawal began right then and it never looked back. The numbness merely got number. A cup of rottenness was hurled into your giggling baby face and repeated year after year until a blind rage rose up where nobody could see it and held hands with the fears that rode your days, the two getting set to support a life of abandon. Never, though, was there a free fall during that 1939-1941 ordeal and so you did not get to the *land of the whole*, but *I* could have led you there by some time-magic. The horns of magnificence that began to blare in 1920 seemed like a real comfort and a glee but really, they were a *curse*. Proof? By the time the 1936 accolades came in from Sweden, you were "too weary" to get to receive the coveted item from the King.

If only you could have seen Eugene, the awful lot that was vested in you was passed on by you to your own kids in "insanity" doings. Eugene, how could you be so wrong and selfish? *I* have that answer! Intolerance of children! Imagine! Come back, Eugene, come down, I can help now. I can set you on the right road, come back, come back, mom, come back Sue, come back everybody. But nobody can come down or back. Too late!

The "fog" that you so often spoke of, it is the state of the public. It is their *trance* and it assaults in the *soft way* all the children of the Earth as it hides the spears of the *hard way*! Eugene, you recall the speech that you put near the end of *Long Day's Journey Into Night*, the dissolving into the sea, the sails and God? That moment that was held there was what is termed "full consciousness". The Hindus term it Sachitananda, the rapture of being in full consciousness, except that for you, it was not permanent or lasting. It *could* become yours, Eugene, if you go into recovery and reclaim the emotional state that you were born with. It awaits you and all who yearn to escape the nagging wretch forced onto them that condemned them only to bitterness. Full consciousness is better than booze, better than morphine or the demerol life that *I* led in 1965 and 1966. I understand Ella's fix.

Let us go to the beloved sea for it holds for me and you the wild, unknown joy. I pledge *my* sea to you as a sign of sincerity and invite you to remember that kind of stirring stuff that you held on the way to Argentina. Just before that moment, you were the grown up child surviving by false ways that were stained into the soul and safe from eradication. But what is this? The *shock* of the *novelty* of laying on a square rigger's bowsprit throws out the history. The intensity of the split open sea water right there beneath, the darkness of night as sort of a protection with punctuation by white sails gleaming, the insulation of this capsule from all the world's woes and memories, *that* is what launched you, Eugene. *That* is what propelled your senses out of hiding and into an intoxication of beauty and singing rhythm, the losing of your "self" the setting free of the only *other* "you" that was possible. Your dissolving into the almighty sea beast and the assumption of its essence and nature made the escape happen or pulled you into itself. A fleet from the past or things to come merged with that "wild joy" as you stated it, the melting into something greater than you, that was a momentary surrender of the false and superhuman self and a salute to that which *is* truly superhuman.

Such elements pass, I am sorry to reveal and the conditions run some cycle and the magic sprint is ended. For such a brief time, you were the baby as yet untainted by James and Ella, so part was nostalgia of a prenatal sort.

The afterglow, so sorrowful, was born of the momentary *seeing*, peering into the very secret of everything and then actually *becoming* that secret and seeing the meaning. It all comes back down and you are thrust back. Fog encircles the head once more, once more and your journey of stumbling off to no place for no reason stutters onward. So, you've had a taste of paradise and *that*, please see it now, *would* have been your reward on Earth. Just by being born does one inherit that euphoria. Quickly is it killed off though by the mean retribution of the cycle. A life of flight ensues for all. The whole soar while the broken flee. But those fractured, you, can come back. Take my road out, Eugene, of the planet. Follow this way! Had we had tea in 1939, we could have made travel plans to do just that! That "Meaning" that was captured there by you is there for whole persons *all the time*! Is that enough of a prize? Does it not rival the King of Sweden's or the Board on Broadway, be it the theater district or way uptown?

The temporariness of your experience there on board matches that of the man who loses his companion, a faithful hound run over by a truck, and who, as a fractured person, is nevertheless thrust into his real feelings for a short time. That awful state of emotional being, rare for him, lasts only for days after which he hides back in his head. That or the square rigger episode, both represent opposite poles of the experience, the intensely pleasurable versus the terribly hurtful. Both push the man to where he was born. The latter kind can be used as a trigger for *recovery* if the grief felt is held on to and nurtured and expanded into the loss of that authentic self, the genuine identity as you called it, Eugene. But, alas! For you it is too late! For me, "No!"

Desperation without equal is the Eugene who wallowed in "walking on the bottom of the sea as if drowned long ago, a ghost belonging to that fog". You called it the ghost of the sea and you as one inside another. Ditto for the idea of yearning for a place where "truth is untrue and life can hide from itself". Follow that up with being born a fish or a seagull and being more of a success at that. Then there is the idea that you were one who does not want, safe that, and who is not wanted. We know this to be so and *I* am your club co-member. But the final notion that you are someone who must always be a little in love with death, that is the kicker because a chink shows up! Yes, these are just words in a play but they are *your* words and *your* life. That "little in love with death" line is patently the antithesis of the often revealed dread of death lurking in you. So, the "in love" part is only a *rush* to the finality that is your bitter fate. You cannot escape death so you run to meet it. Meeting the awful woman of the end a day before your date with her cannot make her very much more terrible to behold, can it, Eugene? The sublime leaps for you. *That* is what *"love"* is for you my nonplussed amigo! But it is *not* what I offer. Mine is a golden path out of the briars that had you strangled!

Then I thought that another crooked-eyed pearl was that man's fate is to glimpse order and unity but to live in chaos and disorder. This is pure abused child stuff. *This*, I could have wrung out of you! Here is a fair question: if that sea experience was so freeing for you, why did you leave the sea life? The answer lies in the simple facts. You were taken by the moment. It happens to us all, all the time although not as dramatically as that. You were able to turn your back on that miracle instant because life as a merchant seaman was okay but you had to *work* and when one is in pain, work is anathema. No, you needed the space to get high, loaded, lazy, no demands, no cares (except your inflamed soul), no interruptions to your vacation of escape.

It is said that you did not pass away a contented writer. You did not die a contented *anything*! They say that you needed to go farther into the under-standing of human beings that were your own family and, therefore, man-kind itself. If nothing else proves the need for an *emotional recovery* by way of *emotional transaction, that* does. One of your self-analyses stated that you had faced reality and that you fled from it in fear. That was just a new way of expressing that the pain of being you was so great that it became intolerable and that you fled, not physically, but into your head. From that moment on, it was a distorted struggle to November 1953. Your pointed query to the effect that "what do we do with the desolate boundaries that we have within us? Is *par* for a child who inherits what you did? The constant attempts to com-prehend yourself, taken along with the preceding stuff, is an admission that you desperately needed to gain admission to the remedy ranch. There, you could have gotten onto a wild but beneficent beast, the real past, and allowed nature to take its usual course with the bucking and kicking of uncontrolled grieving. The torment driving *all of it* springs from the thing that we could have undone had *I* been in charge.

I promised to give you *my* sea, which was *your* sea as well, and who but *we* could grasp the enormity of the thing? It is the blue-green parents that can buoy us up or thrust us asunder and destroy our baby hopes. What can be, I ask you, more authoritative? What greater thing pulls at man's sense of beginnings? Not the night sky! I recall your "mother sea" label and I feel that you were on to the same affection. Only trouble was, your adoration was from behind bars! Would that you could have been drawn out and *then* driven down to the edge of it all. The waves, so dynamic and unrelated to the static land. When graced with a heavy, horizon moon, the seduction is almost too much to take! The rank, salt and kelp air pulls like the aroma of a girl. That rolling possessor, its power ever wandering *under* patterns of gray-green, hidden beneath a shimmering or a waxy cast in late sunlight. *This* is deeply dark and dangerous, yet, mother to tiny schools that flicker parallel. You can glimpse them in front of huge breakers and marvel at their nonchalance! Such a universe! Such unknowing contentment even in the face of likely doom! What odds does each fry have? The waves are alive, constant, like the parade of events in life. The tides are a clock of hours with the waves representing the minutes or seconds. It all makes us *feel* a thing that no other place or object can. It is a source of feelings that is no device or substance like novelty or alcohol. That tapping into the essence of it allows a sense of the ultimate mystery, not only of the sea and life but of God and the entire universe. Cemeteries can come close but there, the scenes are static. In an isolated place, the sea fog can be a sensation of danger, of being swallowed up or overtaken or at the *edge* of one's own annihilation. A feeling of loneliness and alienation are brought to a head at seaside somehow, pointed, magnified, yet with some kind of a comfort with this "companion".

Even when the ocean lies adjacent to a city, New London, it is a savage prospect. There is no match for wild winds and huge insistencies. Yet, the parks and the brethren seem to endure. *Always* does the sea command attention and *never* does one truly turn his back. In that, there is, also, the parental aspect. Sad to say however, that to the extent that it does not stay steady, it reigns ingenuine. The face coming around the corner, the next day, is always unknown and unknowable and capable of great upset. Peace never rests there and the sea itself is not about peace! Perhaps there is some of it in the link, but that remains a whirlwind of flux.

Some days, you are able to *frolic* by the sea, partake of it and the surreal buoyancy and joy. Other times, it is an early morning shroud with a red glow pulsating behind. It gets impressed onto one's presence and overwhelms it. Then there is the *draw* to the sea, to going out to its unsteadiness, beckoning there, advertising even the danger, the peril. Why take such a risk? The sea knows but it *is* the master's silence. Where else lives such savagery and disregard for rules and structure? It hides in a dress of green and beckons all comers. No land mass offers its lessons, yet we cannot say just what those lessons are.

"Refreshing" is the word that now comes to mind as does "freedom" and "escape", but none of that rivals the absolute experience of beholding the curvature of the Earth on the sea horizon. It allows a sense gained no place else. The size and the mass of our planet can be imagined more vividly with that before us.

Pity that you died too soon to experience "Seahunt" which was a popular television show around 1958 starring Lloyd Bridges. It would have delighted you, Eugene! It did me. You went away in 1953 and I recall how the world was then. Had I been able to *lend* you my force, I would have lured you with this bit of verse:

THE SEASIDE EXPERIENCE

When you arrive, you're warm, safe, content,
On solid space plantedly,
But then pushed by longing mystery
And compelled to go into the sea,

It is cold and wet, unpleasant,
Yet persist you on and out,
Gradually aware of the life,
The danger lurking about,

But soon immersed and a part,
The action of water amuses,
Scares, provokes, enlivens,
Curiosity and wonderment fuses,

Lightness of floating has beckoned
A sense of invincible wrath,
But wrinkles descending, though slowly,
Remind of the ultimate path,

A shock suddenly upon you,
Bubbles the eyes' disbelief,
Head upside down in a sandbar,
Frightfully gulping the reef,

Panic and horror and sweeping,
Body shot out to sea,
Current, the ogre of crying,
Holding you down utterly,

Minutes away, a seduction
The looming of rapture of deep,
A grinning at fishes and fingers
And long hair perceived as a weep,

Permanent waterly eyes,
Green glowing shadows delight,
Prenatal bliss upon you,
Lulling you into the night.

Maybe its macabre forboding would have delighted *you?*

I suddenly saw that you were "comfortable" with the sea and fog partly because they are fickle, mercurial, just like alcoholics or morphine-hooked parents!

Back in 1953, *my* world was that of a twelve year old stricken with the sounds of Hugo Winterhalter, Les Baxter, Nat King Cole and many more. Like you, I also was in love with the music of the 1920's and before that, as well as the big bands. It all preceded rock and roll which you missed by about one year. Dizzy Gilespie and Charlie Parker were the be-bop rage. The Song of the Barefoot Contessa was always on my mind and Rosemary Clooney's renditions were a smash. "Wish You Were Here" by Eddie Fisher and someone doing "Slow Boat to China" also spring to mind although the latter one was about 1951, so *you* knew it. Then, my favorite: "It's A Big, Wide, Wonderful World We Live In". And who could shed Frankie Lane and Mule Train or Ghost Riders in the Sky or Vaughn Monroe and Dance, Ballerina, Dance. Then, there was Johnny Ray, the deaf singer who amazed us with the likes of "Cry" and "Little White Cloud that Cried".

My bedroom was a fort and I never really heard of you, Eugene, not even in the news after Thanksgiving this year. *My* freedom was my English bicycle and fishing in the Jersey City Reservoir in Parsippany Troy-Hills. Arrowheads laid around waiting for good eyes to see. The Morris County Fair was annually worth sneaking into and my mother won a blue ribbon for first prize in the pie contest; it was apple. Too bad she couldn't win for love! She tried her best, I guess.

Mars was big that year in the movies and space, the new frontier, was the rage. You, Eugene, no doubt turned your nose up at that. After all, humans had enough to deal with here on Earth…why in hell worry about space?

A persistent memory is of my aunt's banister going from her living room upstairs in Boonton and of Christmas visits there to see the extended family, some of which would turn up or not depending on who was not speaking to whom. That family surrounded me in my feelings even though it was seriously screwed up. I guess that a kid desperately needs a structure and so, will adopt mostly any that he is stuck with and call it okay (sort of). I wonder how such a memory can pull in my vulnerabilities although long ago closed off by the death of nearly everyone, actual or spiritual.

Maybe you're looking down to see me, Eugene? I could have helped you.

CHAPTER SIX:
JUNGLE

My intense sense of Eugene O'Neill's plight on Earth was jungle! Lost in the deep place: no way out, no hint, no comfort, no assurance, just more trees, more spiders, more cats, more jackals, more danger, more injury, more crying, more terror, further wandering, doubling back, more swamps, more reptiles, more teeth, more pretend rays of sun, quicksand, stinging insects, no rest, no real sleep, more fevers, more "medicine", lost weight, more desperation, voices murmuring, further worry, great doubts, self-destruction, other corpses, degradation, hopelessness, despair, final begging, slow, bitter, lingering and then a quick fading of the eyes and a deafness and numbness spread over the head into nothingness.

That is the jungle.

The trees have legs and the arachnids are tall and shady. Many creatures walk the night and suffer. There is milling about everywhere and they swarm over the senses and dull them interminably. Yet, scant sleep revives the awful experience. Death is but a dream, far off, nearly out of reach and tantalizing.

Gone are all wants of centers or solids. Long departed the idea of the life of leisure as one looks down upon jaws on the ankle. Shaking it off contaminates the frame and the effects spread out over the arms and legs. Headaches pound away at the imagined peace, the prize. Wanting is reduced to hysteria for clear water to shut up the raging throat. Nowhere is there an ally, not flying, not burrowing, not skiddering, not climbing up or down, not swimming or skimming, not outside nor inside. All paths let you down. Fake whistling is a clown. Death laughs and hides. Not even the hideous can come when you call it although you grate in your bones that he will take over when hope is at a summit and the last fall down onto diamond-hard cruelty scares the life out of you.

Always, more trees, many short, lots too tall for tops, large bunches, brush uncertainty, dense, thickets, no clear anything, yearning, eyes bugged out, hands stretched out prayer-like, covered in scars, welts, bites, memories. Every place is planted. Nowhere is there nothing. No place where one can sit down unmolested is there. No clear, gentle, calm, placid, thought-gathering areas give grace, not even one!

The darkness comes down every once in a while and holds you in even more. It's not bad enough that the stranglehold paralysis has you caught, there has to be added misery of no light. When will the blessed daylight come? When in good God's name will an edge come into view or even just some clarity?

You drive on and on but the awful giant trunks keep reappearing, Circles are the sole comfort. Mite familiarity soothes minutely. Breaking out, away, is impulse. You take it! But then thrust into some new nightmare city of growth, you regret and pledge not to repeat. Somehow, however, impulse crowds back in and you cannot disobey. Cruel! What deserving is there in this? What story can be told or excuse for self-assurance? How to survive this thicket of weeds in the mind, hardship in the neck, desperation everywhere and no relief to even dream of. What manner of evil is this? What ultimate value or lesson can it throw to you? Can there be this derailed awareness as a way of life on this globe? Could it be in the end the story that cannot be turned off, the tale worms its way into every generation, every toddler wonder, to contaminate and destroy, to take fifty years to play out only to flavor the final days with the bitterest of herbs, sinking or stinking or hating or revengeful or weeping and pale, screaming for mercy, for salvation, for sanity?

A long, repeated, cyclically fierce determination to find the way out only found the failure, the round and round of that. Dizziness rode along as if on a cart and a shedding of all mindfulness came back, the giving up, the throwing up of hands in dismay, the newfound earnestness only met by more trees, more legs, more arms, more crooked smiles and promises, more accolades, triumphs, "progress", more clever-tongued advances, more throwing back, more rejection, more belonging only to the longing, more staked claims, more mirages, more praise, more defeat within, more anything, more everything, lobsters heaped gallantly upon the breast and mind, shrimp nights in the clouds, intoxicating romances with the monkey people, bananas piled up to the ears, stars hanging off the lapel, dropped from above, toilet paper obsessions, "wealth", droning on and on but *never* to see the clearing ahead. Deaths are tallied in faraway ledgers. A sense of oldness climbs onto you, unreal expectation, self-aggrandizment, auto-punishment quickly erased, shower dreaming, sex scheming, but never, never relief!

Cursing God, loving God, threatening God, abandoning God, doubting God, thinking the way out, believing a way out, wishing a way out, inventing the path out, but no way out! Struggling, stammering, clamoring, but no way out! Father, mother, brothers, coming, going, living, dying, but no exit signs. Analysis, structure, lists, crossing off, but no solution.

Clash and hardship, terrors in the gut, imagined worthlessness, Satan, desire, numbness, defeated brow, hands cracked, blood flush behind the eyes, but no path to glory, no lane to the clearing, not even one minute's respite, just this monstrous, undeserved sentence served in the jungle!

CHAPTER SEVEN:
CONSULTING AN
ANALYST IN LIMBO

O n November 27, 1953, Eugene O'Neill graduated from the *Jungle* and was admitted into Limbo. My daydream about what happened is this: This fledgling eternalite languished for a few years in Limbo and was silent until he uttered his first words, which were "God damn it!" A voice, tiny but steady, met his own and instantly indicated that it was referring Eugene to a Limbo psychoanalyst because usually, entrants are not surprised or afraid or even dismayed, such was the nature of their sideways lives and their expectations upon death often linked to O'Neill's last in Boston hotel, cast in bitterness and anger. No deathly peace there!

Eugene asks the voice "Am I dead yet? Has it finally happened? The graceful reply was "quite, sir, rather." "But where am I and who are you?" he continues incredulously. "In the in between area," came the answer. "And now you are to troll down to Summerfields…go along now."

Eugene bumped along in an away direction as if pushed by a clear hand. Summerfields was straight ahead and the path allowed no other. In nearly only seconds, he saw the sweeps of grand grasses that had no color! Things were *like* that here in the area of in between. No one ever remained in Summerfields nor wanted to and in this particular case, as Eugene glided past a stanchion, he saw a parchment that revealed the reason that he had been admitted: "Misled life; debauchery, drunkenness, adulterer, child abuser, abandoner, sower of falsehoods." He went a little farther along, Eugene came upon another one that provided: "Tried with whole heart to comprehend it all, his agony, the cruelty of life, made great efforts to unravel the roots though tangled in them which strangled a doubtful heart."

Eugene could leave the leaves of Summerfields and find the colors of eternity *only* if he could, would learn the ropes of his misfortune and *go straight*. Thus, the analyst. While he was alive, he got an "A" for effort but an "F" for results and the soon to come transaction was aimed at improving that grade.

A wind whooshed Eugene extraordinarily fast right into the lap of Dr.

Kornschucher, a noted Austrian farmer and scientist, who bore a monacle and spoke with a heavy accent but only when excited. Eugene quickly leapt off of the doctor's lap and stood there blinking and kind of stammering.

"I have all the answers, Eugene, you have almost none" the doctor began. "So, here, you will not argue with me…that is not allowed."

"Yes, sir," was the halting reply. "Of course."

"I see," continued the doctor. "That nobody on earth ever tried harder to get it right, to understand the miserable way that life can take us and turn us upside down and shits on us, yes? You've been at it for sixty-five years, no? He asked. "Well, not sixty- five, less than that", he corrected himself, "But you did make a great effort and a strain and everybody saw it, Ja?"

"I guess so," replied Eugene, still a little shell shocked by the new scene he was in.

"Then you will be given the most chances to get a reversal" the doctor assured his charge. "You know what a reversal is?" he queried. "Uh…Uh…" Eugene paused.

"I vill tell you vat it ist", Eugene heard him say. "A reversal is that ting vat takes the rotten journey, the regrets, the death of spirit and mind, the mess, and turns it all around. It does not mend that damage caused but undoes the broken parts in you."

"Yeah?" answered Eugene hesitatingly as though he had no choice.

"*Then*" the doctor emphasized, "You vill get a chance to use your powers to bring a reversal to the whole world. It is vaiting, you know!" said doctor K.

"I guess" was the reply.

"Vell. Didn't you say that the world is sick, society is sick?" asked the analyst.

"Of course; it is very sick" replied Eugene, "Sick and disgusting".

"So who else" remarked the doctor, "To make a reversal than you?"

"Okay" replied Eugene dutifully as if he had no alternative to getting out of this place.

"So, if you take my analysis and believe it, then you vill be half way home, not going home, you understand, you are a dead man, but home in the way of your goal" assured Dr. K.

"All right" said Eugene.

"The other part is that you vill do vat I tell you. That vill be the tough part because it vill hurt you but ist necessary to get a turn around in your guts, you see it?" asked the analyst.

"Oh! I do not know about…I, uh", stammered the patient.

"Do not vorry, my boy, you are smart, no education, hee-hee, but very wise from the street and library, Ja?" the doctor snickered. "Do not be so shy und understand that it is not so easy, a reversal, Ja? It ran away from you in life und was a bitter ting, Ja? It has *got* to hurt, mein Gott, a big rock, a boulder to roll up a hill. You tink it is a pebble?"

Without expecting any answer, the analyst instructed Eugene that if he did what he was told to do, the reversal would enable him to *see* for the first time in his life, not like that time on the ship going to Argentina exactly, but to really get out of blindness and *feel* for the first time as well. He went on to state that his efforts could empower Eugene to eventually understand all the world and all that was thrown into his tender, little path when a toddler and then he might be able to deliver the message to the still living souls in New London even.

"No, the vorld vill not spin the utter vay" he remarked, "But people vill" he said to break the tension.

Eugene nodded that he grasped this even though he did not quite know what was going on.

"I crown you, Eugene O'Neill and command you to listen and receive your charge and your unique place in a world whose ears are still longing for you in a perverse kind of way. It vill listen to *you* but they all but ignore such as me" said Doctor Kornschucher regretfully. "But!" , he shouted, "If you fail here, you will stay in Limbo forever!" was the mext warning. Ve never get anybody in Limbo like you, you son of a gun. Such a guy, you wouldn't believe!" exclaimed Doctor K. Eugene remained silent and awaited the next development.

"Mein Gott! No education und a Nobel Prize, yet?" shouted the analyst. "Do you know I got orders from above to 'fix that boy', you see. *They* are telling *me* vat to do! So, then, if *I* can do it, *you* can do it, Ja?" he remarked, trying to bolster Eugene's confidence.

Eugene watched intently.

"But it von't be so easy. Remember that eleven-play cycle you had going?" he asked.

"You know about that?" Eugene queried astonished. Then he laughed out loud.

"Ja!" was the stern reply, "Ve have files on everybody, every little ting, so, it vill be tough like the cycle. You did not finish it. No 'War and Peace' for you, Ja? But this vill be even harder" Dr. K. allowed as Eugene's face showed a new discouragement.

"But don't you vorry, my son, *I* vill steer you und ve vill work zusammen und someday, sometime, a reversal, no? I can feel that. Your desperation vill guaranty it" he assured his doubtful listener.

"Oh" said Eugene.

"One warning, though", the doctor observed, "One ting: in the end, you vill have to confront somebody yourself but you are not to be scared. You vill be equipped and you can do it. I just know it!" he said.

"Okay" replied the reticent Eugene. He was all too well beginning to get the idea and became semi-scared that he'd never escape Limbo.

"You know vat, Eugene?" asked the doctor, "I made a mistake! Ach, now that ist a joke, Ja? *Me* making a mistake. It vill *not* hurt you. You are *dead*!"

"Is that correct?" Eugene asked with a brighter face, hearing news that he never expected. "It will not hurt me?"

"No, you vill not feel a ting. But, it *vill* hurt the ones who need this. You cannot get a reversal without pain und that is *universal*." assured the analyst. "Zis ist vas Satre meant by 'Life begins on the far side of despair' suffering by grieving forces recovery". "Besides" he continued, "You have had enough pain. It's enough already yet".

"But it *will* displease me, hurt me deeply to stay here in Limbo, no affront to you, doctor," Eugene replied.

"Und that is vhy you *have* to do it, for you and the world so that you can have peace, Eugene. Think of it, boy, better than fog!" Doctor K. quipped. "Better than a ghost within a ghost, Ja?"

Eugene was a little embarrassed by this reference as if he had been caught off guard or with his hand in the till or the liquor cabinet. Suddenly, Eugene heard a funny sound and asked the doctor "What is *that*, a trumpet?"

"Mein Gott, no" replied the analyst, "That ist not Gabriel, Boy, if *that* is vat you tink, nein! Gabriel is far away, up there. Maybe you vill see him some-day but first ve have to verk, Ja?"

"Ja!" kidded Eugene, "I mean, yessir!"

"Tomorrow, ve get started bright und early und maybe I vill be calmed down und use mein gut English, Ja? Anyway, Goodnight, Eugene" said the doctor as he disappeared.

"Goodnight, Dr. K., Korn…Kornschucher," said Eugene as he looked around for a place to settle down.

That night, Eugene slept lying down but in thin air, nothing under him. It was quite remarkable but he seemed to take it in stride and it was not long before he saw that he could point his body in any direction and that it would stay that way he elected to sleep with his feet pointing at a 10:00 o'clock direction and his head at four. This amused him. However, sleep would not come and Eugene's eyes were like large ball bearings rolling around in too-large sockets and his throat was raw.

Soon, the next day came and he was reminded of sunup in New London. People do not, it seems, eat or drink in Limbo or even wash or exercise. Dr. Kornschucher reappeared soon enough and Eugene then realized what that nightlong thirst had been. It was not for water or even to see the water but he *did* catch himself in the silly question of whether one molecule of water inside his eyes had ever been in the Thames at his old haunt!

"Good morning, my boy" chimed the analyst.

"Good day, where's Carlotta?" he answered. Then he, taken aback at himself, was ashamed and tried to undo it.

"It's alright, Eugene," replied the doctor, "You're a little confused, Ja?"

Eugene looked sheepish but composed himself.

"You vill, I mean you *will* not need any notebook or anything because, well, because what I will tell you, you will remember for certain. You have that huge brain that everybody pointed to long ago. Also, what I am about to impart to you will sink in and stay because there are lock and key set ups in that head of yours and the keys I throw at you will fit into some lock, a tiny one, but there are thousands in there," he went on. "So now, ve, I me *we* begin. Eugene, you're such a big shot. You did your own analysis, am I right?"

Eugene was started by this and said "I...well...uh..."

"Come on now" said the doctor, "We have a long way to go, did you?"

"Yes...y-yes, as a matter of fact..." he answered but the analyst cut him off.

"So, *you* were the big shot, huh? Analyzing yourself, huh?" replied the doctor who let a loud, low belly laugh out.

"Uh, I...I... Uh..." stammered Eugene.

"Listen, boy, you answer me right away and tell the truth or you will *never* get out of here, do I make myself clear?" insisted Doctor K. sternly.

Eugene was reminded of his father who was also stern and domineering but this was different and he did not feel threatened somehow. The command sunk into his heart by his own deciding and he vowed to himself to be and do whatever the good doctor wanted. Such was the bright hope cast upon Eugene by the kind intentions and rigid structure offered by Dr. K.

"How did you do?" asked the analyst, referring to the patient's well-known self-examination.

"I do not know, I made diagrams and I wrote down how I felt about everything and everyone, my father, my mother, Ella, Jamie, my brother, others.

Also I expressed *why* I felt the way that I did about them and all," Eugene said. "Yes," replied the doctor. "You did a lot, struggled a lot with it, put your heart and soul into the project and why was that so?" he asked. "Why, Eugene?" "Because I was so hurt and hurting and worn out and sick and at the end of my rope, as they say," he confided. "Indeed you were," assured the analyst. "And you had the absolute motive dead to rights, why who could have desired and needed peace more than a boy, a lad, a man who truly wished that he could be a seagull or a fish or that ghost within a ghost?" replied the good doctor with a grin wryly. "You're *trapped* here," the sudden reply came and this brought Eugene up short. O'Neill let out a shiver. "Trapped," he murmured. "But the good news, son, is that I will not eat you. You *will* be let out of that trap when and if you ever reach the half-way point," assured Dr. K.

"Half-way point?" he inquired with a worried look.

"I have already instructed you that we would get up to a place in this when you will have them to confront somebody, remember?" said the doctor.

"Yes indeed," replied the nervous Eugene feeling strange at forgetting this. He quivered still at the notion of being held prisoner there.

"Am I not right that in your so-called self-analysis, you were still trying to understand people, yourself and mankind, too and that you were even quoted as reflecting on yourself as 'a keen analyst'?" The doctor wondered.

"I guess that that is correct," answered Eugene.

"Superhuman behavior, that is, you see that?" asked the inquisitor.

"Superhuman?" replied the stunned Eugene.

"Ja!" exclaimed the doctor, "Ve vill get into zis more ven ve go mining!"

Eugene sat still because he had no idea what was happening here. "You wrote a good deal about people being caught by cruel intentions or cruel fate or cruel relatives, Ja, Eugene?" he asked him, knowing already the answer.

"That's what's got me nervous right now", replied Eugene

"Well, you got it all wrong that self-analysis, Eugene, all wrong!" the doctor announced as if handing back a corrected test.

The patient was crestfallen and astonished and he let out a cry.

"Do not be alarmed, my boy. You were not a trained psychoanalyst but I *am*, so how could you ever get such things right" inquired the master.

"Oh," was his only reply.

"Never mind, never mind that," said the doctor. "*I* will tell you. It was desperation and ego. A superman can do anything, think anything, write anything." Eugene stared at him.

"All of your endings were *bitter*. You died bitter and weeping for death.

There was no peace, *none*! No contentment graced your final life through the world praised you on high! See it. Eugene?" he asked a stricken patient.

"All men are firemen at heart because they have so much experience with a hose!" quipped Eugene who then covered his eyes in embarrassment.

Dr. Kornschucher wrote this down on his pad and muttered under his breath that that was quite interesting that comment.

"Were you a homosexual?" he asked Eugene.

"I...I do not..." (cut off)

"Or bisexual?" the doctor corrected himself.

"No...I love women, well I *did*," he assured the doctor.

"But you put them in a *lower* place than men, no?" he came back.

"Well, I guess that my mother...she...I..." (voice trailing off)

"I understand, Eugene. But did you ever see a physical relationship with another man as sort of like sex with yourself?" the doctor asked. "Narcissism?"

Eugene remained silent on this and pretended to have a coughing fit.

"Did you ever have such feelings for your father?" Doctor K. inquired but the fit lasted just long enough for the analyst's impatience to force him to move on.

"I always thought that women should pull their dresses up over their heads as a sort of social gesture", Eugene exclaimed to the doctor's dismay. He then passed over that when he heard Eugene laughing.

"Let's get back to where we were," asked the doctor, "You have written nearly everything that you wanted to except that cycle, isn't that so, Eugene?"

"Nearly, but the drive to produce a masterpiece is relentless and..."he said.

"But you were *not cured* of anything. Your kids were estranged from you, your firstborn cut himself to death in 1950, right?" asked the knowing analyst.

"You know he did" replied Eugene sadly.

"Yes, and you didn't even go to the funeral, did you?" he asked demandingly.

"Well, that was back in 1950, doc." Eugene stated.

"I am warning you, Eugene, do not try to con me. You do that again and this is all over and you can sleep at the 10:00 o'clock position until Kingdom come. You understand me?" the doctor shouted.

Eugene was really startled and he saw how his *habit* of lying or dodging or being crooked to others was so automatic.

"You paid for the thing but you did not attend, right?" he asked again.

"Right," he replied now determined to tell the truth from then on lest he never get out of that place.

"So you see Eugene, that in spite of the huge brain and the desperation and the determination and the world's applause, you did not cure a thing. You faked it in the end. Your son died in 1950 but your self-analysis was *way* before that, so you were laying a con job on me. You want to get tough? Tough tears?" he demanded.

Eugene suddenly felt very fatigued.

"You faked it boy. You settled for the best you could think of but it was made up crap!" the doctor yelled. "In the end, you were on drugs, you were an addict, you brought your wife, Carlotta, to Court up in Massachusetts to try to get guardianship over her and she in return filed a petition for separate maintenance, right?"

Eugene looked down in silence dejectedly.

"It was dismissed because you lived in New York and it had to be filed in New York, isn't that the case?" he demanded.

"Yes", Eugene relented.

"And that's how life was going near the end, right?" he asked.

"Pretty petty, huh?" was the reply.

"And still you were smoking cigarettes?" was the next demand.

"So, what importance that has I do not know," he retorted in a snotty voice.

"Plenty!" yelled the analyst. "You were an addict. You had an intimate relationship with a death-dealing substance and it is *sick*! Eugene, do you see it now?"

"Uh, I…uh" stammered Eugene.

"You were an addict because it made you feel good. It made you feel something when most things did not. You didn't care about cancer dangers because what good is long life when it hurts to live even the next day?" the analyst asked.

"I guess," was the tiny reply.

"And all that stuff you put in the end of that play, *Long Day's Journey Into Night*, about *how* the family was and got that way and could be *excused* and the object of compassion and all the rest of it, all rot!" insisted the doctor.

Eugene was silent but looked angry.

"I'm not knocking compassion but the way that you placed it, it was mostly enabling, Eugene, do you know what that means?" the doctor asked.

"Enabling?" he replied.

"Certainly. Allowing someone to get away with false ideas or phony conduct is enabling them. It is usually done for the selfish motives of the allower such as being scared to be alone, fear of abandonment, convenience, avoiding confrontation, like that" replied the doctor. "Enabling is immoral because it hurts both actors and avoids the truth".

Eugene pondered this idea very carefully and silently.

"You and Carlotta were just that", the analyst next proclaimed, "because you each kept quiet, except when enraged, about the other's defects. You both did that for self-centered reasons. *You used each other!* Speaking of 'enraged', Eugene, you *were* violently hostile to women when you were young!" "I don't much care for *that* kind of talk, doc", Eugene said sounding alarmed.

"Right now, Eugene, I am thinking of a concept that appears in that play we just spoke of where there were *tears* and *apologies* between family members for all of the *past deceptions* foisted on one another. Now that sounds good, my boy, but it is no answer! The seeds of deception are deeply sown there and cannot be killed off by apologies. They do not root out weeds", assured the analyst, "and you can be certain that more deceptions are in the works. That was naïve!" Eugene seemed like he had just been told that his best friend was dead. "Don't look so glum, Eugene," the doctor counseled. "What you hear here is the truth so be glad that you are now, finally, aimed at the right thing ahead."

"Gee, I feel so inadequate," replied the dumbfounded patient.

"Entirely understandable," replied the doctor. "After all, we are knocking out a lifetime of false structure. That's how we approach a reversal."

"Why couldn't I have come across this in life?" he asked.

"Don't know," replied the doctor. "But it's rare that *anybody* undergoes recovery from what *you* were stained with. It's just too painful."

"But not for me, not here and now?" worried Eugene.

"Not for you now, you are dead. But for the *living*, yes!" he answered. "I am reminded of an early play of yours called 'Exorcism' where the hero claimed to have gotten rid of his self-destructiveness but without the drawn out grieving process. It was false!"

"You and Carlotta were on sedatives in the end, correct?" inquired the analyst.

Eugene agreed that they were and allowed that they were both in emotional need of them and unable to function without that kind of "help".

"So, you needed artificial support because you were a mess, Ja? Und ist that not the same thing as the characters in *Iceman*, Eugene?" he inquired.

"I suppose," Eugene reluctantly agreed, not wanting to upset the doctor.

"Und your kindern, your kids, you ver not speaking with them in the end, Ja, the vons who ver still alive?" he asked Eugene.

"Right" answered Eugene. "And I cut them off in my will as well. I guess that you already know about that? But they got the Bermuda property years ago, so…"

"Now, Eugene, you did not drive ze car, yes?" was the next question.

"Couldn't manage that, too much pressure, I was too nervous, so I gave that up long ago," Eugene conceded.

Skipping around, the doctor next asked Eugene about mistreatment of his wife, Carlotta, and his shutting himself off from her, refusing to acknowledge her birthday or Christmas and that sort of thing. Eugene confided that Carlotta could be bitchy. Another idea that he reluctantly accepted was that *everything* was off center in the *end* and *along the way*, off center when life *should be* the *grandest.*

"Should be?" asked Eugene, rhetorically. "I have never known how things *should* be."

"Und in the last days in that hotel in Boston, you told Carlotta that there was to be no priest at the funeral and only a simple headstone with the word 'O'Neill', correct?" asked the question-maker.

"True," replied Eugene.

"But you ver a Roman Catholic, Ja?" he asked dryly.

"Oh, shit!" slipped out. "I mean, I'm sorry, yes, I was a Roman Catholic but I gave all *that* up when I was fifteen years old and my mother tried to drown herself in in the Thames at home because she could not get a fix!"

"Terrible," remarked the therapist. "Such a thing to show to a child."

Bitterly, Eugene related how he prayed to god for his mother to get better, to get off of the morphine habit and that no answer came from God and how he then gave up what was left of that in his soul.

"So, the no priest was a protest *or* a sign by you that you were not entitled to a priest?" was the query.

"Uh, well, I guess…," answered a seemingly *confused* Eugene.

"Und the headstone, no special words, Ja? You ver a special person, Ja?" he continued.

"I just didn't *feel special* and I did not want any more fuss, you know," he said.

"So, maybe you ver seeing for the first time the *doubtful product* that you made all your life and the world was fooled by Eugene?" he went on.

O'Neill seemed to flush at that and had the most bewildered look.

"Now, my boy, did you not complain about 'inner shakes' and that they were much worse than the outer ones?" he was asked. "Vat ist that?"

"The rottenness inside of me, that's what it was, collapsed feelings, toppling emotional structure, a threatening sense inside me, terrible, too," he said.

"Well put, my boy," assured Dr. K., "und as a matter of fact, you wanted to be put to sleep, Ja?" he asked dryly. "In other words, Eugene, you vanted death to take you quickly but it refused to cooperate. You couldn't get *life* to do vat you vanted und now, you could not get *death* to do what you vanted, too, Javol?" he went on.

"What more can a body take?" replied a worn out voice.

"You wept bitterly but God and death would not take over!" he went on.

Eugene nodded.

"Maybe you cried so because you ver at zat moment partially in your true feelings and vulnerabilities, Ja?" the analyst asked.

"Who knows?" replied Eugene.

"*You* do," was the response. "Und in ze end, your last vords to her ver something like 'Born in a hotel room, and, God damn it, died in a hotel room', Ja?"

Eugene reacted by pretending to be surprised.

Then the doctor asked him "Did you ever trip over the words of your father, James, in that same tone when he complained about 'that God damned play' as he was blaming *it* instead of himself?"

The reaction was one of being shaken to the core. Eugene turned and looked up into Dr. Korschucher's face as though he were some kind of newly arrived angel.

Continuing with his probing, Dr. K. next inquired about 1912 and the Fulton Street episode where Eugene *also* gave death a chance to take him but was blocked by friends who saved his sorry ass.

"Und for vat vas that saving, Eugene?" was the pointed query. "You didn't vant it."

The look of opening up came over the face of the examined one.

"So. Eugene, my friend," said the analyst. "Ve have adequately shown that all of your efforts in life, some producing objects that most writers would give their nuts to get, and all your suffering as a child, as a young man and the

1939 to 1941 composing of that play and the other big one, what ist that, oh, yes, The *Iceman* von, all the 'blood and tears' as you ver quoted as saying, all would add up to a still crooked life and such a misery".

"Pretty sad, huh? Pretty rotten, yes?" he replied.

"Okay, Eugene, now ve step up a level. Ve know vat you ver, vat you did, how little it helped, so *now* ve vill approach the diamond mine!" announced Dr. K.

"Diamond mine?" Eugene exclaimed, not understanding.

"Javol!" replied the expert, "But first you need to understand that you are in Limbo, not in the Roman Catholic sense, you see, but generically, Ja?"

"Okay, doc, fine with me," was the relieved reply.

"You ver mad at Gott, Ja?" asked the doctor. "Now *that* takes balls… imagine, such a ting!"

Eugene then insisted that he had a right to be angry with him but the doctor cut him off and told him that he was warped and blind and that *that* was why. He also told him that all his carrying on in the plays about idiosyncrasies and human weaknesses and compassionate understanding and sympathizing with such weaknesses and tenuousness of human relationships and all the stuff on needing masks to survive, all of that, would never hold up in the end and that he, Eugene, would soon see it. A reminder to Eugene that he ended up miserable in spite of all that was made vehemently along with the fact that in the end, Eugene had *no* answers.

"I just don't know anymore doc, just do not know," lamented the playwright.

"Here you vil get ze *right* answers and it vill not take so long, mein freund," assured the analyst, losing his English touch. "They vill fit into your tired little mind like keys."

"That's nice," was the dutiful reply.

"I already told you, Eugene, the doctor reminded him. "That I know *everything* about you and *all* that has transpired in your pitiful life. Now you vill, will see that all your projections and representations on despairand damnation, human frailty and alienation, failed lives and tragedy, self-deception and anguish, pessimism and desperation, desolation and fatalism, life tricking us and not belonging anywhere, frustration and sadness, the 'abyss', illusions, man being trapped in his circumstances, a Godless world, guilt, evil in mankind, the so called paradox of the human condition, self-hatred, contradictory emotions, 'truth destroys', 'self knowledge kills', spiritual darkness, human melancholia and the life sentence to 'solitary confinement', all of this list, all your wrenching writing, Eugene, the thinking, the pondering, soul searching, turmoil inside, your poor guts, your boiling head, *all wrong*!" shouted Dr. K.

Eugene fell back in his air chair and slumped but a guttural protest emanated from his throat and the doctor himself was taken aback by it if not downright insulted.

"*Perfect Understanding,*" the doctor mouthed the words slowly for emphasis. "*Achievement of illumination*", he continued. "*This* ist vat you tink you found in those plays, Eugene?"

Eugene appeared to be slighted.

"*In Long Day's Journey into...*where...*Night*, Ja, in that play, you..."

The doctor was cut off by Eugene who protested. "Wait a minute here..."

"No, *you* wait a minute my freund. *I* vill tell *you* vat ist vat und *you* vill accept it, Ja? Otherwise, you never get out of Limbo, Ja?" he warned.

Again, the subject was crestfallen. Moreover, he realized then and there that his *ego* would likely guaranty a life sentence in this colorless place because he was automatically fighting the doctor instead of accepting what was being pushed at him in good faith. So, he resolved to adopt the position of an obedient schoolboy to get a way out of this 'Hell'.

"There was no 'perfect understanding', Eugene," he counseled, "just a sham born of your desperation for *some* kind of answer and some kind of *relief*."

Eugene shook his head affirmatively but in silence.

"Und, no illumination, just *mud*," he instructed without needing a reply.

"Mud...y-yes," answered the schoolboy.

"Don't blame yourself and don't worry. *I* will take you through it and you will get a reversal or my middle name is not 'August', by golly," assured the doctor.

"Okay," replied Eugene sounding very tired.

"Now, here in Summerfields where the foliage has no color, we also have a diamond mine and that is where the diamonds are. Pretty simple, huh, kid?" he remarked. "They, too, are without color but nobody seems to mind that! These are the crystals that almost nobody on earth lives by or knows about, least of all, *you*, Eugene, as I have already demonstrated."

Not daring to disagree, Eugene merely sat watching.

"You ver desperate to find the meaning of life, of death, und equally troubled about vat looked like the absolute *meaninglessness* of it all, nicht wahr?"

he asked. "Und you vanted a place where the 'genuine self' and 'identity' could be nourished and could prosper but saw it as not possible, Ja?"

Eugene agreed with this.

"Und you saw rage and anger and frustration as a block to all that also. Und also, you stated that man is *born broken* and lives *by mending.* Mein Gott! Such a ting vat did they do to you, those awful people...well, they ver victims, too, you vill see, Eugene," Dr. Kornschucher continued.

Determined to nurture his newfound quietude for safety, Eugene just smiled.

"The diamonds will tell us," Dr. K. assured him. "Und they vill show you vat you did wrong and vat *they* did wrong. Also vill be seen vat you *felt* und vat you thought was wrong und vat the *real* cause vas und not just the description of misery that the plays have. Also vill be *a cure!* A *reversal* shown!"

Again, O'Neill just nodded his assent and smiled weakly. He knew though that for the first time in his life, well, death that he was with a *straight person* who was untouched by crookedness and that he would not be harmed or misled. Such a realization boosted his brightness immeasurably! Then, something snapped in Eugene's core and he felt immediate relief. It was as if a magic wand had been passed over his troubles and a broad smile came. Then, tears of gratitude followed and Dr. K. noticed this with silent approval. He went on as usual, however.

"You looked at *sex,* at *passion,* as some kind of a *softener* for loneliness and to offer a glimpse of hope and fulfillment. Does that sound like you, Eugene?" he asked.

"Yes, sir," was the machine-like response. "You saw that as *unselfish,* as *spontaneous* and so it looked like some kind of an absolute to you, right?" asked the doctor.

"Right," he answered tersely.

"But you could be wrong, you admit this, Eugene?" he was asked.

"I guess," was the dry answer.

"It could be wrong, again, because you were desperate for answers and reasons behind the flagrant inconsistencies in life that seemed like a plague upon the people," Dr. K. observed.

"For certain," replied Eugene.

"Und then you insisted that man is a slave to his instincts and to fate, Ja?" was the next area asked.

"I did state such a thing," Eugene admitted. "But so what?"

"But didn't you also at one time go on and on about emotions and that emotions were the true route to the truth because they involved instincts, Eugene?" he said. "So, where is the *slavery* there?"

"Sounds inconsistent, doesn't it, doc?" he admitted.

"Javol! Und 'fate', vat is that but a handle that somebody invented to attach to what seems otherwise to be turmoil! There is no such thing as 'fate' in the predetermination sense. Poppycock! That's vat that ist, Eugene. You vill see it." the good doctor instructed. "Blindness has no bounds, limits, and the imagination of a ruined little boy is void of borders, so sad is it."

Eugene sat and listened and nodded when he had to.

"Und next ve have 'love' and you said, Eugene, that it exists in a family or between people but that 'love' does not stop them from driving each other to despair, Ja?" Dr. K. asked him.

"No good?" replied Eugene. "Not possible…, but I've seen that."

"No gut! Love is selflessness. So is holiness. Ve cannot have selflessness in bed with driving each other to despair., Ja?" the doctor insisted. "Ven you ver born, all you vonted was to love und be loved. That is not vat you got, Ja? The barnyard ist vat you got shoved down your throat und you had to accept it or perish, you see? Love is *giving*, my boy and not more! It escapes the world but it vill not escape you anymore, Eugene!"

Eugene seemed positively inspired.

"The crooked hand and the crooked eye, that is vot hurts the baby. Ven der vater und die mutter ist nicht emotionally available to the baby, the toddler, the baby panics, you see, Eugene?" he asked his charge. "Und another ting: you have stated that the family is chained together by *guilt, resentment* and *hate* along with *love*, but that is impossible. Vot was that play…oh, yes, the *Long Day* one, Ja. Anyway, so much killing in the world in the name of that, Ja? It's crazy," sighed the doctor. "Acht du liebe! Killing is all over the place, common, nobody notices, really," said Eugene. "But linking it with guilt and the other two things in the family, impossible to be and only a warped idea, Eugene," said the analyst. "You *vill* see it."

Eugene straightened up even more and began to see that something was occurring to him. This stuff was started to fall into place, a sensible pattern, a structure that made him feel something secure and it was brand new.

"Soon ve vill have the diamonds and then you vill see better," he added.

Eugene was becoming quasi-exuberant. He did not know how to handle this new sensation and was actually afraid of it.

"Now, Eugene, ve must continue. It is said that you were so far along in the pronouncements about life and *your* life and death in the world that you actually *forgave* your family and ver *reconciled* to your past. Ist such a thing so, did you say those things?" asked the curious doctor who, of course, already knew the answer.

"Well, it *is* so. That *did* happen to me. I needed that *badly*. I got a *complete understanding* of my family members, the whole past, what befell me and I used *total self-honesty* to do it," he exclaimed proudly.

"Tsk, task, tsk," scolded the doctor. "More barnyard piles I fear."

Eugene was hurt by this and visibly shaken. It would not be stretching it to say that he felt beaten down by his newly trusted companion and this kind of threw him into a Pequot Avenue snit. He sort of wanted to just die, but he couldn't.

"You attempted to show in the end of zat play that the characters achieved something wonderful by their *admissions* to each other, *confessions, revelations* that supposedly followed all that but, my boy, where were the explanations of just *how* such a life as that is even possible or *what* the real cure is for such a dreadful state of affairs so artfully described by you over and over?" Dr. K. insisted on asking. He knew that Eugene had *not a clue*. Admissions do not cure the thing that caused the ways admitted to in the first place, nor do confessions. Revelations are nice if they are real, but Dr. K. suspected that *these* revelations were *not* the ones that were coming for Eugene in the diamond mine.

He continued. "There was no complete self-honesty, Eugene. You're smoking cigarettes right up to near the end of your life. Where's the honesty in that? And complete understanding? Vat do ve need mit that stuff that you claimed was the answer, the idiosyncrasies, the human weaknesses, that compassionate understanding if ve have a complete understanding, huh?" he insisted. "Consider, Eugene, that you *might* have understood why your father acted that way but not why he *was* that way."

"Okay," Eugene allowed like a puppy dog.

"Here sits the great 'enigma', Eugene O'Neill, right here! He is such an 'unknown' that it is not possible to grasp it fully, Ja? His mystery is so deep, Ja? You like this stuff, Eugene?" he asked.

"Uh, I don't lament the…well," he stammered.

"It's the roll of meat hanging in the delicatessen of desperation, Eugene, it is despair bologna! Admit it!" he demanded. "Come on, admit it!"

"Okay, I admit it," replied Eugene in a whisper, barely believing his own voice.

"Gut!" cried the doctor. "Ve have proved it anyway. Look at your sorry life! No complete understanding of *anything*…not yet anyway. No, total self-honesty! Und, vat enigma ist this. I vont to know dis hier! Such a simple, little boy warped into a great mystery, Ja? *Bull Stuff.* Ja! The world should be ashamed to show its face, mein Gott!"

"No, no enigma," Eugene complained. "But life *is* and I cannot understand any of it no matter how hard I try!" he waxed in a defeated tone. "All rotten!"

"Vat ist tht you say, all rotten, life? Isn't that vat your father, James, said on his deathbed in 1920, Eugene?" asked the knowing analyst.

"My God," he replied. "I'm back to that. My poor papa lying there wasted. He could not hurt me *then* ,but *it* did. It killed me just to se this human being that was above me for so long now helpless and in pain, no longer able to control me, harm me, make me angry, let me down, cut me off, trample my feelings, make me worthless. He needed *me* now. The morphine was now *his* support instead of Mama's! I wonder if she tried to connive any?" he pondered.

"Yes, Eugene, go on," the doctor urged.

"He never gave me what was right. Always, it was crooked and I hated him as well as her. One thing, though, *he* was not weak. But now, falling away in that hospital, he was no more the great actor but only my poor Papa! I wondered if my own kids would have been in the same spot someday!" Eugene said tearfully.

"Well, you cut them off, didn't you, Eugene? *That* was the *complete understanding crap, Ja?* You understood almost *nothing*, only that you were in pain and *anything* that eased it was fair game! Lying, cheating, smoking, boozing, roaming, distortions, abandonment, all without any limits. What limits did you have, Eugene?" he asked him.

"None, I imagine," was the weak reply.

"*Total self-honesty? Reconciled to your past?* This is what that is made of? Mein Gott, Eugene, do you see it now? A reversal awaits you but hard work is coming first, Eugene. Und, that confrontation, do not forget that, too," Dr. K. said.

"What that man did to me and Jamie, you wouldn't believe it!" complained Eugene. "I hated him…*we* hated him and were afraid all the time! I wanted him to *die* and now he's gone and he *did* die. Jamie, too. Drank himself to death. And *she*, she was just a damned, bad, weakling, sneaky, sly like women are, have to be I guess. I hated her, too. I wanted her to disappear, not to go upstairs, but into Hell the way she made it for me, spaced out house, wigged out of life," he sobbed.

"There, there, my boy, it's alright now," comforted Dr. K. "Listen to me, you thought that death would relieve you of all this, the agony, but here, it's come back to haunt you again. What's this, the ten thousandth time? Anyway, *now* you see the value of the truth and how it will seep into you and soak into that old whiskey and tobacco brain!"

Eugene was feeling very tired but determined to hear more real truth.

"Your two brothers and your mother are also dead and gone now and all together now, yes, Eugene?" he asked, already knowing the answer.

"Right, together, all there now. But in Limbo?" he wondered aloud.

"Do not concern yourself over that right now. The time will come when *you* are prepared," he was assured. "Do not be distraught now".

This seemed to soothe Eugene who thought to himself: "When *I* am ready?"

"Now listen to this list of statements, Eugene. See if they sound like you," the doctor instructed. "The tragic struggle is destined to defeat by the way things are, by the tyranny of man's own conflicting emotions."

"Sounds like something that I would say, yes," admitted the patient.

"Human self-destructive weakness; perverse complexities of human nature, contests between illusions and the will to live; man is a victim of the ironies in life and of himself," the doctor continued. "Sound like you?"

"For sure," was the reply by a hesitant Eugene who figured that a scolding was at hand.

" 'Truth destroys us'; 'We are all victims of life's manipulations'; 'Frustration remains the condition of man'; 'Life seems like a dirty, rotten trick'; Confronted by your most harrowing memories'; 'You put all your ghosts to rest'; 'You've lost your true self forever'; 'Man's fate is to glimpse order and unity but to find and live in disorder and chaos'," Dr. K. droned on. "Familiar?"

"Fuckers!" Eugene let slip out. "Oh, sorry, father, I…I mean doctor. Yes, I said them at one time in my rotten existence or other, yes."

"Did *you* say them or did the critics, the experts say them about you, Eugene?" the analyst asked.

"Bastards, calling me all hours of the day and night, year in and out, hounding me I said, like I was some kind of creature in a cage like a, a, like a gorilla!" he proclaimed in amazement at himself. "Never a damned minute to myself. And what the hell did they care in the end? I was all washed up, the shaking old man, the has-been. Why, I should have poked all their eyes out, rotten, rotten. . .," Eugene complained with bitterness.

"But were those things true, those statements that you wrote or that *they* said in examining your work?" Dr. K. wanted to know.

"Nah, it just sounded good, like it was ultra-important, you know, it sells tickets!" Eugene explained.

"Nonsense!" the doctor yelled. "You believed it all. Admit it, Eugene! You came up with those things because that was the best guess you had and you needed something to hold on to for dear life, right?" he demanded.

"Yeah, you got me there, doc. You're too sharp for me," Eugene conceded.

"I am going to exhibit to you in the mine why and how every one of those things is false, Eugene," he added. "Just wait."

"You see, doc, life never made any sense to me. Right from the start, my mother's crooked eyes and my father's crooked smile and blarney. I never really believed him but I was desperate to have peace and quiet inside me and to understand how life goes, especially when it falls of the tracks," Eugene said. "I was at the end of the road for explanations, so I forged some and got to hoping that they were correct but I never intentionally tried to lie about it, doctor," he lamented. "It all sort of soothed me somehow. God damn it, I had a right to sleep at night, you know!" he said defiantly. "I mean, figure it out, a baby dies, the mother dies in childbirth, the father-husband is suddenly alone heartbroken and maybe even *he* wants to die over it. Where's the sense in this? Where's God now?"

I am thinking of just such a case, Eugene," the doctor said. "It is the Sweeny family in New Jersey, 1906, it was and the baby, Welther Yorke Sweeney died May 24, 1906 and her mother the next day. A huge grave stone is still there in the Washington Boro Cemetery. The husband's name, although carved in, has no dates. He never had that monument completed. So, there you go...heartbreak!" related Dr. Kornschucher sadly to a rapt listener.

"That's what I say. How can such a thing make sense? How can there be any serious human relations with God on earth, salvation, redemption, with *that* kind of aberration?" he asked bitterly.

"Aberration is incorrect, Eugene," replied the doctor. "But your state of emotions have always set you up to see it that way. Really, it is part of the mystery of God that is beyond man's ken," he assured Eugene. "Man is chronically abused as a child in all cultures although the world is usually blind to it and it is ordinarily very subtle. *That* is what is behind the invention of religious stories, which are taken as literal and absolute but which are either just histories or metaphors. Beyond stories are such painful episodes as the Inquisition in Spain, some of the Crusades and various jihads."

"1906! That is the year that I went to Princeton," Eugene recalled out loud.

"Yes," replied the doctor. "1906 was the year of the mess, the little mess for Mr. O'Neill but a big one for Mr. Sweeny."

"God almighty, doctor, I am so sorry, sorry to myself, sorry to you, sorry to the whole of mankind. I have been a drunken, selfish fool and a big mouth and here, I get prizes for that! It's a scandal! That's what it is, a damned scandal!"

"You kind of tried your best, Eugene, considering how damaged you were, that and hardened," said the analyst.

"Yes, but I hurt Carlotta. Also, I tried to force Agnes, tried to drag her by her hair. I get a little drink in me and I get vindictive, well, I did anyway," admitted Eugene. "The unholiness just used to spew out of me!"

"You harmed and damaged your children, too, and many others. Still you were made into a god, the great playwright magician," said the doctor.

"Yeah, a real big deal I was! But just look at me in that Boston hotel room begging for death! Some god, huh, doc?" he lamented sadly. "I was always in a bind inside myself, distracted all the time, never felt alive or right except maybe times like that in Argentina, on the way I mean, with the sails and the foam and the sea and that secret, becoming the 'secret'. They all swooned over that, the miserable, shallow, self-serving, dishonest bastards, the world, I hate *it*, too!"

"But *now*, Eugene, *I* have got you and I do not make dumplings out of souls sent to me by the 'Boss'. I make whole people out of them. That is what you never were except for maybe a few days after you were born, until they got a hold of your poor, little heart and ground it down mercilessly," the analyst remarked, comforting Eugene.

O'Neill nodded.

"Back to babyhood we go," exclaimed the doc, excitedly.

"You mean that you are going to make me into an infant again?" said the worried Eugene. "I couldn't stand to relive that whole thing, please, doc, don't do that to me!"

"It's back to babyhood *purity*, my boy. Don't vorry," he counseled him. "Now, you have had formal psychoanalysis in the distant past, have you not?"

"Yes, indeed, long ago, I and Agnes, my second wife, we went to a Dr. Hamilton for six weeks to try to get at the root of my drinking," he replied.

"Und it did the trick, Ja?" asked the doctor. "You gave it up?"

"Doc, I thought you already knew everything about me, that I *did* that but I also fell off the wagon a few times along the way. But, it was the *fear* that got me to give up booze, not any effects of analysis," said an irritated Eugene. "Fear that my brains would turn to, what did he call it, oh, egg whites!"

"Und you ver afraid that you would not be able to write anymore, Ja?" asked the analyst.

"That's it!" cried Eugene.

"So, that was a kind of desperation, Ja?" he continued. "Dead in the water without your obsession, the pen and paper, Ja?"

"Ah, dead in the water," replied Eugene. "How many times have I wished for that? If only you knew!"

"Oh, but I *do*," responded the doctor. "I know all too well. But honestly, boy, you had a conviction that through endless writing, year after year, you'd get to the bottom of your agony somehow, see it all in a clear light, so that you could *forgive* them and *forget* the horrors, Ja?"

"It's true, I did believe that, that there would be blessed relief, insights, and all that," Eugene said.

"You did not do it for *ego* however, because the prizes meant very little to you, ist that right?" he wondered aloud.

Eugene pondered this bitter subject but did not answer.

"Now, a Dr. Bisch, a psychiatrist friend of yours, you asked him about whether analysis was any good and he told you that it *did* help people, not so, Eugene?" Dr. K. asked him.

"Sounds familiar," he answered. "But a lot of my friends were concerned that going to a shrink would damage my drama talent, ruin it, crimp my artistic abilities."

"But you vent anyway, so?" asked the analyst.

"Yes, again, six weeks and it was paid for by somebody else. I forget who," he admitted, thinking of his own cheap father.

"Und did you know that Dr. Bisch's opinion was that you had too strong an ego to be much helped and that that was par for shy people like you. He also said that you were emotionally starved and that you were antagonistic against your mother. I guess we have seen that here already, huh?" asked Dr. K.

"Yeah," was the reply.

"You loved your father who was sort of an escapist, just like you were with writing," relayed the doctor. "Und that you imitated his alcoholism."

"Uh-huh," said Eugene resignedly.

"Brace yourself, Eugene, because I asked you before about your feelings towards your father, about if you were attracted to him physically, and now comes Dr. Bisch who gives the opinion that you indeed had an *unconscious* homosexual attraction to him and that it carried over to some of your male friends," exclaimed the doctor.

"Gee," said Eugene. "I don't know about him thinking that!" quickly covering himself.

"It does not matter now. Forget it, Eugene," he was assured. "Dr. Bisch said that you hated all women and wanted them punished because of the influence of your mother," the doctor went on. "Is this so, Eugene?"

"Maybe," he replied. "I am not so sure anymore…I…I," his voice trailing off.

"The analyst that treated you saw a *death wish*. Funny topic to come up *now*, huh, Eugene?" he relayed seeming amused.

"Quite drole," was the quick reply.

"I know, my boy, that you are tense with the idea of never getting out of here, so let's move on. Let us speak about the Oedipus complex idea that, I believe, came up back then," lectured Dr. K.

"Do we have to, doc?" Eugene whined. "Isn't that too far past?" he wondered out loud, trying to get past it.

"Yes, the *past*, but so very connected to you getting a reversal, my boy. Now I vonder if there ever was such a complex for you, after all Oedipus is love for the mother and a death posture against the father, no?" he said. "When do we get," Eugene asked impatiently, "to the diamonds part?" like a little kid wanting to know about Christmas treats.

"Soon, my boy, soon, und before you know it, it vill all be over, Ja! It takes only one day, Javol!" the analyst proclaimed authoritatively.

"Gee, so quick?" an astonished Eugene asked.

"Vell, you vont be encouraged to ask questions in that mine, just to listen to me und watch und learn," he remarked. "That *mystery* that you pointed to, that thing, not the true nature of God but the mystery of the dense wackiness of life and people, the seemingly cruel parts, those will become crystal clear. All the stuff that you wrangled over for a lifetime looking for the *answers* vill suddenly *leap out* at you, Eugene, und knock you over," Dr. K. assured him.

A bright light seemed to pass into Eugene's happier face.

"Then when you have learned nearly all of it, minus the parts that vill come when you confront as I told you, only *then* could the world regard you as *another* type of epitome, not that of the ruined child, but of what can be *undone!* The astoundingly complex fakery bakery that you started and built up vill be all smashed to bits and fall down und a green, sturdy, hardy tree of

Eugene vill sprout up mightily in its place!" announced the good doctor.

"I like the sound of that!" exclaimed the mesmerized patient.

"Ja, under your new calling card will say: 'no more pipe dreams, folks, now it's chase that pain and grieve it'!" Dr. K. told an amazed Eugene who wondered if he liked the sound of *this* part.

"Right now, Eugene, you are a crooked fuck!" exclaimed the high pitched voice of Dr. Kornschucher. "Und I am sorry to be so strident und pointed, but at this juncture, at the very edge of you leaving your misery, it has to be all summed up in a way that you'll remember forever."

"God!" rasped the tiny voice.

"You *are* crooked, you know, except for maybe admitting truthfully that the analyst did *not* cure you of drinking, that fear did it all. Other than *that*," the doctor said, "you are as crooked as a stick! But ven all done und said, in that mine, such a ting vill be untinakable, Ja? Und every new day that comes, it vill be dimmer und dimmer!"

"Imagine!" cried Eugene.

"Von ting I forgot, Eugene. I vonted to ask you about something that critics used to say about your work, especially that last play, *Long Day's* whatever; it seems that the experts saw that work as your, and I really have to wonder about them, your *greatest victory* because of that, here we go again, *perfect understanding* and *camaraderie* that you developed for your domineering father and Jamie, that sometimes unfriendly brother of yours. They used to put it that that achievement by you transcended your own selfish feelings and emotions. Also, I saw it that your plays show mankind's struggle to *control* his emotions, Ja?" the good doctor wondered.

"Y-yes?" answered Eugene.

"Did you really feel such a ting and really advise that such an idea as control of emotions was positive?" asked the analyst, already ready for his next pounce.

Eugene was afraid to answer because he knew that he was being set up.

"Vell, let me say to you, Eugene, that it is a lot of schnitzel in the garbage this! Ve already put away the *perfect understanding* part, Ja? But that 'selfish emotions' part bugs me. Didn't you, weren't *you* the one who said that emotions were instinctive and the truth goes deep down and that *that truth* reaches a body through his or her emotions?" Dr. K. inquired deeply.

"Sounds like me, yes," still wary.

"So if this is true, why would anybody want to *control* that avenue to the truth, those emotions and instincts? Und also, vot is 'selfish emotions' and ist this different from the kind *you* were referring to?" was the next kicker question.

Eugene allowed that he was off base on a few things and that the experts and critics often had no idea what they were talking about.

"Anyway, my boy, you see the mountains of crap that punctuate the Earth? Had you had the wisdom that I am about to impart to you, say in 1939 and 1940, during the creation of that play or when you were actually living the events on Pequot Avenue that are that play, then you could have called it *Long Day's Journey Into Light* instead!" he observed as Eugene's eyes bristled.

Then Eugene stood up and growled. "How do you know about that play? It was not staged or published as per my say so!"

"Vell," said the good doctor, not wanting to upset his charge any more than was needed. "I, uh, here in Limbo, ve know everything, Ja? Its content is known." O'Neill seemed to buy this explanation and sat back down in his air chair.

Then the analyst showed Eugene that all he had to do was to take the initials for New London, N. L., and instead of using the "N" for 'Night', use the "L" for 'Light'. No one was amused and the doctor felt very stupid for that silly junk. It was a patent distraction and did not really help.

The analyst tried to right himself by rapidly moving on. "Let's speak of revelation," he insisted. "In that play, you have a brother to brother situation, you and Jamie, only you were called 'Edmund' there, anyway, Eugene, you craft that part to show a confession by your brother to you about how he hated you and was so jealous of you that he led you down the road to destruction. He was ten years your senior and ought to have been looking out for you but he did the opposite, Ja?"

"He used to take me to the whorehouses on Bradley Street. He used to get me into boozing. I guess he was doing something but it seemed just like two brothers having a wild time," he replied.

"Vell, vether ja oder nein, in the play, he confesses that his intent was evil and to bring you down, nicht wahr?"

"Yes," said Eugene. "I was papa's pet and mama's baby and he hated that!"

"So, *understanding* why Jamie did that, that helped you?" asked Dr. K.

"Of course," replied Eugene. "It made his general meanness suddenly open to me so that I could rise above it and its effects and see it for what it really was, you know, not from the same level that pulls you in."

"Und mit your vater, the same?" Dr. K. inquired.

"Well, with papa, it was different. He reveals to me in the play that his lifelong tightness with money, a thing that I railed against and Jamie did, too, and we hated him for it, was grounded in his own family history. So was his theatricality all the time. Hearing the reasons for these awful things that plagued us for decades led us to a final understanding of it."

"Ja, but no healing, Eugene," Dr. K. insisted. "Damages done by parental abuse and neglect to a child is not removed by any amounts of understanding. That just paves the way for the healing that comes with recovery grieving, Ja? You know dis, Ja?"

"Ja!" Eugene said, then caught himself. "Yes, I mean."

"You ver moved by the father's confessions but not healed, you see?" he asked.

"By the vay, Eugene, if Jamie had led you to those awful things when you ver an adult only and you vent along mit it, that shows that you ver damaged already, Ja?" Eugene merely gazed at him. "If you ver a whole person, you would not be so led, you see?" he said. Eugene nodded assent.

"Now, *forgiveness*," said the analyst. "That's OK. You *can* forgive a wrong done to you, especially if you became aware of it's reasons, and *this* without prior healing or grief-work. However," he went on, "it could be *enabling* and it could encourage further transgression, you see?" Again, O'Neill understood. "I forgave Jamie's awful, evil cynicism because I understood it, the underlying roots, yes? But the damage that it did to me when I was a kid, that's not so easy to remove, doctor?" he asked.   "It did, vat it did vas, vell, it continues the abuse and abusive atmosphere there in the home that your parents created," Dr. K. stated. "The real damage done to you by Jamie was to lead you down the boozing and whoring path. Anyway, he was not your parent. With parents, it's different."

"I could have been in church praying, right?" Eugene quipped but the doctor did not appreciate the humor and making light of this.

"You prevailed anyway...in the play, I mean," Dr. K. replied. "You rose above and saw. You were the idealist while your brother just evil and self-dealing from desperation, Ja?"

"True," spoke Eugene in a faraway tone.

"You transcended, Ja?" he asked. "You had illumination, Ja?" he continued. "You were destined to see and see again beyond those illusions that were a matrix. Your recitation to the father Tyrone about the sea and the secret and the lifting of the fog and becoming that secret if only for the second before the hand allows the veil to fall again, that is real stuff, Eugene, you see dis now?"

Eugene's eyes were alighted.

"However, my boy, that is only momentary clarity. It was and will be always blocked by the trance that child mistreatment creates. Only the grief-work recovery can lift that veil forever," assured the analyst.

"Birth of a soul is how I phrased it," the playwright replied.

"I'm sure it felt like that, Eugene. Imagine that all the time!" the doctor wondered aloud.

"Yeah. It never sticks around, does it?"

"It can, my boy, you will find out," he replied to an eager patient. "But zis reminds me. In that play, you are pulled closer to the father because *he* reveals a similar experience but then claims that he forgot about it. How is such a thing possible?" Dr. K. asked. "When you see an angel, you never forget!" This made Eugene suspect that perhaps the old man had made it up in the play but then, he himself wrote the damned thing!

"The Tyrone father never came back to that. He took a path awayfrom such an experience, he wandered away from possible heaven," Eugene recalled wondering out loud. "Gee, hmmmm," Dr. Korschucher mused. "When you wrote *"Long Day's Journey Into Night"*, it was around 1940, Ja? Und you ver fifty- two years old, Ja? Und so, at zis age, you wrote it and only *then* came up mit der understanding of everybody so as to relieve bitterness and find forgiveness, Eugene?"

"Uh…," Eugene replied thinking about it.

"But something is wrong here. If these excuses or explanations by your real father and brother came to you in real life around 1912, the time period of that play, why did it take you until 1940 to find relief? Were these things in your memory the whole time but not acted on emotionally?" asked Dr. K.

"The play is fiction, doctor and a lot of it is made up to demonstrate the truth of what that home was like on Pequot Avenue in New London." he answered.

"But these feelings of forgiveness and illumination and so forth, these had never come to you until around 1940, Ja?" he countered.

"Yes, because I had never faced it all until I wrote that thing, you see?" Eugene assured him.

Doctor K. then asked him. "Is it not so that in most or all of your big work up to about 1931, you were always searching, searching, searching in one way or another for some secret hidden over there?"

"True," replied the playwright seeming far away in his thoughts.

"Und, did you not say along the way that there could be 'truth' in other formulas, not just your own, and that any other life-giving one could be as proper as any other one?" Eugene was queried.

"Sure, doc, that secret to happiness and that perfection of beauty hidden over there beyond the horizon, beyond my and man's view, that is just *my* vi-sion," Eugene announced complyingly.

"Keep zis in ze front of your brain, my boy, for ve are about to enter a thing that will make those words ring!" Dr. K. said in a loud way. "Und, it vill go hand und hand mit your digging at the roots of sickness in society." Eugene's eyes twinkled.

Then Eugene realized that Dr. K. had talked at length about *Long Day's Journey Into Night* and asked him loads of stuff on it, so why was he just *now* seeing that the analyst knew about an unpublished work. Was he that out of it? Or was it because he was dead and not too sharp? He decided to put it all out of his head in the interests of getting the hell out of that colorless place. Of course, he could not know that a very short while after he died, his widow defied the instructions and had the thing published and that it was, indeed staged after that.

The doctor stood up and his mouth took on a kind of a stitching across it so that it looked sewn closed. His brow was furled and visage stern but not displeased. He took Eugene by the nape of the neck, symbolically, and stood him up. The analyst's gaze was far off and he began to slowly trudge back-wards. The two of them then glided along Limbo's luminescence for maybe one hundred yards when the doctor turned to him and demanded that he shut his eyes tightly. Eugene was breathing hard from anticipation mixed with some dread. He dared not defy. It was sort of like the man or woman hauled before a judge for an offense for the first time ever. They do, say, stand, posture, think any way that is demanded of them or expected or even just imagined. It is the ultimate child-like behavior but it is *not* innocent.

With peepers closed, Eugene suddenly felt a whooshing sensation and a spinning but it did not disorient him or make him feel sick. After only sec-onds, it stopped and the voice of his companion took on the helium sound as it announced the black cave that lay before them.

Eugene opened his eyes and right away saw right there in front of him a low, broad arch of a cave, maybe twenty feet across at the base and only about seven feet high. A rather bright light or glowing was coming from that place and it beckoned him.

The doctor paused for a moment, looked over into Eugene's brilliant eyes, saw the Christmas morning beaming in his face, and they proceeding into the cave together. It was like a bride and a groom striding into the unknown or a father and son entering the deep forest for the first time.

Immediately it was apparent that the cave was moderately deep, circular or oblong and seemed to have small rooms or niches as it went around. The first one was to the right and the rest evenly spaced in that roundness. The walls looked dark and Eugene thought that they had to be kimberlite.

"What is about to be given to you, Eugene, is about the behavior of human beings the thing that you've long labored over," instructed the doctor. "It is comprised of knowledge that everyone is privy to but almost nobody sees. The essence of this wisdom is usually kept out of grasp by a kind of blindness that is put upon babies after they are about two days old or so and it is held there against them by one device or another until they come to the ends of their lives," he went on. "And I repeat that it is limited to *nonorganic disorders*."

The two figures entered the second niche on the right and Eugene saw that it was about five felt deep and also rounded. In the center was a crystal table, very small and two matching chairs that sparkled.

"Sit here," commanded the doctor and Eugene obeyed. He put his arms up onto the little platform but quickly snatched them off not knowing if he was out of order.

"It's alright," assured Dr. Kornschucher. "Make yourself comfortable." Then, he disappeared for a minute. Alone, Eugene began rubbing his eyes as if to make sure that this was not some dream. The doctor returned quickly bearing a black cloth-covered plate that bore a bright four-carat diamond.

"Pick it up," the doctor told him. "Feel it!"

Eugene did that and could hold its heaviness. He quickly put it back down on the black cloth like a little boy caught at something.

Then the analyst told him. "Etched on this stone is the first message, my boy and I will read it to you." He picked it up and used a magnifying glass that he got from his pocket. It read:

THE ORIGINAL LIE
The baby idolizes its parents by instinct.
When *they* are the source of pain and turmoil,
The child's second instinct rises up, the instinct to flee.
However, that is blocked by the necessity of its circumstances.
It is helpless.

Eugene's eyes twinkled as if he had just been told that he was getting a new bicycle for the holidays but that it had been accidentally run over by a car in the driveway.

"Do you comprehend this?" queried the doctor and the answer was that he did.

"The first instinct is put there by nature. The baby depends on its mother and father for everything, food, shelter, company, attention, self-esteem, stimulation and so forth," relayed the analyst. "But when those parents hurt the child, be it physically, emotionally, dishonest emotional doings, or ignore that baby or neglect it or abandon it, the infant *panics* and becomes desperate for relief and wants to obey that second calling, to wit: to run away."

Eugene listened attentively as the doctor went on. "That baby, under the urgent need to flee, is *frustrated* by his inability to so do."

"Frustrated," Eugene said out loud as if he were hearing the word for the first time.

"It is blocked," continued the speaker, "because it *cannot flee*. It cannot even walk or crawl away. He is *trapped*!" declared the analyst to an astonished listener. "Trapped," said Eugene who seemed to be shocked. "Trapped!" he shouted and then covered his mouth. "Oh, my God! Oh, my God!" he cried out and slumped onto the table and diamond sobbing heavily.

"From this awful state of affairs," the doctor continued, knowing that Eugene could hear him. "The baby *learns that he does not matter*, and this *untruth* sticks with him the rest of his life. It is a *gross lie*! The baby *does* matter. *This*, Eugene, is *the original lie*."

O'Neill had stopped crying and was looking up at the doctor like he was some type of a god, the very label that was put on Eugene long ago by the star-stricken public.

"The terrible feeling in that child that it is *defective* grows out of this *conflict*, this *clash* of those two basic infantile instincts," the analyst lectured. "That is the *first part*. I think about your creation moon for the misbegotten, Eugene, and its portrayal of an alleged 'self-contradictory' nature of mankind."

"The *second part*," he went on, "goes like this: a baby faced with such an awful emotional or physical ordeal, day after day, soon cannot tolerate it. It is just too upsetting and painful to endure turmoil and hurting caused by the *ones that he loves*. So, the fleeing that is required to escape intolerable pain is not a physical departure, but a feelings-fleeing, a journey out of the child's *vulnera- bilities* and feelings into his *cerebralizing* part, his *head*!"

Eugene could not believe his ears!

"You and your brothers had parents that were alcoholic and drug users.

They knew how to put on a different face at every turn so that you never quite knew which face was lurking around the next corner. Was it cranky, kind, mushy, severe or what?" Dr. K. postulated. "This mercurial home-life taught you two that you could *never trust your senses* and it produced *shifty* children."

You could tell that Eugene was astonished, not so much at this kind of message, but more at the obviousness of it. It had been there all along, but his tries at unraveling that goo bandages were stymied by the goo in his eyes!

Continuing to detail the lesson, Doctor K. said, "That baby now in its own head exclusively for safety learns in time to cerebralize its way into or out of anything and everything. It is living in another world of numbness and no vulnerability. Do you grasp this?" he asked.

"Certainly. It is a foreign concept bitter for certain, but I do see it" he said. "Now, Eugene, this *second part,* this way of being, is the *ultimate life lie.* It is the *offspring* of *the original lie,*" he continued. "And those parents are *forcing* their own baby to *live a lie!*" his voice cracking a little from emotion. "As a result, the child learns and *believes, falsely,* that he can think his way out of anything and this kind of thing is behind most of the trouble in the world although nobody sees it," he went on. "People get so that they believe that they can *change something* just by *deciding.*"

"Sounds like you are on to something there, sounds like *me* actually!" Eugene proclaimed, not afraid anymore.

"Exactly," cried the doctor. "And a person who is aggressive and bold might be instructed to not be so much like that and to be more modest. This is nonsense! He did not get aggressive and bold by just deciding and he cannot escape it that way either!"

Eugene was like a fascinated school child. He stayed silent.

"Now the way that such a person *can* become more modest will be revealed to you in due course," the doctor said assuringly. Eugene was patient.

"Now, one thing, I must explain what the source is of such parental mistreatment of children, Eugene," he stated. "Parental wrongdoing can have several roots. Among them are *mental illness*, which by the way is what evil is and nothing more! Next are the scourges of emotional illness, be they organic or induced by the parents' own parents when *they* were babies. Included are neuroses, addictions and false behavior or roleplaying. Then there are *accidents*, which rob the child of a parent by death or disability. Illness can do the same thing."

Eugene asked the doctor if he could take a small break and the answer was "yes".

After a quick breather, the lecture was off and running again. "Now, Eugene," Doctor K. went on, "all of your past talk about life's frustrations, what which prevents the realization of the human impulse as you put it, the turning of the ideal into cynicism, where faith becomes skepticism, love evolves into hatred or smothering possessiveness and the urge to create is turned towards destruction, all of this, Eugene, is a mere *substitute* for what that baby encountered and could not flee from. It became emotionally warped from it. It got *confounded* and *enraged!*"

"That was *I*?" he replied.

"That was you," the doctor assured him, "bent out of shape and angry, bitter, forced to swallow that pain and turmoil and selfishness for years and years. You could not stand it. No one could, not at such a tender age. You fled into your head as a result and you stayed there until you died. You escaped from your feelings, not in the rage sense but in the vulnerability one."

"Vulnerability," Eugene mouthed quietly. "Very compelling theory, doc!"

"It is *not* a theory!" he countered angrily as if attacked.

"Yes, I was like that for sure," Eugene said, trying to smooth over the ruffled feathers. "*I* was mad all the time, sad, puzzled and angry at God."

"Yes, Eugene, the analyst continued. "There is that rage in there, like the thing you told me about with trying to drag Agnes by the hair. That was a *tantrum* and although Agnes was innocent as a target, *the rage itself was rightful!*"

Eugene was taken with that statement and wondered if he had heard correctly.

"Rightful?" he asked.

"Of course!" cried the doctor. "What they did to you was outrageous and it lived inside you always!" "And whenever I drank, doctor, it really poured out!" he remarked. "That kind of irrational behavior directly matches the irrationality to receiving pain and turmoil and upset from the very ones that you love by instinct!" the analyst assured Eugene. "And the notion so often portrayed by you in your plays about man being *trapped* by life's circumstances is another *irrational idea* and it comes directly from the baby having been trapped with the abusive and neglectful mother and father. Your ideas on this subject are the offspring of being *trapped* with James and Ella O'Neill for so many years."

A look of absolute astonishment graced the face of Eugene and he shook his head in disbelief at the simplicity of this point. A grand smile crossed his lips, too. "*Man* is not trapped, Eugene, and that is *tantrum thinking*. Oh, he might be robbed of a life by lightning or diseases, but it does not lead to untrue thinking and seeing of the world. Only mental illness can do that except for *the original lie* and that offspring I told you about," Doctor K. went on to say.

"I guess you are right," he admitted in a somewhat bewildered tone. "Maybe I was not entitled to those prizes, the Nobel and all," he lamented quietly.

"Mice," said the doctor not hearing what Eugene had just said, "are not trapped, do not commit suicide by leaping off of bridges. If they did, who would see them anyway?" he laughed. "This is in spite of the fact that mice are 'trapped' in a world of vicious cats."

"Now *that is* funny," replied Eugene snickering.

"They are not depressed, Eugene…imagine it!" he went on. "They live their lives gladly and they accept the world the way that it ist. Recall that Sweeny grave, Eugene?"

"Yeah, that's just how life is, right?" he answered matter of factly.

"Javol! No Satan. He is just a metaphor anyway, my boy. No God in control of everyday events! Nor is there any such thing as 'fate' or 'predestination'," he insisted to an attentive listener who did not know what to expect next.

"Is this idea not in conformity with the Greek or Shakespearean view of a moral universe where justice eventually prevails and where mankind was part of a homogenous world that he should not be in opposition to? Didn't such opposition cause his destruction? I think that the characters in some of your plays, Eugene, were confronted by a chasm between themselves and the world. They tried to close that by assertion of pagan continuities in line with Nieztsche or holistic schematics in politics or religion and the like," Dr. K. told him.

"This is very familiar stuff, doctor," he replied. "Very much my work, yes."

"And the reason that you saw mankind as trapped and life as frustrating to the point of rubbing out the ideals we spoke of was because *you were in your head*, a lifelong panic of sorts, desperate to have the rottenness of it all make simple sense so that you could save your imagined 'sanity'," he asserted authoritatively.

Eugene nodded his comprehension.

"You did not see things straight. On top of that, the rage and anger made you stridently cerebral, almost as an act of *spite*. An extremely common example is that old 'mad at God' proclamation of yours!" he said. "Why it's practically paranoid in the delusion of grandeur sense, you see, my boy?"

"It was part of a tantrum, right?" Eugene asked proudly as if he had learned it.

"Indeed!" exclaimed the analyst. "Mad at God is rage-based conduct of very aggressive proportions. It's spiteful for certain. But, you realize, Eugene, that intelligence has nothing to do with any of this. It can strike at any level of brains and respects no degrees of smarts," Doctor K. lectured so that he wouldn't attribute such things to dodo birds or dummies only.

"What I never got, not ever, in my long nights on Pequot Avenue or in some seedy hotel in Providence on the road with my parents on tour, was to be wanted by them *unconditionally*," he cried out. It seemed like the first time he ever faced it. Eugene felt betrayed by them.

"Now, that rage and anger is usually not directed onto the misbehaving parents because it could risk greater mistreatment *and* the 'peace' is needed to be preserved in case they make a turnaround and see the light," replied the analyst. "And the one exception might be at holiday get-togethers where drinking is at hand and the step- mother is kicked or the sibling wrenched from a chair or a fist fight with the father breaks out. Other than that, that rage is usually misdirected to 'substitutes' like homosexuals or the police or women or false blame is projected such as 'that damned play'!" the doctor went on. "Being 'trapped' is one, 'rotten reality' is another. Attacks on Blacks or Jews or Gypsies are others."

"That's too common to, er, I mean, it's *so* common and so virulent," Eugene said.

"It can even be directed against oneself," the doctor pointed out. "Like in wrist cutting or banging the head against the wall."

"Und people under the spell of rage can be irritated all the time, fly off the handle at the slightest thing!" he added. "Then, there's shaming others as in yelling obscenities out the car window. It becomes a way of life and carried like a habit. Then there is spite. You know all too well about that, Eugene."

"Actually, alcohol was my big worry and demon, doc," he replied.

"Sure, and tobacco. Right? Sometimes, substances are used like those not only to relieve 'pain', they are also indulged in as an act of defiance and self-destruction. In *your* case, you wrote about the alcoholic life as a parallel to the fate of mankind, recall?" he queried.

"Did we already go over this, doctor because it sounds so familiar?" Eugene complained. "I thought I already discussed the life of disappointment of

hopes to escape or rise above present reality and the painful realities of dissipation, death and self-destruction, all the alcoholic's fate and man's as well."

"Vell, if ve *did*, you can revisit the idea and see *again* that it is baloney,
Eugene. This first diamond contains the proof of that, Ja?" he insisted. "It is
rage-based, anger-induced, warped, desperate and very personal to you," Dr.
K. said.

"I guess," was all Eugene could say.

"Disappointments in life all come with the territory as does death and
none of it is in any way a problem of children born to whole parents, absent
intervening factors like parental death or diseases. This vas *you*, Eugene, vat
you never got ist vat I mean," the analyst went on.

"My view was crazy, huh?" he asked without wanting the answer.

"Certainly, my boy. Disappointments in life, of one's hopes and dreams or
wishes have *no connection whatsoever* with self-destruction and dissipation.
Und death," he continued, "although not a picnic on a beach, ist nonetheless
a vital and natural part of life that *we cannot do without* and only the child
of the *original lie* cannot see it, face it because he is still digging in his heels.
That's why they rail against getting old."

"Getting old?" Eugene asked.

"Ja, they fear it because they know deep down inside that there is unfinished emotional business. Also ist the eternal hope, while they remain alive,
that those bad parents will turn it all around. Then there ist the idea that
they have not had any fun yet and they dearly desire to have some but they
never can because of the internal distractions," droned the analyst. "They feel
cheated and must *die*, too."

"Gosh, doctor, I never looked at it like that," he admitted.

"The parents were *emotionally unavailable* to you and you were *glued to
them* nonetheless. It's torment!" cried the expert. "Und such unfinished business lives in a *secret hope* that somehow, sometime, somewhere, you will be
forced back into your feelings from your head, the cerebralization life, the
same way that you were forced out!"

"Did we already talk about this, because I am remembering the Outward
Bound theory where troubled persons, usually youths, are involved in certain
outdoor activities that force them into their vulnerabilities, teach them to
trust again and so forth. Did we?" Eugene wondered aloud.

"Uh, ze program that you mention works with victims of the original
lie and the ultimate life lie, Javol, Eugene," he replied. "Vat these kids had to
give up of themselves to survive is *reclaimed* in zat program, Ja? Und so, lives

of lying, stealing, distortion, denial, aggression and rationalization, restored to by kids who experience an interruption in their natural instincts, can be turned around with that principle idea und at is vat we are doing here only you are dead already und so, your reversal vould be intellectually based und not emotionally based the vay it would if you were still alive und kicking, Ja?" he said.

"This is really very amazing stuff, doctor!" Eugene proclaimed in amazement.

"Ja, I know dis, my boy. Now, parental inconsistency, vat we expect in all households of that original lie, make a child doubt his own perceptions while abuse and neglect make him doubt his own worth, you see dis?" he added.

"Do these things cause chaos in the child?" he wondered.

"Ja, in that kinder und in the grown up too, und he never has any fun, never really trusts in an adult way, only a juvenile way, always feels alone or worried about being abandoned by his wife, girlfriend, what have you," the doctor said.

"Boy, I am learning a lot here, gee…," a smiling Eugene said.

"Listen!" the doctor jumped in. "That idea of forcing somebody back into their feelings ve ver speaking about? Ja, this is vat I forgot, Eugene: ven ve do zat, zat person feels everything und it hurts terribly! I vonted to tell you zat this hurting is *legitimate suffering* und zat the 'suffering' that vas felt before vas *not* legitimate because he or she vas in his or her head and the hurting then ist only neurosis hurting, like morbid depression, morbid anxiety, und so forth."

"Morbid?" Eugene asked.

"Ja, morbid," the doctor instructed him. "It is morbid because it is *irrational* and not warranted by the circumstances. So, ve have a man who is *depressed* but he has no event to be depressed about, you see? Or ve got a woman who ist obsessed about something but there is no reason for zis. It is morbid obsession und not appropriate obsession like mit ein new girlfriend, Ja? If your dog gets run over, *that* is a reason to be down, depressed, but when you are down for no reason, that is morbid depression."

"Like *my* life, right, doc?" he asked.

"Of course, Eugene, how could you escape it? You cannot! Und that state of mind followed you right up to that Boston hotel in the end ven you ver weeping for death und so miserable instead of dying in peace after a long life of fulfillment!" the doctor observed. "Und so, you uttered those rememberable words zat ve referred to a while back, Ja?"

"Ja! . . . I mean, yeah, doctor. I was at the end of my rope and just wanted it to be over. Same in 1912, so long before that…amazing to think of it now," he said. "It seemed to me in the end that I'd been as unhappy and puzzled over life as ever and that death would be that ultimate bottle for me. But, it would not come! I couldn't get that bottle open!"

"Yes," replied the analyst. "You and the critics were so very fond of saying that you were a little bit in love with death, isn't that so, Eugene?"

"Bastards!" he yelled. "I hated them all, always grubbing and prodding me and provoking me, a selfish bunch of idiots!"

"Yes?" answered the doctor.

"Oh, Carlotta, she put up with the impossible me, God save her. I feel so ashamed of it. She was a brave soul but had her own idiosyncrasies, too I'm afraid. I was still on pills, the shakes, you know!" he declared again.

You two *used* each other. It's called *codependence*, remember that word from your travels, Eugene?" the analyst asked.

"But I treated her well, I…," said Eugene, cut off.

"You did whatever it took to hold onto her so that you would not be alone, so as to belong to someone, so as to have anybody to look after your affairs and so forth," he said.

Eugene was silent as he usually was when he heard a thing that he did not like.

Then, trying to cover over that he asked, "Doc, all that stuff about driving people into their heads and all, what does that? I was wondering if something else might do the same thing like, say, if a kid were born looking like a coyote or was a fat slob or born with a withered arm, you know?"

"Vell, in ze case of ugly, not unless the parents shamed the child. In ze case of fat slob, same thing except maybe the fat comes from an eating addiction in which case, the child is already in his head. A bad arm could provoke shaming by parents but they vould not do zat unless they ver already victims of child abuse so in zat case, the kid vill be driven anyway, you see?" answered the doctor. "But, zat is not to say he vill not be unhappy with the defect, fat or ugly or whatever. It's just that it vould not in und of itself push him out of his vulnerabilities, Ja!"

"So, they will not become drug users or alcoholics or criminals?" he asked.

"No, not solely due to zat. They vill not be jumping off any bridges with those little mice, you see," quipped the doctor. "Only the original lie and the ultimate life lie are involved in what we are concerned with, organic disorders aside."

"So a kid born into a 'whole' family but has a kisser like a frog, still can see that the Earth is spinning and not the sky?" Eugene pondered out loud.

"Clever," remarked the doctor. "But, listen, Eugene, most trouble in ze vorld ist rooted in those two things," he said, "and the unwillingness or inability to face it, grapple with it or even be aware of it. The misbehavior is a substitute in a way for that. They are in a *trance*."

"A trance," Eugene repeated carefully.

"The crooked hand that holds the baby bottle, the parental eyes that do not, cannot, meet the baby's own remain shifty in their sockets and this is the *first* message to the child that he does not matter! *Then*," continued the explanation, "the *follow up* messages of not mattering, not being worth anything, come along and usually are very *subtle*."

"Subtle, really, not smacking the child around or ...," he replied.

The doctor cut him off. "Usually not so overt, Eugene. The self-dealing parents cannot help but get their smudge on the baby. The instinct clash, though, is the biggest damage maker and it permanent unless the person undergoes a return to his feelings, usually by force!"

"That ultimate life lie, the thinking of one's way into or out of anything, that is like an acorn that drops off the tree of the original lie, right?" he asked the doctor who smiled broadly.

"You *are* very smart und very clever, Eugene, no wonder you got those awards, Ja?" the analyst replied. "So, now you see that *faking it* is not human nature, is not innate and anybody who says that it is *faking* it!"

"My God!" cried Eugene. "That's monumental!"

"People who live by falsehood, a topic that you have written about many times, Eugene, are that way, unless it is organic, because of the original lie and that *acorn*, Ja!" said the doctor. "Und what you said a long time ago, my boy, that it vould take man 1,000,000 years to grow up and to obtain a soul is just that, a falsehood, a crooked view and acorn idea."

Eugene sat quietly in deep thought about the statement.

Suddenly, Dr. K. stood up and, as if handing a long-hidden Christmas present to Eugene, proclaimed that the prospect of the original lie, its effect on children and society and mankind in general, and the notion of its abolition thru grief-work as he'd described all this to him, just might be *the* secret of life, the vision and dream of beauty and perfection hidden *beyond the horizon* that O'Neill had long obsessed over.

Eugene's eyes rolled back in his head. His tongue popped out and his visage took on a simultaneous cast of jealousy, despair and adoration. It was as if his countenance had been reforged in a crucible!

"Pick up the diamond, Eugene, und put it in your shirt pocket," ordered the analyst and Eugene obeyed with delight on his face!

A short time later, he came back into the room with another stone on that plate and he laid it down before a bedazzled Eugene. He was told it was six carats. Doctor Kornschucher read the etched words on it:

SUBSTITUTIONS

Children forced out of their feelings and into their heads grow up to have substitutions for any real identity, real suffering and real pleasure. They are in a kind of a *trance* state.

"Now Eugene," instructed the analyst, "this part is extremely important, critical even, and I want you to pay close attention," the doctor's eyes wide as saucers. "You cannot get a reversal without it!"

"Can't wait," assured Eugene.

"These substitutions are possible only because, as the diamond says, the person is in a *trance*, living in a diminished level of consciousness, less aware than the whole person, and *all* of his conduct of substitutions, false behavior, is facilitated by a conscious deficit and a conscience deficit as well. Things do not bother him or his conscience as they would a normal man. The childhood abuse and neglect are the cause of such *numbness* and *blindness*. The obvious cannot be seen!" insisted the doctor.

"Gosh, doc, numb *and* blind, what's left?" Eugene said thinking of the worst drunk he'd ever been on.

"Just look at the wisdom etched in the *first* diamond. Is it not as easy to see or grasp or maybe even stumble upon in everyday life, yet who does see it?" Dr. K. said.

"*I* never did," admitted Eugene, "or ever read about it even".

"Eugene, have you ever heard the words to the song 'Amazing Grace'?" he asked. "Und the part that says 'I vonce vas blind but now I see'?"

"Of course," replied the patient who then caught himself in a revelation and exclaimed. "Wait! you mean that that is the same blindness that we are talking of?"

"Ja, my boy," answered the good doctor.

"Grace removes blindness?" he asked not believing the simplicity.

"Vell, not so fast, Eugene," he answered. "Grace comes when a person is whole and not fractured. The person who composed this song had to have been the latter at one time and gone thru some kind of recovery to wholeness again. Then the contrast was so great that the tune was inspired by it, you see?"

"But what is the connection between grace and blind?" he insisted.

"Blind is a symptom of abuse and neglect. When you are that, you have no grace. You have only a relief-oriented life, that is, whatever it takes to get by like drinking, drugs, lying, distortion, denial, you've heard it all, Eugene, I don't have to go through the list again?" the analyst lectured. "So ven recovery comes, blindness goes and grace descends."

"Oh, I get it," responded Eugene.

"Und now, let's get down to substitutions, Eugene, the *first* one is one of identity, Ja? Because the baby is driven into its head and remains hypervigilant to all future insults, assaults on worthiness, it never really comes to know or develop its own identity. In fact, Eugene," he went on. "It never really knows what it wants, who it is or what it feels."

"Gosh! That sounds awful. Did I go through that, doc?" he wanted to know.

"Of course, Eugene. Ella and James kept you in a box, made you into a robot and the authentic you was crouched and hidden inside terrified to come out!" said the expert. "Und if you ever get a reversal, similar to that possible in a living human through a process that I will reveal in a while, *that* is the self that will pop out and begin to grow from the point of its former hiding."

Eugene wondered to himself if this were the same idea that *he* had explored when he came up with the notion of breaking through the masks of materialism to unite with the spiritual force and discover a genuine identity?

"Like *my* genuine identity idea?" he asked figuring that the analyst in Limbo knew everything, as he said.

"You ver skirting on the edge of it, Eugene, und you said something about finding zat place vere that identity could be nourished, Ja? Und vere it could grow, nicht wahr, und that it was *impossible*?" the doctor asked.

"I did say that," Eugene replied.

"So, you admit then that identity lost or hidden or whatever, the genuine self, implies an *ingenuine* one, Ja?" asked the crafty one.

"Of course," Eugene readily admitted.

"Gut!" exclaimed the doctor. "Und now, with no real identity operating inside us, vat happens? A void is there und it needs to be filled up, Ja? So, a fake one is born!"

"Yes," said the understanding Eugene. "A fake one".

"Ja, und that is in *two* parts, Eugene, one is made up und zis ist the false role that ve vill get to und the utter is the taking on of the identity of the prison-makers, the parents!" revealed the doctor to an astonished listener.

"Yes, I am amazed at your insights, why I could have used you well in the 1930's and 1940's doctor!" Eugene said playfully.

"Now, Eugene, can you name one or more of those false roles that *you* yourself came up with and lived inside of?" he asked.

"Uh...Uh...I...," was the struggling reply.

"Think! Think, boy!" demanded the analyst. "Vat did you do to try to matter when you felt like you were worthless, when you were sure that you did not matter?"

"Well, I guess I...I...um, I tried to be important by doing the only thing that I was sure that I was good at, a real talent, *write!*" he exclaimed. "Yes, that was it. One day around 1913 when I was back in New London from New York and back at my parents' house on Pequot, I did decide that I was to once and for all become an artist, a writer or nothing at all!"

"New York, Eugene?" the doctor asked implying a correction.

"Uh, Oh! I meant Wallingford. Yes, thanks, doc!" he said thinly.

"That was the T. B. scare and all, Ja?" he inquired.

"T. B., yes, that Wallingford sanitarium," he said.

"Und, you claimed, did you not, that that disease was a punishment from God for all that you had done with your life to that point, Ja?" was the baited question. "All the whoring and the boozing and the pill episode at Jimmy the Priest's?"

"I did claim that it was punishment, yes," he admitted.

"Such an idea, Eugene, *bogus!* It's pure cerebralization and subhuman posturing! 'Subhuman' ve vill get to in a moment, you vill see it. *God* is not in control of punishment of people, Eugene. That is made up by desperate people, wallowing in guilt, trying to explain the unexplainable, you see?" instructed Dr. K.

"Similar to being mad at God," he asked, eyes turned up.

"Ja, except that *that* is not subhuman behavior, that is *superhuman*" was the reply, "Und that also is a false target, Eugene, substituted for the parents."

"Really, it is the mother and father that one ought to be mad at?" he asked.

"Javol!" said the grateful doctor, "You are seeing it now boy. Now, fake identities are never human identities, Eugene, they are *always* sub or super. Und people who go through their whole lives in one or more of these fake roles are never acting *just human*."

"Doc, you mean that I could never indulge in what human beings *naturally* do when I was little, like cry or be in need of love and comfort and understanding and allowed to explore…explore myself and my relations with my family?"

"Never!" he insisted. "Now come on, tell me what roles…yes, the great writer but what else, Eugene?"

"Let's see, I knew that I loved history, devoured tons of books from the New London Library and other places and ate up authors who were considered top notch, if I may say it that way," he continued. "I thought that I could be an expresser of ideas, dramatic ideas set in a dramatic setting, on stage."

"Und did you not ever express that you vonted to go to sea *and* be a poet?" asked the analyst.

"So, you vent to Harvard for a year to develop this talent, Ja?" he asked. "Und zen as you began to write plays, you started to get noticed, say, in New York City, Greenwich Village or on Cape Cod, Ja? Und also you eventually wrote *Desire Under the Elms* where characters make the 'force' express *them*, superhuman thinking, instead of themselves expressing the 'force', normal *human* thinking, Ja, Eugene?"

"Yeah, I did and I could really think of nothing else, doc!" he remembered.

"Und it vas an escape for you, too, Ja?" was the challenge.

"Never saw it like that," he replied. "But I had grand dreams!"

"Maybe began at the Second Story Club, Eugene?" he wondered. "Und, by the way, it's spelled 'storey' not 'story', did you know zis, Eugene?"

"Really?" Eugene asked. "But the dictionary…"

The analyst cut him off. "Even the dictionary caves in after a while, you know, a sign of weakness."

"But the dictionary is a compilation of 'use' and not only of accuracy, no?" he claimed.

"Let's get back to identities, Eugene, und by the vay, I vas just imagining you, caught up in a reversal, a delight light turned on inside you and a crying big shot enigma, the great mystery, all from the *joy of relief*!" the doctor let out. "That re-babyhood glow vill flood you, Eugene, so happy!" he grinned.

Embarrassed, Eugene grabbed onto the former inquiry about identities and said, "My role as a writer was not a false identity, was it, Dr. K. ?"

"No!" said the doctor. "It was not, but the effect of the thing, the world's applause allowed you to become a 'star' or 'hero', which is okay if you really are one, but you were not, Eugene, you grabbed at that to try to matter and *that* is why you were obsessed with the thing!" he proclaimed loudly.

"But doc, I eventually was billed as a star, so why wasn't I really one?" he wondered, his slighted face drooping.

"Because, Eugene, you were the "I can figure it all out' guy when in fact, you were faking it. We have already proved that beyond *any* doubt!" Dr. K. said."Of course, *they* believed it because they needed to believe it just like *you* did and so they all got on your wagon!"

"So my blindness and my thinking up the answers, cerebralization you called it, doctor, those were really a scandal, right?"

"Sehr gut! Eugene, you are so *brave*! You are finally getting used to the truth. Oh, ve have already come a long vay!" an excited analyst cried out.

Eugene sat there in silence but proud. However, admitting to be false was an anti-feeling, so emotional flux was at hand.

"So, when you made all sorts of claims in the plays about mankind und Gott und fate und alcohol und weakness und so forth, the people crowned you King!" the doctor went on. "But really, you were a struggling, lonely addict and ex-boozehound, Ja?"

"I was, wasn't I?" he replied sadly. "And I didn't even have the nerve or guts or whatever it takes a man inside to have a link and a bond to my own children. They were like rags to me. How would I know that two of them would catch fire in the corner from spontaneous combustion!"

"What ist that?" the startled doctor wondered.

"Well, Eugene, Jr. killed himself and Oona married a man who was thirty-six years her senior. I damn near broke my heart to see an eighteen year old girl throw her life away like that, doctor!" Eugene lamented.

"Well, anyway, Eugene, you were trying to be worth something with those plays and it made you feel like no other thing could do, Ja?" he asked rhetorically.

"I called it 'my little bit of truth', doctor, and I really thought that I had hit something that nobody else had. Certainly no one ever staged it like I did!" he stated proudly with a genuine smile.

"Und to *you* it vas truth, Ja, Eugene?" came the invite. "But even though you thought that it was sound und made sense und you *figured it out*, still, the ideas about the randomness of fate, clashes mit people, family turmoils, hypocracy in religion und morals, double standards thriving in New England, the *plea* by you for compassion in place of 'truths', the 'meaninglessness' of it all, the failures of humanity, decadent materialism rampant in the United States, the world without God, the alcohol parallels we touched on already, all your self-analysis, supposed self-forgiveness and the same for your mother and father and brother, Jamie, that absurdity of man's 'trapped' condition, his inability to belong, the very idea that there are no answers, the notion that he is a victim of inheritantly human vulnerability *and the one that I just love*, Eugene, the perverse complexities of human nature!" Dr. K. concluded. "All of that you were *sure* you had it right!"

"Illusions versus the will to live," said the playwright. "That's how I remember it."

"But illusions are never a healthy device in the context of mental and emotional health, Eugene. Surely you see that now? Your desperation to have answers to what your life had shown you was the cause of that aberration. The same goes for perverse complexities! There might be complexities in the whole person, but there is nothing perverse about that. In the fractured, maybe you were right but the implication in your works was that this applied to *all people!*" Dr. K. insisted.

"I imagine that you are correct. You've been right about everything else and here in Limbo, I would expect you to be hones," Eugene allowed readily.

"When life begins, there is no real complexity. We all want only to be loved and to love back," assured the analyst. "You recall such a feeling, Eugene?"

"Honestly, I do not. It was too long ago. However, I imagine, again, that you are right and it makes sense anyway," he granted the doctor. "Actually, I *do* kind of remember when I was six or nine wanting to be hugged and accepted. It never came."

"Javol, Eugene, you were not loved at all. Didn't you tell me, or did I know this independently, that you were an unwanted baby?" he asked in a rapid tone.

"I was unwanted all my life. The start was the year I was born...1888," he said.

"Und your parents could not give you what you needed. *They* were wounded souls themselves and only self-dealing. Pain relief was their primary pastime and they in fact did not love themselves, Eugene. They were shameless in their devices and could not give you or Jamie or Edmund the nurturing and safety required," the doctor announced.

"Boy, that makes perfect sense to me," Eugene agreed quickly.

"Kids see parents or other adults perform and behave and they think that it is correct behavior and they copy it," the analyst went on. "Und this, too, can spread the effect of abuse and neglect upon the child."

"So, misbehaving children are copying their parents, doc?" he asked.

"Well, they might be. But also they could be rebelling against such parents," was the reply. "Children *never* misbehave because they have not had enough pain and fear and any parental policy that embraces the opposite concept presupposes a false premise: that children are born defective and not by nature whole and loving and honest. Use of force and violence on them breeds only robots who then pass that on to their own offspring!," lectured Dr. Kornschucher.

"The use of violence on kids is practically universal, right?" Eugene asked.

"Yes, and it is a sin, by golly, it is *so blind*! Society expects these people to perform, in work, in school, in life generally, and to be in control of themselves, so they have to fake it, do whatever it takes to get through *just like when they were abused and neglected or abandoned to get through*!," the doctor said.

"Fake it to get through," Eugene formed the words on his lips.

"Moreover, my boy, as long as these poor kids are more or less average in their symptoms and miseries, they get by. But people who come out in the *extreme areas*, like child sex fiends or even child killers, these types usually incur the wrath of the fractured folks in the middle of the dysfunction scale. Then, Eugene, the other extreme, the persons who always tell the truth, point out the addictions and the crookedness of those fractured people, these pointers are also condemned because they threaten the artificial structure which is all that they have to cling to. Maybe this is what happened in *Iceman Cometh*?" he asked.

"*The Iceman Cometh*," Eugene corrected him cynically but quickly apologized.

"Jesus Christ was just such an extreme because he saw everything and preached love be heaped onto one's enemies. They blotted him out for that!" Dr. K. lamented.

"So if you're average, you fit in and no waves are made but if on the ends of that scale, you rock the ship and they attack you?" Eugene asked. "Sort of like a law of plummeting acceptance, doc?"

"I love that, Eugene! You *are* a very smart fellow indeed!" he proclaimed.

"Conflict is inevitable anyway, even among the whole people. But the marked difference is that for them, they get over it, see the light, see the other person's point and apologies abound. It's the same with the kids. They fight, they get mad, they throw sand but quickly it seems, they kiss and make up!" Dr. K. said. "The fractured ones, adults especially, hold grudges forever. Und why is zat?"

"Because they stay mad forever?" he asked.

"No, nein, my boy. They hold grudges because they need that to hold on to. After all, their very worth has been called into question and they are daily reminded that they have none. So, a person that they perceive as insulting or worse to them must be made to pay a price forever. Their misery lasts forever, so why not the punishment against others, you see that?" the doctor said.

"No perverse complexities, huh, doc? That sounds pretty complex to me!" he said.

"No, Eugene, we are speaking about no such thing in *whole* people," Dr. K. said. "Und now, let's have some false roles, shall we?"

"What?" Eugene asked.

"By the vay, your take on that perverse complexities was *itself* perverse!" the analyst added. "Anyway, false roles, you recall, we went already over the 'hero' or 'star' ones?"

"Oh, yes," Eugene chimed in, so did I have more?"

"Indeed you did, my lad, you took on the role of *rebel* to try to matter!" said the all knowing one. "Und your rebellion was palpable!"

"Yeah, I suppose I was a bit of a scalawag, huh?" he agreed.

"You under your brother, Jamie, quite a reputation around town, Ja? Und the girls were warned to stay away from you two, Ja? *Rebel*!" the doctor declared boldly. "Also, the townspeople looked down at your reading habits, did they not, Eugene?" the doctor wanted to know. "Wasn't *that*, vat you ver doing und reading, a kind of a rebellion, and did it not make you feel special, apart, above them?"

"Oh, God, yes, they thought that they were so much better!" Eugene said with bitterness in his voice.

"Und ven you ver fifteen years old, you rebelled against the church and your Papa und decided 'no more church', Ja, Eugene?" the doctor said.

"I had had it with them, the phoniness of that place, those people and I had to fight my father over it that day I quit!" he reported to the doctor. "No more orders from the church. God let me down!"

"You had had enough of that job, did you, Eugene? No answered prayers on your mother was the last straw, ja?" he inquired, already knowing.

"True, I was disgusted," Eugene said.

"Vell, I am vaiting for you to tell me the truth," the analyst demanded of him.

"I *am*," cried an exasperated Eugene.

"No, you're not. The truth is that you did rebel against the church, *but*, you did it because it was appropriate in your mind and you did not do it to *matter*, as a part of a phony role or identity as a rebel, you see, Eugene?" he asked.

Eugene pondered that for a moment and his face lit up!

"Und vat about Princeton?" he inquired with a smile. "You didn't study, you did not go to class, Ja? *Rebel!*" the doctor shouted. "You vent to New York City to meet Jamie and go whoring and boozing!"

Eugene looked sort of sheepish about this kind of exposure.

"Boozing and whoring in New London, too, Ja?" he followed up with. "Und no regular job except newspaper work at the behest of my father for a time as well," he explained. "But I couldn't stand it!"

"*Rebellion!*" the doctor cried out and then moved on to other stuff. Eugene was feeling something new and wonderful now. Dr. K. seemed like a genuine ally and his *clarity and force* and *friendliness* were absolutely a stranger to him as people go. He sort of swooned inside at the realization that *that* is how a father ought to be. Eugene was beaming and calmer.

"Vait!" exclaimed the doctor. "I have forgotten, Eugene! Did you ever take on a role to try to matter that was not superhuman like star, rebel or hero, but like victim or scapegoat or lost child?"

"Uh, I guess I was a victim of sorts when I swallowed that bottle of pills in 1912?" he responded matter of factly.

"Yes, maybe, but zat is not a 'victim' role to try to matter unless it was a stunt, Eugene, you see?" the doctor answered.

"It was meant to kill my pain by killing its house," Eugene declared. "I gave up."

"Vat about your words to Carlotta in 1953 about no priest and no tombstone with more than the name 'O'Neill' on it? Was that being a victim, Eugene?" the doctor asked, *testing* him.

"Uh, I don't think, uh, well, No!" he finally shouted. "I was not doing any of that in Boston to try to matter, only to try to deal with the end details."

"Gut!" exclaimed the analyst. "Und why was that your wish about the name?"

"I wanted no references to my life or career or prizes," he admitted.

"But why, Eugene, why," he demanded to know, "would it not be the regular thing to put on a head stone?"

"I didn't want to bother with all that crap," he said.

"Was it a subhuman state of emotions?" the doctor asked.

"I do not really know," Eugene said and the doctor left it at that except to point out that a Nobel Prize winner is regarded by the whole world as *very special* and that it might be a shame to leave that off the stone. He then suggested to him that he felt a little guilt over the prizes because he did not really deserve them.

"Acht!" cried the analyst. "Ve have etwas hier und es ist sehr interessant!" forgetting that he was no longer in Austria. "Ven you were a little boy on Pequot Avenue or on the road with your touring parents, were you not a little bit the role of the lost child and didn't that suit you inasmuch as it brought attention to you that night otherwise be withheld?" he asked.

"I don't remember but it could have happened that way. Yes, I could see that a little kid frustrated and lonely might pretend to be more out of it than he really is just to get the attention," Eugene said with his chin on his hand. "I always felt unwanted and in the way and totally unimportant to them."

"Und you ver a *shy* boy, Ja?" , the analyst asked, "Maybe to the point when you got older of being impolite?"

"I *was* withdrawn and did not want to risk interaction with others all the time," Eugene said, "Bitter feelings were not involved and I did not do that to hurt anybody."

"Und ven you ver drinking, Eugene, ver you shy then?" he asked, knowing the answer.

"When I was tanked, doctor, that fell away and I was more bold, free, you know, and Jamie and I were getting that way more and more it seemed there in New London and New York. He died from it you know...1923 and he's buried over on Jefferson like the others," he moaned.

"Ja, the family, Eugene?" asked the sympathetic doctor.

"Damn! Damn! Jamie!" moaned Eugene.

"I know, Eugene, very sorry, very tragic, so young und your parents ver to blame I'm afraid," droned the analyst.

Collecting himself, Eugene began to speak about his ideas on false faces, masks he called them, and the idea that people play phony roles that way. He asked the doctor if *that* was the same thing. Dr. K. was not entirely sure but he did say that it could be related if the 'masks' were donned to try to *mat-

ter. Eugene then instructed him that often, these 'masks' are borrowed from the past that a person has. Kornschucher then observed that they also could come from legend or from animals or myths or from a foreign culture and Eugene was intrigued to hear this view.

"Alright, my boy," said the analyst. "Now ve move on to the *second part* that is false, the *false pleasure* or *substitute for real pleasure.* Ven you are living outside of your feelings, Eugene, in your head only, there is no genuine pleasure."

"Because you don't feel anything real?" he wondered.

"Correct!" exclaimed the analyst. "One has to be in one's vulnerabilities to have genuine pleasure or *pain* for that matter. So there is no true joy or satisfaction in that state."

"My whole life was a feelings sham?" he asked.

"In a way, Ja, because you ver driven into your head by James und Ella und you ver sort of protected up there, safe und *numb!*" he assured Eugene.

"Okay," he said.

"So, now, people like this, like you, become desperate to feel *something* like joy and glee so they use *mood-altering substances* and do not care that these substances can damage the body und the mind, you see, Eugene?" he asked.

"I guess that I never heard of that term but it sounds correct," he replied.

"Also, these people can use *mood-altering activities* und ve vill get to that in a while, but for now, let's focus on the substances like tobacco or alcohol."

"Ain't had a drink since around 1928 doc!," Eugene said proudly.

"Except for the binge you went on in the Shanghai that landed you in the hospital!" he countered.

"Und smoking, Eugene, vat about that one?" he wondered aloud.

"Ain't had a butt since I died!" he said comically.

"These are the *addictions*, the ways to feel something when living outside the feelings. Tobacco gives it and whiskey gives it. Food also can give it and people who overeat are chasing that mood-alteration.," the doctor replied.

"Really? Gee, I never viewed it like *that!*" said Eugene.

"Sure. Ever notice that you feel different after you eat?" the playwright was asked. Eugene nodded his realization that he did.

"People eat to *feel better* and not to attend a natural, cyclical hunger when they have this eating addiction.," the analyst assured him.

"So fat people are addicts just like the dope fiend?" Eugene wondered.

"Only if they are fat because they overeat and not due to some organic disorder, my boy," he said. "Now, addicts are so desperate to feel what they get from the particular substance that they depend on that they stay in denial about the ill health that is sure to result. Feelings and a sense of power and well-being are attained and these are not ordinarily sensed by them without the addiction substance. It is intoxicating, the effect and the power!" the doctor lectured.

"Morphine," muttered Eugene bitterly.

"Your mother, yes?" asked the doctor, being polite for treatment purposes.

"She loved it and she did not care for me. She also did not care that it was likely to shorted her life," he said bitterly.

"Eugene, you have to understand and I'm sure that you do from your own experience, that addicts have no regard for a long life because the life that they do have isn't worth much. More days are not the goal. Only gaining 'relief' by way of artificially gotten sensations matters.," he relayed.

"Pretty damned sad!" Eugene observed. "And I was one of them!"

"Your claims of 'perfect understanding', or those of the critics and experts that you showed that in the writing of the family defects such as your mother's addiction or father's miserliness or brother Jamie's 'evil' ways and deeds, are *invalid*. 'Objectivity' might be another matter and you might have excelled there, but 'perfect understanding' to go along with the 'pity' and 'forgiveness', no!" said the doctor.

"Well, I...," stammered Eugene.

"It's like an automobile wreck, my boy. You can stop and describe it with 'perfect objectivity' but if you were not there, you cannot ascribe 'perfect understanding' as to its causes, how it occurred. So it is with Jamie. You call it human evil and maybe it was, but the roots are the same roots that held *you* in the ground, the poisoned roots planted by Ella and your father. Just because Jamie was less fortunate and could not muster any kind of 'transcendence' that you claimed to have does not mean that his defects were caused by anything other than what caused yours, you see?" he exclaimed to the wide-eyed Eugene. "No *fundamental human evil* in Jamie!"

"OK, I guess," replied Eugene.

"Forgiveness is another thing and I believe that you did do that if for no other reason than relief inside yourself," Dr. K. allowed. "Maybe it was *enabling* and inappropriate, but if you felt forgiveness, fine," he went on. "You can say that the morphine use was caused by your father and society's ways but that is not really the case. Mood-altering addictions and society's ways but that is not really the case. Mood-altering addictions are caused by child abuse and that was Ella's underpinning. Society does not help, of course. It nurtures child abuse along. It encourages it or it turns its head. And as far as 'transcendence', Eugene, I ask again, was it mere bewilderment and desperation for relief or *real rising above* and seeing?"

"I don't know anymore, doctor," he whispered.

Dr. K. then reminded Eugene that many saw his parents' marriage as successful and hardly likely as a source of tragedy and that they would tend to ascribe same to other forces or heredity or the environment itself, but that they were in the main wrong and not seeing from the above. . Then he told Eugene that his ideas of 'reconciliation' with his father after all the exchanges with him in *Long Day's Journey into Night* was hardly that but more likely a great rush of relief and a wanton need to unburden himself by painting forgiveness over everything bad there."

O'Neill just sat with his head in his hands.

"That's the story on addiction like drinking and doping, my boy."

"Ven you get a *reversal*, addictions disappear. However, those reversals are rare," said the doctor.

"And why is that?" he replied.

"In good time, Eugene, you will find out," was all the doctor could say.

"What about those people who are addicted to being on time or early?" he asked.

"Not an addiction," the doctor said. "It's not a substance but an *obsession*, a neurosis. It is engaged in that instance to guard against being caught off guard or criticized or hurt anymore."

"What do you mean 'hurt'?" Eugene was eager to find out.

"Feelings hurt by those attacking him for being late," he said.

"But I thought he was existing outside of his feelings!" a frustrated listener said in a loud voice but not meaning any disrespect.

"His emotional vulnerabilities he lives outside of for safety. That part is numbed out. When I say 'feelings' in this manner, I am referring to the pain that criticism brings back which reminds him of his worthlessness-conviction induced by his parents," the doctor revealed to him. "And that hurt can sometimes evoke a violent reaction depending on the degree of pain inflicted by them."

"Does being on time or early ever, I mean, sometimes, make a body feel that he is in control when his general sense is that his life is chaos?"

"My goodness, you are something, so bright, Vat a good student!" the analyst had to say.

"Also, he could fly off the handle quickly on some slight reason like being unable to get a jar lid off. He could shout and bang it. This is the underlying rage that he carries and it blows up all out of proportion to the frustration at hand, you see. It lives inside him from decades ago!" Dr. K. said.

"Geeze," replied Eugene. "It lasts that long...well...yes, I guess it did in me as well."

"It hangs there until you die, Eugene, unless it gets worn down a little by age or you get a reversal. Remember," the analyst said, "you are carrying somebody else's pain!"

"Whose? . . . Oh, the parents, yeah!," the bright one stated.

"They forced him to carry it and that forced him right out of those vulnerabilities!" he reminded Eugene.

"My God!" cried the playwright. "*They* forced *me*! They put their awful ways onto the little boy that I was, helpless, needing them so much, I had to swallow it all or be put out or worse!" he cried.

"Und ven yu were fully there, your days became ones of rules to survive and *not* feelings to live in." pointed out the doctor. "You were a robot of their design!"

"I was a robot!" he repeated. "A life of rules and no feelings of love or anything else. That's the robot world!"

"So, remember, Eugene, a reversal will get you back but thinking the right kinds of thoughts will *not* because that is just more robot stuff. So phrases such as 'be yourself' or 'don't you think that you should grow up? ' or 'you ought not feel so sad', things like that, are nonsense," he added.

"Robot!" Eugene said to himself out loud. He was amazed at the simplicity.

"Und now ve move to the *third part* of this unhappy trinity which is the *substitute for real suffering,* and do you know vat ve call it, Eugene?" droned the analyst.

"Uh, gee, no, doc, you tell me, what is it called?" he parroted.

"Ve call it 'neurosis'," he replied.

"Neuroses?" Eugene asked not believing that this common word was what Dr. K. was aimed at.

"Javol!" he said. "It is like a pine goddess whose tits give turpentine, ha-ha-ha-!," the doctor laughed.

Eugene split up over that because it broke the tension and was funny to imagine.

"Ja. Ven you are in your real feelings und your hund is run over, your doggie, you cry. But ven you do not, no tears come out. The suffering stays frozen and not *grieved*. Same if your father dies, Eugene, did *you* cry when your Papa died of cancer in that hospital in New London in 1920?" he asked.

Eugene avoided answering him and just looked down.

"It is like the animal that you will not let out the door. He will tear up the curtains, destroy your shoes, the force will show up somewhere and it will not be denied. This is neurosis. The real pain is suppressed and comes out as obsessions as we already noted, or as hysteria or phobias or anxiety or conversion reaction or depression," the doctor said.

"Conversion what?" Eugene wondered.

"Reaction," replied the analyst. " It is when a person under stress freezes and cannot seem to move from danger or whatever."

"Depression, I had a lot. Some of the others I had as well," Eugene said.

"The *key* is irrationality," the doctor confided. "An irrational reaction to circumstances at hand."

"When my father was dying, I was very depressed, very down and out even if I hated him deep down, his suffering lying there month after month was too much and the end was really a blessing,," Eugene admitted hesitatingly.

"Und ver you also more anxious during zat time?" was the query.

"Probably," he said. "I smoked like the proverbial chimney then."

"Ja, the cigarettes gave you a chemical sense of well being at a time when you were not supposed to feel that exactly, supposed to be crying your eyes out," Dr. K. observed.

"And alcohol helped the same way, you know, both for me and Jamie," he said.

Changing the topic a little, Dr. K. asked Eugene, "You gave up driving at some point, Ja, Eugene?"

"Yes I did," answered the patient. "I *had* to. You see traffic was too much for me. My nerves couldn't stand it so I stopped driving."

"Und this is *irrational* upset or excitement showing up, you see it? Anxiety!" said the doctor. "Und you took sedatives for a very long time, Ja?" he asked.

"Couldn't get on without them…doctor, surely you can relate to that!"

"Ja, Eugene, I seem to remember something about you 'jumping out of your skin', a nervous wreck," he added. "*Anxiety!*"

"And depressed all the time. Oh, I said that already, doc, sorry," Eugene apologized.

"That's okay, my boy, yes, depression, irrational sadness for the event at hand. You had that a lot, Ja?" he asked.

"Lots, doctor, very, very down and moping around. Like when my father was in trouble in the hospital," he recalled.

"But you were not grieving down, just sadness down, Ja? You know the difference?"

"Not really," was his only reply. "Tell me Dr. K."

"Whole people, not you, not Jamie, not your father, not your mother, grieve when they sustain a loss be it a relative, a pet, a job, a wallet full of cash, whatever. Fractured people are down over it but there is no healing. That comes from grieving and the living who go thru recovery, much the same process that you and I are conducting, they break down and grieve the loss of their own authentic selves, that which abusive and neglectful parents rob from them," Dr. K. said.

"Huh?" Eugene asked.

"Vait! Let me say that again. It is muddy, Ja? Okay, whole people break down und cry und grieve and get over losses like a dog. Abused people do not. They might cry but it is *morbid* depression. Recall that term, Eugene? Anyway, when broken people like you, but alive ones, go thru what we are doing here, they break down and cry because they are being forced back into their feelings and *they too* are grieving only this time, they are crying over the loss of their authentic selves at the behest of mistreatment-oriented parents," he said.

I actually followed that, Dr. Korschucher, wow!" cried Eugene.

"Gut!" he said. "I get lost in this stuff myself sometimes," he said jokingly.

"But really, Eugene, that authentic self, the genuine identity that you termed it, that is what is surrendered by the child to the parents who force him to carry *their* pain, you see this?" he wondered aloud.

"Okay," Eugene agreed.

"Ven you lost your father in 1920, then your mother in 1922, was it not a harder hit on you than you would have imagined, Eugene?" the doctor asked him.

"Maybe it was, I don't know," he said.

"Vell, vat I am driving at here is that when they ver both gone, it became *too late*. You had to know that for the first time in *your* life, it was no longer possible for them to sustain a miracle turnaround and love and accept you for who you were. No more change after they are buried, no more chances," the doctor said sadly to him.

Eugene told the doctor that he had never looked at it that way and was very surprised at that slant. Then he told the analyst that he was amazed that such a simple concept about an everyday thing like death or parental loss could be itself *masked* and unseen. Then he asked if this type of 'blindness' were applicable to other areas that they were discussing.

"Damned right!" said the doctor as he slapped his hand down on the crystal table hard which started Eugene.

"I'm sorry," Eugene said.

"For what?" the doctor wanted to know. "For being born?"

"I don't know," he replied. "I'm just awful sorry inside now".

"That is normal for you to feel like that after what you have learned, my boy," said the doctor. "And now, let me inform you that there is a *twin hope* living in everybody who had a childhood like yours, that is, that not only is a fervent wish always alive that the misbehaving parents will undergo a miracle turnaround and give unconditional love and support the way a regular mother and father would, but also lives that secret desire to actually *be forced* back into their vulnerabilities as we discussed a while ago."

"Yeah, and who is willing to do that, doc?" Eugene asked skeptically.

"We, Eugene," he answered. "Are we speaking of being forced back willingly or just who is willing to do the forcing?"

"Both, I imagine," he replied.

"Well, the receiver of the force, remember, has a secret *hope* to get back to where he was before the ungodly interruption of his babyhood, so, although he will seem to resist the force, he truly begs for it inside deep down. As far as *who* is willing to apply it, it can be a family member, a friend, the law or others and perhaps the *law*, as long as I have listed it, is ideally doing such a thing when it imposes incarceration and fines to 'rehabilitate' a criminal. They are in fact trying to make him 'normal' and law-abiding and possessive of a 'conscience' which appears to be *diminished* in the lawbreaker as well as the run of the mill abused and neglected kid", the analyst instructed Eugene, "And, we have to point out once more that we are talking about non organic disorders so that the above does not apply to criminal activity that is rooted in genetics or pure biochemical abnormality."

"This is quite interesting, doctor," Eugene freely admitted.

"Another ting, my boy, ven you have a mistreated child who is now crooked like his parents, it will not do much good to just be nice to him, treat him fairly, be non-shaming. It might help a little because he will feel *safe* and the incidence of his misbehavior might be diminished for that reason, but he will *use you* in spite of your positive treatment of him *because he is still crooked!*" Dr. K. went on. "Und there is nothing that vill alter that in his life except a reversal, the remedy for this that comes

from the process that I mentioned. That is the *grieving* process which is *unlimited* and *uninterrupted*. Again, that cure is not so easy to go along with or even get started on because it hurts like hell!" he admitted.

"I feel it a little now," said Eugene. "Maybe that's the 'sorry' that I just a little while ago told you about was inside of me?"

"The grieving is *constrainstinctual*, Eugene!" he insisted. "Who runs to-wards pain? Nobody!" the analyst declared in a booming voice. "That baby in the *instinct clash* cannot do it because he is just a tiny animal going with what nature put there to protect him, that is, to flee. Of course, he cannot flee to another set of parents, so he does want I told you already, Eugene," the doctor said proudly.

"But doc, that may be nature's protection for the little tyke, but does it truly *protect* him in the end?" Eugene wondered in a bright moment.

"Oh, mein Gott, you are so smart, Eugene! I wish I could get you as my assistant!" was the happy answer, "it seems like it protects the child because what else would an instinct do? But really, it results in a mess!"

"Do you suppose," Eugene next asked, "that it could be likened to the in-flammatory response that the brain undergoes on trauma but which kills the person when the swelling inside the skull becomes too great?"

"Vell, Eugene, it is not exactly the same because trauma-based swelling is a *physiological response* und the baby fleeing into its head is *not*," he observed. "But I get the idea what you are driving at. Very interesting und I vill have to think about this, Eugene. Thank you!"

Eugene sat silent remembering his mission to get out of Limbo and he did not want to risk anything by being too bright or disruptive here.

"Another idea, Eugene, is this. Innocence in the child, the baby, the tod-dler, is *irresistible*, Ja?" he asked. "Everybody is drawn to it, marvels at it, speaks of it. Yet, who lives it as an adult? Almost nobody! Why should such a ting be so?" the analyst quizzed him. "Why in ze vorld ist it so hard to be like them? Mein Gott, you vould tink that a criminal in jail who vould take vengeance upon a cellmate who had been a baby killer could *see*, could grasp what is really at hand in his soul, yet it does not happen! Everybody, almost, lives in deceit and that is because deceit is used to rear them to one slight degree or another which can be much larger!" he said.

Eugene again stayed silent. He was now worried that Dr. K. might sabotage his leaving Limbo so that he could keep him forever as a helper. This terrified him and he was in a tizzy as to how to avoid this. But all of a sudden, he remembered the strange, new concept of an *honest father* and that he was feeling that very thing about Dr. Kornschucher. The worries subsided.

"You know, Eugene," the analyst continued, unaware of his listener's recent concerns, "that the idea of *freedom of speech* is based on the *theory* that people will *say the truth* and that any contrary utterances flooding the public domain will fall away from that truth and be *exposed* for the rottenness that falsity and distortion are, Ja?"

"Sounds right", Eugene agreed.

"But zis is not so!" he replied, startling Eugene. "Remember, my boy, that ve just got done agreeing, vell, I said, *everybody* almost lives in deceit to some degree and to that degree, they are in that *trance* that I brought up some time ago! You see this, Eugene?" he asked.

"So, what does it all mean then?" Eugene replied warily.

"It means, Eugene, that the policy behind freedom of speech is not so sound as the average person might believe if they rely on absolute truth-telling because that is jut not what exists in society," he instructed him.

"Yes, but the policy still is good because its opposite is evil!" Eugene insisted. "Besides, Doctor, this sounds an awful like *my* themes on masks and self-deception and self-destruction and use of illusions to survive a human weaknesses and defeat, doesn't it?"

"Vell, no, Eugene, it does not insofar as 'human weaknesses' goes because those defects that you listed are induced by crooked or crazy or absent parents, are not put in the child by God," he replied assuringly. "Those 'masks' and 'illusions' are, again, devices to cope with the aftermath of child abuse and not some organic dilemma put on mankind as you portray it!"

"Maybe, in society, in the public arena, the 'truth' that comprises the average person's message is close enough to real truth that it benefits everyone and still does dispel the evil messages?"

"Gut!" the doctor allowed.

"So, then, in actuality, Doctor Kornschucher, *nearly everyone* is a truth bender because child mistreatment is so common, although subtle, and therefore, nearly everybody needs *some* recovery work, yes?" Eugene wondered aloud, again fearing being too smart.

"It's true!" the analyst remarked. "Although nobody will face it!"

"Maybe *I* am a symbol of that trance life, doctor, and the public reactions to my works another symbol of the state of things as you just now described them?" he wondered in a profound tone.

"Ja, Eugene, und don't forget the prize givers. *They* are in it, too!" he said.

"Did you say a while back that the crooked person will *use* other people even if they are nice to him, treat him well, are friendly?" Eugene remembered. "I'm just now grasping that."

"Ja, they vill. They vill take advantage of your presence and good nature to lie, tell boasting stories, inflate their egos, maybe borrow money, things like this because they know no other way to relate. Honesty is not what was required for them to survive in a crooked household und so, dishonesty became lodged in the bones, you see?" Dr. K. repeated.

"You know," Eugene said, "I think that I have the answer as to why people marvel at the innocence of children and why they do not copy it. I think that they are reminded by it of their own past, so it seems dear to them. However, they do not use it as a model because they do not know how to be innocent anymore. Again, the crookedness gets in the bones, as the phrase goes, as you said, doctor."

"Very gut, Eugene," exclaimed the analyst. "Und now ve move on here. I believe zat ze very small child ist not vanting to be forced into anything, certainly not his 'feelings' as ve said. That ist only ven he gets older, Ja? You see this, Eugene?"

"Okay," he replied, having no choice.

"But always does the child hope deep down inside for zat miracle that the parents vill get it right someday," he remarked.

"You know, doc, that reminds me of a play that I wrote when I had my own fantasies about New London and visualized life there for me as if it had been a happy and healthy affair instead of the dismal ordeal that it was," Eugene said.

"Ja, und zat play was called vat, Eugene," asked the analyst who already knew.

"*Ah, Wilderness*," was the reply. "Only comedy I ever wrote really except for maybe a few other smaller things."

"Let's continue my boy," the doctor insisted. "Now ve have discussed neurosis number one, obsessions, und now, number two ist phobias, Ja! . Phobias are *irrational* fear or dread. Never ist the reaction appropriate to ze circumstances. So, a morbid terror of spiders, not a healthy fear but a crazy one, Ja, or of being cooped up in a room or fear of open spaces, maybe a ball field, all phobias. Obsession was *irrational preoccupation* with something, now we have *fear.*"

"And you said Dr. K. that these were substitutes for true suffering, yes?" Eugene asked.

"Javol!" he quickly said and then continued. "Next ve have ze *conversion reaction* und zat is a rarer form of neurosis. It is ze freezing up of a person like a deer in the headlights. Ven some threat is perceived, he cannot move or deal with it und so, he freezes up. Next ist *hysteria* und zat is a reaction consisting of an *irrational loss of control.* A good example ist the person who finds that he cannot unlock the bathroom door in an airplane and simply freaks out. That is hysteria."

"I've heard of that kind of thing, yes," Eugene replied.

"Next ve have *depression.* Did ve already cover zis one, Eugene?" he asked.

"Uh, maybe, but tell me again, doctor, please", he answered the analyst.

"Zis von is *irrational sadness.* It ist the blues all the time with no concrete reason for it, Ja?" he explained. "Und zen there ist *anxiety*, Eugene."

"Depression and anxiety," Eugene repeated. "Those have been my problem for as long as I can remember."

"Javol, I know und do not forget, Eugene, ve are *not* speaking about *organic* problems but only ones caused by parents, Ja?" He made sure his patient knew this.

"Plenty of neurosis pops up in my works, doctor, only I do not recall being aware of the roots or remedies as you have put them so as to include those," Eugene remarked in thought. "Plenty of descriptions of misery, however!"

"Ja, I know that," said the analyst.

"Also, I put how hurtful and unfair life is and the struggles over God and my own valiant attempts, if I may say so, to grasp just what it is that mankind's lot on Earth is truly all about," Eugene said proudly.

As if he forgot to dot an i, the doctor chimed in that anxiety was the *irrational* excitement or upset or tension that is out of proportion to facts at hand.

"Anxiety," said Eugene. "That's why I cannot handle traffic, right?" he asked.

"Certainly, Eugene. Maybe ve already said that way back ven we spoke of that traffic, I don't know," allowed the analyst. "I am sure that anxiety and depression followed you around all the time from youth to that day in the Boston Hotel!"

"It was so that I could hardly recognize tension because it was with me all the time," he said. "By the way, I forgot, we were talking about my plays and I neglected to finish up. Many times, I referred to clinging by man to those illusions and..."

Cutting Eugene off, the analyst spoke. "What illusions did *you* yourself cling to, Eugene?"

"Uh, well, I, let me see," he said but did not come up with any.

"Hard to find any, huh?" asked the questioner. "How about the tale that you told about not being cut out to be a father?"

"It is so. I was not. What illusion is that?" he demanded to know.

"Well, Eugene, were you a sociopath? I mean, really, what does that mean? You fathered three kids, so what's no to be cut out about?" Dr. K. insisted.

"When they were around, I was always annoyed. I could never concentrate or produce and my work came *first* you know!" he said strongly.

"But, Eugene, they were your flesh and blood. They wanted and they needed exactly what *you* wanted and needed as a kid and were cruelly deprived of!" the doctor said in a louder voice. "Your excuse is just an illusion that you use for convenience, just like James and Ella!"

This bowled him over and he started to cry and sob deeply. He definitely felt this and the analyst had touched a nerve that was heretofore insulated.

"You made them so that they did not matter. They were relegated to a nonhuman status and your work was above their little hearts! Sound familiar, Eugene? Does this ring any bells?" Dr. K. said acidly.

"My God!" he replied. "I did to them what my parents, my father, did to me! How is such a thing possible, doctor, you tell me!" he demanded.

"You see how the chain goes, Eugene? How the cycle works. ? Und my guess is that this kind of thing goes back farther in your line than you could ever believe!" he postulated. "You pretended not to have the patience, the temperament, but really you were suffering. Intimacy dysfunction, fear, cynicism, the rest of it, these were your barriers. It was illusory, Eugene, do you see it now?" he yelled.

Dr. K moved on quickly so as to prevent Eugene from being too maudlin. He next asked him about his youthful railing against Capitalism and position that it ought to be overthrown. Eugene made the excuse that he outgrew it, but still, there was an illusion about it all and the doctor demanded to know 'who in Hell creates all the jobs' and who provides the efficiency that private enterprise does?

"It's *private money* and *private risk*," he insisted. "And any crazy ideas about the government making jobs or owning the means of production and so forth is way off base and just *crooked*!" he said, emphasizing that word.

"I didn't promote or condone Marxism, you know!" proclaimed Eugene.

"But, in the *Hairy Ape* play, my boy, you carried on with this stuff insinuating that man is not *free* to choose or not choose any work that we wants and lucky as hell that somebody else had the pluck and imagination to create the job opportunity in the first place, to risk the money and time and efforts so that work and profits would descend, right?" Eugene was asked in a challenging voice. "Und ver those workmen not *free* to unionize if they wanted? Sure, there might be a backlash, trouble, strikes, violence, but that is not the point. Capital is not a prisoner to be taken to avoid trouble. *Taking it is the trouble!*," the doctor insisted vehemently. "Und ven you presented what came to be called 'the grinding forces of industrialization', that was pure *spite talking*, false aggression, rage-based, aggressive, self-dealing, violent parents, Ja?" he went on.

Eugene sat silently and listened.

"Go somewhere else und cut bananas!" cried the analyst, " if you vont different verk, Ja!"

Dr. Kornschucher asked Eugene want he had to say about such 'illusory' ideas and he was told that they seemed right and proper at this time. Then he observed that the world is and was full of ideas that 'seemed right and proper at the time' but which turned out to be malevolent or grossly negligent. Eugene agreed with it.

"More illusion-based conduct by you, Eugene; let's hear some more!" said the analyst.

Eugene drew a blank.

"How about marriages?" he asked him.

"You mean Kathleen, doc?" he replied.

"Ja, Kathleen and Agnes too," he responded. "Tell me of them."

"You already know about them. You know about *everything*," he answered.

"Ja, true, but value here is in the discussion, you see this?" he replied.

Eugene asked the doctor what he wanted to know. He was told that the marriage to Kathleen Jenkins in Hoboken, New Jersey in 1909 'on a whim' as it has been referred to, was just such negligent or illusions-based conduct. He pointed out that Eugene had left her *one week* later and pregnant to boot when he sailed off at the insistence of his father to Central America. Eugene again claimed no knowledge of the condition of Kathleen, but he was sharply reminded that he had had sex with her and that such a result was to be expected. Also, the analyst instructed him, letting his father dictate his conduct so as to interfere that way with the marriage was more illusions. Then there were the illusory expectations of what goals would be achieved in Honduras. Next, Dr. K. went into the Agnes Boulton thing. A second marriage, two more kids, making three in all counting Kathleen's so, Eugene O'Neill, Jr., and then a casting off of Agnes in favor of Carlotta and a whim whisking off to Paris in 1929 for *another marriage*! The doctor told Eugene that he didn't see any illusions there. When Eugene bought that comment, Dr. K. laid into him because he was only baiting the playwright who then looked very contrite. But it was *an act*. Eugene was then instructed that his whole life had been a series of life-lies, pipe dreams, illusions and that these were only a few highlights.

"So, Eugene," the analyst went on. "Ve have discussed *false roles* or *identities, false pleasures und false suffering,* the unholy trinity, Ja?"

Eugene nodded and was then told to pick up the second diamond and to put it in his shirt pocket, which he did with delight.

Then, the analyst disappeared as before and soon came back with another plate and black cloth, this time bearing a seven carat diamond which he set down on the table before Eugene's popping eyes. He then got out his looking glass and read it to Eugene. The etching said:

DEVICES TO FEEL
People forced out of their feelings use *devices*
to feel such as a novelty, risk, violence, horror,
sex and pornography and this is in contrast to
    denial which is used to block out any feelings.

"These things are *mood-altering* devices and activities that ruined children us to get a sense of exhilaration and feeling. They are akin to addictions in that they produce 'pleasure' in a body that is wracked by pain and numbed out and void of real feelings," the doctor next told Eugene. "Meanwhile, *denial* keeps the *sham* alive!" he told him.

"Well, how do you mean?" he replied.

"*Denial* is a false device *not* used for false pleasure but to block out reality and truth. It is whistling-in-the-dark stuff," he said. "And amounts to the primary way that any such psychological shenanigans can exist in the first place."

"These 'feelings' you are pointing to as false, they are not what one 'feels' when bad news is replaced by good news, right, doc?" Eugene wanted to know again.

"No!" answered the doctor. "They are not. That is *relief* and has nothing to do with the idea of 'feelings' in the vulnerability sense. *That*, again, is what we are pointing to here, Eugene. Also, they are *not* what one senses when suffering from morbid depression or anxiety. You recall 'morbid'?" he asked.

"Ja!" Eugene replied and then quickly corrected himself red-faced. "I mean 'yes'. Sorry doc."

The analyst saw that his use of the German was a leaning towards Eugene adopting the analyst's identity much as does a child to a parent or a prisoner of war to the enemy. It was a kind of gratitude act here.

"Those 'vulnerabilities', Eugene," he continued, "are what allows us to sense *true joy* or *real pain*. Und von cannot have them separately. Both are needed as a possibility emotionally together to be a real state of being and not a phony one adopted by the child for *survival*. So, imagine this, Eugene," he went on. "Your girlfriend is coming over with something to tell you. If you are open and optimistic, you are healthy. If you are fearful and worried and decide that 'you don't care what she says and that bitch will not hurt you', you're sick and protected and in denial. In such a case, you don't feel real pain. You cannot risk it and only false suffering can 'hurt' you. But the price for the 'safety' is that when she says 'I love you', it does not register in the same place that it would if you were whole. The ultimate *vulnerability* allows the soaring of glee or the dive of *real* despair. Those in between merely float in falsehood."

"It is beginning to sink in and I have to say that such considerations were nowhere in my world and mind, doctor, in life and in literature," he said.

"Ja, I believe it, Eugene. In fact, zat is so for the whole vorld, you know," he observed. "Now, let's look at devices to feel, shall we? *Violence* is all over the place, Ja? Movies, television, books, und why, Eugene, is that so? Why is such a horrible thing so popular?" he asked him.

"Violence, murder, killing, torturing people, arson, revenge," said Eugene, "and all in the name of entertainment and 'fun', yes! Crazy! I admit it, doc, why and *how* is that possible?"

"People get a 'kick' out of it the same way, similar to, a cup of coffee. That 'jolt' is sought because the state of emotions otherwise is flaccid, bland, unexciting und excitement is vat they want. They *need* it because they are in phony pain all the time. Ja, I know, it really does 'hurt' them, that phony pain but really, it is only morbid stuff und not real suffering. It does not bring relief thru *grieving*!" he lectured. "The *jolt* from seeing violence actually alters the mood and is an emotions-based party for these poor souls."

"But why so common, doc?" he inquired.

"That *proves* that child mistreatment is so common," Dr. K. assured Eugene. "Und people into violence do not even realize the sickness, the blindness. *Who can see blindness?*" he added philosophically.

"And novelty, doc, how does *that* work?" asked a truly intrigued listener.

"Easy," remarked Dr. K. "Something *new* always makes the observer perk up, get interested, as in the automobile industry. Think of it, Eugene! All that money that consumers spend every year on *new* cars and such a large chunk of the price covering redesign for no other purpose than to *titillate*! It's outrageous and it, too, proves the commonality of child abuse and neglect. They are the fountainhead of car sales!" he insisted and Eugene just shook his head in disgust at that prospect.

"So it's 'mood-altering'?" Eugene chimed in.

"Certainly, Eugene!" the analyst agreed.

"Same ting for the neighbor's wife," he said. "It's the *novelty* that makes ze pecker go up for her when it lies quietly for ze hausfrau!" he laughed. "Also, it is the sex thing too, another device."

"So amazing," said Eugene, "that I wrote about sex and infidelity and all for so long and so much and never really saw it in these terms. It's amazing!"

"Novelty," quoted the doctor. "*Without content* is *prostitution*, Eugene, you see this? Und it is in bed with *obedience without content* which is *tyranny*!"

"I get that, doc, but what I am puzzled over is this. Novelty is chased after, as you say, to *feel something*, right? But, how is that related to fractured people who use novelty to get *noticed*?" Eugene asked. "And how is *that* different from the same class of persons who do the opposite, that is, they *conform* to try to matter? They join in, they dress and talk the same as the group."

"People who use novelty to get noticed are *rebels* and cannot get any feelings from that kind of novelty like the new car buyer does. Rebellion is a false role to try to *matter*. As far as safety in conformity, that is the *opposite* of rebellion. So in the case of a girl who wears a feather in her hair only because her high school classmates do the same, that can be normal. But if she conforms to a crowd phenomenon that is *abnormal*, say spitting on the classroom floor along with the others, that in an act of *group rebellion*. It also could be a type of codependence to the extent that she gets feelings of worth from the group instead of from inside of herself. *That* will be covered in a little while," the analyst assured Eugene.

"What's next, doc?" asked Eugene who was thinking less about the threat that preoccupied him a while ago about being held in Limbo forever.

"*Risk* is next," he declared. "That is a device used to *feel* something that is mood-altering and a good example, my boy, would be the 110m. p. h. motorcycle ride or making love in public where getting caught was likely or gambling away the rent money," the analyst continued.

"It really *is* a sick society!" Eugene lamented. "Not much has changed."

"Of course, gambling also gives, besides the risk factor, the rush of possible large gain in a short time and this makes the winner feel, falsely, that the hole inside of him, that void, is filled up and *that* feels good, too. Another factor on that is the sense of getting away with something because a large win on a small bet ought not to result but it *can*. Then, there is the feeling that such a 'win' is 'due' because the actor is down and out all his life," said the doctor.

"Okay, what's next?" Eugene asked politely.

"Pornography!" said the analyst. "This is a mood-alterer and *its* commonality attests as well to the ubiquitous child mistreatment in the world. Why else would a pastime like that be so popular? It speaks for itself!"

"How does it become mood-altering?" Eugene asked.

"It does that because it is forbidden. Also, there is the idea that *prurient* sex is involved which appeals to the dysfunctional mind," he replied.

"And I think you mentioned horror movies?" he asked the analyst.

"Right. Horror and fright cause a huge mood-alteration in *all* people. The ones who live life on the emotionally numb side resort to it readily and often. A more common one, Eugene, is sex. That is a very big alterer of mood and is sought a lot for only that reason and not for *affection*," Dr. K. lectured him.

"Now in this area, I have done a lot of writing, as in *Desire Under the Elms* and also have postulated about the connections between sex and love and God and that sex is a bulwark or softener for mankind with regard to loneliness and so forth that seem to be his due. Also, a painful move from sex to love for one another."

"Yes, I know all about that," said the analyst. "But I do not agree with your theories for the most part. I recall, it seems to me," the doctor said thinking out loud, "that for you, 'passion' equals God in that it is unselfish, spontaneous and amoral, a cosmic-type of move that is everywhere and which offers a glimpse of hope and fulfillment. Also, you pointed out that passion transcends man's animal nature. I disagree that it is unselfish for a lot of the time it is very much that way. It is used as a guaranteed mood-alteration device without regard for the partner if there even is a partner, Eugene!" he explained. "It's also not always spontaneous but contrived. As for 'amoral', I challenge that too. Sex and passion can often involve immoral aspects. Take rape. Take underage involvement. Take adultery. These are hardly amoral. It all sounds like gross cerebralization to me, Eugene," the analyst said to a disappointed patient.

The doctor motioned and Eugene picked up the third diamond and placed it with the others in his pocket. Soon, Dr. K. returned with a fourth stone on the black cloth plate. This diamond was eight carats and knocked Eugene's eye out! The doctor picked it up and read the etched inscription on it with the magnifying glass and even gestured to Eugene to have a look, which he declined because he now fully trusted Dr. Kornschucher. It read:

PERPETUAL IMMATURITY
The child frozen out of his feelings remains
in a permanently immature emotional state
although he inherits adult powers. He retains all
aspects of juvenility.

"I am reminded of your theory, Eugene," the doctor said, "that it will take man one million years to grow up and to get a soul. I wonder if this part is what you were concerned with? Anyway," he continued, "please pay close attention to this diamond and I think that you will be quite amazed."

"Okay, I shall," he replied, still interested.

"This section might show you *why* you might have been right, although not in the innate man sense but in the de facto sense insofar as the mass of humanity that seems to fall under such a category. You, Eugene, would have to be included in that, you realize?" the analyst candidly asserted.

"No, I do not relate to *that*," he replied, not happy with the inclusion.

"There is no way in the world that you could have been reared by James and Ella and *not* turned out in a permanently juvenile state, Eugene," he stated.

"No one likes to admit or face even the notion of a previously held self image as having been wrong or way off, you must see. I have struggled all my life to understand man, his plight, the awful things that fate puts in his path and I never really arrived at a 'unified theory' on this. Both Einstein *and* I floundered here, I suppose. Are you sure about me in this, doctor?" he asked, seeming hurt.

"Eugene, your state of mind as an adult, your self image, was understandably solidified in your own way so as to 'guaranty' *some* semblance of sanity and peace of mind. This is to be expected. But no more reason to feel anything except grateful for the insights and the chance to escape the consequences of an ill-lived life, namely, Limbo," the expert cautioned him gently.

"I'm in *your* hands, doc, chip away!" he good-naturedly replied.

"We have discussed what abuse and neglect does to the baby's mind, yes, and you recall, I hope, that when *you* were that baby or toddler, the *fleeing* instinct was blocked by Ella and James because you were too little and powerless to escape physically, Ja?" he asked.

"Too long ago, doc. All I know is that I hated them!" Eugene droned quietly.

"Anyway, you *did* flee, Eugene, into the mind and out of jeopardy. Cerebralization began to assume command of your tiny structure. Und *hypervigilance* became the captain. From then on, you, Eugene, were always *on guard* for the next assault, the awful face about to come at you, the inconsistencies from the father face or the mother's visage. Drugs and alcohol guaranty it. *I* guaranty it!" he announced.

"I am intrigued and 'on guard' myself for the next gem of wisdom, doc!" he said.

"Gut, Eugene. Now, that *hypervigilance* by a child *prevents* inner reflection und inner reflection is *critical* to ze development of that child's, your, maturity and eventual metamorphosis from infantile state to adult state vis a vis world-by-magic to world-by-logic. The codependent aspect, normal in all children, falls away in the whole person at about age sixteen or so but the fractured child remains that way for life absent recovery. Und this is also tied up with that 'genuine identity' development," the doctor went on.

"I am actually understanding this in my bones, doctor," he announced.

"I vont to say here because I do not know if I made it clear before, but the process of delivery of the message to the child that he does not matter comes in *two stages*. One is coming from the way that he is *treated*, like dirt or whatever, but the other comes from the way that the parents *treat themselves*. If they abuse their bodies, their health or safety, either they are killed by that und the child gets *that* message on top of his general worthlessness message *or* they get the awful realization that *they*, the child, are not worth the parent taking sound care of *themselves*," the analyst said clinically.

"Yeah, I can imagine that, remember something like that in my feelings about how they were and I hated them for *that* too," Eugene said bitterly.

"I am sure of that, Eugene, und you have my sympathy!" he answered.

This statement made Eugene feel something winning, wonderful, warm and glowy inside and this was the first time in his life for such sensation.

"Now," said the analyst continuing on. "I am going to enlighten you on the emotional characteristics usually associated with being in the immature state and which are *carried* throughout life absent that reversal or recovery that is so rare," Doctor K. stated gently to Eugene. "First is that seeing of the world by *magic* und *not by logic.* The child who is about nine years old or younger exhibits a normal trait in seeing the world like this. When his father goes off to work in the morning and then comes home at the end of the day, he does not understand the concept and merely sees the disappearance and reappearance as *magic.*

"That I never was aware of," exclaimed Eugene.

"So, a child frozen at such an emotional level has that view of life forever and these are the folks who swear by superstition, ouija boards, *fate* as an active and predetermined thing or force was just a product of an immature emotional state that is normal in the child but abnormal in the adult?" Eugene asked incredulous.

"Correct," announced the all knowing one. "Und a large mass of humanity clings to this very idea to try to *make sense* out of the chaos inside of them and the chaos that they *think* that they see around them. The extra body stuff is just how the universe is. The whole, adult mind grasps it without a problem. Events such as a lightning strike that kills a four-year-old girl has no connection to anything except the existence of lightning and that child on the same planet," said the analyst philosophically.

"No more 'fate', no predetermination, no punishment from God?" Eugene asked in an unhappy voice.

"Vat? You *vant* punishment from God, Eugene?" he inquired with his eyebrows arched as high as they could go. "You *need* this?" he said. "Such a clear and great example of how rampant in the world is the root, child mistreatment!" he exclaimed mightily.

"Seems sick I guess, huh, doc?" he replied sheepishly. "I mean who *seeks* punishment anyway?" I guess it is sick, yes?"

"Ja!" countered the doctor. "Sick for certain und the product of what they did to you and the turmoil of emotions and feelings that got all screwed up like a marble cake. No child can withstand such a thing and come out whole and normal, Eugene, so don't feel so singled out if that's what it is you sense," he said.

"Oh, I don't...I don't really know *what* I feel right now. Mixed up, I guess," admitted Eugene.

"Don't vorry, ve vill get you straightened out. *First you must learn this stuff* und then und only then can you begin to grasp what happened to you und vat would be required to get recovered or a reversal if you ver *alive*. Of course, you are *dead*, Eugene, so that does not apply to you anymore. You vill get out of Limbo ven I certify your new education here *und* you make that confrontation ve spoke about, Ja?" the doctor repeated.

Eugene sat quietly and listened.

"You know, Eugene, I just now had a flash, an insight. Say that you are one-year old and you do not speak and you do not understand what the adults are jabbering about day in and month out. You look at them. They feed you. You cry and they respond und so forth. Eventually, you say 'mama' and they go wild and you see this in their eyes and hear the voices of delight. So, what happens next? You hear another word and manage to say it, too. Again, they all celebrate and praise you. It feels good, you love it and you find yourself seeking it. As you look up in to mama's face and dada's face for new clues and words, *their personality* gets rubbed off onto you. You gladly adopt it because it is a happy time and you want to be a part of it deeply. My question is this," observed the musing analyst. "How much of that child's eventual personality und character comes from that mimicking and what percentage comes from genetics or accident?"

Eugene saw right away that the doctor was baiting him with a question that was too elementary for a psychotherapist to be in the dark about, but he merely shrugged his shoulders and stayed mum.

"I mean, as the tender and innocent elf looks up into a face, how can it *not* be a sponge and absorb all that is there?" he insisted but Eugene would not budge.

Trying to sidestep a scenario that made him uncomfortable, Eugene asked the doctor, "How about those ball players with all *their* wacky moves and superstitions, huh, doc, all the rituals before throwing the ball or going up to the plate. And it is so shamelessly public," he declared.

"True, Eugene, vots the matter, you cannot answer the baby question?" the analyst demanded.

"I don't want to. I can't face that kind of a moment. I remember it and it wrenches me," Eugene lamented in a soft voice.

"Okay, Eugene, maybe ve come back to it, Ja?" he said. "Und so, vat about 'lucky' bingo cards, Ja?" he continued. "It's crazy und also shameless in public and under another good sign of the rampant abuse in the children's vorld!"

"Agreed," was the only response.

"Now, ve go to *fantasy*, imagination, exaggerations, und so forth, Eugene, und see that zees things are the normal child, Ja?" he asked.

"Sure, I guess so," said Eugene. "But don't normal adults, say writers for instance, engage in fantasy and use vivid imagination?" he wondered.

"Ja, they do, Eugene, but it is not *believed* by them or *relied on* by them to attain *emotional security or safety* or such as that, you see?" he asked.

"I see, yes," answered Eugene.

"But in *The Iceman Cometh*, my boy, vat did *you* do mit all those ideas of yours about people being too weak to lie one hundred percent in the truth und zat they need illusions just to survive, or, that truth destroys, or, that self- knowledge can kill, or, that truth destroys, or, that self knowledge can kill, or, that reality defeats attainment of the natural human impulse towards the *ideal*, or, that man is born broken all *zat* is nonsense cerebralization *und* to some degree, Eugene, a fantasy of juvenile proportions, Ja?" he insisted to a dismayed listener.

"Uh, I...," was all that Eugene could muster although he had heard this type of exposure of his past a few times already from Dr. K.

"Your constant agony and despair drove you to invent this stuff to answer the 'unanswerable' questions that you proclaim man is saddled with, Eugene, und that is the engine," he said to a now weeping patient.

The playwright looked as though he had lost his best friend even though he had never really had any friends in life, not truly because fractured people cannot attract whole people and other fractured ones are only self-dealing and never *truly* friends. People will deny it but Dr. K. will say so.

"Come now, Eugene," the doctor prompted him. "Let's move along or ve vill never get out of Limbo, Ja?" he laughed. "But tink, Eugene, pipe dreams to survive? Do you see the ridiculosity of it now, my boy?"

"Does seem kind of far-fetched sitting her in Limbo listening to you doc, I guess I have to admit it," he replied in a kind of relieved way.

"Ja! You *thought* that you ver right und I am sure you did not mean to hurt anybody, Ja, but they *all* say that! You ver 'doing the right thing', but it vas *the wrong thing*, Eugene!," he whispered through the side of his mouth.

"I wonder if I will get *this* diamond, too," he replied.

"Ve vill see", Dr. K. said. "Let's press on. Don't vorry, Eugene, that this seems like you were involved in a *sham*. Your whole life was just *that*!" he stated.

"A *sham*," Eugene said under his breath.

"You faked it at every turn. James and Ella gave you *shamhood* and you carried that banner 'proudly', Eugene!" he replied.

"They gave me nothing and I passed it along, didn't I doc? I mean, my kids and all?" he wondered out loud. "A conveyance of nothingness!" he exclaimed.

"Javol, und a lot of stuff was said about you, that you ver 'fully immersed in life', that you had 'tremendous integrity' ven all ze while, you ver desperate to matter, to belong, to find relief, Ja?" the doctor pointed out to him. "They remarked that you had a personal magnetism und ver a genius who vas wonderfully alive und a unique personality totally dedicated to your work. This might be partly true, Eugene, I don't want to shortchange you, but you ver seriously defective und suffering und it is more likely that this stuff was you being the good-guy-people-pleaser. This is one of those *substitutions* we went over that take the place of a true identity," the doctor went on.

"One of the reasons I am here, right?" Eugene asked as if he didn't know.

"Nobody is saying, Eugene, that you did not have the highest of standards or did not exercise a good deal of good will most of the time towards the public and so forth," Dr. K. assured him.

Seeming to not hear, Eugene repeated himself, "A conveyance of nothingness, right, doctor?"

"Right," he replied unthinkingly. "Of course, some have praised you in terms that seem overblown, my boy. For example, it has been claimed that your sincerity and selflessness left great impressions on people who could come away believing that you were one of the *most honest* human beings."

"If that had been so", Eugene observed, "I wouldn't be in Limbo, right?" he droned, do I recall correctly, Dr. K?"

"That *is* why you are in Limbo, Eugene, remember?" asked the analyst. Now, ve go on here und ve get closer und closer to a reversal, my boy! The frozen emotional level, the juvenile level, carries more. Let's see, there is, I am sure you know this," the doctor said with his hand cupped under his chin. "I am, vell, wait! I just remembered something here," he said, interrupting himself. "I am just so moved by that 'illusion-pipe dream' thing that I just have to tell you that the entire *Iceman Cometh* theory that the *powers* and the *masses* grasped so lovingly, although in a terrified state, was *not* how whole people are! Only fractured ones operate like that, live like that and believe that way. *Hickey* had a good idea, that all those bar people should go out and live a life free from all of the excuses and lies. But, he did not know, *nor did you*, that such carrying ons were possible only if a man is fractured by his parents, organic disorders and accidents of nature aside. I speak only of the hordes of *truly broken people.* They were *not born* that way, Eugene, but were broken only after *birth!*" the analyst explained excitedly. "It is ancient knowledge to me!"

"I hear you," said a suddenly weary Eugene.

"That *good idea* was shunted, Eugene, by a *sham* development that *you* insisted on: the *secret* that Hickey carried. He himself was tainted by a grand illusion that he killed his wife to *help her,* which was only an excuse, a disguise, for his *hatred* of her and *her* indulgence of *his* wayward emotions. It was a twisted world by magic exercise!," the doctor explained further.

"Maybe," Eugene sputtered.

"Und I *must* again apply the same to the ending of *Long Day's Journey Into Night,* Eugene, where everybody *confesses* or makes *admissions* or has these grand *revelations.* That is all bull, Eugene! *There is no finality in it,* if that ist vat you meant to convey, Ja? A crooked family or person does not get whole and honest und straightened out by mere confessions und such, Eugene," he stated emphatically. "The public bought it. The prize givers bought it unless they were awarding them merely for superb but inaccurate drama! But everybody missed the notion that people cannot think their way out of such a dilemma. *That* is the *ultimate life lie* again, Eugene, you see this?" the confident analyst exclaimed. "It takes not a cerebral transaction to put a stop to fakery and false lives. It takes that emotion-based transaction, Eugene, that grabbing onto and *grieving* of the loss of that genuine identity or authentic self that you already acknowledged!"

"I'm getting it now, doctor and thank you so much for this gift of relief!" he said lovingly. "I'm getting it now, slowly but for sure."

"You also attributed at the end of *Long Day's Journey* your *own* failures as a human being to similar ideas and that, too, was a sham," he assured him. "You had no idea what was behind those failures and all zat nonsense about 'compassion' und 'idiosyncrasies' und 'human weaknesses', Eugene, was just a *default explanation* of how misery is allowed to exist in families or between people," the analyst continued. "You were sure that that was the true light shining on your awful childhood, but it was a dim flicker. No place does one find the suggestion that your father, or Mr. Tyrone, or your mother, or the wife, or your brother or self portrayed as 'Edmund' were in any way connected directly to the abuse and neglect sustained by the kids that they once were, that it is usually *very subtle* and not physically violent, and that there is an effective remedy that has nothing to do with idiosyncrasies or compassion or the other excuses that you laid out on the play goer," Dr. K. lectured. "That stuff was largely 'feel good' invention made in desperation by you to get relief from a lifetime of bitterness!" he continued. "I am reminded here, my boy, that it has been often claimed that you had achieved a perfect understanding of your family, felt a deep pity and a forgiveness, and expressed it in *Long Day's Journey Into Night*, Ja?" Doctor K. went on. "Und also, that there was perfect objectivity by you instead of some kind of condemnation."

"OK," Eugene replied.

"But do you see a difference, my boy? Perfect understanding and perfect objectivity are not the same, you know?" the analyst remarked. "Tell me the difference, Eugene, please!"

Eugene looked weary and stayed silent.

"I tell you. Objectivity is a lack of bias and maybe you did do that but understanding is quite another thing and I wonder if you understood deeply or just on the surface?" Dr. K. lectured quizzingly.

"Huh?" said Eugene.

"You might claim that you understand your father's tightness with money, for instance, but do you understand it in the way of knowing its real cause? I mean, if his clan in Ireland was miserly, that might tell you *why* he was too, for understanding purposes but it does *not* explain the actual reason behind the tendency to be a tightwad, you see?" Dr. K. said.

"OK," replied Eugene.

"The *real* reason and path to a *perfect* understanding might go something like this, my boy: The clan was more or less comprised of adults who were mistreated as children, physically and emotionally. They grew up to suffer what all such children suffer only in their case, the hording of money represented power-a power that they felt robbed of as kids. With money, they had a defense, an escape, a way to smash back, you see? The horde stayed intact if the money was only dribbled out!" instructed the analyst.

"Makes some sense, I guess," countered Eugene.

"Und another ting, ve have the idea of *transcendence* being kicked around a lot by the critics and the experts and even you, Eugene, especially in regard to your last few major works," replied the doctor. "Und I am tinking of the notion that *you* yourself arrived at a transcendence of personal egotism in the face of criticism of those and other works, that you also no longer pursued romantic dreams or railed against the "selfishness" of materialism und merely applied objectivity and a realism."

O'Neill's eyes seem to brighten a bit.

"Ja, Eugene? Und now you tell me if this idea of transcendence was not just you giving up from bewilderment?"

Eugene looked like he'd been shot.

"I don't say it is, my good fellow, I'm asking!" Dr. K. quickly said.

"No! I do not think so," replied the playwright indignantly. "Why Edmund in the play that was kept hidden undergoes a tragic transcendence in stark contrast to the rest of the Tyrones and *that* is anything but bewilderment! So, maybe it is a rising above, a giving up of seeing a ting from the same level and viewing it from a higher perspective, Eugene?" he asked.

"Maybe," he answered hesitatingly.

"But couldn't such a ting as that be done and no judgment made but at the same time lack true understanding of the actions you are witnessing?" he asked him. "Couldn't there be such a new feeling merely out of weariness of a struggle to grasp, in other words, a bewilderment?"

"Not if there were that true understanding. Why then, there'd be no weariness, just elevation of consciousness," Eugene replied strongly.

"What if I told you that the critics called *Long Day* your 'greatest victory' and an achievement of "perfect understanding?" Dr. K. stated and then, without waiting for a response said, "Und another von, my boy, ist the idea in dat other von, *The Iceman*, Ja, that *transcendence* was at the most just coming to grips with the idea that there is after all is said und done, no final secret over that horizon?"

"That particularly *is* bewildering when one remembers the glow of the days spent sure that such a secret beckons, but that was so extremely long ago, doc, and I have gone thru so much since and been made aware of so much," Eugene admitted. "Now I have your wonderful suggestion about the abolition of the original lie!"

"I know, Eugene," assured the doctor.

"You never achieved any appreciable elevation of consciousness, did you?" he asked Eugene knowingly. "I mean, you were an addict right up to the end, nicht wahr?"

O'Neill suddenly appeared crestfallen.

"Come on now," Dr. K. prompted him. "Don't vorry, you vill learn in ze end."

"I didn't know most of the things that I am now learning here," Eugene said.

"Neither did the world!" he said in a louder voice. "All those experts were just as confused and ignorant as you were, I'm afraid."

"But you do not find fault with 'compassion', do you doctor?" he asked, already figuring the answer. "And surely you do see that there are such things as 'idiosyncrasies' that have absolutely nothing to do with child mistreatment and which exist in the world as a natural variation in people and which need to be made room for, doc?"

"Certainly, my boy," he assured the playwright. "I have nothing against those things, in fact, I ever can encourage what you say. However, one must learn and be on guard against similar stuff that is not really 'compassion' and so forth and which is really enabling due to the enabler's own weaknesses or fear or insecurities."

"I did get several prizes of great magnitude remember, doc," replied Eugene.

"Yes, I know, my son, I know, and perhaps they were given for dramatic content rather than accuracy of message, eh?" he asked him. "I do not quarrel with technique or the revolutionary aspects to your work or the novelty or the actual descriptions of misery in the family and the world. I quarrel merely with the ideas explicit or implied in those plays and in your public sayings that the stuff is inborn, innate and the omission by you of the remedies that await," he said. "The de facto falsehoods in those works were spun off like tornadoes that swept the country if not the world!"

"I *was* the rage there for a while, yes indeed!" Eugene said proudly.

"Made up whitewash! That's what it was!" the analyst said in a loud voice that started Eugene. Much of that stuff in *Long Day's Journey* was candy coating on crap!"

Eugene stayed silent at this sudden turn but he understood the vehemence.

"Any *true* weaknesses, like genetic or accidental or pure, innate personality stuff," he declared. "Of course must be taken into account in clashes in families or other relationships, but the vast mass of emotional 'junk' in that play, not to mention several others, is induced by the parents into innocent children who then grow up to repeat that cycle and any renowned work of art, like yours, that allow this stuff to pass as 'truth' is junk and should be exposed!," he yelled.

Eugene was withered by this but remained on his beam of getting out of Limbo and so did not speak. He *did* begin to feel that the analyst was correct.

"Would they allow a defective one to run this program here in this other world?" he wondered aloud and then responded quickly that it could *never* be so. Eugene also remembered for some crazy reason his father's last words about 'all rotten, no good' and so forth and he began to understand that his Papa was not right, that it was *not* that way at all although a large part of society and people *were* rotten in the sense of leading grossly defective lives. However, he now saw, thanks to Dr. Kornschucher, that it was not inborn and did not have to be that way. So, his, Eugene's, portrayals of life that way were wrong just as his father's idea that the world was rotten and no good and that after death was a better place.

"Life for the Tyrones would have gone on as before," assured Dr. K., "because no remedy was at hand for the dysfunctional family members. Admission of deceit is a *start*, but it does not remove the cause of that deceit and it will continue indefinitely for the *same reason* that it began," he continued. "The reversal and cure are possible only by the emotional transaction that I already referred to!"

"And admissions of jealousies that I put in there, failings, unrealized dreams making people 'turn against' others rather than face their own 'guilt', that's all the same thing, doctor?" Eugene had to ask.

"Of course, my boy, of course. How could it not be? 'Unrealized dreams' are no source of turning against somebody. That's false fare and made up crap, Eugene," scolded the analyst. " It's the *unresolved rage* against the *parents* that makes people turn against anything that is not connected. It's a phony target, a misplaced aggression if you recall, Eugene?"

Eugene quietly pondered this again.

"Such unfortunate people and *you*, Eugene, did not know the source of the pain, the crookedness, the false blaming, the verbal violence because it is buried in the baby past and the survival structure is so firmly in place that the affected person has no real conscious idea of it all. Had you known all this, Eugene, it would have been placed front and center stage in your plays. The experts and the analyzers were roundly fooled. They all swallowed hard and it *went down!*" he said.

"I cannot express how terrible it feels to be on to something so profound as the *Long Day's Journey Into Night* seemed to me," Eugene whimpered. "And now to find out that it was largely junk!"

"Do not feel bad, Eugene," counseled the analyst. "You are on the right track now. Acht!" he cried. "Look at the *irony* here. You tried desperately to matter and to feel better by staging productions that publicly displayed the very dysfunction that you were attempting to escape from! Now that's something!" the analyst cried. "Trying to heal the hole inside by showing it off and waiting for some 'curative' reaction."

"Yeah, I guess that accurately describes it," Eugene admitted.

"What did some of the 'experts' say about you? You admitted during the final part of your life that you were *still* trying to understand people. That was proof that you were still lost, Eugene, yet, these critics and analysts were piling it on higher and higher with stuff such as the absolute demands that you made upon life with your *acute* awareness of humanity's failures!" the doctor smirked. "Hell. Eugene, you might have had an acute awareness but it was just an *inventory*. Where were the explanations? All we got were 'self-destructive tendencies' which is crapola, or 'perverse complexities of human nature', more of the same fantasy junk although humans *are* complex. There's just no perversity in it. That comes by way of warped children made in the image of warped parents. Period!" he said.

"Don't forget the 'victims of the ironies of life', doc, or 'fate' or 'innate weakness' or 'human frailty'," Eugene reminded him.

"Yes, those too, Eugene, all junk stuff that the public ate up. But no revelation of the true roots of this, again, nature-made diseases and accidents aside?" the analyst went on. "Why you made it sound like *freaks* inhabited the earth and not whole, calm, rational, productive, happy souls! Those inhabitants were mostly born that way but got bamboozled from the start!"

"Geeze, what a mess!" he replied.

"But everyone was fooled," said the doctor. "Nearly everyone, that is. The public ate it all up with a spoon. I am referring to the plays *and* what is force-fed to babies!"

"I wrote only of life as I saw it, not more," explained Eugene. "It was the truth as *I* saw it."

"I know, Eugene. I've heard that already," said the analyst. "But the idea of 'victims' is a concept that defies reality really because it presupposes an *evil force* and, excluding mental illness which is the only evil on Earth, there are no other truly evil forces as portrayed in your plays. 'Victims' is the nice thing again and it is not in touch!" insisted Dr. K. "There *are* no victims of anything innate or inherently human. *That* was made-up stuff born of your desperation as I have pointed out. Escape from your own agony and misery, sadness and depression, that was the driver and it clouded your perceptions fatally," he went on.

"Sounds like I was an idiot!" Eugene said in a thin voice.

"No, Eugene, you *were* a victim, but not as an adult. You were the victim of adults when in the baby state. That is not the same concept that I am talking on. Children are green and unprotected and unwary. Victimization is easy there. But in adults, it is not. The malaise that parents put onto kids, that thing that makes them *subhuman* at first, although maybe *superhuman* later as a device, results in emotional illness that is spread out over the globe like a thin haze of smoke," he said.

"I wonder, doctor, I am now thinking, right now, of my words on the 'fog people' the stammerers, that I portrayed as always bumming a cigarette. They've got the habit but not the means. Are *they* subhuman?" Eugene asked.

"They could be either. Plenty of superhuman persons who are bigger than life, the big shots, the heroes, the stars, the can do guys, also cannot manage to buy their own smokes!" he replied. "Both can be that way but mostly 'fog people' *are* the *lost child* or the *scapegoat* role."

Eugene sat and pondered all of this and thought about his coming escape from Limbo. But first, he had to endure more education and acceptance of the truth.

"I do not recall if we covered this already, Eugene," the doctor said. "But it is so important that it will not do anybody ill if we go over it some more."

"Oh?" asked Eugene.

"Your idea that the *pressures* and *causes* of family dysfunction existed *in spite of the love* that each family member felt for the others and that such *causes* compel them to drive each other to *despair* is the most bogus thing that I have ever come across, Eugene!" the analyst yelled for effect.

Eugene sort of hunkered down, slouched, and waiting for more, smiled thinly.

"*There is no love in that family. Period!*" he stated flat out. "*Love is giving* and nothing more. But *that* family never experienced love because they did not love *themselves*! It is a *prerequisite*. Love cannot exist along with jealousy or hate. Such is not giving, Eugene. *It is pure taking!* It is pure self-dealing!" he said.

"I understand, doctor," he said, but the analyst could not tell if he was being patronized or not.

He continued. "Then, I see the Tyrones as being 'chained together by guilt, resentment, love and hate'. Same thing, Eugene! Throw the 'love' part out. Then, I would agree."

"Agree?" Eugene asked, not believing is ears.

"Sure!" was the quick reply. "Throw out the thing that cannot exist with hate, that is the love part, and the rest make a nice, neat little package of *codependence*. *That* is what chains them together!"

"You know, I think that we *did* go over all this already, doc, can't we move on?" he asked in a childlike way.

"Soon my boy, soon. Meanwhile, let's finish up with those awful public comments about your work. They stated somewhere back a long way that the *Long Day's* play was a *vehicle* used by you to *forgive* your own family, although they were already dead by 1939. They said with a straight face that it was employed to *reconcile* you with your past and that it resulted in a *disintegration* of your *lifelong resentment* through a *complete understanding* of that past and a *total self-honesty*. Ah, yes, I am sure now. That does ring ze bell, Eugene. Ve *have* done this part. I am sorry, kid. Ja, I vas saying that it vas a lot of barnyard piles!" the analyst apologized.

"And I know that I *did* leave strict instructions with Carlotta about no books on that play until twenty-five years passed after *I* passed and no staging either," he repeated. "So, she cut me right out and did it anyway!"

"Ja!" said the doctor.

"Some wife, huh?" he said resignedly.

"The void vas clamoring for it, Eugene. It vonted its 'fix' und she could not deny them, I guess. Then, they ate up the junk! They all missed the obvious!" he complained and the two of them shook their heads.

"Anyway, Eugene, *all junk* or mostly so. All that stuff that they said was puffery. It was not science for certain, but who demands science? Not the Creationists! Not the flat-Earth people. Not the wiggly souls of superstition!" he said in a funny voice. "Und 'disintegration of lifelong resentment'! That's a joke, but I do not say it to hurt you, Eugene, just to get it out clearly!" he said. "You still had enough resentment left in you in that Boston hotel to feed a pile of people."

"I *was* pissed off, that's for sure!" he replied loudly.

"The pills for the inner shakes I recall, Eugene, and almost *no* understanding is how I would put it," he announced. "Und here's another von. Listen to this," he said. "Another critic or drama expert had you harboring a fellow-feeling for your tyrannical father and hostile brother and that a transcendence of your own selfish emotions was at hand which achieved *illumination*! That kills me!" exclaimed the analyst. "Where do they get such crap?"

Eugene stayed silent.

"What fellow-feeling? Or did you put that wording in *Long Day's*? If so, this is the same negative stuff. If you really did think that such a thing was inside of you, it was maybe, at most, a mellowing of old angles and sharp parts but the basic breach of father-son was intact. It had to be, Eugene. He treated you like a nonperson and was sort of an ultimate self-dealer. So was Ella. There might have been your own 'selfish emotions' but they were well based. You had a good reason for feeling hatred and resentment. They were supposed to love you for Christ's sake!" the doctor yelled.

Eugene looked like the client in the courtroom after his adept attorney has just spoken irrefutably to the opposition's case.

The analyst continued. "Maybe you *did* achieve a little bit of understanding in the way of *pity* or that 'compassion' for them, James, Ella and Jamie, for the struggling human beings that they were and that is laudable and noble. But the way that the experts put it, you'd think that you had struck 'curative gold' and gone straight to heaven, which, we now know, you did not, at least not yet."

"Don't remind me, doc," said a passive Eugene.

"Listen," said the analyst. "You're darned lucky to be here with me and doing all this after a couple of years of languishing here. All you need is to pay attention to our transactions and wind up the *exact opposite* of the way that you were on Pequot Avenue, were *required* to be by *them*, to survive those long years there and on the road with the troupe of Monte Cristo," he continued.

"Opposite," Eugene mouthed the word.

"Of course," replied the doctor. "What do you think, that you can be the same sneaky creature here and get away with it, gain something, get a reversal and get out of this place?" he said sharply!

Eugene now really felt the thing. He knew in his bones *now* that Dr. K. was bona fide and that the interaction with him was a model for father-son or parent-son and he began to rejoice quietly. There was a sort of a letting go inside of him.

"You must tell the truth all the time, you understand?" asked Dr. K. "It is that 'opposite' of which I speak, the very thing that was *not* ongoing in New London. And don't bother telling me anything else, Eugene. I already know already. You are having feelings now that I am your father the way he could have been and maybe the way he was in the *Ah, Wilderness* atmosphere?" the analyst said.

"You read my mind, doc," he replied. "Makes me feel naked!"

"Ja, und zat ist the vay you vere born, naked, und so, you are being sort of born here except that you are permanently *dead*. No point in any more twisting or stalling or complaining now," he assured Eugene.

Eugene's face grew very bright but then drooped out of habit.

"Here, you tell the truth, hear the truth and are *free* from turmoil or punishment or loss or any other terrible thing that comes with deceit. No more jumping out of the bushes and nailing you!" he said confidently to a receptive Eugene. "Life itself might 'jump out' but no monsters from 'within' can anymore. Lightning can still strike you but no derailments from the secret agony because *it, too* will be dead."

"No more pretense," Eugene said out loud to himself.

"Correct!" exclaimed Dr. K. "No more pretending that everything is alright just to avoid more trouble. Here, you do not have to keep your mouth *shut* because of a fear of the consequences. No secrets and no 'no talk rule,'" he said.

"No talk rule?" Eugene asked. "What is *that*?"

Dr. Kornschucher told him that this rule was the one prevalent in most households that blocks any mention of 'mother's drinking' or 'father's gambling problem' or so and so's bad temper. It keeps the calm, or so everyone believes. Meanwhile, turmoil is churning up everybody's guts and the pot will boil over sooner or later be it a new black eye for mom or the setting on fire of dad's car.

"I get it," said Eugene. "Gee, I have to say that it is the most unusual feeling to be as you instructed me to be, honest and open and truthful and not shy or reserved or worried or doubting or suspicious! I've been that way all of my life," confided Eugene. "Sixty-five years," he remarked, still not quite believing it.

Continuing with prior discussion, Dr. K. then said, "I am not done, Eugene, with the phony public responses, the critics' pronouncements. One was the remarkable statement that O'Neill has finally reconciled himself to being the man that he really is and that this came through *penetrating self-analysis*. Wow! What crap!" exclaimed the analyst. "You, Eugene, never knew who in hell you really were or what you really felt or what you truly wanted. Only the whole know such things," he commanded. "The fractured ones never find out because their identities are buried inside of them and terrified to come out. This was *you* for sure."

"I wonder who in hell these people really are, were?" Eugene remarked, referring to the critics and drama talkers.

"As far as 'penetrating self-analysis,'" the doctor observed, "you discovered nearly nothing there. How could you? All your waking hours were cerebralizations just as in the themes of those plays as we have shown already. You agree?"

"Yes, I am beginning to agree," he replied hesitatingly.

"You are not *required* to agree but you *are* required to speak the truth,

Eugene," he demanded politely.

Eugene reported how he *did* try to analyze himself, made quite a project out of it and that it was mostly to get at the root of his drinking binges. He made charts and diagrams. But he told Dr. K. that he failed to hit on most or all of what was on these diamonds.

"It was in you but hidden," he reminded Eugene. "Then I read somewhere that you 'confronted' your most harrowing memories and put your ghosts to rest. They reported that your delving into the stuff for *Long Day's Journey Into Night* appeared to have been 'partially therapeutic'," he went on.

"You disagree?" Eugene wondered aloud.

"Not completely," replied the doctor. "Partially is close to what you *might* have achieved but 'partially' is not worth that much because the remedy like that is similar to one-half a dose of anti-venom. You'll feel something but the poison lingers and is devastating. Insights are gut but only a start. The stubborn monster of falsity stays in power or it is ousted. There is no in between."

"What about the 'putting ghosts to rest' part?" he asked.

"There could have been *some* relief in your belief that you *were* forgiving your parents or were understanding them more, but the real ghosts, the loneliness, the agonies, the struggling, the doubts about God, apparent meaninglessness of life and the not belonging, those ghosts haunted you right up to the end and no more need to be said about that!" he said loudly.

"I see," said a solemn Eugene. "Yes that sounds right."

"You know that they did, Eugene, come on!" he demanded.

"I was a pain in the ass, yes," he replied. "Moody, loss of temper, extremes of emotion, on pills, still smoking though I hated the stench."

The doctor mused a second and then said, "For some reason, I am again reminded of the topic of materialism and what you have said about this over the many years, Eugene."

Eugene watched his face in anticipation.

"Man is by nature materialistic and sinful and his tries to find his own dreams must lead him into evil. This he tries to escape and the very nature of those dreams dooms man. His romantic vision of perfection in his race becomes the source of all evil," Dr. K. proclaimed. "Sounds like you?"

"Gee," replied Eugene.

"A fundamental fact of human evil?" asked the analyst.

Eugene sat waiting.

"Well?" asked the doctor.

"Well," replied Eugene. "I…uh…I remember…yes, *The Hairy Ape*, my ape," he said, "*That* was where I started to attack this awful American blight of possessions…materialism as a way of daily life. Then, later, I attacked again. Let me see," he said, with his hand on his chin thinking. "Ah, yes, that salvation cannot be had until man *renounces* all of such things and goes back to a spiritual way. In attempting to get what he needs, day to day, man shoves aside the ideal things that he needs or needs to be."

Having heard him but seeming to ignore it for the moment, the doctor next asked him, "My boy, the spiritual way, have you not at some time in your miserable past said straight out that mankind's loss of faith was the cause of the sickness in society and that such loss was itself caused by his abandonment of *traditions* and that his heresy from abandonment of *orthodox religion*?"

"I see where you are headed," Eugene stammered, embarrassed.

"Ja!" exclaimed the doctor. "Pretty bad, huh?"

Eugene blinked his eyes waiting for the bomb to explode.

"Now," in a loud challenge, "now, you explain what's wrong mit dis, Ja?"

"Vell, I mean well," Eugene stuttered. "What I said there, it ignores that these various things were only *symptoms*, not real causes. Oh!, it pains me to have to admit that, but what choice is there, anymore?" he said, voice trailing away.

Impatient to get it all out, "Javol, Eugene!" the analyst exclaimed. "Und, vat else? I tell you! Not only is 'abandonment' of orthodox religion just a symptom and not a cause, the same for ignoring old traditions, any preaching of this anywhere by anyone implies that robot rules will work! You see dis?" he asked.

"Oh, yeah, robot rules," O'Neill recalled. "Robots obey and go back to the orthodox and the traditions because it is a rule jammed down their throats, not because something is newly healed in their heads," cried out a proud Eugene!

"I am delighted! Und, the udder part, der material possessions ting, zat ist too a symptom, Ja? A warped life of chasing material tings, Eugene, is not any cause, you see?" he inquired in a voice that implied that Eugene could not get this wrong anymore.

O'Neill smiled silently.

"It is an imagined feel-good way of thinking und acting und is engaged in because an emptiness inside of them craves *something* to fill up the hole," he lectured. "Und *renouncing* that way of being without more, just doing it cold, is another robot behavior, Eugene, you understand me?" he continued almost unaware of Eugene's presence. "The spiritual way comes only when recovery comes and never before! Only that grief-work to heal the damage will open a real gate of heaven, Eugene!" he said, seemingly be aware of his charge. "Never do we change from that just by deciding! *That* would be more robotics."

"And the fundamental evil stuff, doc?" O'Neill asked.

"More baloney, my boy und I tink you know dis already, Ja?" he replied in a warm voice. "Man is no more materialistic or sinful by nature ,organic excluded, of course, than the man in the moon! Ve are born whole and spiritual and not sinful or any other such defective way. That is grafted on beginning with the original lie, you recall?" he asked assuringly.

"And my old ideas about 'possessions' as being self-destructive and ending up ultimately dispossessing, that is bogus, too, right?" Eugene wondered aloud.

"Maybe the State's Attorney missed this, Ja?" he replied like Santa Claus and Eugene went into an internal fit of memory-feelings chaos, a shadow of a recalling but not enough to admit to himself. He was now like a beet!

"Now, Eugene, there was a piece that was published about your work, something to the effect that existing society did not have the ability to change family or individual personality predicaments and that the so-called 'rational enlightenment' would have no place in enabling moral reform. *This* I quarrel with strongly! It seems to be stating that such predicaments and good old moral behavior or *reformed* behavior could not be induced or corrected by the wherewithal that society possesses," complained Dr. K. "Vat kind of hogwash ist that? Are they insinuating that people who are in the everyday kinds of struggles and problems that *you* were or even the average emotionally troubled family cannot be helped by a rational or learned process?" he asked bitterly.

"Sounds hopeless, doesn't it!" he replied. "Crazy stuff!" .

"Javol! Vat insult!" he replied. "Crazy stuff!"

"You'd think that they would know more than that," Eugene said.

"I vont to ask you, Eugene, about some lines that you put in for Mary Tyrone that vent something like this. 'None of us can help the things that life has done to us'. Und a little farther on, 'you've lost your true self forever'. You recall this?" he asked.

"Yes, I do, very well," replied the playwright.

"Now I realize that these are not matters brought up by the critics or experts," Dr. Kornschucher said. "But I just now recalled them and they are remarkably on point! The, the mother figure, Mary, says something like 'the things that life has done to us! ' or to *me*, maybe, 'cannot be explained'. She says these words to her husband, does she not?" Dr. K. asked rhetorically.

"Correct," said Eugene.

"My direction here," said Dr. K., "is that these lines reveal something very important to me and show *only now* to you! Can you see it now that you have learned a little something from the diamonds?" he asked Eugene.

Eugene told the doctor that he thought that the things that life has done to us or does to people, are sometimes things that *can* be helped and that not all of such events are mere chance occurrences. Dr. K was very pleased and asked Eugene to continue. Eugene added that 'losing your true self forever' was not a valid concept because it lies hidden and fearful to come out, but that it *can* be brought out. Again, Dr. Kornschucher was delighted to hear this. Eugene claimed that he did not know the actual remedy yet even though he *had* already heard it described a few times by Dr. K.

"Und vat about that line 'things that cannot be explained', Eugene. Can you explain that?" he asked him and Eugene replied that life's little jolts or large ones are often just physics, such as lightning, or biology, like diabetes, or happenstance, like a flat tire. He said that they were *not* a punishment by God or anyone else.

"But they *could* be caused by someone's misery being pushed onto you either intentionally or carelessly and that this notion was either onto the baby who then internalizes it and lives it or onto a fractured adult who has no true resistance to such things and is affected one way or the other by it," Eugene said confidently.

"So you see now," said the doctor, "that these ideas were mere pokes in the dark to try to slay the monster, Ja, Eugene?" He then pointed out to him again that despair and depression kept him from realizing such a thing, that it was so false. Also, he allowed that maybe whiskey had a role.

"You asked me about the word 'codependent', Eugene. I don't know if we touched on this yet or not but codependent is what *normal* kids are and the thing they lose when they reach about age sixteen or so. It is the gaining of a sense of self-worth, self-esteem, from outside sources instead of from inside of one's self naturally. Kids do *not* lose it however if they are abused and ne-glected. It stays with them and it shows like a *neon lamp!*" he proclaimed. "In such cases, the affected adult is constantly seeking approval and praise to feel like he is worth something."

"People who brag a lot or drive flashy cars, sport tattoos, chase women to get that 'kill' of new conquest, this is what you mean, doc?" Eugene asked.

"Exactly, my boy, except that tattoos *can* be 'normal' and not a sign of codependency. Now, when you were a regular in New London, you were known for use of catch words or phrases and slang, colloquialisms, Ja?" he asked Eugene.

"Don't recall, doc, too long ago," Eugene pretended.

"I have it on good authority, Eugene, that you did. It is meant to shore up the spirit, the image, a try to guaranty that one gets attention. Flashy clothes is the same thing. *You* were a codependent long after sixteen, Eugene," Dr. K. said. "The seeking is never-ending and the affected soul goes from low to the next high day after day always riding that rush of imagined self-worth or falling under the crush of rejection. A simple unkind look or word can *destroy!*" he said.

"Any nexus to my 'alcoholic' parallels?" Eugene asked the analyst.

"I don't really see that but those parallels we already dismissed as the desperation moves of one caught in the web of chaos and booze!" he exclaimed. "I *will* say, though, that the alcoholic's life and the codependent's life both embrace illusions, the juvenile 'fix' transferred to the adult seeker. Both seek oceanic peace and euphoria," he said.

"Uh, yeah," Eugene said.

"Your marriages, Eugene, show a defective emotional state. *You* probably attribute them to more or less 'regular' flow of life but the ditching of Kathleen after one week, the actual marrying of her on a whim in the first place, the subsequent over the side treatment of Agnes and the two kids with her and then the twenty-four-year relationship with Carlotta, your third wife, stormy as it was, all speak to dysfunction and codependency. We know that number three wanted a famous husband and one who was a genius. We also know that you yourself pleaded with her that you needed her. She was the buffer to being alone. She made you belong to something. You two *used* each other," he said.

"I could not stand to be without Carlotta for more than a short time, yet, she got on my nerves a lot," Eugene said bewilderedly. "She filled up a void and gave me a sense of power of sorts," Eugene said.

"But no *love* in the sense that I told you about, right?" he was next asked.

"I *did* love her, doc, I really did!" Eugene insisted but the analyst reminded him that love is giving and not more. He told him that many relationships are *mistaken* for love but that they are really just gratitude, comfort, sex, not being alone, convenience and the like.

"After a while, chinks appear but there are *no chinks in love*," he told Eugene. "Flaws rise up and rejections come, violence can flare, pettiness takes root," he went on to instruct him, "and adversity soon rules. It is *self-dealing* all the way," he told him.

"So much for marriage," Eugene said dejectedly.

"Nothing wrong with marriage," Dr. K. said. "Just codependent marriage is bad." Then the analyst went on to introduce Eugene to the related topic of *enmeshment,* which usually exists in dysfunctional families such as his was. He told him that this was the abnormal encroachment of roles upon one another like the ten-year old boy whose mother sets him up to play the father position in the family vis a vis her own status as wife. It is *sick* and a symptom of child mistreatment. Eugene sat and wondered about his own family and whether there had been any enmeshment in it. The role of "child" on the part of his mother in connection with his father, James, came to his mind as a possibility of this.

"Aside from codependence," the doctor continued a prior thought, "a dysfunctional family can feel chained together by fear of the outside world. They might have a vague hope for better days but they usually never come. Only *more* days come. 'Strife' can actually represent comfort to that kid of family unit," he went on, "because strife is familiar and more or less constant. If there is yelling, they all feel at home. Thus the 'comfort' notion."

"In my case," Eugene interjected, "religion also held the two of them together because it was forbidden by the church. Otherwise, they'd have split up long ago," he conjectured to the analyst.

"Perhaps you are right, Eugene," said the doctor with a sympathetic tilt of the head. "Now, because we seemed to have strayed so far from the traits of the immature personality, and that is okay in analysis because too rigid a schedule can shunt progress, let's go back to that, shall we?" he asked.

"I almost forgot," he replied.

"Me, too," the analyst added. "Now, left are the traits of immediate gratification, the characteristic being easily led, the one of shamelessness, and the trait of rebelliousness which is not the same idea as the 'rebel' role, a superhuman role that we discussed that aims at *mattering*," he continued.

"And *that* will do it for this diamond?" he wondered aloud.

"Pretty much, Eugene," replied the analyst kindly. "Immediate gratification is what every juvenile *must have*. Ever see a kid pester his mother when she is on the telephone? When these kids grow up whole, that tendency disappears, but if the child is fractured, it does not and the man demands this in life! You see it in traffic all the time! Can you relate?" the doctor asked.

"Maybe," he answered. "I remember when Jamie and I would go up to Bradley Street for some fun and thinking that it was so much better than having to court a girl and treat her well and buy her stuff and get cornered. The babes up there were ready whenever *I* was. No waiting! I couldn't bear delay anyway!" he admitted.

"Very gut, Eugene. Now, the *shamelessness thing*. Kids have no inhibitions and will talk to strangers about the most intimate stuff, you know? Grown up kids who cannot outgrow shamelessness will talk to anyone in a bar without knowing that person at all and again, reveal the most embarrassing things," Dr. K. went on.

"I am very familiar with that bar stuff, doctor. And flashy clothes that make others cringe is shameless too, right? Seeking attention in an outrageous way carries the same root, right?" Eugene guessed.

"Excellent, Eugene! Und now ve move to, let me see, to *irresponsibility*. Did I put that one in the list? Anyway, irresponsibility is normal in der kinder but ven he grows up fractured, he keeps this. Thus the wrecklessness in the world, Eugene!" Dr. K. said.

"Sounds like you are ready to pin *that* label on me, doc?" he winced.

"Vell, Eugene, vat vould *you* call your life?" he replied. "Leaving Agnes and the two kids by her was kind of like forgetting a valise at the train station, Ja?"

Eugene stayed silent.

"Und then the 1906 Princeton thing, Eugene, that too, Ja?"

Eugene stayed silent.

"Now ve have *selfishness*. Did I list it, Eugene? Anyway, this one is *normal* for the youngster but not the adult. It gets carried over, however, the same way and the predominance of selfishness in the world proves once again the preponderance of child mistreatment!" he lectured sternly.

"Sounds like me in a way, huh?" Eugene finally spoke. "I guess I was that guy!"

"Javol, the great playwright, the enigma, the mystery. Big deal! No time for his children who were being made into miniature Eugenes!" he yelled *kindly*. "Pulitzer Prizes *und* the great Nobel crown! Selfishness abounding, Eugene!" he said. "Next ve have 'easily led', Eugene, und this von is simple. A child is easily led because he or she is inexperienced and has no ego bulwark yet. So, they can be talked into or out of anything! The grown up who is fractured retains this and thus, the naivety in the world, Ja?" he said.

"Boy, you sure do cover it all, don't you?" Eugene said gingerly to Dr. K. "*Immaturity* comes next," Dr. K. told him. "Und zat is simple to grasp. The child who grows up broken by chronic maltreatment does not lose this und so, behaves like a baby. Everybody is always saying to him 'why don't you grow up' but he does not know how! Only emotion-based recovery can do that trick," he said.

"Okay," said Eugene, eager to get on with the task.

"By the way, immaturity does not mean in *taste* or *education*. It is emotions only, Eugene, Ja?" he asked.

"Sure," he replied. "Like tantrums, right?" he asked.

"Gut!" was the reward.

"I was considered a false pose by many in town," Eugene admitted, "a pain in the ass, a difficult, dandy type, demanded that I get my own way, flew off the handle when I *got* a handle on a bottle!" he confided to the analyst.

"Immature! Javol, my boy. Und how about *rebelliousness*?" he asked him.

"Not a rebel but rebelliousness, right, doc?" Eugene remembered.

"Correct!" the doctor assured his bright listener.

"Is it normal in kids? I really don't have any experience with them!" he admitted sheepishly.

"James und Ella robbed you of the treasure that is fatherhood. They *also* robbed Eugene, Jr.,Shane und Oona O'Neill of the treasure that should have been their *father, you*!

Eugene bowed his head very low on this and sobbed a little.

"Rebelliousness," the doctor said to distract him, "is normal, Ja? Und a healthy breaking away to test the vorld, Ja?" the analyst posed the query.

"Like when I was fifteen and refused to go to church anymore and had a tussle with my old man about it?" Eugene chimed in.

"No! That is not it, Eugene. That was not rebelliousness, not the false role of 'rebel'. That was *rebelling for just cause* and was a healthy thing to do even if you were a basket case," the doctor lectured him. "Vat ve are speaking about now is that testing tendency that is seen so much in teenagers but in toddlers, too. If the child grows up not whole, he leads off many aspects of his life with rebelliousness for its own sake and is troublesome for everyone!" he added.

"What about my rebelling against the American way of life in my plays?" he asked the doctor. "Wasn't some of *that* constructive?" he wondered.

"I imagine that it vas, Eugene, Ja?" the analyst said. "Oops, I forgot one, I tink, the seeking by the immature personhood of a child of *novelty*!"

"Okay," replied the playwright.

"You know, Eugene, I just remembered your 1909 trip to Honduras leaving a pregnant bride behind. *That* was your father's doing, Ja? *He* was scared that Kathleen was plotting to take over his 'riches' so he led you to dump her, Ja? Don't answer, Eugene! You ver *easily led*!" the analyst said triumphantly.

"Geeze!" was the sole sound.

"Pick up that stone und put it in your shirt, Eugene," the doctor ordered. He complied and in minutes, Dr. Korschucher returned with the familiar black cloth-covered plate bearing another diamond. It was *nine carats* and a dazzler! He read the etched inscription as before:

SPIRITUALITY
Spirituality is innate in human nature. It is diminished
or eradicated in the fracturing of a child but returns on
recovery.

Dr. K. began by telling the wide-eyed Eugene that this ought to be of the utmost excitement to him in light of his lifelong struggle with the question of God, a society without God, the problems with redemption and salvation without God, the seemingly random allocation of 'dirty tricks' in life by 'fate', what the actual meaning is in all that man beholds, if any, or if there is nothing but 'meaninglessness'. He also pointed out Eugene's occupation with his sense of lost connection to God complete with his anger at him and puzzlement over it, his ideas of 'spiritual darkness', and faith turning into skepticism.

Eugene's face was a mixture of shining and eagerness at this.

"You had a hole in your soul," he was told, "and you strove to heal it, fill it in, by displaying it in public thru your works and waiting for some kind of reaction to boost your sense of well being and make you feel worthy and that you mattered," said the doctor. "Typical codependent behavior," he asserted to an absorbing Eugene, now free of most or all of his heel-digging in and cynicism. "You got a sense of your own value from the outside world when there was none inside, all persons with backgrounds at home like yours being similar."

Eugene just sat quietly and waited.

"One of the heavy and dear prices that you paid, my boy," he added, "was the *loss of spirituality*! On top of that, your Roman Catholic upbringing was taken by you eventually as a con job because its structure did not serve your spiritual needs and yearnings while the stories foisted upon you as part of its dogma were patently unbelievable and you had had enough falsity at home," Dr. K. said.

"They were so 'distant' if you understand my meaning, doc. Not physically, but held away from me," he replied.

"They were *emotionally unavailable* to you, Eugene, and that confounds a child. It is an unacceptable puzzle to a young heart and it twists it immediately!" he added. "And the split at age fifteen over the unanswered prayers to God on your Mama's morphine habit was the last straw. That was enough for you!" he said.

Eugene sat patiently.

"Listen, my friend, I want you to now visualize your three children and see *yourself* as emotionally unavailable to *them*!" the analyst ordered.

"Oh God! I know. It's terrible, but what can I do?" he begged.

"Too late!" exclaimed the doctor. "Damage done!"

"I am a beast!," Eugene cried out desperate.

"You are the beast of James and Ella!" replied the doctor. "They created you and then you created three of your own," he said to a drooping man.

"What can *I* do?" he sobbed.

"I know, Eugene, very sad. It's always *very sad*," the doctor claimed philosophically. "But nobody ever truly knows what to do about it. *Here*, Eugene, *you* can *do* something about it!" he proclaimed excitedly.

"I'll do anything, doc, just name it," he replied eagerly.

"*I*, Dr. Friedrich August Kornschucher, *have* the answer, but the vorld vill not listen!" he said defeatedly. "They always know better than me," he said. "*They always think that they can think their way out!*" he complained. "It's the ultimate life-lie, Eugene, the virulent offspring of The Original Lie etched so plainly on the first diamond, you remember?" he asked him.

"So, what do I do, doc?" he wanted to know with that expression on his face that only *a child* can have.

Ignoring him for a moment, the analyst said, "Do you know *why* they pay no attention, Eugene? I'll tell you *why*. They are *afraid*. They live in *terror*. The same thing that gripped their baby hearts in the beginning has them by the throat *now* and they cannot bear to face it!" he exclaimed. "So they think their way *around* it all!"

The playwright seemed stunned to hear it all framed like this.

"*You*, Eugene, can help by learning all of it and doing what I *tell* you to do," Dr. K. exclaimed vehemently.

Eugene nodded obediently.

"You yourself have yet to know of a heavy toll, a heavier toll, to be collected and I cannot tell you of it's coming," said the doctor mysteriously.

A furrow knit Eugene's brows but his lips stayed sealed.

"*That* fear is a panic that the baby gets when it deduces in the baby way that *it* is worthless and unworthy so as to cause the unloving visage of the bosom, Eugene. They yearn to be cherished. *You* yearned to be. It was a dry hole, however, and in some case, physical pain and neglect are heaped on," he lectured. "These masses of children march onto the Earth and all around it in that 'defective' state, self-fulfilling as it were," he said.

"Children should be seen and not heard is how I recall it," said Eugene.

Dr. K. nodded his grasp of this awful legacy and then continued. "Spirituality, be it Muslim, Christian, Jewish, Buddist, Hindu or any other religion, or just the idea that there is something greater than we, than humans are," he said, "is *taken away* when the child is thrown into that *panic*! The loss of that and what is left behind, namely, the bare superhuman or subhuman self, leaves the victim exposed in a most cruel manner. It is most ripe for protective invention," he propounded.

"And what is *that*?" Eugene asked.

"What you see as the status quo in religion, my boy. *That* is what it is!" he cried out. "The emotional wasteland state of mind breeds desperation which garners its own brand of dark-management. The falsehood of the baby's infliction by its parents is the *standard set*. That ingenuine state of affairs allows copies to take the form of 'comfort' at any price including *self-deception*," he added.

"What about criticizing those religious falsehood like *I* did, doc?" he replied.

"Wonderful notion, son, but the world is terrified of attacking anything that bears the sacrosanct status of religion!" he lamented. "It is a *block* in the mind of humanity. If it's religious, we cannot 'touch' it!" he cried.

I'm loving this, doc," Eugene admitted. "You were *right*! This stuff is just *my* cup of tea! I have thought for years about the schism between spirituality and logic. Are they in conflict or not?" he pondered. "And does the rigid doctrine of those organized religions set up the impossible? One would think so because so much of it is only metaphor but the masses grasp it eternally out of the same desperation that drove *me*! So, there are *two* blocks: that metaphor one and the impossibility of the versions set forth as gospel," he replied.

"The whole person perceives the world by *logic* yet retains a sense of the force that is greater than human force in the universe. The broken mind does not, cannot, do that. *It* sees everything as if by magic, remember, Eugene?" he asked. " For *him*, logic is out. The variation of course is the atheist. For him, it is *all* logic. Both forms of the latter are ego-oriented and driven. It is the ultimate formula for loneliness," the analyst went on.

"But he can't help it, right, doc? He's stuck in that trance, yes?," Eugene asked.

"Correct!" was the grateful answer. "Und *you* are so brilliant, such a student I tell you! I vish I had you in my class in Vienna, Ja!" he beamed.

Eugene beamed as well and leaned forward.

"The stories that make up the status quo are not so different from the ones that you, Eugene, made up in your works to explain all of the chaos that was your life and surroundings, Ja?" he asked in a baiting way.

"It would so seem," he answered dutifully but genuinely.

"Und the vorld vas *astounded*, Ja?" was the next worm on the hook.

But Eugene refused to bite. He saw the light and smiled broadly!

"That vorld ist the *same creatures* that think that they are *smarter* than me," doctor Korschucher said strongly. "*They* bit deeply onto *your* hook, Eugene, but there merely circle around mine," he complained. "Can we force a fish to go for the worm?" he wondered out loud. "Or can we only deprive him and starve him into it?"

"The vorld looked on and saw an 'average' family in New London. Some well-known experts have had the amazing naïvite to publish statements about them such as or to the effect that by all ordinary standards, the marriage of Ella and James O'Neill was *successful* and should not have resulted in tragedy! Astounding ting to say, Ja? Sure, your father was a famous actor, but nobody picked up on much that would cause alarm. Such is the blind vorld, Eugene, the very same one that is smarter than the doctor und dug in against him," he said. "Maybe *you* can change this?"

"What a mission, doc. Why *that* would puff me up one thousand times more than that stinking Nobel that I didn't want anyway!" he exclaimed.

"Stinking?" Dr. K. asked. "I would never view it as that, Eugene," he scolded.

"You're right, did I say that? I'm sorry. It was just so inconvenient for me back in 1936 to have *that* hung around my sorry neck, you see?" Eugene explained.

The analyst understood, of course. They are trained to. "The loss of your spirituality turned you into a struggling *beast*, Eugene, one with great mental powers. That is how the world is always misled. Look at Hitler! Look at all the bloody tyrants!" the analyst enunciated. "There was no end to your energy or your *compensatory carryings on!*" he declared.

"It was my lot in life!" Eugene admitted.

"But it didn't *have* to be!" replied the kind man. "That's what ve are aiming at stomping out!"

Then Eugene waxed profoundly with a faraway gaze in his eyes. "I am seeing an automobile wreck," he said. "A man is climbing out of his car all bloodied and torn and he cries out for help without shame! He is 'naked'. Those in an *emotional* auto wreck do the same but *nobody* hears them it seems, and worse, no one even knows what to do if they did hear! The morphine sought by the actual wreck victim is as well sought after by the other one, *my mother!*" he said. "Kill this awful pain!" he concluded. "That is the sole aim in life!"

"Oh, *that* is good, Eugene. Vould you like a job here?" the analyst asked jokingly. "It pays a sliver of diamond dust a week!" he laughed.

"I'd like to be in heaven," Eugene assured the good doctor who understood all too well. "Ja, Eugene, a reversal vill do it but do not forget vat I told you!"

Eugene instantly recalled the warning about a 'confrontation'.

"Ve must take away his *distractions*," interrupted the doctor. "Ve must take away his *excuses*, that *fish!*" he exclaimed, and Eugene knew what he meant! But vill the law allow us to force him?" he added. "No! unfortunately," he said sadly. "The vorld insists on a *right* to screw things up including its *children!*" Dr. K. continued. "They vill put *you* in a prison if you try to prevent *them* from putting their *kids* in a 'prison'," he declared in a scholarly tone.

Eugene stared off into space as if thinking of a ship on the Atlantic.

"Meaninglessness of life is an invalid concept," the doctor suddenly said. "There is no meaning to life nor is one required. A flower is just there. It performs without ultimate significance except that it *is* life. Same thing for a bear or a mouse. But *your* life was so *tormented* and *horribly empty* and your *great intellect* demanding an *answer* to satisfy what you saw as your *feelings place*. Trouble was, you *had* no feelings place!" he said. "You were a *head* man."

"I figured that the loneliness and emptiness were due solely to the fact that I had not yet discovered the *meaning of life*," Eugene declared.

"Meanwhile," said the analyst, "the empty soul, the lost self, demanded relief right away and that resulted in what we term 'insatiability'," he said.

"What, doc?" he wondered.

"Insatiability. It's that void in you, that hole in there. You tried to fill it up with whiskey, with sex, with reading, with writing, with money, with power. Und there could never be enough! The praise was never enough, nor the booze nor the girls nor the *ideas*! That hole cried out for fulfillment, satiation. It is the polar opposite to the part that found secret refuge in your head. The spirituality fled and the void opened into that '*abyss*' that you always talked about, Eugene," the doctor pointed out.

"Those awards never filled it up one iota!" he said.

"Your true self-esteem stayed on the floor," the doctor answered. "Und you could never really receive love, Eugene, both because no *whole person* would get near you und whole people are the only ones who can love and be loved, and because you had no love receptors, only *use* receptors. All you could do was *use* people, like Carlotta," he answered.

"Sounds dismal, doesn't it?" he replied.

"Remember, babies want only to love and to be loved. *You* were a baby so *you* had that once but James and Ella pushed you off the tracks of life," he said.

"I can see that so clearly now, thanks to you," he answered gratefully.

"Remember, Eugene, you cannot love if you do not love yourself and you did not. You were self-centered but that is different! And as far as women went, yours was a hostile view so that lets them out for real affection. Then there was the stand off posture on children. More evidence! Then there was that idea of the instability of human relationships! All phony, Eugene. More evidence! Then there was the notion that you mentioned of Agnes keeping you feeling guilty about Carlotta! More evidence! A person cannot keep another person 'feeling guilty' because that is a false perception and emotional state. It implies that silence makes him not feel guilty which is nonsense! It's all cerebralization *again*!" the doctor concluded. "The hallmarks are, by way of review, lying, denial, rationalization, false roles, distortion, exaggeration, ego-dealing, downplaying others' views and needs, gross invention. You recognize it, right?" he asked a sheepish listener.

"Yes, it's the *Ultimate Life-Lie* again!," he responded correctly.

"My, my, my, vat a gut lad you have become. I predict great things for you, Eugene! I am sure that the public did *not* know that you were crooked for the most part und now ve have a very different prospect here: a reversal Eugene. He *ist* coming!" cried the glad analyst. "One cannot speak the truth if one does not know what it ist, Eugene, und now you are beginning to!"

Eugene was starting to look like a man possessed by hope, not only to escape Limbo but eternal hope as well.

"Once upon a time, you ver such a mess, Eugene, a basket case, haywire, hateful, yearning, resenting, drinking, whoring, escaping, marrying again and again, obsessed, bewildered, angry, bitter, walling your kids out. Where was the love there?" the analyst asked.

"A mess," he replied.

"Love cannot be received by one such as that and neither can criticism. It is usually taken as attack and reconfirmation of 'worthlessness'. *Never* ist it considered as loving and constructive!" he went on.

"It used to irk me no end. I felt like smashing them when they did that. Or, I'd withdraw to punish them!" he admitted.

"Missing was the spirituality that whole people carry and sense and recognize instinctually as a *great mystery* that cannot be *dissected*. The masses have, however, been mad to tell the details and frantic to insure what God was and does. It is, in fact, not a subject truly capable of being known or is it necessary to know that. Live the whole life and be oceanic in the natural spirituality, Eugene!" the doctor preached.

"Now *that* is simplifying it for certain," Eugene replied.

"Wars have been fought, inquisitions, laid upon the people, cruel crusades launched, killing done in the name of religion. It's sort of the ultimate scandal!" the doc said. "Just look at the chronic turmoil in the Middle East where Jesus reigned! It's amazing!"

"I've done a great make God *fit him*. It's sick! Pitiful!" Eugene relayed.

"You had to endure a lot, my friend," the analyst said. "relying on such a strict Catholic upbringing only to have it all come tumbling down on you! You were a sponge and they made you soak up the eternal falsity-fear! It must have alarmed you greatly," he said sympathetically.

Eugene looked down at his legs and a pain came over his countenance.

"The 'tricks of fate', as you called them, that seemingly random setback that life can deliver, those Satan-like twists thrown up upon the innocent, why it must have been enough to make you think that it was all just a nightmare and that you would soon wake up," the doctor guessed.

"People try their hardest, they strive mightily as they say, try to be moral, make some difference in the world, to help out the less fortunate, yet then comes the slap in the kisser by fate. It was enough to make me spit!" said an angered man. "It reminds me again of that Sweeny grave. How in hell can such a thing happen when God is looking down?"

"Eugene," the doctor said, "natural spirituality allows such things. God is a 'good God' only in man's desperation. Actually the force responsible for the Earth and its creatures is neither good or bad. It just is. God has no control over everyday things. Only man's despair and fractured state say otherwise. Prayer, remember, is only a focus, a consciousness raising device, and an act of community," he assured Eugene.

"So I now come to believe," he replied.

"The world by magic outlook is bogus when you're an adult," he reminded him. "Yet, you could get yourself *killed* over it! People are *not* superhuman, just human. For them to have the power to actually change the future hands off, they *would* have to be superhuman!"

"Radical stuff, doc. You're a *rebel*!" Eugene mouthed the words playfully.

"I am recalling your theme of 'faith' turning to skepticism, Eugene, and I am thinking that it could hardly be otherwise. It needs only for a person to wake up and see the view that the vast majority of Earth's inhabitants harbors, namely, that 'faith' is some kind of a magic charm that will 'protect' them," Dr. K. lectured. "And maybe, you can hear your old mother's words there on Pequot Avenue complaining that 'if only I could find my faith' as if it were a lost watch or get-out-of-jail-free card!" he went on, and slapped his knee.

"Gosh, doc, you remember that?" Eugene asked.

"There was never any emotional safety in that house *ever*!" he said. "Your entire life was spent seeking relief usually by false means. Denial was always in the air and you duplicated that for the Tyrones, didn't you, Eugene?"

"Uh, I...," was all he could say before Dr. K. spoke again.

"Denial is sort of the right hand man to the no talk rule, is it not?"

Eugene nodded his assent.

"*That* and blocking out are measures, along with twisting the truth, wielded by the desperate, those confounded by *the original lie* and its acorn, that *ultimate life-lie*," he said.

Eugene sat silently.

"Battles that are produced by that state of man are monumental and unnecessary, like the one between the *Creationists and the Evolutionists*. It is a mere substitute, a mask, a disguise for the clash of instincts that diamond number one revealed. Sides line up, black eyes are planned and it is a sad sham, my friend," Dr. K. said. "Creationists are in denial re parents as *the* source of pain."

"What about the Bible?" Eugene asked innocently.

"Vell, vat about it? It is, again, largely history with wisdom thrown in and a load of those metaphors that I told you about. The battle between those two groups is really one between groups that are largely fractured and those that are largely whole. The Creationists' line is just a symptom," he said.

"Of just what?" he was asked.

"Of dysfunction born of abuse and neglect although they do not see it. It reminds me of the statement attributed to St. Thomas that said something like 'the Kingdom of Heaven is spread upon the Earth but Man does not see it," Dr. K. said. "The Evolutionists are a false target for the Creationists."

"You are telling me that their version of the truth is just a symptom?" he said.

"That or nothing," answered the analyst. "Of course, I exclude the organic disorders," Dr. K. answered.

"Dealing with chaos, emotional turmoil, is a lonesome trail, eh, doc?" he asked.

"And the world was had to fight that primary battle it seems forever," he answered. "Stridency and shameless proclamation are thrust out and the masses scramble to gobble it up, so desperate are they for any kind of 'light," he remarked. "And I find that a good deal of folks substitute God for misbehaving parents because God will give to them unconditionally what the mother and father are supposed to give the same way but fail to do."

"Yes, I can see such a thing," Eugene replied in deep thought.

"Religion becomes," the analyst went on, "a mere shield, a lollipop, another *device* to *feel something*, but there is *no spirituality* in it and that bloom of first encounter soon wears off. Meantime, you get outrageous statements by so-called religious leaders or movements that such things as state-sponsored violence, the *death penalty*, is proper. *This*," he added, "is the horrible status quo as well. Add the specter of abortion, in most cases killing for convenience and as a means of birth control! If ever there were a symptom of child mistreatment, *that* is it!" he continued.

"Gosh, so grave," Eugene remarked.

"Again, I am reminded of the parade of youth corruption across the television screens on killing of criminals by the government!" Dr. K. lamented again.

"A terrible possibility, I agree," stated Eugene.

"When children are not given the 'luxury' of being taken care of, they cannot ever graduate to become the care takers. They remain hungry for care! It turns them into copies of the parents, a cruel and ultimate irony!" Dr. K. stated. "The *real* mysteries of the world never get a thorough consideration because the wars started by the crooked-heads and sly-eyed saps steal the soul's treasury every time!" he continued.

"I am reminded of my own grappling with those mysteries," Eugene said quietly.

"Not that those unknown things *need* to be solved," he quickly added. "They really do not."

"I see now," Eugene chimed in. "That all I managed to do was to come up with a bunch of clever stuff that was easily swallowed by the eager-for-leadership crowd, anything to give relief!"

"As were *you*, Eugene!" Dr. K. was quick to add.

Eugene turned red.

"Don't worry. Here you are in friendly territory! But don't get any ideas on staying here, Eugene. This place could become too crowded!"

Sort of missing the joke, Eugene then said "They tell you about God's love and the rewards to come after death and that you *are* God's love but that is an insult to somebody as bad off as I was because catch phrases are the last thing to help. Reversal is what is desperately needed to match the desperation that plagues us types. They hide, if they even know, the idea of *not* being able to love because a lack of love for self! It's an outrage! It's a public obscenity! Why, it's a *robot remedy!*" Eugene suddenly remembering that concept.

"My, my, you are certainly responding well, Eugene," the encouraged analyst said. "And now let's see how elaborate are the assurances by the status quo about God's caring, God's love, God's powers, God's goodness, all the while suppressing the idea of God the destroyer!"

"Sweeny!" cried Eugene.

"Perpetual immaturity, my boy. That's behind it. The powers cannot preach the truth because the masses will not accept it. Those masses are not adults! Well, they *are* adults legally, have adult powers but are five years old or eight years old, wherever they got stuck, emotionally, and need to be spoon fed. Reality does not fall down to the swallow. *These* are the ones who hold their heads and shake in bewilderment when a tornado wipes out a church. They are puzzled!" Dr. K. said.

"Bravo!" shouted Eugene.

"Book writers, not playwrights, Eugene, who tell us so confidently of 'God's plan' for us, his 'purpose' for us, that we were put here 'for a divine reason', and all such stuff, are five or eight or ten years old inside as are the devourers of their product! It is a great example of the *parent-child relationship between adults!* It perpetuates the awful cycle!" the analyst said sadly.

"So, what's the answer?" Eugene asked him.

"Education to increase awareness," said the doctor. "And then wholesale reversals thru grief work which is highly unlikely *because the masses run from pain instead of embracing it and grieving it and recovering from it.* They are reenacting the fleeing of their babyhood from pain into their heads. *That* refusal to face it as *adults* now ensures the immature status quo," he proclaimed.

"That's the remedy that I would have had to undergo while alive, doc?" Eugene said.

"That's the remedy that I would have had to undergo while alive, doc?" Eugene said.

"That's it," he replied. "And it would have taken at most three months. Instead, you toiled in the 'recovery' mine for decades and yielded barely one-half ounce of recovery at most. It was largely *cerebral* and did not work. It was mere thinking instead of grieving which does not require any intellectual input."

"Can you or I or anyone get this idea of *the original lie* or its 'acorn', as you say, doc, the *ultimate life-lie*, out to the public in any kind of meaningful way?" Eugene asked.

"You'd think that people would *see it* without prompting, but the fear and the pain are so strong, it keeps them in that *trance. Force* is the best guarantor of starting the process but it's illegal. The no talk rule, the 'kindness' idea as cure, public skepticism, the 'why don't you grow up rule', the ubiquitous notion of thinking one's way out, all guaranty the cycle. Blindness stays on the throne and rattles the newborn.," cried the doctor bitterly.

"Evil rules, too, right?" he asked.

"Evil does rule but evil is mental illness, Eugene, and that is the province of physicians, not us here," the analyst assured him. "But the idea of 'evil' as some earth roaming force or 'divine intervention' as an entity are bogus and the product of the juvenile state of emotional development only!" he asserted. "There is no 'mystery of evil', Eugene, as some higher ups would *want* you to believe!" he proclaimed.

"And what causes this? What is evil, mental illness?" Eugene asked.

"Mental illness and its own offspring, the abused and neglected child," answered the analyst. "Evil is not Satan because 'evil' is real and 'Satan' is only a metaphor as I have instructed you already, Eugene," he added.

"And the idea of 'divine intervention' doc, tell me again," Eugene asked.

"No such thing!" demanded the doctor. "Remember that four-year old little girl that got run over by that truck?" he asked.

"Yeah, no divine intervention, right?" Eugene said.

"Where is it?" Dr. K. demanded to know.

"But *I* was taught that God works in mysterious ways," he replied.

"Yes, by taking the lives of innocent children!" the doctor exclaimed cynically and sarcastically. "That is just a *cover up phase*, a peppermint stick for the juvenile masses who figure out that killing a child is not God's expected handiwork. It's a turn-the-lights-out-because-there-is-no-boogey-man remedy," the analyst stated. "It's *'just go to sleep'*!" he complained.

"The baby birds peeping and squawking in the nest demand it, do they not?" the playwright wondered. "And after their *dose*, they nod off to slumber!"

"God, what a crooked world," cried Eugene. "How could I ever have hoped to succeed, not in print, but in my guts?" he said bitterly. "It's heartbreaking!"

"Heartbreak, Eugene, in life is not that it is imperfect or interrupted by tragedy nor even that it has to come to an end. Heartbreak is the face of the little child, ready for *anything*, open to *you*, and the wonder of it cannot be ever fully grasped or possessed. Then there is the question of why would you ever think of that. That's heartbreak. It's akin to 'wounded by her beauty' if that is somebody's saying or *will be*," waxed the analyst.

Eugene began to cry and then sob. "*I* was that little face!" he exclaimed in a hopeless voice. "That was *me*, that was *I* !" he corrected himself.

Allowing Eugene to flow with the tears, Dr. Kornschucher then said, "Holiness is a state of transparent selflessness and when it is engaged in towards others without regard for one's own safety, it becomes *heroism* or *heroinism*. How's *that* for an ideal?"

Recovered a little bit, Eugene responded by saying, "I like it! But *why* is there so little of that in the world?"

The doctor told him that it was because nearly everyone is *twisted*, some a bit, many moderately, some grossly like any severe pretzel, and confounded by *the original lie*.

"Oh, yeah!" replied Eugene. "So easy to forget that!"

"Prophetic!" exclaimed the doctor. "*Forgetfulness* is *the 'protector'*!"

"I always drank to forget," Eugene recalled out loud.

"Now standing up, the doctor told Eugene that he was going to give him a test. He handed him a pen and piece of colorless paper and told him to turn his seat away from where he was and to mark an answer to each question.

Eugene took the items and turned his chair away from the analyst.

"Zis quiz, Eugene, vill be on the Greeks and on *Mourning Becomes Electra*," he announced.

O'Neill began to tremble so hard that the doctor saw it from behind. Just when Eugene felt in his bones that he had confessed all that was in him, he got a look on his visage as though there were a fifth pocket left to be emptied, one that no one knew about.

"You remember, Eugene," the analyst began, "that your frustration over the impossibility of the dream of human perfection led you to compose zis play und also Strange Interlude, Ja?

"No!" answered Eugene. "I mean 'yes'...uh, No...yes, uh...," he stammered.

"Now Eugene," assured the doctor, "just apply the *truth* and you vill stop shaking. You also vill pass the test!"

O'Neill sensed that getting out of this desolate place depended on his score and he was desperate.

"Now, give me the correct answer. You wrote this one to express the idea of the romantic dream of human perfection being the *source* of all evil and that such a ting comes to a head in zis play in the form of almost perfect human depravity and insanity, Ja?"

"True," replied Eugene.

"At zis time, you ver into the Greek Classical ting, Ja, Eugene, und you ver studying it und also, your first son vas in Yale, Ja?" he inquired rhetorically.

"Yeah," answered Eugene. "He was a brilliant kid, too brilliant actually, and he was well known there for his prowess in this field, yeah."

"Und maybe you wrote this play which you based on the Orestes Trilogy as a way to connect better with Eugene, Jr., Nein?" he asked.

"That was a part," he replied. "But my love of Greek tragedy was intense and," cut off, "it gave me something I was missing inside history, moral structure, certainty, intense feelings, concrete circumstances!"

"You worshipped that Greek think, Ja...you ver deeply into it even ven you ver young boy, er, man, in New London, Ja?" he inquired.

"I read everything classical that I could get my hands on, yes," he said.

"Und so ve know vat ve are talking about, the Greek tragedy is a serious tale where there is always a hero, a man in position of power or prominence, a great and a good man, who nonetheless thru some flaw, a tragic flaw, suffers downfall and loses his ability to perform the great and the good and this downfall is inevitable, preordained by the gods," Dr. K. asked.

"Pretty good," replied the playwright. "And the *audience* feels pity or fear or loathing at this prospect and undergoes enlightenment, a catharsis, a purging, a cleansing, a resolve not to imitate such a fate."

"Now, the Greeks believed, did they not, that the gods had supreme power over man and that man could not escape his predetermined destiny and this they called 'fate', Ja?" Dr. K. went on. "But also, the Greeks felt that a man was responsible for his own actions and a criminal, for instance, was punished even though his behavior had been predestined," the analyst asked in a challenging manner.

"I know," replied Eugene. "And a hero with no power over destiny and who suffers defeat and downfall as a part of that because of some tragic flaw, sounds crazy, no?"

"But they brought in the element of 'free choice' of action among alternatives, Ja? Und the hero always chooses the wrong way, Ja? Und zen there ist the idea of 'an involuntary flaw' in the hero's *nature* and that this defeats the noble human being that he ist, Ja?" Dr. K. droned on, setting the stage for the test.

Eugene took on a lecturing tone, "That tragic flaw is never *vice* in the usual sense of the world or a *baseness* but is usually an excess of a nature," he continued. "The Greeks saw the tragedy as part of their religion and the main point was always that the hero committed a sin and confronted the gods. Then punishment came. It was in response to a *sin of excess*, uncontrolled excess, and in gross contrast to what the Greeks loved which was moderation."

"Ve vill have some questions in a little bit on the Greeks, Eugene, but I leave you for the moment with this scene:

It was not by the hand of a man that the sheep of Iotothes were laid to earth but an electric bolt! His loss was suffering as well as wool, and somebody, something, had to explain this! Perhaps, then, an explanation can be had for why his wife ran off with the neighbor's son, too. Thus began the imaginary world. Eugene just sat with the pen in hand and waited, blinking.

"Zis play, *Mourning Becomes Electra*, it was touted as a 'masterpiece' und one of your best, Eugene, Ja? It was called a milestone in the American Theater and it was very deep, clever, ambitious and a novel ting, und also, that Nobel Prize, that had to be partly based on this piece, nicht wahr?" he asked.

Sheepishly, "I was proud of it, yes. Damned difficult feat, you know!" he said. "I believe this was the last play trying to find that damned perfect beauty, that secret hidden over the horizon and it described my failure to ever do so."

"Und the story, the plot, involved ideas of mourning, guilt, love, frustration, Ja? There vas a replacement of those ancient Greek ideas and supernatural retribution with modern psychology, then-current ideas on that?" he asked Eugene and was told that it was so. "Und zen, ve have ze themes of a longed-for happiness and peace and freedom as symbolized by the South Sea Islands you put in there where the Mannon family members visualized free love and no hang-ups?"

"Very good, doc," he replied. "I put psychology in there in place of the old idea of 'Fate' I figured this thing would raise the public's awareness! Man's conscience was to take the place of the Greek Furies to punish the fallen. His *innate* sense of right and wrong would gradually get him good after the fact."

"Javol, und so ve have zis Mannon family modeled after the Greek one in that Orestes Trilogy, Ja? und zer ist bloodshed und adultery und poisoning, und incest stuff, und suicides und revenge, und so forth, Ja, und passing on to ze children of zis rottenness, zis jealousy, hatred, murder. Now tell me, Eugene, is it true what they said about psychoses and neuroses in zis play, zat these people labored under such stuff?" he asked.

"Well," answered the playwright. "I guess I put those in there, I mean, these people, Christine, Lavinia, Ezra, Orin, Electra, all Mannons, and Capt. Adam Brant, they were 'crazy'. They stopped at nothing! Insidious!"

"Zis plot is taken, more or less, from the trilogy only with modern day setting, right after the Civil War, and modern concepts about human acts?" he asked.

"Exactly," he answered. "Only here, the tragic flaws of the hero were destructive family pride along with a Puritan state of mind and morals. Actually, the whole Mannon family suffered from these defects. In the Orestes Trilogy, the hero's tragic flaw was, and this was the Atreus family and predecessors, well, there was murder, adultery, revenge, treachery, a lot like my piece!"

"OK," said the doctor.

"Hey, doc, where's that test?" Eugene demanded in contrast to his former tone.

"It's coming. Be patient, my boy, remember, you're here for eternity, maybe," he replied and Eugene's face dropped like a bottle of Ouzo!

"Again, Eugene, so I recall correctly now, the idea, at least on the Greek scale, was that the audience would undergo a purging or emotional cleansing or an enlightenment from watching the tragedy and feeling pity or fear or a revulsion to the outcome, Ja?" the analyst asked. "Und also, the falling hero would see what was occurring and himself undergo something?"

"That's the idea, Doc," he replied.

"Und in the modern version of the Greek play, like in *your* play here, is it not the idea that that old catharsis thing is now described as a process of getting rid of *frustrations* and *complexes* by having the *conscious mind* bring them into focus and then expressing them in some way, maybe orally. In other words, the result would be a *facing of the truth* about oneself whereas before that, illusions or denial reigned?" Dr. K. inquired knowingly.

Eugene knew that he was being set up but he played along smilingly.

Next Dr. K. asked if the old Greeks did not believe that suffering had a great value, a *divine* purpose and that it was *inevitable* and that it gave rise to *wisdom*. Eugene allowed that such was the case. Then Dr. K. asked him if the old Greeks did not have a concept that embraced the practice of *moderation* in things in contrast to *excesses*, he called it *Hybris*, which leads to sin. Eugene assented readily but warily. Then he was asked if those Greeks did not also have the idea that emotion like hate, fear, violence, etc., should be replaced by reason, harmony and cooperation and Eugene again agreed.

"In your trilogy, my boy, did you not express that hatred, jealously, love, revenge und so forth were real human emotions?" Dr. K. asked next, "Und also, portrayed incestuousness, crime, murder, punishment und so forth so as to prompt the audience to be purged of such feelings themselves by instilling in them that catharsis of pit or fear or loathing?"

"I did," he replied.

"The idea of death bringing peace from the Puritan life of emotional struggle, you

expressed that as well, Eugene?" he asked him. "These poor Mannons dream of sin-free sex and love and freedom in the South Seas, Ja?"

"Yeah", he countered, "The Puritan way is that man is born to sin and punishment. Life is punishment for being born!"

"Zis play is a wacko concoction, nicht wahr?" he slyly inquired and the playwright looked quite hurt. "*I* am supernatural and a lot closer to the gods than any old Greeks, Eugene, so listen to zees questions, now und write ze answers!"

Number one: Silliness is the idea of being a victim of flaws *not* of one's own making like sins of fathers, you know, yet the idea of a *fate* being created by a man for himself and personal responsibility or punishment, yes or no?

Number Two:The actions of the characters in Electra which destroy each other mirror the destruction reigned upon them as children, yes or no?

*Number Three:*Those characters are in a juvenile state but have adult powers and use those powers to indulge immature tendencies, Ja oder Nein?

*Number Four:*A romanticdream of human perfection is the source of all evil and *not* mental illness or child abuse /neglect, yes or no?

*Number Five:*The Puritan way of repressed sexuality und so forth und the idea of destructive family pride are robot rules and robot life coupled with superhuman conduct to try to matter, yes or no?

*Number Six:*Moderation or excesses are practiced merely by *deciding* and are *not* symptoms of child maltreatment when excesses occur and can be eliminated by habit alone. Flaws like excess pride can be rid without lengthy grieving? Yes or no?

*Number Seven:*If flaws exhibited in the hero are mental illness like psychosis or neurosis, organic or not, the audience can be purged of like maladies merely by watching a tragedy and feeling momentary fear or pity, yes or no?

*Number Eight:*A character can be "noble", great, good, yet suffer from excess pride or any other excess, true or silly?

*Number Nine:*An audience can have a pleasurable and uplifting reaction by such a pity or fear or revulsion by realizing that they do *not* themselves possess something inside to make them worry or be apprehensive? Yes or No?

*Number Ten:*The Greek concept of the *divinity* and *inevitability of suffering*: Is their view valid that it brings wisdom and is this not merely a recognition that suffering can force one into one's feelings and out of one's head und is this not an admission of culturally prominent child mistreatment, yes or no?

*Number Eleven:*Is it accurate to say a hero has "A flaw in his *nature*"?

*Number Twelve:*A man's "innate"sense of right and wrong would plague him after a sin and there would be no diminished or lack of conscience, yes or no?

Number Thirteen: Can emotion, what you called a route to truth, be replaced by reason, harmony and cooperation and is zis more silliness, Ja oder nein?

Number Fourteen: Can frustrations and complexes be resolved by "facing the truth" about oneself without an emotional transaction, yes or no?

Dr. K. beckoned and Eugene handed him the colorless sheet with a hug and relieved grin. The analyst shoved it in is pocket without inspection knowing that his patient had made great inroads and was ready to continue.

"Being in the center of yourself, Eugene, unleashes perfect courage and contentment, not 'satisfaction' with the state of humanity as it now stands but with one's own powers and 'raison d'etre,'" declared the analyst.

"And how does a body get *there*?" Eugene quickly queried the professor.

"You were born there and immediately knocked off of that center by James and Ella, I am sad to say," he replied. "But you know now that you *can* get back. It's a world of robots and none is listening, but *you are* and there is finally hope for you, Eugene."

"Hope for me," he repeated. "But I'm dead!"

"Deader than a doornail, yes!" he joked. "But still you could bring the critical message to the world, no?" he asked the playwright. "That and that God will come back into you."

"God into me?" he wondered as if it were a foreign concept.

"A higher power will become sensed by you. It might not be what you expect exactly, not an everyday force looming or whatever, but the freedom from the life sentence that your mother and father passed will make you cry in relief!" Dr. K. assured Eugene.

Eugene stood up and let out a sound that defies description as he lunged towards the analyst with opened up arms to hug him. As he did this, the doctor disappeared in a flash and suddenly was standing behind Eugene where he motioned for him to pick up the final diamond and to place it in his shirt pocket along with the four others, which Eugene did do.

Then he spoke. "Eugene, you will live in Heaven and will be unperplexed by all the contamination plaguing earth and there will be no mysteries to confound you anymore. Those that remain will be just for your eternal gaze. You will leave with this peace in your soul and be restored completely even in the face of that Sweeny family's existence. That is reality. *Denial is the monster*. It, along with devices and substances and blindness and all the rest of you have learned about here with me, are all brought to the forge of coping but that is a battle that cannot yield victory. Only confrontation of what lies before oneself at the hands of that *original lie* and its *acorn* can deliver triumph," he recited solemnly.

"Am I cured now?" Eugene pondered out loud and was reminded by the good doctor that he still had to confront someone to learn the *critically pressing question* of *how did you become your mother and father*?

Eugene let out a yelp and stood up again and sort of staggered a bit. Then, Doctor Kornschucher steadied him and said, "You see it now? You *are* James and Ella, your ways, your shallowness, pettiness, ego life, drugs and drinking, your selfishness, resentments, the meanness, the struggling inside. You actually became them, Eugene!"

"Oh, God, I am they. Their awful ways are in me and I passed that on to Eugene, Jr. and Shane and Oona!" he cried out in shame.

"You must go and confront and find out how such a horrible and 'unlikely' travesty could occur," the analyst ordered Eugene, and both men began to walk out of the cave. "You cannot have a healthy relationship with any other soul if that soul is fractured," Dr. K. told him. "They will just *use* you. You know that now!"

Then, half way out, Eugene tripped over something or only his own feet and he went sprawling forward. The five glittering diamonds got thrown out of his pocket and in a dream-like moment, he saw his own trajectory forward and the sudden vanishment of the stones in a burst of heated air! For a second, his guts were wrenched, but then, a low glow descended onto his senses and his newfound awareness grabbed him by both hands and infused him with gladness.

All at once, Eugene was alone and he just stood there, bedazzled and exhausted and not aware of how time passes in Limbo. His after-session rest took around twenty-five years but to him, it seemed like maybe a few hours. Then, as Eugene felt the new strength and courage, he rose to meet that "confrontation" by instinct alone.

My mind-dream on the foregoing was then continued into that netherworld.

CHAPTER EIGHT:
VAPORS

L aid before the sky is a vast cornfield, partitioned with ancient stones and clods of dirt. The crop is now stubble of a golden kind and the rows penetrate the horizon or swerve in parallel unison over nearby mounds and valleys. Crows are very black and in scattered groups or else solitary. Their hue sets off even more the color of the stalks and a spare but wonderful sense of life in all forms, for all times, in all ways is presented insistently to the gaze.

This is Massachusetts and one cannot tell just from looking what century it is. The feeling of a hard life permeates the sullen air but the sun, weak and pale, is just there in its mood ready to turn up the glowing at any instant. No wonder. After all, that same presence keeps our planetary house running and in good order and this scene here is but a tiny part of what is made and made possible by the overwhelming star.

Just over the way lies a group of houses, smoke rising, orchards growing, barns bursting and children scurrying or at chores. It is life as God expected it insistently and one beholds the meaning of the spectacle, crows and all, as if it were a religious vision. It is! All manner of clergy abound but the place is so huge that a body seldom ever comes across one except maybe on a Sunday in a village or hamlet. There are rabbis as well, but rarer still.

A latent squirming pervades the human experience at every turn, at every time in recent times and going back quite a ways. It is comprised of certainty lamented over struggle so as to ease the ordeal. It is found in the preaching of both the formal and the informal. There is a conflict abounding and many a soul has gotten an eye poked out over it or just shot dead by somebody's incensed father, brother or insanely angry women. The passion rises up in the gun barrel or the loins. It is hidden behind those barns, fuller than before or else inside in a loft where the rafters creak and cry out a tribute to the earnestness of the joined animals. It also can lie hidden, denied, kept in ice and icy lives where the urge to get out is stymied. Arguments seldom rise more furiously than over that sort of forced order. Jealousies run the Sundays and the Mondays. The ugliness over such a primal rest has to make the Creator shrink back. The extramarital tremors threaten to disrupt the placement of all facets of a civilized presence. Men of God soothe the fevers with words but soon enough, they behold their awful impotence. Skirts rise in defiance. Outright hussying by both sexes forms a carnival that all attend, though some not in person but through peeks or wishes.

This, too, is Massachusetts! The aforementioned 'sparity' of life seems suddenly not so difficult. Yes, it is the land of the blunderbuss, large buckles and strong hats, if not in the meadows, then in the museums. It is the center of New England and hub of the pulse or the pitiful thriving of hope. In the woods there are witch trees with sharp, blackened sticks ajut. Near the North border, the signs point the way to two upright states and a large cap one. In the opposite direction lies Woonsocket. Such an expressive name! Then, there is Connecticut and the sea-soaked place they call New London. The Puritan way is not as severe down there, but the struggles and the squabbling and the righteousness do fill up the ears just the same. All try to avoid being hurt again and all manner of devices are leaned on to shield the cringing soul.

There is art but it's potential to move or disrupt is somewhat attenuated and often a scandal erupts over it. In no manner, however, is this piece of God's ground anything like New York City where the local forms parade around with their art on their faces and party without shame even on a Tuesday.

Some, it seems, are or were steeped in that New York City soup but still gravitational towards the New England peculiarity at the same time. The perception of moral battles there and a failure to deal with the sin of original lie or its offspring, titillates the spinal awareness as a possible gateway to grasp man's ultimate nature. No matter. Indelible history lies there as well and such appellations as The Boston Massacre, The Battle of Breed's Hill, Lexington and Concord, Paul Revere, The Old North Church beckon to us all as do the familiar tea party, burdensome taxes, men dressed as Indians, and all the rest of it. They live in the place, in that hub, so far from that other center, the partying one with the debauchery, the scandalous drinking not covered up, the *rebels* of all shapes and sizes and the books by radicals, which our Eugene partook lo those many years ago.

So, it seems a mite peculiar that his bones should rest in that upper place, there in Forest Hills Cemetery on the outskirts of Old Bostontown, stuck in the earth early December 1953. He has been quiet now for some long spell. He could have been interred in New London. More likely, though, might be that party pot, New York. He had so many connections there: birth 1888, Bronx school 1895. Preparatory school 1900, lived upper Westside 1901, Fulton Street Bar where suicide attempted 1912, lived Greenwich Village 1915 onward, Broadway play 1920 garnering first Pulitzer for him. But bones usually remain and his did where the last wife dictated when *her* opinion took the reigns.

An otherworldly nexus linked Limbo to the gravesite and one deep night, Eugene arose as a vapor, a spirit, from that earthen place and attained some undetermined height where it then turned towards the southwest to obey Dr. Korschucher's directive. The essence proceeded about ninety-two miles, as the crow flies, and it took along one of those field crows to verity that. He would disdain any bird-walking.

In what seemed like an instant, Eugene got over the St. Mary Cemetery where it was also rather darkened. He did not see that this was in fact New London but merely yearned for and hovered over the O'Neill tombstone that has been heretofore described and right where I had trod! He, as well, had spent many a long minute there over the years.

Eugene's vapor then addressed the gravesite:

EO: Hello! Hello there!

JO: Who, Gene? (James O'Neill replied) What's this?

EO: Yes, Papa, it is I.

JO: Gene?

EO: Yes, I've come to speak with you

JO: Eugene, my son, been a long time, eh?

EO: How are things now, Papa?

JO: Well,…

EO: I've come…er, I'm talking about…to ask you something.

JO: Ask me? What's this…I'm dead you know.

EO: Yes, Papa.

JO: Say, what year is it, Gene?

EO: Uh, I have no idea. I'm dead as well; who'd a thought…

JO: Ask *me* something?

EO: You remember, the God awful time, after the first play in New York, those crazy reactions, you know...

JO: I got sick and wasted away and you came to visit, Gene.

EO: And we lost you that summer, Papa and...

JO: And you were all sorry *then*, eh?

EO: Listen, I have realized something about myself and had a little bit of help doing it and I need to ask you...

JO: I can't really see you, Gene. Where are *you*, next to me?

EO: No! I'm in Boston, but...

JO: Boston! Jesus Christ, Gene, Boston! What the hell?

EO: (growing impatient) Never mind that, Papa, I ...

JO: Why aren't you with your family. That's where you belong!

EO: Why am I you (shouting)

JO: What?

EO: That's right. I've become you...you and *her!*

JO: What in Hell are you talking about, Gene?

EO: It's true,I'm *you*, Papa!

JO: I'm James O'Neill, actor, why in my day, I was in public all the time. People could come see me anytime!

EO: You're in public now, too, Papa, and everybody can come see you *now...*

JO: You're not *me*. Gene. What's this nonsense? I act the play, you compose!

EO: No, Papa! I am talking about becoming what you were, what *she* was! She's right there next to you, you know!

JO: Eh? Next to me? Ella? She's here?

EO: Of course, Papa, don't you know your own wife?

JO: No, Gene. Here in Limbo, they don't tell me anything. Why, you can be with somebody a long, long time and not even know who they are, what they are, that they're even there, really.

EO: So, you're in Limbo too, eh? (surprised but not really) I didn't see you there, or Mama, is *she* in...well...I guess she would be. Died in twenty-two.

JO: Twenty-two? So soon...so soon...followed me in practically!

EO: *I* have become just like you both...callous, hardened...what you did to me; how'd you do that, make me like you...now *I* am the *child hater*!

JO: (ignoring that) Say, Eugene, how much did your mother's funeral cost me?

EO: (annoyed) Nothing! *You* didn't pay for it.

JO: Wait a Goddamn minute! Callous? Hardened? Why I ought to wash out your mouth with (cut off)...

EO: Listen to me! That's how you were and that's how *I* came to be. You kept your emotions away from us, stayed unavailable all the time, and I got the same way, Papa! (shouting)I *demand* to know how you did that to me, you and *her*!

JO: I just don't know what you are speaking about, boy! I just do not!

EO: Are you in a better place? Better than you were, Papa?

JO: What better place?

EO: Remember near the end, at the hospital there in the heat, you whispered to me...remember?

JO: Damn! No!

EO: You said it was no good, all rotten and you were going to a better place.

JO: Oh...Hell no! It's no better, eh? Better? I said *that*? I'm in Limbo for Christ sakes!

EO: But it *could* get better, Papa, you believe that...I mean if you can escape Limbo and...

JO: Can you arrange it, son, I mean for your Mother's sake?

EO: We'll see, Papa, but meantime, answer my question.

JO: (sidestepping) How'd the play go, Eugene…did they eat it up, the Broadway bums?

EO: A 'smash'…come on, tell me…

JO: It's cold and wet and dark and lonely and miserable and dirty, *eternally.*

EO: That's how you made *me* feel…you and *her!*

JO: Ah, go on…you're exaggerating, Gene…I know you…

EO: When I was little, you bastards…you…I hated you both. Jamie and I, you made us feel that same way…mad, actually, scared!

JO: Hey, Gene! We gave you a roof over your head and four squares, three squares a day, so don't usurp the limelight! (Actor's voice) "Now, come gentlemen and free thine eyes to gaze upon this heap of Earth…(cut off)…

EO: You *hated* me, my even being there.

JO: No, Gene, we *loved* you…a father's lot is a hard lot and everyone makes demands! Takes shots at his countenance!

EO: And *you*, Papa, *you* took shots as well…bourbon, rye, rot gut, bootleg, a little milk thrown in for, what, appearances?

JO: Hey! I held my own, never was late once for my calling hour; showed up every night; bought lots of rounds for everybody…everyone *loved* James O'Neill…why they even asked me to be Mayor!

EO: I don't want to hear it all again, Papa…just tell me what I want.

JO: I have no idea, really, no idea. Is *that* all you want?

EO: Yes. You never gave me a thing, not anything that counted. I was unwanted, a nuisance, always *dealing* with the two of you instead of basking in your…well, whatever you were supposed to give your son. Now I'm the same son of a bitch that you two were! You made me treat my *own* kids the same way.

JO: You are wrong, Gene. You are *not* me. You are a playwright, and I can still recall that opening night in February...(cut off)

EO: I got a Pulitzer for that, Papa...not that you could know it.

JO: You kidding me, Gene? When was this?

EO: After you passed on, I was so surprised!

JO: Dying is abandoning your feet.

EO: (Coughing to cover up the comment)

JO: Surprised! . . . me too! You *were* good, son...I said that!

EO: You don't know the half of it, I got *two* more of those. Two *more!*

JO: Imagine! My son, a *star!*

EO: And a *Nobel*, Papa!

JO: What? What was that, Gene? For what? A Nobel? What the hell are you talking about?

EO: They gave it (cut off)

JO: You're not *that* smart, Eugene, really now...

EO: Got it for writing, Papa, for *writing*, not some discovery. It came in 1936 and they brought it here all the way from Sweden to my hospital room.

JO: Hospital? What...

EO: I was ill...so they came to me. It was for (cut off)

JO: A Nobel Prize, Gene?

EO: For my plays. I didn't want it really...

JO: So you scored with more stage stuff, Eugene? Must have been *my* influence.

EO: Yes, more. Many more, Papa, right up to 1943 when I had to quit.

JO: Hey, Gene, you still got that moustache?

EO: (ignoring him) Some were crap and others big, Papa! Bitter lessons...

JO: I always hated it!

EO: Yeah, I guess it's around here somewhere…

JO: Made you look sinister, goddamned thing!

EO: Like *you*!

JO: I'll try to forget that you said that, damned ingrate! Shave it off!

EO: The question, Papa, the question!

JO: (ignoring him) Must've made you feel wonderful inside!

EO: What, what did?   Oh, the prize? Actually, I hated it. An anchor around my neck!

JO: Geeze!

EO: My son made Phi Beta Kappa, Yale, 1931, Papa, Eugene, Jr. Some kid, huh?

JO: You don't know… (cut off)…

EO: Slit his wrists and one ankle in the bathtub, Papa! What ya think of that? He was carrying what *I* was carrying and I want to know how the hell that can be.

JO: If *he* was carrying what *you* were, why don't you ask yourself, then?

EO: I was the awful bastard that *you* were…mean, drunk, distant, always running my life, shaming us instead of supporting us. A bar creature you and I got your disease! Tel me, Papa, tell me!

JO: You are being too hard on yourself, Gene. Kids! Hah! They drive you nuts.

EO: All I ever wanted was for you to put your arms around me like you mean it, like you really cared about me, your son, made me feel like I mattered.

JO: I tried, Gene, I was always under the gun, what with money and that Goddamned play always tugging at me, you know…

EO: I didn't even feel like it was okay for me to be there. I was an intruder and always having to hide my feelings. And Moma, she was the same only different.

JO: The same, only different? You see how mixed up you've become?

EO: Neither of you ever really cared a whit about anything except yourselves!

JO: Your mother and I, we gave you what we could.

EO: You did not *love* me! You did not love each other! You even did not love yourselves!

JO: That's crazy talk! Where'd you get that crap, New York? Why everybody loved James O'Neill, the whole town, the whole world.

EO: Not the *whole* town Papa, not everybody. A lot of them just used you.

JO: Yeah? Like who?

EO: All the land that you bought up, that's what.

JO: We had a grand business idea, a great notion to *triple* the investment if only, if only…the Port of New London could have been made into a receiver for transatlantic ships, you know we could have…(cut off)

EO: I know, I known, I've heard that story too many times, Papa. You were just a machine, a damned machine. And, they saw you coming! Did you ever make a dime profit on all the real estate? No! You always lost money!

JO: Hey, watch it boy, I'm still your father!

EO: And I'll tell you again: I *hated* you! I hated the both of you so badly that I could have spit on you! That's come back, you and that church. Then I put my foot down and you tried to force me but I was too damned smart for that garbage!

JO: That's blasphemy, Eugene. You could end up in Hell for that!

EO: We *did* end up in Hell, Papa, *your* Hell, me and Jamie!

JO: Jamie's alright, you know.

EO: No, he's not, Papa, he's dead!

JO: Oh, God, Jamie's dead? How? When?

EO: He died in a sanitarium in Hoboken in 1923, right after Moma, and Eugene, Jr., bled to death all over the stairway and carpeting in 1950. *He* was only forty, Papa! Forty! And Jamie only forty-five!

JO: But what happened to Jamie?

EO: He drank himself to death, what else? First to blindness, then to stiffness! And it was all your fault, Papa, *your* fault!

JO: Bull! I never hurt him, how's it *my* doing, Gene? You're just trying to get even because you're still so damned mad! *That's* why you came here, to get even.

EO: You are impossible! What do *you* think made Jamie into a drunk, huh, Papa?

JO: Well, everybody's different. He just couldn't handle his liquor like me, that's all! And what about you?

EO: Jamie is lying there right next to you and Moma.

JO: He's a good boy. He's not up in Boston.

EO: *Moma* hated you, too! Only she never let on. Jamie would have cut your throat if he'd been able to get up the guts. He despised you, Papa!

JO: I was always covering for her, her damned needle…Why in hell would she stay on with me for all those years if she hated me, huh?

EO: Because she *used* you! She was co-(cut off)

JO: Used me? You're nuts! Get outta here! Go on, get!

EO: Moma was selfish and horrible and weak, never there, up in bed all the time. Sarah did all the attending. She was like a saint to me, like a real mother, that is until you took her away from me! Papa, how could you?

JO: Well, Gene, we couldn't keep her *and* send you to school in the Bronx!

EO: Oh, how I *hated* it there, so cold…

JO: Education…very vital you know, and your mother and I were on tour all year except for summers, so that's no place for a growing boy, you know.

EO: But stuck away in some New York Catholic boarding school is? Sarah was my only joy and you robbed me. You robbed me *again* and I wished you *dead*!

JO: I was a fine actor, my calling, why Edwin Booth even (cut off)

EO: Please! I cannot stand to hear it again! I just wanted to tie a rock around my neck and jump into the harbor and never come up!

JO: Your mother was at times like a rock around *my* neck, you know. Actually, all of you were, but I guess that I shouldn't say such things. Anyway Gene, she never got over the loss of that baby. It was always so damned sad in that house, unless she was on a high.

EO: When I finally moved away, in 1915, and went back to New York, I thought that I would feel better, get happier, less lonesome, desperate, have something unobstructed to wake up to every day.

JO: But No! You had to take a bottle of sleeping pills, you damned fool!

EO: Papa! That was in 1912, way before what I'm referring to. *That* was when I sailed back from Honduras.

JO: So, what happened to you? Fall off a bar stool?

EO: Life never got better, just change of scene of misery. You didn't have to be around for your influence to be potent and stinging, Papa! It was like a tattoo that I could never wash off or even gouge out with a knife!

JO: *This* is the thanks that I get!

EO: You and she should never have had children. It was not *fair*!

JO: If I was so bad, why didn't you just be the *opposite* of what I was?

EO: Believe me, Papa, I did think of that. It seemed so logical. Yet, you were inside of me like a stain. I could hear myself saying things that only *you* would say! It was a nightmare!

JO: Tiring, very tiring.

EO: Too bad! I want to know how it was possible for you to do that to me, to us, and I'm asking *on doctor's orders*.

JO: "Doctor's orders" is it? Now I've heard everything, Gene, ha-ha-ha-ha!

EO: I'm under counseling in Limbo, yes, in Limbo, just like you and Mama and Jamie, I guess, except that the three of *you* are staying there and *I* am getting out. *You* are stewing there!

JO: Can't *you* get me out?

EO: (ignoring him) The other things about me not wanting to be you is that I have learned recently that one cannot be 'opposite' just by deciding. I didn't get like you and Mama by deciding and escaping cannot take such a road.

JO: Who filled your head with that stuff?

EO: Same doctor.

JO: In Limbo, where *we* are?

EO: Yes.

JO: And what is the whole point?

EO: I am instructed that if I pay attention and *learn*, apparently various things that almost nobody alive is willing to do, I could get a *reversal* and get out of Limbo. One of the chores was to *confront you* to ask that question I posed.

JO: Oh, so *that's* why you're here, not to see your old man or your mother but on some errand, is it, laddie?

EO: Okay, bad word. 'Assignment' is a better one. How's that? Gee, I thought that you'd have gotten a little more gentle about life, the shit that passes for life, but I guess not, huh?

JO: I don't have an answer for you, Gene.

EO: I can still remember when they put up that monument in town. I was only eight years old. "Don't Give Up The Ship" it read and I was so moved, maybe more by the size than the words but ... anyway, I felt like I was okay *then*, but I imagine that I was already a little you! Now look how I ended up! I abused my own kids! I cut them off and cut them out! And *you* had a hand in it. You sent me off to Central America when I was just one week married and Kathleen pregnant!

JO: But nobody knew that, so *there*!

EO: Yeah, Papa, but we did consummate the marriage. I could have stayed with her. I know it was in the air that we got hitched on a whim but youth is like that, you know!

JO: Not Catholic youth! Besides, she was after my money and you know it!

EO: That is ludicrous, Papa. Anyway, you didn't have much except all that real estate and...

JO: Boy! I just realized... you would not have had any dealings with the theater and plays had it not been for me, so I guess that I was the cause of *that* too!

EO: You were the cause alright. You ruined me and then drove me to suicide and then towards the theater as an outlet. Some inspiration!

JO: *I* never drove you to suicide, Gene. Your mother maybe but that was your own choosing. I'll be damned. He's blaming *that* on me, too!

EO: Well then, who *should* I blame?

JO: You blame yourself! You were a man, you were twenty-four years old for Christ's sake!

EO: Oh, I see. I was a man, so I have to blame myself. God almighty!

JO: That's right, sailor! Nobody held your hand on that pill bottle or any other bottle. It's your own doing!

EO: *You* did it. *You* held my hand on it, screwed my fingers to the glass just as sure as if you'd been standing right there in that dump.

JO: Sounds like you've been at a wee bit of that *other* bottle, yes?

EO: (ignoring that) And to continue, I did more or less the same thing to Oona and Shane. Then, there's Eugene, Jr. ! I abandoned them all in my insides.

JO: Well, except for him, the others made out okay, didn't they, Gene? (a stirring and rumbling was heard by the two men-vapors)

EO: It's *Edmund*, Papa, he just now whispered something into my ear. He *is* here too, you know, 1885, measles and all.

JO: Yeah? And what did the baby tell you, Eugene?

EO: I'll let you know later.

JO: (changing the subject) So, who was in charge, who put you in that grave?

EO: My third wife, Papa, Carlotta. She did it.

JO: Third! What happened to Agnes? Geeze!

EO: We split up and I went to Paris with Carlotta and we got married in 1929 and we stayed that way.

JO: Where the hell did you dig her up?

EO: She was an actress. She played Mildred in The Hairy Ape, a play that I composed in 1921. It was one of the productions of it long ago.

JO: So, your life didn't end up so bad.

EO: Not so bad? Dead at sixty-five, no real home, addicted, on sedatives for nerves, Parkinson's-like shakes all the time, no longer able to write, can't drive a car, still confounded about the agony and turmoil in me that *you* caused, you and *her*. Three kids off on some tangent, one of them dead by razor, the other two cut off by me in my will and nobody speaking to anybody. *Now* Edmund tells me *this*!

JO: What did he tell you, Gene?

EO: (ignoring that question) I *did* give them the Bermuda property, it was called "Spithead" long ago but that's it. The whole thing was rotten and it was just what you gave to me! I just passed it on, Papa! (Then Eugene got a hot rush when he remembered being told that a *mystery* was coming. That was the thing that Edmund told him *secretly*!) You know, Papa, little Shane used to spend countless hours there all alone, none of us really kept tabs on him and he was quiet and tentative. Sort of reminded me of my own shyness. Then, Eugene, Jr. came to see us there. I remember it. It was Easter vacation and he had been told not too long prior that *I* was his father. He was reported to be overjoyed at this because he hated his stepfather, I guess. Anyway, the kid had been writing! Can you believe it? He was about seventeen years old, I guess, and had been working on writing *plays*! He did change over to poetry, however. I was told that when he learned of being related to a *famous* writer, he flipped! Now, he's gone. I can't help thinking that I held that razor, Papa, just like *you* held my hand onto that bottle!

JO: I cannot bear to hear that sort of drivel, Gene, *please!*

EO: Then there was Oona, my little girl. (Eugene's thoughts wandered off)

JO: Oona? Strange name, Gene. Where'd you dig that up?

EO: She ended up age eighteen married to a famous comedian, Charlie Chaplin! I wanted to wring her neck! Practically never spoke to her again, Papa. The bastard was fifty-four!

JO: What? ! Oh, hell, that stinks, Gene. Couldn't you put an end to it?

EO: Like me and Kathleen, you mean like *that*, Papa?

JO: (ignoring him) Maybe you got throngs of bad messages from your mother…

EO: And you.

JO: But you did get a Nobel Prize out of it! That's worth more than kids any day!

EO: Why does it not shock me to hear you say that?

JO: Kids are just a damned pain in the ass, dragging you down all the time, cost a fortune to raise, sapping me…

EO: Pain in the ass, Papa? Where's your Catholic Church now? (His father had to remain silent on that) I felt your resentment every day of my life, yours and *hers*. "Tightwad!" That's what Jamie called you. That Nobel was not worth a whit to me Papa. I hid from it!

JO: Geeze! What a thing to say!

EO: Ours was not a home, never a warm feeling, not any heart, no belonging feeling, no kindness, impossible to relax, no gentleness or understanding, no support of the type that I *craved*… from *you*. Papa, it was all just a *pretense* to those things, like *you*, Papa, all 'rottenness, no good… oh, my God! I'm quoting *you*!

JO: Where are you getting this stuff, Gene. It does not seem like you.

EO: It doesn't matter. From my Doctor. I told you, in Limbo.

JO: And what's *he* got to say about it?

EO: If only I could tell you, you and Moma, *really* tell you. If only you'd listen, but you never did!

Ella: Eugene? Is that you, Eugene?

EO: Yes, Moma, it's Gene. I'm here to visit.

Ella: Oh, to visit *me*! How nice, Eugene!

EO: I've been speaking to Papa here.

Ella: Gene, son, are we near the river?

EO: I don't believe so, no, Moma.

Ella: Oh, I tell you, I do so *love* that river... if only I could find my...

JO: (cutting her off) Shut up, Ella! Don't you see, Gene's come to ask me something.

Ella: Eugene's visiting *me*, James, so *you* be quiet, dear... skunk!

JO: I can't hear anything.

Ella: I'm in Limbo and it's dreadful. I guess your father is too?

EO: I guess we all are, Moma, and do not know it yet but he... (cut off)

JO: Kicked the bucket, I am told. Drank himself right into the ground, so our son's informed me not twenty minutes ago.

Ella: Oh, my God! Jamie! Jamie! Please hear me! This is Moma calling. Are you in heaven, son?

Jamie: No, Moma. I am in Limbo. I hear you very well.

Ella: What happened to you, son? *When* did you die?

Jamie: In 1923, right after you, I guess. As to what happened to me, I am not sure. Maybe I indulged to excess? Yeah! That's got to be it.

EO: So, I lost you, brother, you, Moma, and you, Papa, all in the space of three years. And now, I'm all alone. No! Wait! I have Carlotta! Oh, I *had* her. So, I did not cry over the three of you... I wanted to, I was *told* to, that I *could*, but I *couldn't*! Tears were there but too deep to come out.

Jamie: You lost us all!

JO: Geeze, all three of us, boom, in a row, eh, Gene? Must've figured you were next!

EO: Nah! Not really. Never entered my mind.

Ella: We're all dead, Eugene, did you know that? They put us here and we stay here but we don't want to. Too deep to come out! (mildly joking)

EO: That's Limbo, Moma, that you don't want to… (cut off)

JO: *I'm* the skunk? You're a polecat!

Ella: (begins crying)

JO: Be quiet! I'm talking with Eugene. He came here specially to see *me* and to ask me something, right, Gene?

EO: Right! Well, actually, I've *been* asking but not getting any real replies.

Ella: Answers? What question, James?

EO: Moma, I came to find out how it is possible that I was turned into the two of you when I was once a pure and happily free little boy?

Ella: Oh, *Edmund*! What about pure, little Edmund? *He* was pure, happily free, wasn't he, Gene, James, Mommie?

Bridget: I'm tired, so tired. What did you say, dear?

Ella: Edmund was free, wasn't he, mother?

Bridget: I guess he was. But he was only two years old or…

Ella: He got the measles from Jamie. Bad boy, bad boy, Jamie, you have killed your little brother… bad, shame!

JO: Leave him alone, Ella, he's innocent!

Jamie: I'm *innocent*!

Bridget: It was *my* fault, I guess. I could have taken better care to keep them separated… I don't know…

EO: Grandma, *you* are in Limbo, too?

Bridget: I suppose so. It's been so long.

JO: Eugene spoke to Edmund.

Ella: What? How?

JO: A little while ago… well, not spoke. Edmund spoke to *him*.

Ella: How do you know that?

JO: Gene said so, that Edmund whispered to him.

EO: Edmund's in heaven, Moma. He told me so!

Ella: And we are *here* in St. Mary Cemetery. I love Mary… I pray to the Virgin regularly, that way… (cut off)

JO: That way, she's bound to hear you, yes, Ella I think we know that!

EO: I wrote a play, Moma, and the main character, the female, was fashioned after *you*. The setting was our place on Pequot.

Ella: Hear that, James… after *me*… gee, Gene… after *me*!

EO: And I named her "Mary", Moma… your role was Mary.

Ella: Oh, delight of delights! Halleluiah, James!

EO: The piece was entitled, well, I, uh, Listen! It's getting on in time.

JO: He needs to know how he became *us*, if that is possible, how he became me and you when he *hated* us so much!

EO: Excuse me! (to offset embarrassment)

Ella: Hated us?

EO: Now, I never said that I hated *you*, Moma.

JO: No, just *me*!

Ella: Well, who could blame him… I mean, really…

EO: *This* is not helping. My analyst told me…

Ella: Analyst?

JO: Yeah! He's got one in Limbo! In Limbo! Can you believe it?

EO: They've pegged me for somebody special and want to teach me all about whatever it is that pushed me off the tracks.

JO: Or, you just *fell* off. Inebriated? Now, *I* have never missed a performance from booze, no sir! Hey! Why doesn't that doctor, what's his name, teach you how you became us if it is the truth, huh?

EO: Because he wants me to confront *you*, Papa, and I guess, you too, Moma.

JO: What's so special about you? You said you were deemed 'special'.

EO: Yeah. They figure, I imagine, that I am the *epitome* of what can be done to ruin an innocent child with the ultimate effect resulting in a *Nobel Prize* and some lesser stuff, the *Pulitzers* and all. Maybe, too, they imagine that I can serve to complete a *cycle*. Hey! I just realized! Maybe they remember my abandonment of the *Cycle* of plays and decided to pin me to a more vital and critical *cycle*!

JO: That's ridiculous! What cycle, Gene. Come on!

EO: A reversal!

Ella: A what, son?

EO: If I do what they tell me in Limbo, I get to get out! I become *whole*!

JO: What cycle?

EO: You all are *blind* to it. I was born pure. You ruined me. I became thru my wits and desperation a Nobel Prize winner! But in Heaven, they see that it is wrong, that what happened to me was aberration and not human fulfillment or just destiny. So, they want me to complete that *epitome* role by ending up whole and completing that terrible cycle that nobody else has the courage to do! Theirs is a pain buried too long! Their denial keeps them in prison, you see, Moma?

Ella: Imagine that…James!

EO: A, if only I could see the *green sea* again! If only I could…the foamy play on those grey swells!

Ella: But what about *us*, your family?

EO: (Ignoring her) Oh, to wake up in a hammock at dawn and be pulled in again by that giant, wonderful, invasive air. It can wash you right out of your mind! That's the life I want! Yessiree!

JO: Too late for that, laddie, you had your stint on the briny, gave it all up, you know…

EO: Just to put my poor feet in it, surely not too much to ask. (Then Eugene recalled the diamonds and saw their unimaginable glinting and sparkling in his memory eye.)Oh, if only I could tell you all. But I'm on a mission. Yes! I must learn the answer as I've already told Papa.

JO: *That* again! He insists that we tell him how in hell he became us. Do you hear this? He became you and me when he *hated* us so much!

EO: You were always gone, Moma, one way or another. What is *that* to a four-year old who needs you? Sandy did all *your* loving for you and you stayed up there in bed doped up all the time. I hated *that*!

JO: The pity train and the needle express it is!

Ella: But I *loved* you, Gene. I gave birth to you, you know.

EO: Like hell. You *resented* me. I was *unwanted* so don't be giving me any more of those lies, Moma, *please*! I cannot take another one. Never got a thing I could use from you, never anything that mattered. *I* didn't *matter*!

Ella: You hear that, James? That's what the world's come to!

JO: Yes. He demands to know how he got so rotten. Well, I'll tell you, Gene, you were born rotten in a rotten world. What's the big puzzle?

EO: No! No, I was not! I was born in a diamond world, a world of hope and solidity. Not in *your* world, Moma and Papa!

Jamie: He's right, you know. *I* saw it all.

EO: I was so lonely and scared! Half the time I was cringing where you couldn't see it until, until…until I somehow got ruined, turned around and *I* became crooked and mean like you, like you still are, no offense to you, Jamie, poor slob!

Jamie: Gee, thanks!

EO: They *made* you that way, drove you to it, to a terrible end in Paterson!

JO: I thought you said 'Hoboken', Eugene.

EO: He died in Paterson, I never said...oh, wait. Maybe I did. I had 'Hoboken' on the brain. *That's* where I married Kathleen before *you* ruined *that* too!

JO: All crap, Ella, he's nuts! Don't listen to it!

Ella: Gene, where do you get this awful stuff?

EO: It's in my guts, Moma, that's where it's been stuck all the years that you pitched it at me and I had to stand there and take it!

JO: Well, you didn't have to stand there and take our money, all we spent on you, the TB in Wallingford, the trip to South America, Central, whatever it was, all the years, that damned Princeton education that you just chucked out the window. All that money! My God!

EO: Money, Papa, is that all you ever think of? It's just like the Nobel... who in hell needs it? It's not hugs and understanding. It's not solidity inside. Just more surface junk by some team and a king who think that they've got it right, but what do they have? Did they ever see my suffering, that awful despair. Did *they* ever put a hand on my shoulder and ask me what they could do for me? I'd a told them to just put their arms around me and hold tight!

JO: Ella, Eugene, Jr. is dead by his own hand...

EO: (avoiding the topic) You made sure I knew I did not matter, Moma. Moma!

Ella: Dead? Gene's little son, baby Eugene, dead? By *what* own hand?

JO: Gene tells me that he slit his wrists in a bathtub in 1950.

Ella: Oh, God! Oh, No!

EO: Yeah, his ankle, too. Couldn't take it anymore either, I guess...and it was *my* doing!

JO: And how is it *your* doing? More of that special learning, I suppose?

EO: *I* am to blame. *I* was the one who left him and his mother and *you* father, *you* had the biggest hand init of all sending me off like that and setting up the divorce. It's *you* that separated me from my boy... eleven years!

JO: Oh, so now it's *my* fault again! Always *my* fault!

EO: He inherited *your* pain and it was channeled through me!

JO: Well, let me tell *you*, I never cut *my* wrists! What pain is *that*, Mr. Genius?

Ella: Oh, my goodness, our grandson, dead by his own hand. I cannot take any more.

EO: What kind of a life is it to take a baby, me, on the road for seven years, living out of trunks, hotels, no home life except summers in town, and *that, that* was the nightmare you already know!

Ella: Well, Gene, I *had* to follow your father. He was my husband. Besides, you were always well tended...

EO: Not in the heart, Moma. Never in the heart. All I ever got was your emptiness and his big boasting, big chest, grand actor!

JO: I resent that! It put food on the table, didn't it? A roof, didn't it?

EO: Please! Not again! *Just shut up*!

JO: I'll be giving you the back of me hand, lad, tell me to (cut off)

EO: Stop it!

JO: I was a *star*! A *star*, I tell you, why, I ...(cut off)

Ella: Be quiet, James, listen to our son.

EO: Then, you put me in a prison for seven years, six years, in the Bronx. You stripped me of my Sarah, *she* loved me. She loved *me*! Why did you have to do that? *Why*? I had to take it! (Eugene cries)

JO: Just look at what you've done now, Ella...

Ella: *Me*? You're the bastard! We should have kept him at home while you were out on tour, him and Jamie. Or else, you could have given up that damned Monte Cristo role. The raves were too seductive for you, James.

JO: But you did not mind the money, did you dear? Skunk!

EO: Stop it! *Please*! Not another word! I'm getting sidetracked here.

JO: All we did for you and now this!

EO: I needed you desperately! I needed you to *love* me, surround me but all I got was a *wall*, a siege, a puzzle and ended up hating you instead of loving you! I guess (thinking) I *was* surrounded…surrounded by a wall! It was nightmarish!

JO: He won't let go of that I'm afraid, Ella…

Jamie: And why would he? He's right! I never had the wherewithal to say it, but he *has*. He *has* and he said it exactly right!

JO: You're *both* off base, delirious maybe…

Ella: Maybe he's come to reject us in finality. Oh, Gene, don't …

EO: No, Moma, I have not. I have come for one reason only.

JO: Bully for you! Blasphemer of St. Mary…get out!

Ella: No, son, don't listen to him, not anymore. Listen to me. I'm your mother! Now, if only I could find my…

EO: Yes. Moma, I know.

JO: That goddamned play! That's what's to blame for all of this! If only I had…

Jamie: I was only forty-five. What about *that*? Nobody cares.

Ella: We *do* care, son, it's just that we didn't show it all the time.

EO: When did you *ever* show it, Moma? *When*, tell me!

Ella: I gave birth to you, you two. *That* was caring.

EO: But you *resented* me. You thought that God would punish you for having another baby when Edmund was dead. *God*? Didn't God *make* that baby, Moma? That's the *craziness* that you are about!

Ella: Edmund was killed by Jamie's doing. I've got *that* straight!

JO: Ella! For Christ's sake! Jamie was only seven. I mean, even if he *did* mean to give his brother the measles, so what? That's kids playing.

You cannot go heaping blame on him like that. That's adult stuff!

EO:　　If we make kids be responsible like and behave like adults, they will remain as children even when they grow up to be adults. But if we let them be human and child-like, they will be real adults when they're grown!

JO:　　Rot!

EO:　　Jamie was not to blame. It was *God's* doing. Jamie did not invent the measles. God is not only a loving God. He is also a *terrible* God! He is the one who ends it all!

JO:　　Oh, what an awful thing to say, Eugene! You've lost your mind!

Ella:　　We were afraid of God for what we did, afraid he would kill us.

EO:　　Afraid of God, Moma? That is wacky! Why fear what is? How can the world go on if it shakes in fright from what *is*? It is a crazy view and you are just that!

Ella:　　You hear how he speaks to his mother? James? Are you listening?

EO:　　Cursed by a baby being born! Moma, don't you see it?

Ella:　　Oh, if only I could find my faith…Mary! . . . Mary! I'll pray to you! I'll be safe again…you'll see.

EO:　　You are delirious, Moma.

Ella:　　No! It's *you* that's the one. *You* are to blame!

EO:　　You two paralyzed me from the beginning. You are damned lucky that I came here from Boston…

JO:　　Now that is dishonest. We are *not* 'damned lucky'. You came for your own reasons!

EO:　　Partly true, but not selfish reasons, Papa. There was never any safety with you two. No safety, Moma, not from praying or being a good boy or being nice or from hiding inside myself.

(Ella and James stayed silent)

EO:　　Then I slowly went over to the other side. I became the two of you, my own, mean parents. I got mean, too!

JO: And was there any safety in that, Gene?

Bridget: You know, Ella, there is something in what Eugene is saying. I mean, it strikes a chord in my memory.

JO: The old bat speaks!

Bridget: It is as if I were wishing that I could have said some of those very things to my own mother and father because *that* is how they made *me* feel! Go on, Eugene, tell us more.

EO: Well, Grandma, maybe you became *your* parents and you carried *their* unhappiness because they *forced* you to. You became them.

JO: All a lot of Blarney. Don't listen to it!

Ella: How old are you now, Gene?

EO: I'm sixty-five, Moma.

Ella: Sixty-five! Imagine that!

EO: Died in 1953 in a Boston hotel, Moma.

Ella: You died? Sounds funny. Boston, you say?

EO: Yes, with Carlotta, my third wife.

Ella: Carlotta; what a lovely name, Gene. Third?

EO: I am still determined to find out…(cut off)

JO: I know: how in the hell you could get like us…roof over your head, food on the table, a good education up to a point, yet I am the bastard. Geeze, I wish I had a glass!

Jamie: Me, too!

Ella: And I wish that *I* had something…

EO: I give up! You'll never tell me what I desire to know, *have* to know.

Edmund: *I'll* state it, brother that I never knew, *I'll* tell it.

JO: What? What's this, the baby talking?

Ella: Baby talking? Edmund! My precious one, my dear lost child, Oh my!

Edm: I'm in Heaven, Mommie and Daddy, not in Limbo like all of you. I know *everything* that has happened after my death and I can see it all in a way that you cannot or do not.

Ella: If only I could hold you, find you again, you're not dead, Oh, Edmund!

JO: Leave him alone, Ella.

EO: Yes, leave him alone, Moma, he was addressing me.

Ella: But how can he talk to us, he's only an infant?

EO: He whispered to me a while ago, before you woke up, Moma, and he informed me that he was with us and his spirit was in Heaven.

JO: It's magic, I guess, what the hell!

EO: You see there! When it's a rumor or dogma or catechism, it's the law, but when it is right there in front of you, it's 'magic'! *That* kind of tells it all, I'd say, Papa. Hypocrit! All the pig of convenience *I* say.

Edm: You were speaking a little while back of the suicide of Eugene, Jr. recall?

EO: Yes, we do.

Edm: Well, brace yourselves, folks, I have more bad news. *That* was in 1950, but in 1977, it came again. Shane!

JO: Cut himself?

Edm: No, jumped out of a 14-storey window I'm afraid.

EO: God in Heaven, help us all! Shane! My boy, my little son…I loved you, but…

Ella: You see?

EO: I kept myself from him, his sister, too. I held back. I punished them because they were acting in a way that I didn't approve of…now, this!

JO: Ella, this is terrible, two grandsons, two suicides. Took after *you* maybe…you know, that time in the river?

EO: That year, 1977, twenty-four years after I went…For some reason,

Moma and Papa, it reminds me of your *great grandson*, Eugene III. He also died an infant…

Ella: Dear Lord…more? James! Put a stop to this!

EO: Yes, that child, *my* grandson, dead on arrival. St. Vincent's Hospital. It was winter time. I think it was 1946 and the doctors there saw signs in the baby of *child neglect*!

Ella: (hysterical) So! Gene, your grandson died in the city just your brother, Edmund. Strange! Very Strange!

EO: I know. I know, Moma. What can I do?

Edm: *That* was a symptom. The child neglect, soiled-diaper-skin-deterioration I believe, chronic signs, were indications that its parents were carrying their *own* parents' pain. You understand this? Eugene, I *know* that *you* do because of the diamond mine.

JO: Diamond mine? What's this? What mine?

Edm: That is a place where souls can go to find out that lives lived by *default* are more tragic than a baby death from measles and where hordes of children indoctrinated by a catechism that convinces them that they do not *matter, the Original Lie,* can be *reversed.* That lie is far more insidious than any other!

EO: I struggled right up to the end in 1953. In 1912, I wanted to join Edmund. The whole world made me feel just like the two of you did-alone and worthless! Why, it was like they were working for *you*!

Edm: The masses, all here included, are but pawns in the cycle of it all, a cycle that *can* be broken, ended, just like your play cycle, Gene, and your substitute rush to freedom. That trail awaits all. I will instruct!

JO: *If* we care to hear it…

Ella: James! He's in Heaven! He's innocent! How could you say such a thing? If *he* tells us, it *has* to be the truth!

JO: Yeah, I suppose so, but don't *we* tell the truth? Don't we?

Edm: In a word, father, 'No.'

JO: Well, I like that!

Edm: Eugene was correct to label the world a sick place.

JO: When did he do that?

Edm: Well, father, quite a while after your death, but do not worry about it. He himself was sick and a part of that world, just a zebra seeing his brethren's stripes with no known escape from that banded life absent some miracle on the plains.

EO: Well put, Edmund.

Edm: *You* were the powerful equine, lethal kicks, no carnivore but worthy of great public attention and *dismay*, fear even. Great speed and agility, deadly!

EO: Gee, I do not know what to say!

Edm: Yet, I am seeing you at that player piano, Gene, that well-known photograph where you are grinning…

EO: I so loved that thing…Rosie! Ah, Rosie!

Edm: Yes, but there's fraud about!

EO: What?

Edm: Sure! Look at it. You're smiling like you swallowed a canary. It is because you knew that *they* knew that you were not really playing it. You were putting them on and that fact exposed you for an instant, bared the falsehood of *it* and your entire self.

EO: Wait a minute, here…

Ella: Now, gene, don't argue with the *angel*. He *is* one, you know.

JO: Don't pay any attention to him! He's a baby for Christ's sake! Damn!

Edm: Well, know this! We three O'Neill brothers, me, Jamie and Eugene, represent the range of extremes. *I* died in infanthood and escaped. Jamie at forty-five and *he* escaped sort of. But Eugene lived a full life of misery and did *not* escape. *His* suffering was eternal. People can avoid a future comprised of such a thing.

Ella: James, he knows what he is talking about.

JO: I doubt it! He cannot know about adults, about life, not that I know what in hell this is all about anyway!

Edm: *First*, I hereby set the record straight. Jamie was not to blame for my death. He was only a child himself and it was not possible for me to avoid the measles anyway since we were brothers and living together!

Ella: I see that...I believe you, baby son!

Jamie: Thank you. Wow, it feels so good to be free!

Edm: Oh, you're not free yet. *That* was a part of your prison but there are many bars left.

Jamie: Many bars! That's funny. Can we go in one?

Edm   (ignoring that) *Second*, society is still very sick. Eugene was entirely correct on this except that your diagnosis was quite *off* as you have since learned from Dr. Korschucher.

EO: Agreed.

Edm: The world is still selfish and ego-driven. Why, do you have any idea that the planet is getting hotter because of what is called 'greenhouse gasses' like carbon dioxide coming from cars and coal-burning furnaces. The temperature rise will cause significant melting of the earth's ice. As a result, sea levels will rise and in decades, lands will be flooded. Your own grave, Gene, in Boston could be under water!

EO: Golly! I *love* that!

Edm: Yes, I figured that you would but the rest of civilization will not. Why won't they stop, you wonder? Because it is not convenient for the world's economies to stop producing carbon dioxide and they all just shut their eyes and minds. *It's man's primary defense...denial!*

EO: Gee!

Edm: And society is so screwed up that it is locked into a robot waltz. Fads are dreamed up and then anyone not joining in is shamed. And, we are not allowed to say 'colored' anymore. Now it is frowned upon. Now, it is 'negro'!

EO: Well, it always *was* 'negro', Edmund, but 'colored' is slang, 'negro is not .

Edm: But they make a big deal about it.... like 'colored' will keep them down and 'negro' will not! It's false! It's façade stuff. Catering to closed thinking, I call it!

EO: Preposterous!

Edm: Then, there is abortion. It is legal now. Who would believe that this absolute taboo would fall like that? The Supreme Court made it legal. Except for it being used as a method of birth control, I offer no view on the matter. My point in bringing it up is the sick way that society deals with the terms.

EO: Terms? What terms?

Edm: People in favor of this call themselves, are you ready? . . . "Pro-choice"!

EO: Not pro-abortion?

Edm: No! Pro-choice! They're terrified! And the people opposed are calling themselves "Prolife".

EO: *That* sounds okay. It's logical. Why isn't it just *pro* and *anti*?

Edm: Sickness! Then, there is 'computers'. Lots of people have one but it cannot compute a thing!

EO: I want to say something about 'pro-choice'. Don't women make their choices when they spread their legs? Don't they choose when they shun regular methods of birth control? There must be six ways! Of course, the Church does not condone that!

Edm: It's an ego-driven society. Fun and pleasure take the place of responsibility and killing a growing baby inside its mother is the norm!

EO: Now that *is* sick! My God!

JO: I can see it if a woman is raped and gets with child or if her life is in trouble or she has sex with a brother, thank God for no girls in *this* family, but...

Ella: Yes, James, but abortion is against the Church in *all* instances.

JO: I know but I don't agree with *that* part...

Edm: Then there is rock and roll...

EO: What's that?

JO: You mean 'Rolling Rock'? It's a beer and I wish I had one!

Jamie: Me too!

Edm   No, it's a form of new, well, new to you all, music and the kids are just wild about it ! Began around 1954 or so. Too late for you, Gene.

EO: Thank God for small favors!

Edm: Anyway, I bring it up because it is still going strong and the kids do crazy dances with it and the parents are still upset. Too uninhibited! Too 'black' they'd say!

JO: Black? What's black?

Edm: Negro. It's slang.

EO: Oh, so 'colored' is wrong because it's slang but 'black' is okay?

Edm: I'm telling you, the world is sick!

EO: But 'black' is not a color anyway!

Edm: So the parents are scared to death *still* about rock and roll and condemn it.

EO: But weren't they teenagers themselves in 1954?

Edm: Sure, but the new rock and roll is much wilder!

EO: I am wondering if I should tell everyone here about the diamonds, Edmond?

Edm: By all means, do. It can only lead to them being sprung from Limbo.

JO: Those diamonds again? What are these diamonds, boys?

Eugene began to describe his experience in the cave with Dr. Korschucher and he listed the five diamonds in detail, explaining it *all* to them just as it had been presented to him. Thus, the *Original Lie* was revealed with a lead in to the *Ultimate Life-lie*. Edmund showed his approval and because of his Heaven status, all believed and accepted this. Then Eugene moved on and showed how diamond number *two, substitutions,* sets forth the truth that nearly *everybody* is in some kind of *trance,* thus the ridiculous behavior set

forth on rock and roll, race wording, computers, abortion, and a *host* of similar stuff. Again, Edmund assented and all present absorbed it. They seemed
to eat up the 'unholy trinity' of falsity. Next, Eugene set out the principals of
the *third* diamond, *Devices to Feel,*. Again, Edmund gave his blessing and the
listeners were wide-eyed. Then came the stone that read "*Perpetual Immaturity*" and Eugene explained it in great detail while omitting, of course, all
personal aspects that the analyst had discussed with him and again, Edmund
tipped his hat. It was thusly all taken as most serious by the O'Neills. Last was
the *fifth* stone on 'Spirituality' and all, especially Ella, loved this part because
they were, or fancied themselves as, a religious family. Edmund underlined
this section by his comment that Mary herself was right there in Heaven with
him. Ella swooned at the thought. After all, Mary was the creator of Jesus
Christ, the Prince of Peace, so what could be more bona fide than that? She
knew that even the other religions regarded Jesus as a holy Prophet. Ella was
simply thrilled! She was comforted beyond imagining. For the first time in
her life, she was at peace inside although she did not really know why.

Edm: Has anyone here ever heard of a 'hate crime'?

EO: No! What is a hate crime…you mean that there are *love* crimes?

Edm: Certainly. Easing the suffering of a terminally ill spouse could be
        called a 'love' crime, no?

EO: Yeah! Like Hickey! "Love! Hah! More like a despisement crime, I'd
        say.

Ella: Who dear?

EO: Oh, Mother, you'll find out by and by.

Edm: Anyway, a 'hate crime' is now a term used and I think a symptom of
        that societal sickness, you agree? (All were silent)

Edm: Then we have people making fun of retarded children just to matter.
        They pretend to be dumb to get sympathy, attention.

Ella: Imagine such a thing!

Edm: Then we have the idea that nearly everyone shakes his head at how
        the beaten child grows up to become a *child beater*! They don't grasp
        it because *they* are in that *trance*! Now, you folks get it. *The diamonds
        say the truth.* (All looked at Edmund as if he were a God of some sort.

They were amazed at what they had learned but more at what they had *not known*. All seemed exhaulted. The father, James, was just reduced to a puddle of gratitude at what his young son, the measles-dead baby that had been the launching pad for his wife's tyranny, that along with her beauty, had done for him and to him. No more the boasting actor. No more that domineering bastard, cheap to the end! Jamie was resurrected in a sense and he was smiling as never before. Ella was still giddy over the Mary part. Bridget, as well, was something of an amazed sight to see and she was heard to remark something to the effect that "No one ever really knows what is possible". Bridget's long-suffering burden of a life after the death of Edmund had suddenly been relieved. No one ever came out and blamed her for the baby's demise but the atmosphere was often dense over it. Edmund explained that parents are the last ones to be blamed in many instances because of the common notion that kids preserve their parental status to accommodate any miracle turnaround. He also pointed out that since kids become their parents, maybe there was a trace of 'self blame' involved as well. He did allow that *this* was under examination. Ella now saw that *she* had become her own parents and that Bridget did, too. This revelation *astounded* them! Jamie had a similar one but the most tumultuous one was that of James. He was downright flabbergasted that he had become his mother and his father and was drastically moved to realize that his dad's abandonment of him to go back to Ireland, along with the totality of the parental misbehaviors, were rooted in the same ideas that those diamonds exhibited. The look of relief on his face was much more expressive than any that he had ever mustered on stage as the great actor!

EO: Tell us, brother, about the *breaking* of the cycle that you mentioned a while ago.

Edm: Yes, well, that cycle of passing on the sickness, parents to child, where that child takes on all the symptoms, then becomes his parents, can be *broken* in only a few ways. One way is to not have any children. *That* breaks it. *But* the cycle can arise spontaneously by way of parents who *become* defective as child rearers from the spontaneous appearance of mental illness or accident or unintended abandonment of the kids or in a few other ways.

EO: So, I almost cut the cycle in 1912 at Jimmy the Priest's, huh?

Edm: Yes, indeed! Same for Eugene, Jr. . His death without living children did, too. Let us move into the realm of the *why* and the *how* a child, like you, Eugene, can actually become his parents.

EO: Finally! My mission is to be fulfilled!

Edm: It is really quite simple. A child takes on the identity of his mother and father because an unfilled hole exists in him or her. The driving of the child from vulnerabilities into cerebralization prevents development of the true identity and allows *false* ones to spring up. The pain from ones idolized by instinct is thus shunted. The fleeing is done. The shaming, the neglect, the emotional starvation, the physical mistreatment and so forth were too much to bear so the refuge is safe in *the head*! The child is forced to stay with those parents, but it becomes thusly tolerable. Meanwhile, *hypervigilance* guards the door. *That* too, blocks formation of real identity. The days are made of pain avoidance and not *true life*. Along with those false identities comes the awful adoption by the child of the wrongdoers' identities! The child joins the enemy and this phenomenon is akin to the one seen with *prisoners of war!*

EO: This is astounding!

Edm: What could be safer than becoming one of the malfeasors? You become split off from the prior you. You kind of lose your target status. Also, they see themselves in you, which is more imagined 'protection'.

JO: Let me just say that never in my life have I seen a plot such as that. A wondrous stage piece, that!

Bridget: May I say something here? I am sure that it is correct because I could feel my own heart, what's left of it, respond in a way that signifies connection. It was nearly like learning a secret *code*. Once you learn it, the messages are very clear!

EO: But *how* does a body get out of this, Edmund?

Edm: That would be the *reversal* that your analyst spoke of, yes?

EO: Yes.

Edm: One gets *out* of it by doing the very thing that babies do best *crying*.

EO: But I have cried all my life. That never did any good!

Edm: That is because you were *not grieving*. Tears that *you* shed were from morbid depression, not healthy tears.

EO: Go on.

Edm: Morbid unhappiness, neurotic misery, produces crying but it is not the same experience as true grieving. Neurosis activity is in one who is *outside* the feelings and vulnerabilities, remember?

EO: What does grieving have to do with it, Edmund?

Edm: It produces biochemical changes that morbid tears do not. And what is the grieving over? It is over a loss! And what is that loss? It is the loss of your authentic self, the one that *they* robbed or 'killed'.

JO: Truly unheard of!

Edm: Crying and grieving as a *remedy* are *not instinctual*. Who seeks that except whole people? A healthy person loses a parent and he cries. But a fractured person who loses one has no tears! Why is that? It is because his feelings are *frozen*. He is unvulnerable as protection!

EO: Can a person get a reversal just from that?

Edm: It takes a long time, months. The process is an *emotional transaction* and not a *cerebral* one. It is not a matter of thinking the right kinds of thoughts or thinking the 'right way'. The malady did not result from thinking the 'wrong way'. One cannot change such things just by deciding to be different. *That* is *not* emotions-based!

EO: Continue, please!

Edm: Just getting started is the trick. Frozen tears do not yield to ordinary fare. So indelible is the survival scheme, *extraordinary means* are usually required. And once it is turned on, that fountain, it is hard to turn it off. People get scared and fear that they will *break apart*!

JO: Amazing!

Ella: Well! I never!

EO: Go on, Edmund, please!

Edm: Of course, they never do fall to pieces in that way and after unrestricted *free fall,* perhaps for eight weeks or so, they begin to get a sense of having been purged, cleansed, like a laxative effect. It's unpleasant but welcomed!

JO: Now that's funny! "Laxative" from a baby! You little crapper, Edmund. Just funning, son. (covering his bad taste) Just *how* did you learn all this...we didn't.

Edm: Actually, you did but it was suppressed, buried, denied. I know because I was still pure and had clarity before I died. It was so obvious in you people, pressed right up against your faces but you all balked!

JO: How do we get started?

Edm: You don't. You're dead so it is not needed. All that is required for *you* all is to learn it all so as to escape Limbo. But the living need to engage in that grieving to *escape*!

JO: How do they get started?

Edm: Well, Papa, it takes some tricks to do that. Advancing age wears you down and *that* sets you up for it because the youthful invincibility is gone and denial is partly made of that. Then, if a person suffers a *true loss,* death of a pet or being fired or going thru a divorce, it can set you up to go to general grieving above grief for that particular loss. The latter weakens the safety resolve.

EO: What a plot!

Edm: Then there is direct confrontation of things that will remind you of what was done to you and the times that it occurred. Letters, photographs, direct talks with your parents much as Eugene did *here.*

EO: *Now* I see what Dr. K was up to! (excitedly).

Edm: You see, you all had lives of *pain avoidance.* The lying, denial, dishonesty, falsity, drugs, alcohol and so forth, Eugene's life for one, is a kind of a *block* to any such contrainstinctual remedy such as I have described. Again, who seeks more pain? They do not, cannot see the difference between real suffering and morbid suffering. *The misery must be embraced!* Crying it out beats a life of constant contamination by it. Eugene tried something like that when he composed Long

Day's Journey Into Night.

EO: I was hoping to avoid that; can we, Edmund?

Edm: Sorry. Your attempts were stymied by all of the distractions around you, Carlotta, your obsession with the idea of a successful work to prove that you were *not* a pseudogenius, the war in Europe, your other motives. Yes, you *did* suffer in 1939 and 1940 but the grieving was not quite *free fall*, which is essential to success in getting *a reversal*.

EO: I *did* feel some permanent change after 1941. Was it from that partial grieving?

Edm: Could be. I am reminded of the four classic steps that persons are reported to go through when faced with impending *demise; denial, rage, bargaining, acceptance.* These steps do not happen for whole people, only fractured ones. Whole people accept demise as a natural event and do not have the heel-digging response based on the miserable history of struggle and bewilderment. I was just wondering to myself whether those four steps have a parallel to recovery? I think that you, Gene, never got to the 'acceptance' stage in 1941.

EO: Who the heck knows, Edmund?

Edm: Anyway…(cut off)

EO: Babies cry all the time and everyone pays attention but when adults do it, they get uncomfortable and try to make them *stop*!

Edm: And *that* could be a *block* as well. It's part of the sickness. It's societal denial.

EO: No more do I yearn to be a 'ghost within a ghost', Edmund, you remember that, right? You *do* know about everything, yes?

Edm: "Damned peaceful", didn't you say?

EO: Hooray for you, Edmund…savior!

Edm: Same general thing for The Iceman Cometh, you know, all cerebralizations and almost no truth.

EO: I was so *proud* of that, though…

Edm: I know, but so was Adolph Hitler. He thought *he* had it right but my God!

EO: Yes, I'm afraid you are correct. The analyst showed me the wanderings of Iceman only he did agree that it was an accurate portrayal of *how* life is and was for a vast majority…illusions, self-deception, pipe dreams, life-lies, all just to survive or so they think. But nowhere is it shown *how* it gets like that or what is needed to escape to 'sanity'. Also, doesn't 'self-deception' imply a personality duality? What of that?

Edm: (Ignoring that) There is something else that I am *pressed* to reveal, Moma and Papa, and that is that when I was your little baby, 1883 to 1885, you were both beginning to get to me when I contracted that disease. Already I was panicked from your ways, Moma, your eyes, always a coldness, far away. It made me doubt myself and dislike myself. *I just wanted to die inside*! I wanted warmth and loving and bouncing happiness to let me know that it was alright for me to be there. Jamie and Eugene never got that assurance, you see this now, Moma? You two were like a stone! So when I *did* die, it was a tremendous relief.

Ella: Dear God in Heaven, James! (screaming)

JO: We are *so* sorry, son…please forgive us!

Edm: Yes, I forgive you both and I think that everyone here can forgive everyone else. Be whole and up front and no more need for artifice like 'respecting each others' weaknesses' or having compassion in place of truth, those types of Eugene-invented remedies. He meant well but the diatribe was made strictly of desperation from a life of agony that he was loath to grasp in spite of enormous effort. True idiosyncrasies are okay but not those made by child abuse. Compassion is fine but not if it is really *enabling*.

JO: Yeah…God sees this!

EO: So, man is *not trapped by anything*! When one views life and mankind from the whole perspective, not the sick and warped one, it is all so clear! *Man is not a victim at all*!

Edm: Indeed! There is no tenuousness of human relationships either except those tainted by maltreatment of children who grow up warped and needy. Of course, disorders of the biochemical kind are excepted as well.

EO: And there is no *dark side of man* except for what produces this anomaly to begin with?

Edm: Absolutely! Man needs no pipe dreams to be content.

JO: What about Satan, son? How do you deal with the Devil?

Edm: Papa, there is no Devil. Satan is mental illness and its offspring.

JO: But what about the Church?

Edm: It's only a metaphor, Papa. The Church is *stuck* on a metaphor!

EO: And *fate* is just physics and God does not have an active hand in running day to day events, tragedies or triumphs like the Sweeneys or the poor little run over girl?

Edm: Correct again. You have it down, Eugene...all of you, I earnestly hope.

EO: And man does not *need* to grasp all of the mystery of God, the force that is responsible for us being here, the universe?

Edm: Well said! It is sufficient that man just lead a whole life and that he *give. Love is giving*, remember?

EO: And man's tendency to think his way out of everything, that is bogus, correct?

Edm: Correct! Bogus! *That* is the *Ultimate illusion*, so seemingly real but only born of desperation. The *Original lie* is its *parent*, that *instinct clash*, you know.

EO: And those in that plight live in a secret desire to be forced back into their vulnerabilities. They beg for it in 'silence'?

Edm: Amazing, huh? Who would have believed it?

JO: An *understatement*!

Edm: The freezing water of facing the original lie and clash, the forced 'march' back into real feelings, the weeks and weeks of overdue grieving and unstoppable tears, that shock, believe it or not, unfreezes the icy soul and it emerges and *blooms* with a smile like *that* one over there! (points to Jamie and James). Suddenly, the vapors seemed to move, Eugene's, James', Ella's, Jamie's, Bridget's, all connected to Edmund's essence. In a great rise, this joined mass of swirl ascended to an indeterminate height. It was now daylight at St. Mary Cemetery in New London and as the vapors soared even higher, they passed through a circle of cavorting seagulls who were chasing their own imaginations. Then moments later, it reached a critical level out of the view of anyone, not that anyone was around, and it began to spread out over the earth in a thin veil matching the haze of emotional illness heretofore described. It was at last the future, the hope for all of mankind. A *real* reconciliation for the Tyrones and the O'Neills was in Heaven and could have been called "*A Long Night's Journey Into Light*". All of them were in Heaven now.

I snapped out of this startled but in wonderment.

CHAPTER NINE :
A TOMATO MORNING

I gazed at the city and down State Street and let my imagination go.

"C. O. O. L." That is what the 'cool' people will call *Children Of Original Lie* but they are not so clever. The cool folk imagine that they are hip, with it, unperturbed by life's events. They stay outside the arena of emotions.

Such a disease of adult juvenility is the offending beast which roams freely up and down the main drags of our towns and along the sea shores. And so, some far off morning, at the sea, in Rhode Island, I will be pondering the secret that every mature artist knows: 'do not struggle, just let it come' and looking forward to that unimaginable high that graces every worthwhile creator when some new res bursts into being! It's intoxicating!

As Eugene O'Neill had to know all too well, that rush, that high, wears off very soon and a new one is chased unless a mere blank is the vision. Then that 'mature' part kicks in. He might not have ever drawn a blank but that would not likely have figured in his obsessive bent for writing. Then there was all that important element of his attempts to unburden himself and explain his 'fate' on earth.

Too, on that coast on that morning, I might recall again that remarkable irony, an ultimate irony I believed I termed it, that he strove to matter, to free himself of a lifelong agony and emptiness by displaying it all in public. It would be trying to matter by exhibiting one's status of not!

He *has* made it easier for me to live *my* life and in the end, he will have made it easier to die my death.

Yes, it will be one of those mornings at the sea and its cast will extend over that bridge towards the West. There will be a light red clarity in the air and it might remind me of that day in 1991 when I pledged to give up stealing. I was locked into an ongoing recovery phenomenon which daily dazzled me. It will occur to me that most days, most things, are for our own time only. So struggle-oriented is the plodding plight in most of us that we never really see. A great urgency and priority is attached to every little thing and nuance of need. Who really perceives that the transformer of forgetation is coming, inching up to wash over us all and that it is the very few who escape. Even then, a rescue lasts only for decades or, rarer, centuries. Take Aristotle or

Plato or George Washington. That which one leaves behind can be regarded before the departure as equal in stature to the life led. I do not speak of wallets or buckles of gold. My own father's was sterling with inlay of red gold and yellow gold and I adored it, if not him, but it is lost these thirty-eight years later. Someone holds that jewel! I have to forget about it.

So if a man dies and is forgotten, he had then that own life for that own time and so it must be for that clump that is seen from a satellite. But something left behind that lasts, that *moves*, that lives on because it seems to compel so, *that* can ease the dying brow and alight the face one more time. Who is remembered in history as having passed on with such a thing? Maybe for me, I'll be in the midst of a silly Spoonerism but the pain will bring me around and I will set out to the last effort. At that moment of this reckoning, I find myself wondering if the driver of the vehicle that must bear my remains back to New Jersey is truly aware of anything? No matter. All to me now is the vitality of the message to come from my pen, from Eugene, to *all* who languish. His *unwitting* legacy *could be* a resurrected awareness passed on to me and then by such power of words passed on *through me*! I could write of this excursion!

Others might ponder whether O'Neill has truly become 'irrelevant and overrated', but if he has, *what to make of the Nobel*? The drama was the highest. The private ardor was most laudable. It is also said that nothing mattered to him but his plays. Such is an infinite attestation to the awful and terrifying nightmare from which he had to constantly run. I say to a hesitant world that in all things, in his birth, ruination, in his crying life and in his death, he has become one more epitome and *that* is of the *ultimate vehicle*.

I will drive my car a one last time over that bridge and take the downtown New London exit. Some lonely parking space will be waiting near the old Courthouse early in the morning. No trace of my relatives recently passed by as I drive will linger and the heavy importance of the occasion will impress me and suppress the pain, I hope! I suppose that a note on the windshield and a larger explanation inside the car would be the responsible thing. It would also highlight the town event about to unfold. I will no doubt think of the exact spot as having been chosen from a small list of important places such as George Washington's Crossing on the Delaware. This gesture will be for *love* and not for escape. It will endeavor to prevent that very thing for all of humanity and force it to finally look instead of cringe.

Something in the living of *his* days; Spithead, Puget Sound, Sea Island, California; Paris, New York will live in me. His woes were my woes and I can now take a real walk down State Street, the Bohemian, with a grim smile, our old Harpies a flying again, memories of fathers who perished *before* we made much of ourselves, ever 'alone'.

Down the slope I shall parade, left side or right, the fancy of 'fate' like two weapons on a plate. But no duel this at least not in the Burr-Hamilton way. It will be more like me against you. I will pause a moment to remember a place of far ago heartbreak there at the pier where the awful hurricane of 1957 blocked my boat trip to the island in the sea. His was in that place as well. Then one last memory will infiltrate, that is being my presence in the Courthouse Law Library September 11, 2001 at around 9:20 a.m. when the sudden chatter drew me to learn the awful news!

As I carry myself closer on the water, there will be cradled in my hands a ripe, good-sized, red tomato. It will be the kind that when you cut into it, it delights you!

The yards will tick off. I will approach the little statue unaware of those landmarks anymore. As I focus on it, I will be for a second transported back to 1895 when his world was one by magic and not by logic, when those 19th century schooners approached to his amazed delight and their captains actually related tales of the sea to his eager ears. The lovely waters will be alive to me and I will go over to the child, to his spirit, and I will offer it to him, place it in his presence. The mystery of the whole thing is no greater or lesser than in that fruit. It will be an offering from God and not humanly-contrived. The tomato will sit there with him and I will want to know that there is no lurking force to be remained of vodka!

Then, I will kiss him on top of the head with feelings in him parallel to Edmund expected to seal it. At last, I shall turn and not look back. A short distance later from that finality will come the real one. I imagine that a duplicate note pinned to my sleeve would assure everybody. My nearly worn out form will surrender *theatrically* to make the people listen, to make them take their eyes off that all important *next fix*. They'll really see what hidden secret of life and wonderful dream of beauty and "perfection" *do* lie beyond the horizon, just as Eugene desperately yearned for. It is the *seeing* of the original lie and the abolition of its effects on man's otherwise shaky future. And any idea of the impossibility of a dream constituting its real beauty need no longer apply.

I did not suffer for nothing, nor did he. *That* can be the label on the gift of life and *hope* for the masses who languish alone.

The thirty-eight caliber report will punctuate my last words.

THE END

ABOUT THE AUTHOR

Richard Heim is a NYC metroploitan area native who received a B.S. in science locally and a juris doctorate in Boston.

He practiced civil and criminal law for 23 years and is a member of the Bar, U.S. Supreme Court, Second Circuit Court of Appeals, Federal District Court (Ct) and Connecticut State Bar.

Heim has long been interested in the effects of child mistreatment/ neglect on society, the law, government and individuals and the many gross and rampant misconceptions abounding.

He is the author of "ORIGIN OF MISERY", 2002, revised 2005 ISBN 1-4208-7975-8, a nonfiction work exploring the famous Changewater Murders of Warren County, N.J. 1843 and execution of two innocent men in 1845 for the ice axe slaughter of a young family. Parallels to modern thinking and society are drawn.

He also authored "VERTICAL VERSE", 2006, Brunswick Publishing Corporation (ISBN 978-1-55618-213-6) a thematic collection of verses focusing on various aspects of child maltreatment/neglect and the banishment of human joy. It sets forth two pieces of cure and contains a "Declaration of New Human Rights".

Heim also wrote "GRACE UPON THE RACK", a 25-stanza verse published April, 2005 Venture Literary Magazine, Boston, Massachusetts.

Among his past jobs are laborer, musician, tutor in languages and science and pharmaceutical researcher.

He has had solo and group exhibitions of his oil paintings in Soho, NYC and has worked as a volunteer 1972-2004 in various hospitals, chairman Local #23 Selective Service Board, ACLU-NYC death penalty matters and PBS-TV 13.